BROKEN

COVINGTON SECURITY

DR. REBECCA SHARP

Broken (Covington Security, Book 6)
Published by Dr. Rebecca Sharp
Copyright © 2022 Dr. Rebecca Sharp

All rights reserved. No part of this book may be reproduced, distributed, or transmitted in any form or by any electronic or mechanical means, including information storage and retrieval systems, photocopying, or recording, without permission in writing from the publisher, except by reviewers, who may quote brief passages in a review and certain other noncommercial uses permitted by copyright law.
This is a work of fiction. Resemblance to actual persons, things, living or dead, locales or events is entirely coincidental.

Cover Design:

Sarah Hansen, Okay Creations

Editing:

Ellie McLove, My Brother's Editor

Printed in the United States of America.

Visit www.drrebeccasharp.com

PROLOGUE

Stevie

FIFTEEN YEARS OLD

"STEPHANIE!"

My pencil veered on my calculus homework, messing up the neat lines of the problem I'd been solving. Some might think that being homeschooled made school easier, but I was pretty positive that no calculus teacher in regular school would take off points from homework if it wasn't done neatly, regardless if the answers were right.

Mom and Dad were strict about my schoolwork, but I couldn't complain. It was because of them that I'd tested well above my grade level for as long as I could remember.

"Stephanie!" Mom's footsteps pound quickly up the stairs. She sounded upset, and I wasn't sure why. She was supposed to be resting.

At dinner, she'd said she felt a little sick. Mom always got sick easily, but Dad always had a reason for it. Today, he claimed it was because she'd overdone it cleaning out boxes of clothes and toys to give away from the basement; we usually donated a lot to our church, but there was some stuff that had been stored down there since they'd bought our house before I was born.

Dad insisted she stay home while he went to church for the three-hour CCD class he taught every Wednesday; I was given a reprieve too, instructed to clean up from dinner, do my homework, and make sure Mom was okay.

She didn't sound okay when she called my name. She didn't sound sick either.

"Yeah?" I called back, sliding off the edge of my blue comforter.

My room was covered in posters of the beach. Everything from my towels to my bedspread to my binders was blue because I loved the ocean. I'd never seen it because we lived in Wyoming and were surrounded by mountains, but I loved it from the pictures. From afar.

Dad said if I got all *A*'s this year, we might take a family vacation to the beach. He also said that last year, and we hadn't gone, but I wasn't going to risk it, so I kept up on all my schoolwork. *Not that I had much choice about that either.*

We'd never really gone on a vacation. I used to ask about it when I was younger—that and why I couldn't have a pet. As I got older, I realized that maybe they just couldn't afford one with Mom being home to teach me and Dad only working for our church, so I stopped asking.

Mom used to teach high school math and science. Then she met Dad at a church community dinner and, according to her, fell for him that very night. When she ended up pregnant, he made her quit working so she could be a stay-at-home mom. It was sweet... *sort of.*

But if Mom missed teaching, she got satisfying doses of it with me as her sole pupil.

"Mom—"

The door to my room swung open and banged against the wall, scaring me, but not as much as how she looked.

She'd been crying. Her makeup was smudged, but her eyes weren't sad. Her hair was pulled up in a ponytail and she had a coat on over her clothes.

Why was she wearing a coat?

"Stephanie, you need to pack a bag." She went immediately to my dresser, pulling out underwear and socks from the top drawer and throwing them on my bed like cotton confetti.

I stood there. She was panicking, and I didn't understand why; she'd been calm—quiet but calm—at the dinner table only a little bit ago.

"Mom, what's going on?" My lip trembled; she was scaring me.

"Pack a bag right now, Stephanie, we need to go."

"I don't understand," I protested, approaching her. A few T-shirts and a couple pairs of jeans all added to the growing pile of clothes that completely buried my homework.

She spun and her hands shot out, gripping my shoulders with a strength I'd never felt from her before. She bent until her face was even with mine.

"We're not safe, and we need to leave. Please, help me."

Safe? We lived just outside of Casper, Wyoming. The only danger out here was the cold or a wandering bison.

"*Stephanie!*"

I jumped. Mom never yelled. Sometimes, Dad did, but never Mom.

"Bag. *Now.*"

It wasn't her yelling that made me comply, it was how she looked at me. I went into my closet and pulled out my duffel bag, shoving all the clothes on the bed into it. Mom grabbed my toothbrush and a few things from my bathroom, and I added them to my bag, waiting for her to tell me what was going on.

"Put on your sneakers and coat." She zipped up my bag.

I did what she said, my fingers shaking a little when I tried to tie my laces.

"Okay. Let's go." She slung my duffel over her shoulder, her head whipping through the room to make sure she hadn't forgotten anything I would need.

I saw my homework on the bed, so I went to grab it when her icy fingers clamped around my wrist tightly. "Leave it."

That broke my scared silence. "But what about my homework?"

"We'll figure it out."

Tears burned in my eyes.

"Mom, what's going on?" I pleaded as she pulled me down the staircase; I saw her own bag sitting at the bottom landing. There was no way she could've packed all that after Dad left; she must've packed before... and waited.

"Does Dad know we're leaving?" I blurted out, stumbling as she pulled me faster. "Is he picking us up?"

Her fingers loosened for a second and then retightened their grip.

Something painful tore my chest, and I yanked my arm away, crying, "Mom! What's going on? I'm scared."

She spun and pulled me in for a tight hug, holding me as I panted and fought to not burst into tears. Mom always gave the best hugs—the kind of hugs that could stop the world from ending, which is what it felt like was happening right now.

"I'm so sorry, baby. I know this is scary, and I know you don't understand, but I need you to trust me right now, okay?" She drew back and pressed her palm to my cheek, quickly wiping away the tears that iced to my cheeks. "Please. I love you, and I promise I'll explain."

I shivered. I wanted to argue, but I couldn't. Whatever was happening, she was trying to save me from it.

"Okay," I choked out, my throat too thick to swallow.

And then she was leading me again. Outside.

Dad wasn't waiting in the drive for us like I hoped. Instead, there was a cab idling at the curb.

I'd never been in a cab before; it smelled like a thousand air fresheners were put in a microwave and the plastic seats groaned when I slid over them. I sat in silence, staring at our house through the window until I couldn't see it anymore.

Somehow, I knew I'd never see it again.

The cab took us to the bus station. The bus took us to Salt Lake City, where we got on another bus to San Francisco. My eyes shut as soon as it pulled out of the parking lot; all I wanted was to sleep and then wake up to all of this being a terrible nightmare. It never happened, and a whole day later, we arrived in the city.

Grabbing our things, Mom walked us a few blocks from the

station to a park. She got us gyros from a food truck and we ate in silence on one of the benches, her eyes constantly looking around like someone was chasing us.

"This way," she instructed when we finished, taking my hand and leading me along another few more blocks.

We slowed in front of a large church and then stopped when we reached the adjacent administrative building next to it.

I recognized the space immediately since most of my social life consisted of church and church-related activities, many of those activities revolving around community outreach and assistance. Dad had very strong opinions about drugs and sex and morality, and did his best to educate those around him.

Dad.

He would've realized we were gone by now, and I hadn't seen Mom use her phone once. I actually hadn't seen her phone, so I was pretty sure she left it behind. *Just like she left him.*

She promised she'd explain, I reminded myself when we walked inside.

There was a bulletin board immediately to my right with flyers about assistance programs for those battling addiction, those seeking shelter, those looking to start over from abuse.

Had he hurt her? Threatened her?

I shook my head. No. None of those things made sense. Dad might be weird about certain things, but he'd never hurt Mom; he loved her.

Hadn't he?

The more I thought about it, I'd never heard Dad say "I love you" to Mom. While I'd seen enough movies and TV shows to know most people used it as a precursor to goodbye, my parents had always said *"God bless you"* before ending a call or walking out of the house.

But that didn't mean he didn't love her.

That wouldn't be a reason to leave him, would it?

The tears welled again as Mom ushered me into one of the chairs in the small lobby, leaving our bags next to me as she went up to the receptionist. A minute later, a woman appeared and began talking to Mom, a sad expression on her face as she reached out and seemed to comfort her. Then a man joined them. He wore a suit and seemed like he was in charge of something.

They talked for another minute before Mom pulled out an envelope from her coat, the kind that was big enough to hold cash, and handed it to the man, ending their conversation.

"Mom..." My lip trembled when she returned to me.

"Patience, Stephanie," she pleaded.

The building housed a small hostel upstairs that we stayed in that night. The following morning, the same man and woman approached us after breakfast. Mom sent me to get our bags, and when I came back down, she was alone but holding a large yellow envelope that she hadn't had before.

"We're almost there," was all she offered before she threaded her fingers through mine and took us back to the bus station.

Two more tickets. Two more uncomfortable seats. At least this trip was only an hour, our destination a place I'd never heard of; Monterey, California.

Once the bus got rolling, Mom opened up the envelope, her hands shaking as she dug inside it. She pulled out something blue and handed it to me.

A passport.

"We're starting over, baby," she said.

She'd called me "baby" so many times since we left our house. More times than ever before. Dad didn't like it when she used that endearment; he said it was childish and I wasn't a baby anymore. I never knew how to explain to him that wasn't what she meant.

I peeled back the cover, and my face scrunched.

Stevie Michaels.

Who was Stevie Michaels?

A small cry escaped when I saw the picture. It was my photo, except it wasn't me.

"What is this?" I shoved the passport back at her. "That's not my name."

Her lips drew tight. "It will be when we reach Monterey."

My shoulders started to shake. "My name is Stephanie Turner—"

"No." The word was sharp and angry. She took my hand and

forced my palm back open to take the new passport. "We're Mary and Stevie Michaels now."

I shook my head. That was what all that back and forth was about; she'd paid to change our names—our identities.

And then it hit me. We hadn't just left Dad... we were hiding from him.

"What happened, Mom?"

I was only fifteen. I was homeschooled and hadn't seen anything beyond a fifty-mile radius around Casper. I didn't know a whole lot, but I did know that the only people who hid were people who were afraid.

She took my hands in hers, clasping them tight and pulling them to her chest.

"Your dad loves you, Steph—*Stevie*. He loves you a lot. But he's not a good man, and we weren't safe."

I flinched when she changed my name. This wasn't... right.

Dad hardly got mad or yelled. I'd never seen him raise a hand to Mom or to me. He was a minister. He worked at our church. Taught CCD. I had no proof he wasn't a good man.

Except that Mom had left him when obedience had always been her most prized virtue.

I felt like I was staring at an algebra problem that Mom had solved but wouldn't show the word to her answer.

Dad = bad.

It seemed impossible to believe her, but I did.

Mom always answered my questions that Dad would brush off. She talked to me about grown-up things, and we even listened to grown-up true crime podcasts together when Dad was busy at church. She tried to prepare me for the world with knowledge and honesty while Dad tried to shield me from it.

I never doubted his intentions were good, but with Mom, I never doubted her. And when she looked at me, trying to hide how much the truth hurt her, I didn't doubt her answer even if she wouldn't share the proof.

"So, we'll never see him again?" I didn't know why I asked such a silly question.

"For your sake, baby, I hope not."

My head lowered slowly, tears falling and landing on the dark blue of the passport in my lap.

Mom put her arm around my shoulder, but I turned away. I believed her, but it hurt. I knew she was protecting me, but I was angry at how she had to do it.

"The place we're going to—Monterey—I picked it because it has a beach."

She was trying to make this easier, but even the ocean wasn't enough to make me smile.

CHAPTER ONE

Stevie

"It's just an interview. I haven't gotten the job yet," I told my friend, my cell pinned between my cheek and shoulder.

The GPS beeped, reminding me I had a turn coming up. Even though I could connect my phone to my Ford Focus, I chose not to. I'd been moonlighting as an Uber driver in Carmel Cove for over a year now, and even though it was only for a rideshare app, it felt unprofessional to have my car start ringing while I was midtrip with a passenger.

"I know, but you're going to get it," Carina insisted, her voice just as hopeful and glowing as the rest of her.

Carina Damiani had gone from being one of my passengers to one of my good friends. We were around the same age; Carina just about two years older than me, but we couldn't have been at two more different points in our life; her, married and expecting a baby in the next month. Me, trying to scrounge together funds for the college education I'd dreamed of for so long now.

"We'll see."

"I sang your praises, and unfortunately, it's not like he has a lot of options right now."

Carina had the kind of personality that made friends with everyone. Case in point: she moved here *after* I did and already had connections with everyone in town. However, she did have one distinct advantage: she was married to Rocco, one of the members of the Covington Security, and was the younger sister of Dante Lozano, another member of Covington's team; and no local in Carmel Cove didn't know the guys of Covington Security.

Her popularity wasn't a complaint, just fact. I'd always been more reserved in my relationships; life had taught me it was safer that way.

"I know, and I'm really grateful, but it doesn't change my lack of experience." Even though I was going to community college for early childhood education, I hadn't been able to get a nanny or babysitting job in Carmel.

Not for lack of trying.

I applied to every position posted on the community board at the local coffee shop, Ocean Roasters, and at the community center. I'd even had a few interviews, but it never went further than that. Apparently, no one wanted to trust the no-experience newcomer with their kid.

Or maybe everyone could sense the poisoned soil I came from.

So, I started with Uber. It paid the bills, and it quickly familiarized me with how the streets of Carmel Cove were stitched and seamed together.

"Well, I'd say the two of you are on equal footing then."

"Yeah, I guess so." My chest squeezed as I headed south along the Coastal Highway.

As the town faded in my rearview, the towering cliffs of Big Sur plummeted in the panorama on my right, diving into the depths of the cold Pacific below. The jagged rocky edges were a favorite spot of mine; the way they stood strong and stoic against the fickle sea who could be calm one moment and stormy the next. Sometimes, I felt like the crags of Big Sur—*Big Stevie* —trying not to erode from the waves that life continued to crash into me.

I loved the ocean when I was a kid only because I didn't know the cliffs existed. Now, I accepted every Uber trip out this way and spent whatever free time I had exploring the iconic vistas.

"I thought he'd live in town." *Another two miles.* I passed the turn for Sea Lion Point.

"I think having a little bit of space is probably good for him and Lainey right now."

Duh, Stevie. I remembered how I felt when Mom died; I'd wanted space. I'd wanted out of the city, so I came to Carmel Cove. The town was surprisingly quaint for being a tourist destination only an hour south of San Francisco. And even with those flocks of tourists whose presence provided my income, Carmel still proudly glowed with her small-town vibe even more than Monterey.

I'd thought about moving back there first, but every inch of it was covered with memories of Mom and me. Memories of the new life we'd grown in the ashes of our past. It was all the good memories before she got sick.

We'd lived in Monterey for two years before moving to San Francisco, so she could get better medical care. It turned out, all her sudden bouts of fatigue and chest pains were because of a rare autoimmune disease. She was diagnosed with autoimmune myocarditis, but even with a regimen of immunosuppressants and steroid therapy, she'd passed away a little over three years after her diagnosis.

I tried not to wonder if regular medical care at an earlier point in life would've made a difference; it only made me angrier at Lee.

Lee. *Not Dad.*

He stopped being Dad when I turned twenty.

When Mom knew her time was running out, she finally explained everything, and that moment defined me. A secret and a burden she'd tried to spare me from, but time wasn't on her side, and she wouldn't let me continue life... *unprepared*... for what could happen if I didn't know.

"Have you seen him?" I slowed, approaching Spindrift Road.

Him. *Roman Knight.*

Even his name sounded as chivalrous as the man who'd quit his job and moved across the country all in order to take care of his orphaned niece.

I knew the basics; Carina told me the basics when she said she'd given him my information when she heard he needed a nanny.

Roman's sister and her husband had died tragically in a car accident three weeks ago, leaving him as the guardian of their six-year-old daughter, Lainey. He'd immediately resigned from his job at the FBI and brought her here. I tried not to ask too much more. I didn't want to cloud my opinion about a man I might not meet and a job I might not get.

"Two days ago," she said. "We went over with some of the other guys from Covington to help Roman move in and welcome him and Lainey."

Having a support system to lean on was invaluable in times of trauma and crisis. I knew because we hadn't had one. It was just Mom and me starting over from nothing—with nothing. *Nothing except new names.*

"Oh, that's good." I let my foot off the gas, braking hard as soon as I turned on Spindrift, not expecting the road to narrow into one lane. "How was she?"

"She wouldn't come out of her room."

My heart squeezed. "Poor thing."

Outside my window, a tall wooden fence turned into walls of dead brush on either side. It was nearing the end of September, so the thicket of foliage that normally framed every undeveloped inch of Carmel had started to thin, allowing me to see some of the houses set back from the road. Most were small, single-level homes, but as the numbers on the street lowered, the homes grew bigger.

"I can't wait to hear what you think of Roman."

"Why do you say that?" I slowed even more as the road took a blind bend to the left.

"He's just... not what you would expect from an FBI agent," she replied cryptically. "And he wears these glasses..." She sighed.

"Okay..." I wasn't sure what wearing glasses had to do with anything, but my GPS beeped again, alerting me to my approaching destination. "I'm about to pull up, Care. I'll talk to you later."

"Call me when you're done and let me know how it goes."

I should've known she wouldn't let me off that easy.

Hanging up, I dropped my cell into the cup holder and really took a good look at my surroundings. The houses were impossible to see now, and even though the ocean was out of sight, too, I heard the waves getting louder and knew I was getting closer to the bluff.

The road curved to the right, and I took the left-hand turn onto Spindrift Lane. The first house number was sixteen. Then twenty-four.

"Where the heck..." The road veered sharply to the right once more and then the sign for one-seventy appeared.

Slowly, I coasted down the drive until it ended in a square parking pad in front of a single-story house.

My eyes widened as I took in the fairly unassuming front facade made of stacked, narrow stones that matched the rocky gray of the iconic cliffs it rested on. Potted plants and bushes decorated the exterior, blending it in a natural way with the majestic location of the property.

The single-car garage sat to the right of the front door—a door that was rounded at the top. It instantly made me think of the Hobbiton houses from *Lord of the Rings*. On the other side of the garage, a tall stone wall extended out from the house, arching over a large, also round-topped, wooden door. Or gate? I wasn't sure.

What I was sure of was that though the house appeared modest, where it was built was anything but.

The gnarled extremities of the coastline butted up to the left side of the house and then wrapped around the back.

Man, the view they must have from inside...

I swallowed hard, forcing down the swell of hope that I'd get the job—that I'd get to work right next to the cliffs I loved.

I shut off my car and flipped down the visor, combing my fingers through my midlength brown hair that naturally curled into soft waves. Next came a coat of ChapStick across my lips and a quick sip of water before I got out of the car.

I wasn't even completely upright before a gust of brisk ocean wind knocked into me. It was always noticeably colder on the cliffs, the wind able to pierce right through you.

Shutting the door, I used my reflection in the window as a mirror. I'd worn my favorite polo shirt and dark jeans for the interview today. They fit in all the right places—not that it mattered for a nanny position—but I wanted to look as personable and professional as possible. *I wanted to look confident even if I didn't feel that way.*

Maybe it was because Carina got me this interview, and I didn't want to disappoint her. Maybe I was tired of driving Uber, sometimes late into the night while trying to stay on top of my online classes at Monterey's community college; even now, my textbooks were piled in the front seat where I'd tried to study for my two quizzes this week between trips last night. Maybe I was tired of only taking one or two classes each semester because I couldn't afford any more.

Maybe for once, I just wanted to feel the kiss of the ocean against my life and not its crash.

The sound of waves ebbed in my direction and before I realized what I was doing, my steps carried me to the very edge of the pavement instead of to the front door.

There was a sliver of space between the trees lining the road and the house that opened with a clear view of the rocks and rich blue sea.

I loved the ocean in the fall. The color of the water would take on this deeper, somber hue that was cracked by the coarse, white foam of the waves. It was broken, but beautiful.

A little like me.

A familiar sense of calm brought on by the sound and smell of salt water settled me. A quick whip of wind took a strand of hair across my face, sticking it to the ChapStick on my lips, and I turned. There was only a small porthole-like window on the front of the house. I hadn't noticed it at first, but now that I was looking, I swore I saw a pair of eyes watching me through it for a second before they disappeared.

I shouldn't be standing here; I should be knocking at the front door.

Peeling my hair from my mouth, I glanced back at the sea and filled my lungs with the saltwater breeze when a warm shiver cascaded down my spine and crashed low into my stomach.

"Excuse me," a voice rumbled behind me, deep and somber... *just like my sea.*

I spun, my filled lungs emptying with the strength of an ebbing current.

Him.

Roman Knight.

The rush of the waves had masked his approach.

Holy handsome.

His dark slacks molded to his legs, black loafers peeking out from the bottom. I followed every buttoned button of his starched white shirt up to the collar, marveling at how he could be comfortable when every article of clothing seemed to lock him into place.

His mocha-brown hair looked tossed by the wind, and it was the only part of him in disarray. The hard cut of his jawline was dusted with a day-old shadow, drawing me up to the matching shadows-in-gray gaze. Untouchable pain blocked by a pair of square-framed glasses.

The glasses...

No wonder Carina wanted to hear my impression. Roman looked nothing of what my imagination envisioned as an FBI agent. He was more soldier than suit with all that bulk. His biceps stretched the sleeves of his shirt and his broad chest tested the limits of its seams.

He rose up like a bluff of man and muscle, as rugged as the rocks stacked into California's coast though he'd done everything to package himself into the picture of composure.

BUT THE GLASSES... I swallowed hard. He was hot without the glasses. *With them?* He was impossibly sexy. Maybe even deadly so.

And that was a very bad impression to have of the man who was not only, at thirty-seven, fifteen years older than me, but also the man I was hoping would become my boss.

"Can I help you?"

The question spurred me into action, and the rich tenor of his voice spurred the lower parts of me to respond, too.

"I'm so sorry." I strode toward him and extended my hand. "I'm Stevie Michaels. I'm here for an interview." I glanced over my shoulder, but only for an instant before my eyes were drawn back to his.

"I know."

Of course, he did. A house like this—*a man like this*—would have security cameras.

"Sorry, I just couldn't help but admire the view." *Oh god.* I flushed, instantly worried he thought I meant him. *Crap.* "Of the ocean." I jabbed my finger in the opposite direction like he had no idea what ocean or what view I was talking about.

Genius, Stevie.

"Roman Knight." He folded his arms, raising the swells of his strong pecs.

"It's a pleasure to meet you, Mr. Knight." Something in my stomach fluttered.

Note to self: don't use the word "pleasure" around him again.

"If you're ready, we can go inside."

Way to go. Gawking at the man's house before even meeting him.

I flinched ever so slightly, but of course, he noticed it. It felt like he noticed everything, even things that couldn't be seen. But at least he hadn't ended the interview here. I could pretend like I still had a shot at salvaging this.

He didn't wait for me to agree before leading the way.

My head tipped up as I walked through the arched doorframe that led inside the house where my attention was quickly diverted.

We entered between the kitchen and dining area. Everything from the cabinets to the flooring was colored in off-whites. The roof was a warm-colored wood, though I had no idea what kind. The furniture was new; some of the dining chairs still sitting in their IKEA boxes against the wall.

In front of me, the walkway led into the living room, a large stone hearth eating up the center of the back wall. There were two navy couches, and a TV that was still in its box. More boxes lined the walls. Some opened. Most still taped up. This was definitely the home of a man who'd just moved in, that much was obvious. What wasn't obvious—*what should be*—was that a child lived here, too.

Roman stopped just inside the space, but I took another few steps forward. I couldn't help myself. On either side of the fireplace were floor-to-ceiling windows that overlooked the cliffside.

The rocks. The ocean. It was all here.

"So, Ms. Michaels, you came very highly recommended by Carina even though you have no babysitting experience."

I spun and nodded, unable to deny the truth.

"That's correct, however, I'm currently in school for my degree in early childhood care, so even though I'm inexperienced, I'm knowledgeable," I offered, watching the color of his eyes shift underneath the gleam of his glasses.

Desperate to not be caught gaping at the inside of his house after he'd caught me doing that very thing outside, I kept my back to the amazing view and rounded the far side of the couch. There I noticed a hallway to my right, a closed door on either side and an open one at the end; the master bedroom with its stark white bedspread clearly visible.

His bed.

"You're in school?"

I jerked my eyes away, blotting that last image from my mind. His voice was like a fog, too cloudy to tell whether he thought my being in school was a good or bad thing.

"The classes are online," I assured him. "So, it won't have any effect on my work schedule."

He hummed, the sound much smoother than the rest of him.

"I assume you've been told about my situation." He strode up to the couch, clamping over the back of it with both hands. It sent a ripple cascading down the cords of his neck, down to the bulge of his biceps, along the veins of his forearms, and right down to the twitch of his strong fingers.

This was a man doing all he could do to hold on—to hold everything together.

My mouth opened and shut once, feeling strangely dry,

before I replied, "Yes. Carina told me what happened to your sister. I'm so, so sorry."

I knew what it was like to lose a family member, but I couldn't imagine losing that person and then becoming a father because of it.

The full arch of his lips narrowed and he nodded. "Between closing up things with my old job and starting my new one, this position could get pretty time intensive. Are you sure that's something you want to handle in addition to your schoolwork?"

"It's something I need to handle, Mr. Knight, whether it's here or somewhere else."

I wasn't about to burst into a sob story about how I was living on my own and trying to put myself through college; I needed to work. I didn't have a choice.

I didn't have a man like him to swoop in and help me... and I didn't want one.

"But you have no previous nanny experience," he repeated. "What about babysitting?"

Heat rose in my cheeks. "No. None."

"Not even for family or cousins? Even if you weren't paid?" He sounded as frustrated as I felt.

"No." My throat burned. This was a bad idea.

"Do you have any experience with children at all, Ms. Michaels?"

Do you? I wanted to shoot back.

"No, but I'm patient and reliable and compassionate," I returned. "And if you talked to Carina about me, then you already should know *both* about my lack of hands-on experience *and* my character."

His eyes glinted, surprised by the backbone in my response.

"Ms. Michaels, you have to understand that my niece has been through significant trauma, losing both her parents."

And it didn't look like she was the only one, I thought.

"I understand." And I did. I'd also lost both my parents.

"Of course, I'm taking Lainey to see a therapist, so that's not what I'm looking for, but I need her to have someone..." He trailed off with an audible exhale and speared his fingers through his hair.

That grip was the force that wrecked his thick brown waves.
The knot in my throat tightened. *This was a mistake.* I wasn't getting the job. Experience mattered, just not my own.

A creak entered into our conversation from the hall, and we both turned.

A skinny, brown-haired girl stood in the doorway of her room, peering up at me curiously.

Lainey.

She had on a tie-dye sweatshirt and matching sweatpants. Her hair looked like it needed a good brushing, but even though her eyes looked sad, she didn't look like she'd been crying.

I glanced at Roman, but strangely, he stared like he'd seen a ghost, afraid if he moved a muscle that his niece would vanish.

Well, this was awkward.

My eyes returned to Lainey; this time, I saw a younger version of myself in her big brown eyes. Sad. Confused. Scared. Searching for answers like they were a life raft in the middle of the ocean.

Except Lainey was only six. Not fifteen.

Her gaze dropped to the floor and widened. Mine followed it to see the ladybug that was crawling on the floor.

"Oh, don't worry about her," I murmured soothingly, quickly crouching over the bug.

I carefully angled my palm directly in the bug's path, watching the red-and-black dot pause at my hand before climbing onto it.

My eyes flicked upward, surprised to see that Lainey had come closer and was watching me intently.

"She just got a little lost," I said softly, lifting my hand with the ladybug in the center so Lainey could take a better look. "She lives outside. Do you want to help me bring her home?"

Her little head snapped up and she stared at me for a long second before nodding.

"Do you want to carry her?"

Her eyes widened and then another nod.

I extended my other hand and she hesitated a moment before giving me her palm. Lining it under mine, I gently brushed the little ladybug into Lainey's hand.

"There you go, little bug," I cooed.

Lainey stared at her little bug passenger.

"Alright, let's get her back outside," I urged, about to turn toward the front door when Lainey took decisive steps into the living room leading over to the sliding glass door instead.

I gulped as I straightened and hesitantly followed her. I thought she'd go with me back to the front door since it seemed pretty obvious that I'd be on my way out of here as soon as this rescue mission was done.

But now, I didn't have a choice.

I followed her to the back door, feeling Mr. Knight's gaze lapping hotly at my heels with each step though he said nothing and made no move to stop me.

I unlocked the door for Lainey and pulled it open so she could go outside first.

Oh my... It was beyond beautiful back here with the sea framing the edge of the property. But it was more than that. There was a serenity that screamed sanctuary.

"Alright," I said and quickly tore my attention back to my task. "Now just put your hand down here." I gently took her wrist and lowered it to the grass. "And scoot her off."

Two gentle nudges with my fingertip and Miss Ladybug was back into her wild home. *And I envied her.*

Lainey watched the bug intently for a few seconds while I watched her and while I felt Mr. Knight's gaze on me.

"I'm Stevie, by the way," I belatedly introduced myself and extended my hand. "It's nice to meet you."

Seconds stacked on top of one another, building the awkward silence. I didn't dare look back at Roman, afraid of what I'd see. *Afraid he'd still be paralyzed.* Or worse. *That he'd tell me it was time to leave.*

Who was I kidding? I wasn't going to get this job. I shouldn't introduce myself into her life only to walk right out of it. I didn't need a degree or a therapist or *nanny experience* to know that.

"Okay, well it looks like my work here is done—" I sucked in a breath when tiny fingers squeezed my lowering hand.

And then, in the smallest whisper known to man or decibel measurements, she whispered, "Hi."

Her voice was so tiny, so innocent and yet it trembled with the trauma of what she'd been through.

"Hi," I repeated back, knowing that it probably sounded like I was talking to myself because there was no way he could've heard that over the sound of the ocean.

But I couldn't stop myself from glancing over my shoulder, and what I saw twisted a knot into my chest.

He stood in the doorway, hands on either side of the frame like he was holding himself back from stepping outside. *Like stepping outside would shatter something so important yet so fragile.*

And his expression. I couldn't decipher it. Confusion? Pain? Hope? His eyes connected to mine with an electric magnetism, firing the muscle in his jaw.

I'd overstepped. *And I should go.*

"Nice to meet you," I murmured to Lainey, about to pull my hand away when his voice sounded behind me.

"Lainey, I have—"

As soon as he spoke, she dropped my hand and darted by him inside. I couldn't see where she went, but the sound of a door shutting made her bedroom a pretty safe assumption.

Well, that was unexpected.

My brow furrowed as I straightened, but when my focus returned to Mr. Knight's handsome face, it was wrought with devastation—the big, broad bluff of a man eroded by his niece's suffering and solitude.

The sight swept over me and almost drew me under. I wanted to go to him. To assure him it would be okay, that little girls were so strong even when they hurt; they just needed time to heal. But I stopped myself, crossing my arms and biting into my lip hard.

A low sound that approached a growl rumbled from his chest. His eyes were locked on my mouth—my lips. It was because I'd said something. He was angry, and it was all my fault. I'd talked to her. Engaged with her. Introduced myself when all I was going to do was leave.

"Mr. Knight, I'm sor—"

"You're hired."

What? Why?

I gaped, swaying slightly with surprise. "I... am?"

His jaw was set. His gaze daring me to disagree.

I wasn't going to. He was the one who'd thought I was ill-equipped not even five minutes ago; I still desperately wanted—*needed*—this job.

"You start Monday morning, Ms. Michaels—"

"Stevie," I choked out, reeling from the sudden and swift change of course.

He grunted low, refusing to reciprocate the gesture of familiarity. "Please be here at seven." He made for the door, the expectation that I was to follow.

Roman Knight was a riptide come to life. Strong and powerful. Devastating and dangerous. A break in the waves that could leave you broken.

I managed to keep myself calm as I followed him; his goodbye was as short and swift as the door closing in my face, leaving me gaping on the stoop. But I couldn't care how gruff or curt he was; he had his reasons, and I had the job.

A nanny position. Steady, stable pay.

Excitement brimmed inside me. *I got the job.* A job that involved me spending my time in my most favorite place—along the cliffs.

The fact that my new boss was both beautiful and broken was something I'd just have to ignore. *But that should be easy, right?* The whole point was for me to watch Lainey while he wasn't home.

Out of sight, out of mind.

I turned my key in the ignition, my eyes drifting back to the front door.

Why did I have a feeling that Roman Knight was good at keeping out of sight, but had no intentions of retreating from my mind?

Maybe it had something to do with the fact that I'd seen the bed where those bulging muscles and tossed chocolate hair slept at night. *Maybe it had something to do with the fact that I'd seen the place where those glasses and all his shields came off...*

CHAPTER TWO

Roman

"That's quite the haul you've got there," the woman, her name badge read Stacey, remarked as I unloaded my cart at the register in the grocery store.

"Yeah," I grunted and grabbed another package of Oreos, sighing as I set it on the conveyor.

I spared a glance at the clock. *Forty-five minutes.* That was how long I'd been roaming the aisles, trying to figure out what the hell to buy—what the hell a six-year-old liked to eat. *What kind of comfort food could bring any comfort to a little girl who lost both her mother and her father?*

It took forty-five seconds to come up with that answer: none. The forty-five minutes was my attempt at finding a delicious distraction.

I cleared my throat and stacked the boxes of frozen pizza, bags of chicken fingers, and an array of mac and cheese on the conveyor next.

My stomach tightened painfully. Val fucking loved mac and cheese. Any kind. Any cheese. Made from a box or by Anthony Bourdain, she'd loved it from the time we were little. But no matter how many kinds she tried, she always said her favorite mac and cheese was mine.

"There's just something about the way you make it, Rome."

I always said she was full of shit. A half-decent mac and cheese would turn me into a chef no more than becoming Lainey's guardian would turn me into a father.

I rubbed my throat like there was a rope knotted around it, and every time I tried to pull on the rope—to pull my head above water—the knot tightened.

"New to town or just visiting?" the cashier—Stacey probed, an easy smile on her face.

"New." My voice cracked over the word.

Everything was new. New place. New home. New life. New job. New role. *Guardian.*

I didn't want new. Lainey deserved better than new. She deserved her damn parents, not a man whose only company for the last decade had been government employees and serial killers; *I refrained from making commentary on which group was crazier.*

We'd been in Carmel Cove for two weeks, and I was just getting around to stocking the kitchen. *Great start to being a dad, Knight.* I winced. I wasn't her dad. Never would be. I would always be Uncle Roman. I had no fucking clue how to be a father.

No fucking clue how to do any of this.

"Oh, well welcome to Carmel Cove," she said warmly. "Hope you're getting a warm welcome from all the locals. Be sure to stop over at Ocean Roasters for a coffee if you haven't already, assuming you like coffee; their tea is excellent, too. But the coffee..." She trailed off with a sigh. "A little taste of heaven."

Heaven. I flinched.

Dammit, Val. I blinked, the shutter of my eyelids opening the memory I'd relived over and over again for three weeks now, wondering just how the hell it had become real...

"Is everything okay? It's not the baby, is it?"

Val smiled and chuckled, patting my shoulder as though she were the oldest and not the one seven months pregnant.

"The baby is fine, Rome," she assured me and scooted her chair closer. "I needed to talk to you because Bill and I are updating our wills... for the

baby, and I wanted to ask you if we could put you in the will as Lainey's guardian should anything ever happen to us."

"What would happen to you?" I asked dumbly, as though I didn't deal regularly with the unexpected and abhorrent.

"Oh, you know, that we would decide to flee the country on a pirate ship and leave our infant behind," she tossed at me, unable to keep a straight face let alone hold back a laugh.

She was always light. So damn light.

Maybe that was why I hunted all the darkness in the world because I never wanted any of the shadows to touch her brightness. *Hers or my niece's.*

"Nothing is going to happen to Bill and me. Just promise me you'll take care of her."

"In case of pirates?"

She frowned. "Rome…"

"I will." I heard myself say, unsure of who I was responding to at that point—the cashier or the memory. Thankfully, it looked like my answer made sense because Stacey smiled.

Unfortunately, being friendly was low man on the totem pole under grief, responsibility, desolation, fear, and worry.

I loaded the rest of my things on the conveyor.

Fifty minutes.

Addy told me not to rush; she thought I could use some time to myself to process everything that happened instead of just reacting. I refrained from telling her that there was no such thing. For a man who dedicated his life to saving the world from its worst, there was nothing I could do to save this little girl's world from the worst thing that could happen in it—losing her parents. That kind of unfixable failure was the kind of thing that would forever haunt me.

"Sorry you're coming into this weather," Stacey went on; if my clipped answers bothered her, she didn't let it show. "It's supposed to clear up in a few days, and I promise, when you can see that ocean horizon off the cliffs, you'll just fall in love."

I managed a tight smile in response.

I owed Addy and Carina big time for offering to come over and sit at the house with Lainey while I ran to the store.

Since the accident, Lainey cried every time she had to get in a car; not even the loud, sobbing wails. Silent fucking tears. Like she didn't even have the capability to protest the torture. Of all the horrible things I'd witnessed in my life—in my career—nothing compared to my niece's silent tears.

On top of that, this morning the dark-gray clouds had loomed like a malevolent fist in the sky, unfurling as I pulled out of the drive to release torrents of rain from their fingertips as the day went on.

I definitely wasn't going to put Lainey in a car in the rain; it was raining when the drunk driver crashed into them.

"Thank you," I mumbled when she finally handed me my receipt, half hearing her second welcome to town as I gathered my bags.

I dropped the cart back into the trolley and split my ten bags between my hands, beelining for the parking lot.

I needed to get back.

Rain pelted my face and shoulders as I jogged to the new Bronco I'd purchased the day we arrived. I wanted a big SUV—something so big that it would convince Lainey she was safe riding in it because I didn't know how many more trips of silent tears I could take.

I tossed the groceries into the back, rounding the SUV when a blue car caught my gaze.

I shouldn't have even seen it through the rain, and I definitely shouldn't have stopped. But decades of searching for patterns and training to pick up on familiar details were instincts that were hard to break... especially when what I was noticing was her.

Stevie Michaels.

My—*Lainey's* new nanny. The girl—woman—*fuck*—with no formal training, no experience, no... nothing... except the ability to rescue ladybugs and get my niece to speak.

I stood in the rain, the tiny balloons of moisture sliced open by my jagged edges, bleeding their contents onto my clothes and skin until I was soaked. But I couldn't stop watching her car like there was some kind of magnetism that held my attention to her.

She stopped right out front, and I thought she was going to run into the store for something. Instead, she pulled the hood of her sweatshirt over her head and went to her trunk. She had on sneakers and black leggings and even from here, there was no mistaking the way they shaped her legs and ass.

Generous curves for a small frame.

My dick twitched.

Fuck.

Before I could thoroughly berate myself for looking too long at Lainey's damn nanny who was a few years shy of exactly half my age, a cart appeared next to her. *And a guy.*

A different emotion I refused to deign with a name dug its claws into my veins like an animal I tried to cage. My teeth clenched. The two of them talked for a second before he walked to the passenger side... *and got in the car.*

What. The. Fuck.

Did he really just leave Stevie to unload their cart of groceries into the trunk in the pouring rain?

Propelled by a revolt of anger, my feet carried me toward her. I was fuming. Angry that her boyfriend left her in the rain. Angry because she had a boyfriend. *Angry because I shouldn't fucking be angry.*

Dammit, Knight. Every step echoed that this was a mistake. A giant fucking mistake. Just like looking at her. Just like hiring her.

But she'd gotten Lainey to talk to her; *she'd gotten Lainey to talk.*

As if I didn't feel like enough of a failure to Val, Lainey hardly ate two bites of anything I put in front of her and hadn't spoken to me since the accident. Hell, I wasn't sure she'd spoken at all since the crash until *her.*

The niece whisperer.

I caught a whiff of her through the rain as I approached. Soaked peppermint and sugar. She wasn't paying attention to anything except her task, trying to get out of the storm as quickly as possible.

She'd picked up a single bag from the cart, needing both hands to support the weight when I got to her.

"Give me that," I ordered, taking the bag from her hands.

Stevie recoiled with a loud gasp until she recognized me.

"Ro—Mr. Knight?" I felt her confused gaze.

I grabbed two more bags from the cart, both filled with liters of soda. I ground my teeth together, wanting to pull that fucker from the car and punch him in the face for leaving her to load up all their *heavy* things.

"What are you—you don't need to do that," she insisted, trying to shoulder in front of me.

I stopped and glared at her through my rain-caked glasses.

Her eyes were so damn wide and surprised—like she never expected anyone to help her. And fuck, if that didn't spark a burning in my blood. *At least I could help one fucking person around here... even if it was just with her groceries.* But it was the way even the cold, bitter rain clung to the pink pout of her lips that made electric desire crack through me.

Wanting her was just as dangerous as the mix of electricity and water. *Especially since she was now working for me.*

"Move, Ms. Michaels," I snapped and shoved by her.

I hauled the over-packed bags into the trunk of her car. It couldn't have taken more than a minute to load everything up, but it would've gone a helluva lot faster if her—*that guy* would've helped.

Her head tipped up. "Thank you."

"Don't thank me. Get a decent boyfriend," I snarled and slammed the trunk shut like my own crack of thunder.

Her sudden inhale was strong enough to stop me for a second and burn the sight of her parted lips into my brain and leave the memory to haunt me later. Growling low, I stalked back to the Bronco, my fists balled at my sides the entire way.

"Fuck." The curse erupted from deep in my chest as soon as my door shut.

I gripped the steering wheel, vibrating with rage. It was a miracle I hadn't pulled that asshat from her car and made *him* unload the bags after giving him a good piece of my mind... and my fist. Except it wasn't a miracle; it was because of Lainey. Three weeks ago, this scene would've played out differently, but now, I wasn't just... me.

I wasn't able to play hero for everyone anymore, only Lainey.

In retrospect, I shouldn't have even gone over. Stevie and her relationships were none of my goddamn business. But dammit, seeing her there, struggling in the rain, something unstoppable came over me and I needed to be the one to help her. *I wanted to be the one she could depend on.*

And the way she looked at me when I did... *Shit.* Now, I wasn't sure I'd ever get that feeling out of my system.

I was soaked. My seat was going to be soaked. But all I could think about was the fucker who sat nice and dry in his girlfriend's car while leaving her out in the rain.

I should be grateful she had a boyfriend. It was one more reason to add to the laundry list of why wanting her couldn't even be a ghost in my mind.

"Did she come out at all?" I asked Addy, brushing off her attempt to help me with the groceries.

"Once." She offered me a sad smile, tucking a strand of blue hair behind her ear. "She walked over and looked out the window, and then went over to Carina and touched her stomach, and then went back to her room."

I set the refrigerated items on the floor next to the fridge, the thud masking my defeated exhale.

"Did she say anything?"

"No." Addy shook her head. "I'm sorry."

I pulled my lips tight and nodded.

It wasn't a secret that I was struggling with my niece, but there wasn't anything that anyone could do. I just hoped the therapist I'd scheduled us with next week, Dr. Shelly, could figure out what was going on in Lainey's head because every moment of her silence was like another nail being driven into my sister's coffin.

"Sorry about that," Carina entered the conversation, coming from the hall. "Just wanted to use the restroom once more before we head out."

Her hand cradled her very pregnant stomach.

"Are you sure you don't want us to stay?"

"I appreciate it, but this was more than enough," I said and dumped a whole bag of frozen pizzas of every kind into the freezer drawer.

Pizzas. Chicken nuggets. Ice cream. Mac and cheese. Oreos. I was going to throw every kid-favorite meal I could think of at the wall, praying that something would stick.

"I'm glad you hired Stevie," Carina went on, and I stopped short for a second at the mention of her name—*and the too vivid memory of her dewy lips.* "She's really great."

"I hope so," was all I managed to get out through tight teeth as I straightened. "Thank you both for sitting with Lainey. I'm going to see if these might do the trick before I get on a call." I held up the package of Oreos.

It wasn't healthy. But neither was not fucking eating.

Desperate times...

"Of course. We're all here to help, Roman, so just call if you need anything. Really," Addy said and placed her hand on my arm. "You're doing good."

Good but not good enough.

Addison Covington was a miracle worker. Aside from being my friend and new boss's wife, she'd helped countless women survive and recover from all kinds of abuse and trauma with her nonprofit organization, Blooms; if Lainey were an adult, I knew Addy could help her, too.

But she wasn't. She was a little girl who'd lost her parents and was left with an uncle who knew nothing about raising a kid.

I could get into the mind of a serial killer, but figuring out the mind of a child? Forget it.

"Just give her time," Carina said as she stopped next to me, drawing me from my thoughts. "She's a strong little girl, and little girls can do hard things, too."

I pulled together a tight smile.

Carina and her four sisters had lost their father when they were pretty young. I couldn't remember all their names let alone their ages, though I knew Dante had mentioned them to me before, but I didn't think any of them had been as young as Lainey.

"Thanks."

I watched them get into Addy's car and then locked the door. With a silent prayer to the Oreo gods, I took the snack to Lainey's door and knocked softly.

"Hey, Bug." I swallowed. *No response.* Somehow, the times when she didn't respond to the nickname I'd given her when she was a baby were even more painful. "I grabbed a snack for you at the store."

Another beat passed. *Nothing.* Silence was the sharpest knife.

"I'll just leave them out here if you want one," I rasped, crouching down and listening once more for even just a shuffle of movement, but there was nothing.

Of course, I could just open the door and check on her; she never locked it. But just like she could hardly bring herself to come out, I couldn't bring myself to go in. If she didn't want to see or talk to me out here, I was afraid I'd only make things worse by forcing my way into her grief.

I set the Oreos on the ground and returned to the kitchen for a water bottle. I'd worry about eating once I was done with my meeting.

Sliding into one of the chairs at the small dining table, I flipped open my laptop and pulled up the video conference app, seeing that Ace was already waiting.

"Sorry for the delay," I greeted Ace Covington, the owner of Covington Security.

The former SEAL sat in his office wearing a Covington tee, his glassy blue eyes penetrating the screen. He was an imposing hulk of a man—but so was his brother, Dex, and the rest of his team.

Ace and I had been friends for a long time. He'd been a SEAL, and I'd been working an international serial killer case the first time our paths crossed. Over the years, we'd remained friends. I'd consult on their cases; they'd provide on-the-ground assistance on mine. Now, after all these years, I was finally going to work at Covington Security—something I honestly never thought I'd do. Not because I didn't like or have the utmost respect for Ace and his growing team, but because I could never imagine doing anything other than working for the FBI's Behavioral Analysis Unit.

But hunting serial killers didn't go hand in hand with raising a child.

"Promise me you'll take care of her."

I'd called Ace the morning after the accident and put in my resignation with the FBI immediately after. Within the week, I was preparing the both of us for our cross-country move.

"Don't worry about it, man. Addy called and said they just left your place, so I figured you'd need a few."

"Thanks." I flipped open the case on my iPad and tapped on my task app.

"You sure you want to be doing this right now? You can take more time."

My head jerked. "You're already letting me work from home. I don't need more time."

He stared at me, jaw clenching all the way up onto his skull, twitching the tattoos inked to the side of his head. There wasn't anything subtle about Ace. Not his size. Not his head tattoos. And not the Viking-style haircut he sported, one half of his skull buzzed, the other half grown out and pulled back.

"It's only been three weeks."

Only? Those three weeks had taken longer to pass than the last thirty-seven years of my life.

"I'm good, Ace," I told him, my voice carrying a hint of warning.

I had to do something. Sitting around in the silence, a bellowing reminder of all the ways I was failing Lainey, wasn't an option.

We both needed a consistent new normal—a firm path to follow even as we walked in grief.

"How's everything going with the BAU?" he probed.

I notched my glasses higher on the bridge of my nose. "Slow," I replied. "But it's going."

Losing the senior supervisory special agent of the East Coast field office wasn't a blow that the agency was prepared for. Even though my team was top notch, and I'd personally recommended Sally Koorie to take my place, the powers that be still requested I remain available to them in a consultative capacity for the next four months to wrap up the cases we still had open and provide support until Koorie's spot on the team was filled.

"There are three open cases I agreed to see through remotely. Two should be wrapping up within the next couple weeks. The last…" I shook my head. "I think the Bureau is going to have to take that one as a loss."

At least, I was.

Agent Aarons, my predecessor, had warned me there would always be cases that stuck with you. Ones where we didn't get to the victims in time. Ones that would cost me members of my team. Ones that would make me question not only humanity, but my sanity. And ones that never got solved.

The Archangel was *that* one. A violent serial killer who'd remained in the wind for decades. A rare breed of psychopath who'd killed consistently across state lines, across the country, only to seemingly and suddenly go dormant for a decade and a half—unheard of in a breed of human that, for one compulsion or another, typically escalated in the frequency of their crimes rather than taking a break.

The working theory was that he'd been incarcerated for a lesser crime during those years, but that explanation sat like bad fish in my stomach especially since we hadn't come across an inmate who fit the mold.

"You'll figure it out. Always do," Ace assured me.

I swore I was going to catch the Archangel before my career was through, the task like my personal quest for the Holy Grail.

"If not, it's not my problem anymore," I brushed it off, pretending like I'd ever get a good night's sleep knowing that man was still out there—taking young girls, assaulting them and strangling them before cutting into their bodies all in the name of religious redemption. "So, what have you got for me?"

His stoic composure broke for a second as he drew a deep breath. "Well, what I have for you are a couple of cases the team is tackling that we could use some profiles on the suspects, but I'm going to shoot those over in an email because I just got off the phone with Hazard over at Armorous Tactical," he explained. "He said they're dealing with a serial arsonist, and he wants you to give them your thoughts on a profile."

"Got it." My eyes lifted above my screen while he added everyone to the call, drowning my focus in the sea of gray outside the glass panes of the living room windows.

Gray sky. Gray ocean. A murky canvas that seemed more like a mirror than it did a window.

"Roman," Ace spoke and my attention snapped back to the screen, the video conference now split into several squares with familiar faces of my new teammates and old friends.

I'd seen almost all of them since the move out here, but this was the first time I was meeting with them as a fellow employee.

"Hey, man. Welcome aboard." Rocco Damiani was the first to speak, a flash of white slicing through the dark mat of his beard as he leaned back in his chair in his office. Former CIA spook. Married to Carina. Specialized in security systems.

"Glad to have you. Can't wait to pick your brain about serial killers," Dante Lozano chimed in before tossing a handful of popcorn into his grinning mouth.

Dante was Carina's older brother and a Backstreet Boys fanatic. He lounged in a desk chair in the ops room at Covington headquarters which doubled as Dex Covington's office.

"Roman," Dex grunted and tipped his head; though his size rivaled his brother's, his technical skills were the ones that formed the informational nervous system of the company. Dex handled anything from tracking to hacking—everything that occurred behind a computer screen was his domain.

"Dex," I grunted back and shifted my eyes to the last man in Dex's office who stood with his arms folded, his blond hair buzzed, and his winning smile unmistakable. "And Reed Lockhard... so the rumors are true."

The former San Francisco policeman chuckled. "Another cop claimed by Covington."

Reed and Dante had been on the force together several years ago. Dante had been the first to leave after his partner was killed; he'd joined Covington as their protection specialist and that was where he'd met his famous wife, Lenni.

The last time I'd seen Reed was almost two years ago when he and Dex worked with me to solve a case; he'd still been with the force back then.

"The whole city has signs up looking for San Francisco's Hot Cop. Just wait until they figure out he's hiding in Carmel," Dante joked between bites.

Two years ago, Reed had been caught on camera by a tourist as he jumped in front of a trolley—shirtless—to save a dog that escaped its leash. It earned him the infamous title of Frisco's Hot Cop. Even the locals, who hated the abbreviated name for their city, didn't let it deter them from turning Reed into a viral sensation.

"So, does this mean I'm not the proby anymore?" Reed wondered and glanced around, eager to escape being highlighted as the new guy on the team.

"You're the proby until Jackson says you're not the proby," Roc informed him firmly, hiding his smile by dragging his hand down his beard.

The only one missing from the group was Jackson Pyle, a SEAL buddy of Ace's who'd joined Covington a little over a year ago. He was also the one I had to thank for this house. The housing market was complete shit right now, especially for someone moving from the other side of the country. Addy started to look at places for me when Jackson stepped in and offered to sell one of the unused properties owned by his family's corporation, Pyle Petroleum.

Normally, I was the kind of guy who'd graciously refuse that big of a gesture, especially when the price he set was well below market value. But there was nothing normal about this situation. Nothing normal about losing my sister and gaining a child in the blink of an eye. And while my knowledge of what it took to raise a kid was sorely lacking, the one thing I did know was that what I needed or wanted no longer mattered.

I acted for Lainey. I made decisions for Lainey. *I lived for Lainey.* So, I accepted Jackson's price and bought this house because I refused to bring anything temporary into her life. Not when she'd already lost more at six than most people had by sixty.

"Jackson's on baby duty at the moment, so I'll fill him in later," Ace said as though reading my thoughts.

Jackson's girlfriend, Isla, was also pregnant, so I guess he was with her at a doctor's appointment.

"So, where are we at, bossman?" Dante balled the popcorn wrapper up and tossed it in the trash. Dex's eyes narrowed.

"Well, I just wanted to have our first official meeting with Roman. I just told him that Hazard is sending over a case of theirs. Serial arson near the city. He wants a profile from Roman, but if the rest of you want to take a look, too."

"Jesus," Dex grumbled. "First serial killers, now serial arson. What are they putting in the water up there?"

A brief laugh blew through my lips. Dex was referencing that case that he, Reed, and I had worked on in the city. We'd thought it was a serial case at first, but it veered more into organized crime than psychopathic tendencies.

"He's going to send over everything they have to you, Dex, for review. I guess Detective Werner reached out to him because the police are a little short staffed with citywide events."

"Just got the zip file," Dex said, clearly opening up the information while on the call. "Once I download everything, I'll put it on the server so everyone can review it remotely."

"Great." Ace clipped his chin downward. "Let's take a look and reconvene on Monday with ideas, leads, and possible suspects."

The team muttered in agreement.

The rest of the meeting went by quicker, everyone reviewing the cases or projects they were working on before new clients were discussed. For a split second, I felt some semblance of my old life return: meaningful work. Good team. *Zero personal distractions.*

"Is there anything else we can do for you, Roman?" Ace asked, timing out that split second.

"No, thanks." I cleared my throat, and Ace adeptly read the sound, moving on and concluding the meeting a few minutes later.

I closed my computer and set my glasses on top of the shell. Pinching the bridge of my nose, my eyes drifted shut for just a second.

For weeks now, anytime I closed my eyes, I saw my sister's face—her smile. Val was always smiling. Hell, it was the one thing I knew Lainey inherited from her. Not just the shape of the smile, but its ever-present glean. From the moment I first held

Lainey in the hospital the day she was born, I swore she'd smiled even in her sleep.

And it killed me that she hadn't smiled in weeks. It killed me worrying if she ever would again.

But this time, the face behind my eyes wasn't my sister or my niece; it was gleaming wet hair sculpted to pink, porcelain cheeks and eyes the color of worn leather bookends, binding too much knowledge in their depths for someone her age, and lips…

The way those strawberry-red lips paused on the *o* at the beginning of my name. *Fuck.*

I groaned low, feeling my cock stretch against my pants without any fucking restraint. It was ridiculous. I'd never had urges consume me like this.

Maybe it was the grief. Maybe it was the massive change. Maybe it was the months I'd gone without sleeping with a woman because I was too damn focused on my career. But holy hell… The chair skidded back as I abruptly stood, needing to adjust my sudden raging erection.

Air escaped in a hot hiss from my lips that were pulled tight. Just the thought of Stevie made each of my cells scratch with a clawing hunger that it should be illegal for me to satiate.

She was twenty-two and my goddamn nanny, for fuck's sake. No matter how far upside down my life had turned in the last three weeks, it would never be far enough to put me on the right side of wanting her.

Shoving my glasses back on my face, I stood and returned all my thoughts to Lainey. Maybe pizza would lure her from her room. So far, it was the meal I'd gotten her to eat the most of. I headed toward her room to check on her, but when I reached the hall, I stopped short; the package of Oreos was gone.

I tipped my head back and heaved a sigh. Val could never resist Oreos either. It was such a small thing, but the relief I felt was fucking massive.

We were going to get through this. One Oreo at a time.

CHAPTER THREE

Stevie

I FLATTENED MY PALMS ON MY THIGHS AND RAN THEM ALONG MY jeans.

Were jeans appropriate attire for a nanny?

I paired them with a simple blue T-shirt, but looking down, questioned that, too, when my cleavage stared back at me. My chest was a solid *C* cup—and *C* stood for conspicuous; there was no bra I'd come across (within my budget) that could do anything to make my boobs less obvious. Even the sports bra I'd picked today only seemed to press them tighter and higher.

And I was pretty sure Mr. Knight wasn't looking to hire Mary Popping-out-of-her-shirt.

Staring into my window once more, I tugged the neckline up, but that made the shirt bunch weird. Sighing, I pulled the fabric back down and ran my hands over my front to smooth the fabric once more and then walked away from my car before I wasted any more time.

The level to which I'd overthought my first day on this job was Olympic. What I should wear. What I was going to say. What I was *not* going to say.

Three days had passed since the grocery store run-in, but I still hadn't gotten over the way Roman helped me. It had been so long since anyone helped me—so long since I'd even had anyone to ask for help—that the gesture had stopped my world on its axis. Our eyes locked through the raindrops as though they'd been paused midfall, and for a single electrifying second, I saw someone who cared. Gone was the fine facade of the man who'd interviewed me last week and, in his place, stood raw masculinity carved from stone.

And anger. Lots of anger. And all because of a misunderstanding.

He wasn't my boyfriend.

The correction sat at the tip of my tongue like a mint that wouldn't dissolve, the truth fresh and strong and waiting to burst free. Instead, I swallowed it whole because setting it free would only bring trouble.

Confessing that Colin wasn't my boyfriend would require me to explain that he was only my Uber passenger and had offered me an extra fifty in cash to load up his groceries in the rain because he'd just had Lasik done and couldn't get rainwater in his eyes. And if I explained that, I'd have to explain how much I needed the money.

The only thing worse than the off chance that my rideshare gig would jeopardize my new job would be if Roman—*Mr. Knight* offered to pay me more so I wouldn't have to drive.

I didn't want pity, and I didn't want help. I wanted a job, an income, and to get my education. Complete independence.

It's the surest thing—the safest thing. Pieces of my mother's advice flitted to the surface of my thoughts, and I carefully tucked them back where they belonged.

I was already cutting back the time I spent driving by taking this job, but I wanted some childcare experience on my résumé. I just needed another month or two of additional income to pay for my next semester.

I'd already registered for my classes and paid a deposit with my summer earnings, but then my car needed new tires and brakes, the rent for my closet-sized apartment (that arguably had several code violations) went up, and the rest of my savings was suddenly depleted. But I was going to figure it out.

What other choice did I have? I needed to be able to drive. I needed a place to stay, although living out of my car had crossed my mind more than a handful of times since the fourth email from the school reminding me of the balance I had to pay hit my inbox this morning.

I couldn't lose my spot in those classes. If I lost that, I'd lose a whole semester.

And quite frankly, I was tired of losing things.

So, if that meant working as a nanny and moonlighting as a driver while keeping my grades up, I'd figure out a way to do it. It certainly wouldn't be the hardest thing I'd had to overcome.

I didn't stop to gawk at the ocean views this time, instead walking directly to the front door. This time, I noticed the security cameras tucked into the seams of the house.

Crap. I pulled my lower lip between my teeth and closed hard. *Had he seen me adjust my shirt and boobs?*

A husky groan tumbled from my chest just as the front door opened, catching me before I could knock.

"Ms. Michaels." Roman filled the doorframe.

My lip popped free, causing his attention to drop to my mouth for a fraction of a second before he turned his head and the sun glared off his glasses.

"Stevie," I insisted softly. "Good morning."

His nostrils flared, and the glint on his glasses parted just enough for me to see his stare rake down my front. Maybe it was my imagination or my insecurity, but I swore it paused for an extra beat on my chest, the attention making my nipples harden.

Because their level of conspicuousness could always be topped.

"Please come in." He stepped back and ushered me inside.

I folded my arms, but couldn't stop myself from examining him as I walked by. He had on a button-down shirt and khakis, and everything from the cut of his hair down to the socks on his feet fit him like pieces to a puzzle. The fabric snapped around the swells of his shoulders, meshed over the planes of his chest, and locked along the muscles of his thighs. He was a study in stony composure, but those glasses... they were the corner piece that held every inch of his picture-perfect sex appeal in place.

My mouth dried.

For the first time, I felt the full weight of Dad's lectures on temptation that had been vacuum-packed into my head. *The desire to sin comes straight from the Devil, and if you give in, Stephanie, he won't stop until he's led you straight to Hell.* Whether that was true or not, what was certain was that having the hots for my new boss could only lead to disaster.

So, I needed to focus on the *only* reason I was here.

"Where's Lainey?" I asked, glancing around.

"Still in her room," he said. "I figured I'd give you a quick tour and then let her know you're here."

"Sure."

"Good." He clipped his chin down and then walked by me, pointing and talking as he went. "Obviously, the kitchen, dining, and living room."

My gaze snagged on the view from the windows; the blue ocean spread like a silk blanket tucked into the horizon. But the shimmering sea was no match for the specimen of a man walking in front of me. I found myself enrapt by the sway of his gait, authority oozing from each step.

If I hadn't known it before, I did now: this man was meant to be in control.

"Lainey's room." He indicated the room she'd appeared in yesterday, and then turned to the door on the opposite side of the hall. "Powder room." He took another step forward and then stopped suddenly as though recalling that he didn't need to go any farther. "And the master."

The way he said master sent a ribbon of heat unfurling down my spine.

Before I could catch my breath, he spun and crashed right into me.

"Oh—"

"*Christ*," he swore and grabbed my arms even though I wasn't off balance—just shocked.

His eyes stormed when they found mine, but without anything more than a tic of his jaw, he purposely moved me to the side and continued on.

"Each of the bedrooms has a silent panic button installed next to the bed in case of an emergency," he said as though these kinds of things were normal. "It will alert my phone and

Covington and the police when pushed, but won't make a sound."

"Does Lainey know what it's for?"

He strode through the living room to the back door we'd gone through the other day.

"I told her it was a special button that can only be pushed to call me when I'm not here."

"Is that... necessary?"

He stopped at the door and faced me... cautiously this time. "In my line of work, you can't be too safe."

"Of course," I agreed, feeling foolish for asking.

I went to stand beside him, assuming he wanted to show me something outside, but as soon as I did, he visibly tensed and something burned in my chest, like he'd ripped a scab off a wound.

I knew I didn't have experience, but he acted like he couldn't even stand my presence.

Could he still be upset about what happened at the grocery store?

Again, I tasted the truth on my tongue, but if he was upset thinking Colin was my boyfriend, how much more upset would he be to learn that he was a stranger—a stranger I was driving around alone with in my car?

For some reason, I was positive that the man who needed to be in control would *not* like the idea of that at all.

"There's a single camera in here"—he pointed up high where the stone of the fireplace met the ceiling—"that gives a wide-angle shot of this space and Lainey's door. The rest of the cameras are all over the exterior of the property, front and back, and down by the guesthouse," he continued. "They're all wired to my phone and to the office."

Translation: he would always be watching.

Miss Conspicuous meet Mr. Control.

I opened my mouth to ask about the guesthouse, the spired roof of which I now saw peeking above the path that led from this building to it, but Roman walked back into the kitchen.

"If you want to knock on her door, you seem to have better luck getting a response than I do," he said hoarsely, his eyes falling to the counter.

My brow creased, and then I saw it. The plate of pancakes still on the counter. Untouched. The glass of orange juice. Still full.

Lainey hadn't come out of her room at all this morning, and if his comment was any indication, this was the normal situation for the two of them.

Two people thrown into a situation neither of them could've imagined. My heart wrenched. I might not have any experience as a nanny but broken families were my expertise.

"Is she not eating?"

He turned and grabbed something—a package of Oreos and set it in front of me.

"She'll eat these. Sometimes pizza." His expression fractured and his shoulders drifted down; the man in control was slowly losing it. "But other than that, she doesn't really want to eat. Or come out of her room. Or talk to me."

I tried to swallow, only to realize how big the ball in my throat had swelled.

Roman shook his head and let out a strained exhale before reaching for the cup and plate to clean them up, obviously giving up on the idea that his niece was going to eat the breakfast he'd made.

"Hold on for a minute," I pleaded, my hands shooting out to stop his without thinking. His sharp stare sliced to mine, and my heart jumped. "Please."

While looking at me, his finger slid up the strong bridge of his nose, seating his glasses higher. The movement was thoughtless and swift, but it struck my stomach like a bolt of lightning, burying heat down deep in its depths.

Drawing himself straight, one eyebrow lifted, daring me to accomplish this monumental feat.

Breakfast.

Lowering my head, I turned and made my way to the hall, feeling his stare bore into my back the whole way. Reaching Lainey's door, I rapped gently.

"Lainey? It's Stevie," I spoke calmly and with a smile. "We saved Miss Ladybug together last week, and I've come to see you again." I heard movement, so I kept talking. "I just wanted to let you know that I'm going to go out back and scout for pirate ships if you want to join me."

Step one, done.

Spinning, I returned to the kitchen and to Roman's doubtful stare; he didn't think it was going to work.

I smiled, picked up a napkin and a single pancake in one hand, took the glass of juice in the other, and walked to the back door. After a moment of finagling, I wedged my foot and nudged the sliding door wide enough to slide through, pressing my butt and pushing to shut it.

Step two, complete.

Salty air hit my lungs like a cool mist, and the temperature was already reaching toward the high of sixty-five.

I walked to the edge of the wooden deck and looked in awe. I could see farther down the lit cobblestone walkway from here. It unraveled along the shoreline to a small paved patio containing two wicker chairs that overlooked the sea. Just beyond that spot, it merged with another path that came from the small garden grove where we'd freed the ladybug, the entrance to which was the door in the wooden fence that I'd noticed from the driveway.

From there, the path wove closer to the bluff and down to the guesthouse.

I could make out a similar rounded door, a stone exterior that blended with the craggy cliffside, and the turret-like structure that rose up and rounded out with windows toward the sea. If a hobbit lived in a castle by the sea, this guesthouse would be it.

I didn't know how I'd missed the absolutely magical setting of this backyard before. *Maybe because I'd been so focused on him.*

Without thinking, I brought the cup of orange juice to my lips and took a sip, citrus bursting along my tongue; Roman had bought the good stuff.

Of course, he did. Of course, he bought fresh-squeezed orange juice, let his niece eat Oreos for breakfast, helped an almost stranger load groceries into her trunk in the pouring rain, and lived in a house that had a tiny castle in its backyard.

Who was this man?

I drifted toward the structure when the sound of the sliding door squeaking open broke my fascination. I turned.

Lainey.

I didn't know why I felt a breeze of disappointment blow through me. Of course, I wanted Lainey to come outside; that was the whole point of this. But apparently, I also wanted her broody, grumpy uncle to follow me, too.

"Oh, good. You're here." I beamed, but didn't approach her, waiting patiently as she pushed the door shut with both hands.

Lainey had on a different tie-dye shirt than the other day and a pair of gray joggers; her hair was pulled back in a messy, lopsided ponytail with a blue scrunchie—something she'd clearly done herself. The little half-moons of purple under her eyes made my chest tighten. Not only was she not eating well, but she clearly wasn't sleeping well either.

Her boots clunked on the wood as she walked over to me.

"Have you seen any pirates yet?" I asked.

Her eyes widened and she shook her head, half her hair sliding out of the tie and in front of her face.

"Oh, let me help you," I said and crouched, then extended the food and drink. "Can you hold these for me for a second?"

Just like I hoped, she took them, staring hungrily at the pancake while I fiddled with her hair. As soon as I had the tie secure, my gaze drifted above her head and was instantly captured by Roman's.

He stood on the other side of the glass door, watching us. *Watching me.*

My lips peeled apart, heat zigzagging through my body in waves.

"Have you?" Her tiny voice jolted me, and my attention immediately returned to her.

"Not yet." I smiled and cleared my throat. "But I think that is the perfect lookout spot." I angled my body and pointed to the two chairs a few feet down the path. "Should we go look for them there?"

Her head bobbed.

"Okay, but I can't take the cup with us." I nodded to the orange juice. "Can you help me finish it? I already drank some."

Lainey looked into the cup for a second and then brought it to her mouth. A spur of relief washed over me, and I immediately looked back to the door, hoping Roman was seeing this, too.

He was.

But now, he had one hand pinned on the doorframe like he had to hold himself back from coming outside. For a moment, I almost felt guilty for getting her to drink the juice because it was obvious how much it hurt Roman that he couldn't help his niece.

Cold glass touched my fingertips and forced my thoughts away from my boss. Lainey pushed the empty cup into my hand and wiped her mouth with the sleeve of her sweatshirt.

"Perfect." I set the glass down on the floor of the deck and nestled it against one of the railing's support beams so it wouldn't tip over. "Let's go."

I let Lainey walk ahead of me, giving her the sense of purpose of being the leader and also allowing me to watch her carefully because the rocky path was a little uneven. The farther we walked, the less I could feel the intensity of Roman's gaze.

We reached the chairs, and I sat in the first one. She took a minute and then climbed onto the other.

"Are there really pirates?" She stared at the pancake she still held.

"Oh, there are definitely pirates," I assured her.

Her eyes went even wider. "They'd come here?"

"Well, that sure looks like a fairy castle." I pointed to the guesthouse. "And pirates always deliver their treasure to the fairy princess."

She considered my answer and then looked back at the food. I swore I heard a small stomach rumble over the roll of the waves.

"Do you want that pancake? It's really yours."

Her button nose wrinkled.

"You don't have to." I shrugged my shoulders. "I'll eat it if you don't want it. Chocolate chip pancakes are my favorite. I just don't want you to get hungry and have to go inside and miss the pirates."

I didn't think I'd seen anyone take a faster bite.

I exhaled the breath that was knotted in my chest, relief untying its tethers as Lainey devoured the pancake. I lifted my eyes and sent a silent thank you up to Mom who'd unknowingly given me a guide on how to handle a grieving little girl.

There were some things in life you had no choice but to miss. *Like lost loved ones.* Sometimes, the way to keep moving forward was to remember there were still parts of life you could choose *not* to miss.

For a six-year-old, she could still choose pancakes and the chance to scout for pirates.

I sat back in the chair, staying quiet so I didn't distract her from a solid meal.

"Who's the fairy princess?" A crumb spewed from her mouth as she talked while chewing.

"You are."

Lainey stared and then shook her head. "No, I'm not."

I blinked, faking confusion. "But you live here, and that's the fairy princess's castle."

Her small brow scrunched, and I bit my cheek to hold back a smile at just how adorable she was.

"If you're not her, then who is?" I tipped toward her and added in a fake whisper, "It can't be your uncle. He wouldn't look good in a dress."

It took a fraction of a second, but then her smile appeared. Wide and dimpled, her missing two front teeth making the sight just as craggy as the coastline and equally as beautiful. And then came the giggle—low and bubbly like gentle waves rolling on top of one another until it got bigger and bigger, louder and louder.

And I laughed with her, both of us cackling in our seats.

Roman Knight in a dress. *Could I even imagine?*

A ladybug flew in front of her and she squealed in delight.

"Look! It's Miss Ladybug!" She launched a small hand out to catch the bug and released the empty napkin from her hand in the process.

"Yes," I squeaked and pushed out of my seat to catch the flyaway napkin. "Oh!" I exclaimed breathlessly as it grazed my fingertips before the breeze stole it higher.

Crap. I didn't want to litter.

My gaze tracked the napkin, directing my feet across the narrow path. I could catch it before it got too far, if I could just reach a little higher. I saw it start to dip, so I jumped, letting out a yelp of success as I pinned it in my fingertips.

But as my feet landed back on the ground, my yelp turned into a cry of distress. The grass on that side drifted down a few feet before turning into the vertical drop of the rocky bluff, and I immediately lost my balance on the uneven footing, my weight propelling me forward.

"*Stevie!*"

The booming shout crashed like a wave over me right before my body was yanked back with the force of a riptide into a wall of hot stone.

I panted, processing first that I had *not* just tumbled to my death over the rocks to be buried in the sea below. *And all for a piece of litter.*

Then, I processed him.

The immovable strength of his arm locked like a steel anchor around my stomach, each of his muscles like a chain link wedging into my skin. The musky scent of him lodging with the sea salt into my nostrils. The flat of his torso riveted to my back. And the heat of his breath as it came in heavy waves melting the skin along my neck.

My eyes fluttered shut—not wanting to waste a sense when all I wanted was to memorize the feel of him.

I'd never been this close to a man before—never held like this by a man before.

My idea of men had been rendered as undeniable as my idea of a father. Of course, I knew good men existed. Good, strong, protective, and caring men *did* exist in this world. *Just not for me.*

But for a moment… on a windswept bluff while watching for pirates, I could pretend that they did. *That he did.*

It was only seconds before his hold released and the anchor of his arm retreated back to his side, leaving me with the chill of his absence.

I turned and met Lainey's worried gaze first. I held up the napkin and stretched my smile so wide there was no way she could see any cracks of lingering fear in my expression.

"Got it!"

Lainey's smile started to flicker and then died when she

looked at her uncle. One glance at Roman, and I wanted to punch him rather than thank him for saving me. The anger that rolled off him darkened the moment like a layer of soot, suffocating the pocket of happiness we'd been enjoying.

"Lainey, why don't you move on ahead." I pointed to the fairy house where a thick concrete wall edged around a paved patio at the front. "I think we'll get a better view from down there."

She slid quickly off the chair, her eyes trained on the ground as she marched down the path, eager to avoid the confrontation I was about to face.

Once she was out of earshot but still within sight, I hazarded a glance at Roman.

He wore the same expression he had in the parking lot, only wilder. Like a warrior who'd just come from battle but knew the war had yet to be won.

I shivered and apologized. "I'm so sorry, Mr. Knight." I gulped. "I was trying not to litter."

He folded his arms across his chest, both hands gripping his biceps hard as though he were physically imprisoning himself so he couldn't reach out and throttle me. Meanwhile, I couldn't help but trace the veins of his forearms that distended from the effort it took to catch me back.

"With the napkin or with your dead body?" His jaw wrenched so tight, I could practically hear its gears grinding.

I blanched and bit my lip, but that made him growl louder.

"I'm sorry. It was really stupid of me, and I will absolutely be more careful from now on," I assured him, hoping there would be a *now on* and that I wasn't about to be fired for setting an incredibly dangerous example of what *not* to do. "Thank you for saving me, my—Mr. Knight."

Good grief, Stevie. He's not your knight, he's your boss.

Roman's silent glare raked over me several times, each pass feeling like he saw through one more layer. First, my clothes. Next, my skin. Then, my thoughts... I shifted my weight, worried what parts of me he'd see if I let him keep going.

"How did you do that?" he demanded with a coarse voice and then glanced to Lainey.

"Almost die?" It was supposed to be a joke.

Mr. Control didn't like my jokes. "Get her to eat her breakfast," he grunted.

"Oh." I licked my lips and swore I heard him suck in a breath. "When my mom moved us to California, I was really upset." I paused and chose my words carefully. "I didn't want to lose everything she'd forced us to leave behind."

"So, you refused to eat?"

The ball in my throat burned, but I ignored it. The way he looked at me was dangerous—as though he could see all the broken parts of my past that I'd worked so hard to sever myself from. *Unfortunately, I couldn't sever my own blood.*

"I was an angry teenager… but angry because I was sad," I explained. "At first, I would only eat Girl Scout cookies. After about a week of trying to coax and plead with me to come out of my room, my mom finally knocked on my door one morning and said she was going for a walk on the beach if I wanted to go, too."

"She left you?"

Great, now he was angry at my mother.

"I was fifteen, not six, and our apartment building was a block from the beach." A shadow of a smile teased the corners of my lips. "And she hardly made it through the door before I caught up with her."

His eyebrows lifted above the rim of his glasses, emotion breaking through the structured expressions he tried so hard to maintain.

"I was upset, but I also didn't want to miss the ocean." My shoulders relaxed further, and I cautiously allowed my gaze to chart all the hard planes of his face up close. "She's lost a lot." My eyes connected with his. "Sometimes, to get through what you've lost, you need little reminders of what you still have. Even at six. She has ladybugs. And pirates. And fairy princesses."

He watched Lainey, pain softening the angry lines of his face, and making him appear even more devastating.

You've lost a lot, too, Roman. What are you missing?

"Where's your mother now?"

My heart stumbled, and I swallowed hard. "She passed away three years ago."

"I'm sorry." The coarseness of his voice filled my body the way sand spills into every corner of a jar.

"Thank you. She had a lot of health issues." I wasn't sure why I was talking about Mom. I tried to avoid talking about my family when at all possible because no one could ever know the whole truth. *Why open a door if I could never let anyone walk through it?*

"I'm sorry about your sister."

His jaw flexed, the muscle pressing against his skin.

I wanted to reach out and soothe it. I wanted to knead the knot with my fingertips until it released—until it was relaxed enough to allow his smile.

Roman's smile.

I bit hard into my lower lip, deciding maybe it was better that his smiles were locked away; I wasn't sure I was ready to withstand the full force of what was sure to be breathtaking.

"Lainey is just like her," he rasped, sadness sucking the strength from his voice like a leech. And then his head jerked to the side in a swift shake. "I need to get back to work. Be more careful."

My mouth parted at the brusque order, and he glared at my lips for a second before turning on his heel and stalking toward the main house.

"Yes, sir," I grumbled under my breath, but the way his steps slowed and he almost looked back, I worried the breeze carried my retort up to him.

Turning my attention to my charge, I saw Lainey waiting for me with her arms folded on the concrete wall, her chin propped on top of them. I smiled and joined her.

Time to scout for pirates...

And that did not include searching for signs that Roman was still watching us, no matter how deftly his attention pillaged away all my senses.

We spent most of the morning outside, roaming around. Looking for pirates shifted to searching first for ladybugs, and then any kind of bug. My second success came when Lainey asked to share the peanut butter and jelly sandwich I'd whipped up under Roman's steely gaze.

He'd been sitting at the dining table like he was now, but I felt him watching me the whole time I made it. And that got me thinking... *shouldn't he be at work?*

This whole time, I'd prepared myself thinking that it would be Lainey and me, and that my interactions with Roman would be limited to hello before he left for work and goodbye when he came home.

But what if he was going to work from home?

What if I was going to be in his vicinity... in his presence... all the time?

The thought was just as unsettling as the tension that only seemed to pull tighter the more I was around him.

"Same time tomorrow?" I asked at the end of the day.

He mentioned when we came inside that this week would only be half days, ending at just a little past noon, on account of Lainey's therapy appointments in the afternoon. I realized I hadn't even asked about my schedule at the interview, too shocked that I'd landed the job in the first place.

Roman looked up from his computer and pushed his glasses up.

"Yes," he answered, squeezing his eyes shut for a second before opening them wide. He'd been in deep focus.

I hesitated and then blurted out, "Are you going to be working from home then?"

Because I wasn't sure I could keep all my focus on Lainey if he was going to be around...

His head tipped, scrutinizing me before he answered, "This week, I am. Next week, I'll need you to pick her up from school and bring her back here until I get home from the office."

"Oh, okay." I tried not to show my relief as I walked toward the front door.

"I want to make sure this transition goes smoothly for her." He cleared his throat and stood. "It seems like it is; this is the most she's eaten in weeks," he confessed. "I just… have to be sure."

I nodded. "Of course."

He reached for the doorknob to open it for me but then stopped and rasped low, "Thank you."

The weight of his gratitude overwhelmed me, and tears burned in the corners of my eyes.

"You're welcome," I said thickly. I wanted to say more—ask more. *Know more.* But I knew better.

Roman Knight might be a savior. A protector. A modern-day knight in shining armor for his niece.

And he was entirely off-limits for me.

CHAPTER FOUR

Roman

I RESTED MY SHOULDER AGAINST THE DOORFRAME, CAREFUL NOT to make a sound from my post in the hall.

In the corner of the room, Lainey sat cross-legged in the white leather chair with a book in her lap. Across from her, leaning forward in an identical chair, was Dr. Shelly Goldner, who smiled and pointed at something on the page. From her ash-blonde hair to her light-gray skirt and jacket, the well-respected therapist's appearance cemented her place in the room: as an observer, not the focus.

At our first appointment, I was surprised to find Dr. Shelly was younger than I'd expected though still probably around my age. We'd talked at length on the phone, and she'd consistently spoken with the steady confidence of someone who knew her field well, something that usually came with age.

Dr. Shelly's office was in the heart of Carmel, the room a study in shades of white. The only splash of color was the deep green of the snake plant on her desk. The clean space was supposed to feel neutral—the white furniture and walls void of distractions and bright triggers. But after a decade trained to get into the mind of serial killers, the blank walls made me feel like I was going insane.

I'd expressed my concerns over the phone last week—how Lainey wouldn't talk, would hardly eat, and how she only wanted to play in her room. That was on top of the way she cried anytime she was in the car and in her bed at night. *She's shutting me out.* Those were the words I'd used, and they'd never hurt more than when I'd had to explain how we'd previously had such a close relationship.

Dr. Shelly reminded me of some things I already knew, pain and worry blinding me to my own knowledge of psychology; Lainey was young and this was her trauma and grief response, but that didn't mean it would be forever. What mattered now was support and consistency. So, we'd come to her office every day this week at one thirty p.m. sharp and would continue with weekly sessions for as long as it took for my niece to heal.

She was all that mattered.

I refocused on Lainey, desperately hoping today would be the day she allowed me to hear her say something.

She'd been poring over the same book for twenty minutes with Dr. Shelly beside her. I couldn't see the exact title from my position, but I had noted the cartoon pirate on the front and swore I heard the word "Neverland" mentioned.

I adjusted my glasses, the movement making the doorframe creak.

Lainey's head snapped in my direction and then shot back down to her book. Dr. Shelly tapped on the page, encouraged her to keep going, and then rose from her seat to join me on the other side of the room. She picked up her white notepad folio and silver pen along the way.

"Mr. Knight." She nodded toward the hallway, and we took a few steps away from the room where Lainey wouldn't be able to hear us.

"Anything?" I rasped.

For all of our previous sessions, I'd remained with them in the room while Dr. Shelly tried to engage Lainey in conversation. Forget talking about the accident or her parents, I just wanted her to talk about something. *Anything.* But it felt like we were getting nowhere, so Dr. Shelly suggested trying a one-on-one scenario today while I waited in the hall.

The therapist inhaled deeply and then gave her head a slow shake, her white-blonde hair hardly moving along the side of her head.

My breath released in a hiss. *Dammit.* When I blinked, I saw my sister. First, her smile. Then, her pleading eyes. And then her body that I'd had to identify at the morgue.

I couldn't grieve when guilt bombarded me with unrepentant blasts.

I'd sworn to take care of Lainey, and at every turn, my niece only showed me how I was failing—how the man who could get inside the minds of humanity's worst wasn't good enough to comfort the heart of its best.

"Children are surprisingly and admirably resilient, Mr. Knight," Dr. Shelly continued. "And your niece is no different. Being in the accident—surviving the accident that killed both her parents, she's been through a horribly traumatic experience, and to process that will take time. She's not as reclusive as when we started our sessions just a few days ago."

I grunted, hating how I couldn't be content with small changes—small improvements. I wanted the little girl I knew back, so I could fulfill my promise to Val.

"How has her eating been?" She flipped open her notepad.

"Yeah—ahh…"

"Does that mean it's improved from the Oreo days?" she asked, her pen poised to write something I wasn't even ready to speak out loud.

"A little." *A lot when Stevie was there.*

I wondered if that first day would be a fluke—if Stevie was a novelty that Lainey would soon retreat from. But every day that passed was the same. Stevie lured my niece out of her room with the promise of pirates or bug-catching adventures in the secret garden or fairy princesses in seaside castles, and for a few hours, I saw Lainey start to come back to life.

Meanwhile, I lurked in the background. When I should've been working, I was instead watching the two of them turn our new home into something magical.

But when Stevie left, the misery returned.

"And how about speaking at home?" She asked, the ink of

her pen flowing like a vine along the paper, marking our progress. *Or lack of it.*

"She won't say anything to me," I replied, making sure my voice remained steady.

"But she's still talking to the nanny?" Her eyes flipped up pointedly.

"Stevie," I corrected her without even thinking even as my throat tightened. "Yes. She talks to Stevie."

Only to Stevie.

"Yes, I'm sorry. I thought I wrote her name down…" Dr. Shelly shook her head as she spoke, making a point to scribble Stevie's name with a flourish. "There we go. Well, that's good—very encouraging."

"That she's talking to practically a stranger over someone she's known her entire life?"

Once more, that serene smile painted over her lips. "Because thinking about what she's known her entire life means thinking about all the things she's lost. A stranger doesn't come with that hurt."

"And she knows that at six?" I slid my eyes back to my niece, her attention locked on the story in her lap.

"Kids know when something hurts and learn how to avoid it," she replied. "I realize you've dealt with a lot of psychology for your job—"

"Psychopaths, Dr. Shelly." My fist balled at my side.

That was the most frustrating thing about all of this. For a decade, I'd decoded the inner workings of some of the most sadistic criminals the world had ever seen. I deciphered what serial killers and rapists and arsonists wanted—what triggered them—and ultimately, what would be their downfall. Arguably, calculus-level psychopathy.

But why my six-year-old niece who always ran into my arms whenever I'd come for a visit, who smiled and laughed when I tossed her over my shoulder, and who always wanted to tell me about every part of her day… that was harder to decipher than the mind of any murderer.

Or maybe I just cared more.

She nodded. "What you're dealing with now isn't the faulty

wiring of a murderer, but an immature mind trying to process. It's not something for you to solve for her, Mr. Knight. It's something she needs to work through, with your support, of course, but for herself."

My teeth fitted together tight, watching Lainey turn through the pirate book. Pirates and princesses. Magic and castles. I didn't believe in fairy tales, not when I'd chased monsters for so long.

"You're doing all the right things, Mr. Knight. Just give her as much time as possible with Stevie, if she's the one unlocking the door. It's only a matter of time before Lainey will let you in."

Maybe Dr. Shelly was right. Maybe Stevie's gentle kindness and sense of adventure and out-of-the-box thinking gave Lainey a haven from her hurt, and I would never begrudge her that. I would however begrudge Stevie her impossibly deep eyes, full pouty lips, and soft, supple curves that haunted me every time my eyes closed for the way she turned my dick into knots. The way I thought about her... and the number of cold showers needed to temper those thoughts... were all kinds of wrong, especially when it could jeopardize the only person who seemed to be getting through to Lainey.

She was too young. Twenty-two. *Might as well be twenty-too-fucking-young.* But more importantly, she was my niece's nanny. *And that was all she could ever be.*

"And how about you, Mr. Knight?"

My head whipped in her direction, leveling her with a stare that I'd formerly reserved for hardened criminals. "What about me?"

"Have you talked to anyone?" She asked, unshaken.

"I'm fine." I gave her a tight smile and walked back into her office to collect my niece.

The kind of person I had to become to catch the kind of people I did wasn't the kind of man who could be helped. Nor was I the kind of man who could be anything but alone.

BROKEN

By the time I turned onto the driveway, my palms were sweating on the steering wheel.

I drove slowly because I wanted Lainey to feel safe, but the way the tears leaked down her cheeks the entire way made me want to floor it and see just how quickly the Bronco could get us back to the house. Anything to end her pain as quickly as I could.

"What the…" I trailed off, seeing Stevie's Ford parked in front of the house. "Why is Stevie here?"

The mention of her name sent Lainey's attention eagerly out the window.

I pulled into the garage, helped Lainey out of the SUV, and then followed her to the driveway. Stevie wasn't even out of her car before my niece was running for her like she couldn't get away from me fast enough.

Stevie greeted Lainey with that tender smile of hers, and I noticed she'd changed from what she was wearing earlier. Now, she had on a pair of black leggings and a long, loose tee that dipped lower in the front than the shirts she normally wore over.

If there was any doubt in my mind about the fullness of her ass or the generous swells of her tits, it was sufficiently eliminated. No one used the word *voluptuous* in this century, but if there was a body that could resurrect the description from the dead, it was Stevie's erotic curves.

"Miss Michaels…" I folded my arms, slowing my approach. *How long had she been waiting for us?*

"I'm so sorry." She flushed and her smile dimmed. "I left my bag here earlier with my books, and I have a lot of studying to get done this weekend." Our eyes locked for a second before hers broke away to Lainey, and she crouched down. "Back again."

Her brow furrowed. I knew she was seeing Lainey's tears, and my chest burned. I felt like a fucking failure. All I wanted was to make this easier—better for her. And I was failing.

Stevie said something to Lainey, but I kept my distance, willing to trade anything to hear my niece's voice. But nothing came. Lainey nodded and then went inside the house, the look on her face like she was on a mission.

"What happened?" Stevie asked immediately.

"She cries during car rides." I sighed and felt my jaw pulse.

"She was in the car the night of the accident. They said it was a miracle she survived."

"I didn't..." Stevie blinked rapidly, her tongue sliding along her full lower lip to wipe away the knot of hesitation from her voice. "That's horrible. I'm so sorry, Roman."

My body tensed, and I sucked in a sharp breath. *Roman.* My name was like the sound of the apple falling from the tree of temptation, ripe and begging to be bitten.

My cock thickened in my pants. This was my fault. I hadn't been with a woman in so damn long that one look at her luscious curves packed on a petite frame, and chemistry did as chemistry does: it reacted.

Stevie's eyes bulged, realizing her slip. Her lips peeled apart, but she didn't say anything else for a moment. No apology. No change of subject. Instead, we treaded waves in a sea of chemistry in the middle of a damn lightning storm.

"I should get my bag," she mumbled, and I realized I'd let out a low noise that was more threat than growl.

She bolted inside, and I followed the bounce of her sweet ass. Every time I was around her, all I could think about was the way the soft swells of her body promised to hold the cure for all the hard aches in mine.

Fuck. I speared a hand through my hair. I couldn't be doing this—be distracted like this.

I had enough on my plate figuring out my new world. Lainey had the best parents in the world; forget living in their shadow, I wasn't even parked in the same zip code. Kids. Family. All things I'd written off after my first case with the BAU—all things I'd written off after what happened to my predecessor and mentor —his family targeted and murdered by a serial killer we'd been hunting and failed to catch in time.

I stared up at the rapidly moving clouds. Normally, I'd reach out to Val and ask her what to do in any personal situation. She always knew what to do. Even though she was younger than me, she was wiser. She knew how to handle life—how to be a human; I only knew how to be a hunter.

But no more.

Heading inside, I found Stevie bent over the coffee table in the living room watching Lainey work on the new puzzle they'd started yesterday morning when the rain forced them inside. *Forced them into my domain.*

"Mr. Knight," she said, correcting herself firmly this time when our eyes met.

I folded my arms, forbidding myself from telling her she could call me Roman. *Forbidding myself from wanting her to.*

Lainey tried to hand her a puzzle piece, stealing her attention for a second as she murmured, "I've got to go, Lainey. I'll see you next week, and we'll work on the puzzle." Her coffee stare caught mine from underneath her lashes. "Or maybe you could ask your uncle to help you with it over the weekend."

For the first time all day, Lainey looked directly at me, her eyes the mirror of her mother's, and my heart stopped. But then she jerked away, focusing on the puzzle as though her little life depended on it.

Dammit, Val. How the hell do I do this? My fist flexed against my side.

Stevie bent farther forward, my eyes straying traitorously to her ass, her leggings hugging the full curves like they were made to show them off.

"He looks like he'd be good at puzzles," she added. "And I think he'd really like to help."

My niece didn't look at me again. She only reached for Stevie when she started to walk away.

"I'll be back Monday," she assured Lainey and peeled her fingers free.

Lainey shuddered and her lip quivered, on the verge of crying again. *Dammit.* I scrambled for a solution. After a week, I was exhausted from trying to win over words from her silent hold.

And then my phone began vibrating in my pocket.

I didn't care who it was. At this point, I'd happily learn about my expiring car warranty if it gave me a reason to do this.

"Can you stay?" I blurted out, holding up my phone. "I need to take this."

Stevie's mouth dropped open, about to refuse, when Lainey

reached up and grabbed her hand, tugging her back toward the table with pure hope in her eyes.

"Please," I begged with a low rasp.

I pretended not to see how she shivered before agreeing, *and I pretended not to notice how hard it made me.*

Leaving the two of them, I stalked into my bedroom, needing a moment of privacy to get my dick on straight. But when I looked at my phone, I was a little shocked to see that it was Special Agent Sally Koorie calling me.

"Koorie," I answered.

"Hey, Knight. Sorry for the late Friday call," she apologized with that familiar "sorry but not sorry but for a good reason" tone.

Sally Koorie was my right-hand agent for the last four years. Sharp, dedicated, and determined, she was an excellent asset to the FBI and the BAU team; I'd given her the highest recommendation when I'd handed in my resignation, letting my superiors know in no uncertain terms that she was the only one I would trust to take over my lead.

"What's going on?" I strode into the bathroom and turned on the faucet, running the ice-cold water over my fingers.

"Well, the team and I are on our way to Phoenix."

"Oh?" I stared at myself in the mirror. "A case?"

"Your case."

I let out a rough laugh, and reminded her, "I don't have any cases to close up in Phoenix."

The handful I was still finalizing paperwork on were all East Coast based.

"You have one."

I froze, those three words icing the burn from my blood.

"The Archangel." *My Holy Grail.* "He's in Arizona?" I rasped, my fist tightening with the instinct to be there—to help them.

Dammit. Catching monsters wasn't my responsibility anymore.

"He was." She sighed. "The body wasn't found right away; the girl was a vagrant, so no one reported her missing and we still don't have any ID. Hikers found the shallow grave and reported it to the police."

"Same MO?" I placed my palm on the window frame and

stared out at the ocean, the waves frothing and foaming at the shore, as eager to capture the land as I was to capture this piece of shit.

"Sexually assaulted. Strangled. She was seventeen," she confirmed.

Motherfucker. I gritted my teeth. "And the mark?"

His signature. A cross-shaped piece of flesh cut from the victim's chest.

"Due to decomp from the elements, the coroner hasn't been able to confirm that yet, but I'm going to send Torres there as soon as we land." Alex Torres. Another member of my former team. Another piece of my former life.

I glanced at the door. Stevie was right. I did like to do puzzles —these kinds of puzzles.

"If it's him, we'll see what new info we can learn," Sally went on, claiming my attention again. "We're going to find him."

"It's him." I felt it in my bones. When she didn't respond, I probed, "You're still not sure."

"It's just… you know what this would mean… if it's the same killer. A decade and a half…" she trailed off into silence.

I knew.

I knew how unlikely it was for a serial killer to quit cold turkey. I knew that it was even more unlikely for them to change their victimology. But I was also positive we were dealing with the same man.

He'd killed twenty-five women on a path stretching across major highways between Chicago and California before disappearing for a decade and a half. My predecessor profiled that those victims would've been around the Archangel's age, and the working theory was that he was most likely good-looking and personable, making the women easily attracted to him. However, when they gave in to temptation, so to speak, it triggered the Archangel's moral compass to swing widely in the opposite direction, driving him to kill them because they'd been "loose" with their bodies.

He turned the women into sinners and then killed them for sinning, though in his mind, their death was their redemption.

In the last seven years, a dozen bodies had been discovered with a similar MO, but too many other differences.

The victims had stayed young. If it was the same killer, precedent showed his victims would've aged along with him. The newer victims were also nobodies—half of them we still hadn't been able to identify; the previous victims had all been well-known members of their respective communities, especially their church communities. It was one of the strongest ties between the first round of victims—they'd been devoutly religious. The new victims lacked that, and they lacked a clear route of trade or transportation that linked the locations where their bodies were found.

Of course, we'd spent hours exploring copycat options. Hours investigating how someone could've learned the Archangel's signature since the cross marks to the chest were kept out of the press.

But it was just as unlikely for a serial killer to go on sabbatical and change his victimology as it was for a copycat killer to emerge knowing the Archangel's signature, so I couldn't fault her hesitation.

Until we knew for certain which one we were dealing with— *and what his motivation was*—it made solving the case a thousand times harder.

"I guess we'll know more when we know more," I repeated the adage my predecessor would say to me when a case seemed to be stalling.

"I'll keep you updated, but I wanted to let you know."

"Thanks, Koorie."

There was a pause, and I lifted my fist to the frame of the window above my head, the looming stance similar to the one I took when I watched Stevie and Lainey on their outdoor adventures.

I knew what was coming; I'd worked with Koorie for too long to not anticipate her next question.

"How are you? How's Lainey?"

I swallowed over the knot of failure in my throat. "Managing."

"If you need anything, Knight—"

"Just catch him," I broke in. "Just catch him for me."

We hung up, and I went back over to the bedroom door, opening it slowly so I could see what was going on. Watching the two of them—watching a flicker of life come back to my niece's eyes when Stevie played with her—it was the only solace I had. Except they were no longer in the living room hunched over the puzzle table.

Tossing the door wide, I strode into the space and stopped short when I found them in the kitchen. Lainey sat on the edge of the counter, *smiling* at Stevie who was laughing at... the pile of chicken nuggets on the baking sheet.

Damn, she had dimples.

I rarely got to see her laugh up close, but here, her unfiltered smile pinned the most delicious dimples under her cheeks and dusted them pink.

As soon as they saw me, the entire mood shifted. Lainey's smile disappeared and Stevie's laugh stifled as she rolled her lips between her teeth. I always arrived like the thundercloud there to rain on their parade.

"Lainey picked out chicken nuggets for dinner, but I... ahh... accidentally dumped the whole bag onto the sheet," Stevie explained, trying to pick apart the frozen chicken pieces and put some back one by one. "I'll just fix—"

"Just make them all." I reached my hand out over the pile of chicken to stop her and her hand collided with mine.

Heat zinged through my cells like the hot snap of a rubber band, and I quickly jerked my hand away with a hiss, folding my arms across my body.

Too late, I realized my reaction made it seem like I thought she'd done it on purpose and I was angry.

"Make the whole bag and stay for dinner," I clipped, trying to make the situation better but now it just sounded like I was ordering her around. "If that's okay with you, Bug?"

I looked at Lainey. It was a cheap shot, bargaining Stevie's presence in exchange for an answer—not even an answer. An acknowledgment. But the fact that I never planned on being a father or a guardian and had no idea what I was doing or what was acceptable was already pretty fleshed out.

Her eyes rounded, but she didn't retreat. She wanted Stevie to stay, and one simple word was the price I was asking her to pay.

I didn't get a word, only a rapid nod that quaked through the air just as forcefully as a sound wave before she slid from the counter onto one of the stools and climbed down onto the floor.

My small win quickly deflated as she retreated to her puzzle, and I pretended like her small footsteps weren't capable of breaking a grown man's heart.

I faced Stevie, seeing all her reservations stack into the silence that my niece had left us with.

I wanted her to stay. Not just for Lainey—not just so my niece wouldn't take her dinner and run to her room for the rest of the night, not to be seen until morning. But because there was something about Stevie that calmed me, too. Something that forced me to focus on what I had—*what I wanted*—rather than what I lost.

She came for her books, so it was safe to assume she'd planned on going home and studying. It was not safe—*no*, it was downright dangerous to assume anything else, but I couldn't help myself.

"Unless you have somewhere to be," I charged gruffly, daring her to say she did—daring her to tell me she had plans to meet that piece of shit who made her load their groceries in the rain.

I refused to let her look away, caging her with my stare until her head slipped side to side.

Her pink lips peeled apart slowly. "No, I can stay."

CHAPTER FIVE

Roman

I went to the freezer and reached for the bag of waffle fries.

Stevie moved to the side, anticipating that I'd need another baking sheet from the cupboard by her. Of course, the damn thing was wedged against the muffin tray. I jiggled it with more force, and when it snapped free, my arm brushed against Stevie's thigh.

Damn. My teeth ground tight, steeling myself against the heat that blasted straight to my dick. *So much for that time I took to collect myself.* I straightened but kept myself angled away from her so the bulge in my pants wasn't so obvious.

"How did everything go at the school?" Stevie asked and turned on the faucet.

I lined the sheet with aluminum foil and dumped the fries onto it. "Fine." I winced at the harshness of the word, wishing this new life of ours came apart as easily as the frozen potato slices.

Lainey was joining the first-grade class at Our Lady of Mount Carmel elementary school on Monday. I'd had countless conversations with the principal and the nuns, and Lainey's teacher in particular, Sister Mary, and we all thought it was best to introduce the school to her slowly; she was going through enough change.

I started with just driving by the building on our way to our appointment with Dr. Shelly; the stone structure and adjoining playground were a few miles north of the house and right on the south edge of Carmel Cove. Though fenced in and secluded, the property butted up against the beach.

It was two days of driving by. On Wednesday, we'd stopped in, and I walked Lainey around the grounds; she'd even wandered onto the playground though she wouldn't go on the swings or slide. Yesterday, Principal Prior and Sister Mary met us on the playground and introduced themselves.

"Sister Mary took her inside the school today and showed her around—showed her where the classroom was and which desk was hers." I'd stayed outside, unwilling to risk how being around me somehow made everything worse.

"That's good. Did she like it?" Stevie asked, jumping into action and opening the oven door when I picked up both trays of food.

I slid the sheets into the oven, and when the door shut, we both reached for the timer at the same time, fingers bumping. *Christ.* It was like there was something magnetic when she was around that kept pulling me to her no matter how hard I tried to keep away.

"Sorry," she murmured and linked her hands behind her back, the stance pushing her chest forward.

I bit back a groan. The rise and fall of her tits... the deeper *V* in her shirt... I was half tempted to climb into the damn oven to cool off with the way she made my blood boil.

I punched in the timer and let the clock tick down.

"I think she liked it, but I wouldn't really know," I replied hoarsely.

Her blush deepened and she realized her mistake; I wouldn't know if Lainey liked it because Lainey wouldn't talk to me.

"She told me about the playground," Stevie offered, biting her lip. "She told me the one part of it was high enough for her to look out for pirates."

My mouth pulled tight, laughter and pain mingling in my chest like thorns and petals on a rose.

"My sister homeschooled Lainey for kindergarten, so she has no reference for what school is or how it will be different." I swallowed hard. "I guess it's a good thing."

"She'll make it her own," Stevie replied confidently. "Now, if she were a hormonal teenager, I'd tell you to brace yourself."

"Oh?" I arched an eyebrow.

"I was homeschooled until I was fifteen; I was *not* happy with my mom when she put me in public school." She grinned.

"Why were you upset?"

Her face shadowed for a split second. "More change. New home. New place. And then my mom wasn't going to be my teacher anymore."

"Why did she stop?"

"She had to work." Her chin dipped like she was desperately thinking of a better answer. "She also told me it would be better for me for college. I was always ahead in school, so going to public school gave me a chance to take more advanced classes."

The investigator in me clawed for more answers. The background check I'd run provided the bare-bones information of Stevie's life after the age of sixteen. *Which was not that fucking long ago for me to be looking at her the way I did.* But when she talked about herself, it made me want to know more.

What her childhood was like. Why she never mentions her dad. What made her want to become a teacher.

And it made me want to know the kinds of things a man had no business knowing about his nanny.

Who gave her her first kiss. Why she was dating someone who left her out in the fucking rain. If he pleasured her the way she deserved. If she pleasured herself because he didn't.

If she was still a virgin.

The oven timer interrupted our conversation.

Stevie grabbed plates while I pulled out the hot food. Lainey drifted into the kitchen, watching us work to put the plates together. I felt my jaw twist tighter, wondering if this was going to be the first meal I'd eat with my niece since I'd become her guardian almost a month ago.

"Hey, Lainey," Stevie began, grabbing the ketchup from the fridge. "What if we ate dinner while we worked on the puzzle?"

Tiny brown eyes whipped between us, uncertain if her new friend was betraying her for inviting me into their bubble.

Stevie handed a plate to Lainey, crouching as she did so and whispering loudly, "We can make him find all the end pieces for us."

Lainey's head tipped, considering the offer. My breath glued to the walls of my lungs, unwilling to inhale one more sign of defeat. And when she reached out and took her food with a tiny nod, it expelled in a whoosh of relief.

Just like that, I'd been snuck through a crack in my niece's wall. *We were going to have dinner together.*

I followed them into the living room, letting them pick their seats on the floor before taking my place on the couch. Staying silent, I focused on my task to find the border pieces to the puzzle, stacking them in the center for the girls to take. Stevie took up the entirety of the sparse conversation, talking about the puzzle, and then school, and then bugs.

Lainey replied with nods and shakes, and I kept my few responses to a low hum. I was treading on thin ice, afraid one word would make it crack. For tonight, I was happy to be a silent star orbiting in their world. *More than happy.* Even if every time my fingers brushed Stevie's in search of the same puzzle piece, it threatened to send the whole thing up in smoke.

This was the first time Lainey had eaten with me—the first time I'd seen my niece eat dinner since our lives had been thrown together. And I'd do anything for it to not be the last.

When dinner was over, I collected all the plates and carried them into the kitchen, watching the two of them out of the corner of my eye. They organized the rest of the puzzle to finish later, took one last look at the darkened horizon for pirates, and then Stevie sent Lainey off to get ready for bed.

For a second, I felt the shadow of normalcy creep over the scene like a passing cloud. But then it was gone, leaving only the blinding tragedy of what brought us together.

Maybe Dr. Shelly was right. Maybe Stevie was the key— the bridge I needed back to my niece. I could only hope I wouldn't burn that bridge to the ground with the way I wanted her.

"I'm going to head out, if that's okay."

I winced, hating the thought that she felt forced to stay.

"Thank you for staying," I muttered gruffly, wiping my hands on the kitchen towel as I faced her, noting how tired she looked.

And she was still probably going home to study. *Way to be a selfish ass, Knight.* Whether it was my training or my personality, the handful of days I'd spent around Stevie was enough to convince me that her determination and dedication were not only genuine, but made her unstoppable.

The admirable combination something that I was glad to have around to rub off on my niece.

"Of course. I'm glad we all got to eat together." She made it seem so easy to express the things bottled inside me, and I wondered if that strength of hers could rub off on me, too.

I walked her to the front door.

"What's my schedule for next week? I forgot to ask earlier." She blushed and crossed her arms, the movement dragging my gaze to her tits.

Fuck.

"Lainey will be in school until two, and then I should be home by six," I clipped, my tone harder than required but anything softer would let desire bleed through. "I told the school you'd be picking her up."

My level of presumption was astounding, but I wasn't willing to risk the alternative.

All week I'd gone back and forth about calling Ace to tell him I would be doing half days at the office for a while. However, all week, I was reminded over and over again that for whatever reason, I wasn't helping Lainey—that no matter what I did or how hard I tried, I wasn't making things easier.

So, standing outside the school earlier today, I succumbed to the unwelcome but no less truthful admission that the best thing I could do for my niece was surround her with the people she did open up to. No matter how much it wounded my heart.

I cleared my throat. "If it's okay with you…"

"Of course." Her head bobbed.

"I have an extra car seat," I said, having bought two from the get-go. "I just want to make sure she's in bed, and then I can put it in your car now if you want."

Again, she nodded and waited while I checked on Lainey. My niece was fast asleep, curled in her bed... and there was no sign that she'd cried even a little.

Another small miracle for tonight.

The first couple of nights, when I'd heard her cry, I'd immediately gone into her room to comfort her, but as soon as I opened the door, she would stop and pull the covers over her head. I assured her it was okay to cry—that it was okay to be sad. To miss them. But nothing I said comforted her. If anything, I worried it made her try to hide it harder from me.

And the last thing I wanted was for her to bottle up her grief.

Now when she cried, I didn't knock. I simply stood right outside her door and listened in case she called for me. She never did.

"It's in the garage," I mumbled to Stevie upon returning to the kitchen, leading the way outside.

I inhaled the cool night air, the etch of salt infusing deep in my lungs.

The car seat was in the back corner of the garage. Tearing the box open, I lifted and carried it over to Stevie's smaller Ford, wondering with each and every step if I was making the right choice.

She unlocked the car, the light flashing once in the dark, and then held the door open for me.

Steadying the car seat on the back seat, my gaze caught on a small basket tucked on the floor on the other side. Water bottles. A few granola bars. Tiny bottles of hand sanitizer. In all, they weren't strange things to keep in the car, but in such individualized quantities it struck me as odd.

"Here, let me," Stevie broke in, and as soon as she brushed against my side, I stepped back and let her take over.

I couldn't let myself be so close to her, but even space couldn't stop the caress of sound.

At first, her small pants made my jaw slowly tighten. Then her little grunts as she worked the seat belt through the loops made my lips curl. But it was the way she was bent over, her ass dipping and bobbing while she finagled the attachment, that made my dick start a riot in my pants.

I tried to think of something else—look at anything else. But it was night. The private location of my house was doing its job—shielding everything from my sight.

Everything but Stevie and the sway of her damn ass.
Focus.
Focus.

The small blue car was the only other thing in front of me, so I blurted out, "Have you ever been in a car accident?"

I hadn't even thought to check her driving record for any citations before deciding to trust her with my niece in her car. *Guardian of the year, right here.*

"No," she grunted, tugging on the belt once more.

"Have you ever gotten a ticket?"

"No—" She moaned.

"Ever been pulled over for speeding?" I spoke faster, needing to block out every other erotic noise that slipped through her lips.

"No—"

"Running a stop sign?"

"No—" Her shoulders sagged and I thought I heard a click.

"Violating any other traffic laws—"

"No!" She exclaimed, exasperated, and whirled around too quickly, banging her head on the doorframe in the process.

Her pained cry sliced straight through my chest, and I reached for her when she started to sway. My palms framed her face and held her steady.

"Jesus, Stevie." I inhaled sharply, cursing myself for letting her name spill free.

She shuddered, her eyes springing open.

Shit. "Are you okay?"

"Mmhmm." She moaned again.

My stupid dick swelled, not caring that the noise was borne from hurt. I brushed her hair from her face until there was nothing between her skin and mine.

"Stay still," I ordered when she tried to reach up to feel her head. "Let me check."

Her movements stilled instantly, and she lowered her arm with a deep exhale.

"Good girl." Two little words, innocuous yet illicit.

Fuck. I'd just praised my fucking nanny. And not in the normal way.

No, not with the husky hunger in my voice that was impossible to hide. *Fuck.* The phrase was worse than when I said her name. Worse than me touching her. Worse because it told her just how fucking turned on I got when she let me take care of her.

"I just need to make sure you're not bleeding," I said because I had to say something. I couldn't let *good girl* linger like a damn smoke signal in the air that would lead her straight back to my body that burned for her.

I tightened my lips together and tried to filter out desire from the oxygen I inhaled but all I got was peppermint and sugar.

Sliding my right hand back, my fingers threaded through her hair, the thick waves were even softer than I'd imagined—like silk spun from the thread of clouds. Gritting my teeth, I splayed my touch wide and roamed it over the back of her skull until I found the growing knot where she'd bumped it good.

"No blood, but you're going to have a nasty lump for a few days," I rasped, dragging my hand back to its starting point. I should've let go of her, but I couldn't. "Are you sure you're alright?"

She nodded slowly, her throat bobbing as she tried hard to swallow.

But instead of making any move to leave, she surprised me by saying, "I drive slowly and very carefully."

"Stevie," I tried to cut her off, tipping her face up to mine.

I wanted to knock my own hard head for making her feel like she had to strain to give me this answer.

"My mom was very sick for a long time," she murmured, her voice cracking at the end. "She was especially carsick, and I was the one who took her to all her doctor's appointments, who took her to the hospital for testing and treatment..."

Jesus.

I was a fucking ass. A giant fucking ass.

"I'll keep her safe. I drive with the speed of a geriatric sloth."

I couldn't help the low rumble that burst from my chest. How she managed to make me laugh in a moment like this was beyond me. At the sounds, a flicker of wonder glimmered in her eyes with the fleetingness of a shooting star. I recognized the feeling because it was what I felt every time I watched them through the window and saw Lainey's lips move.

Her throat bobbed. "Roman..."

Heat spilled like lava through my veins. *Who was the last person to say my name like that?*

Like she needed me.

Not professionally... not for my job... but for me.

I hunted serial killers for a living, but nothing made me tremble quite like the sound of my name from her full lips, husky and forbidden.

My eyes stalked the moonlight as it flitted over her face. I really should've let go of her. Stepped back. Maintained space. *Preserved sanity.*

Instead, my head drifted closer.

"I'm sorry," I muttered, but I wasn't sure what I was sorrier for.

Doubting her. Or kissing her.

Her breath didn't catch, it pulled. It drew the air out of the space between us. It evaporated the invisible barrier that came with age and professional boundaries. It eliminated what restraint remained to keep me from tasting the lips that could break through to my niece, wondering if they were warm and sweet enough to break through to me, too.

Closer and closer. Even slower to offer her the chance to stop me. But she didn't.

She didn't because god help me, she wanted me to kiss her, too.

A rip of thunder tore through the sky, and Stevie jumped.

I froze. My mouth was so close to hers that a twitch was all it would take to tip into the first taste. I exhaled with painful slowness as the sky boomed around us, and I felt like I was standing in the eye of the storm—paralyzed in place because one wrong move, *one little taste*, was all it would take to toss me into the hurricane and tear apart what was left of me.

A fat raindrop fell with icy warning onto the bridge of my nose. My hands snapped from her face like rubber bands returning to their rightful shape. *Returning to reality.*

"You should go before it pours," I rasped low.

"Yeah." She ducked her head and stepped to the side and closed the door to the back seat.

I held the driver's door open for her, ushering her out of my reach as fast as was civilly possible.

Stevie slid into her car, the low lights of the dash enough to punish me with the outlines of her hard nipples against her shirt.

"Good night," she said and looked up at me.

My jaw flexed and released. The words were on the tip of my tongue to reply, but I didn't trust my tongue with anything at the moment. *Not around her.*

So, I nodded and closed the door just as the rain started to come down. Cold drops pelted me with unrelenting force as I stood in the drive, watching her pull away.

Good girl.

I needed to do better. *I needed to stop thinking with my damn dick.* Stevie was too good—too wholesome while I would never be whole.

The safest place for her to be was out of my reach, no matter how much denying her drove me insane.

CHAPTER SIX

Stevie

A TINGLE RACED UP MY SPINE. LIKE A BREEZE ALONG THE TRUNK of a tree, leaving no trace except the way it fluttered every nerve that branched from it.

He was watching us.

My head tipped in the direction of the house, the wind pulling my hair from my face, but I stopped before my eyes reached the windows. *And his penetrating stare.* The moment I acknowledged Roman's observation was the moment it would disappear.

It hadn't taken long to relish the routine I'd fallen into over the last few weeks. The mornings spent on schoolwork from my apartment, the old insulation starting to struggle to hold in the heat. Then I'd leave and pick Lainey up at school and bring her back here to her seaside sanctuary. *And mine.*

We'd do her homework, usually outside on a blanket. Then it was time to play—either capturing new bugs to add to a quickly growing collection of homemade terrariums or imagine pirates tracing the horizon; while we watched the far-off sea, I'd continue the story I'd made up about the fairy princess who'd fled from her evil father and lived in their guesthouse.

At some point, Roman stopped asking me to stay for dinner and just wordlessly assumed I'd be joining them.

And I did. *I wanted to.* In many ways, this place had become a haven for me, too.

Even though I should've been out taking Uber trips and saving as much as I could for the courses I still hadn't finished paying for, instead, I chose the adorable little girl who wanted to hear my pirate stories and her too-handsome guardian who'd almost kissed me.

Two weeks had turned me into an expert in the unspoken. At least when it came to my reclusive boss. Every interaction felt like I was walking around unfamiliar territory with my eyes closed, and only my other senses to guide me. Unfortunately, he made all of those go haywire.

"Stevie!" My thoughts broke at Lainey's exclamation, she crouched by the trunk of the cypress tree in the garden.

Nothing compared to this place.

The private seascape that greeted me every time I walked out the back door. Then there was the garden tucked next to the house filled with willowing trees and colorful plants, and the wandering path that led down to the guesthouse that, though I hadn't been inside, provided a wrapped deck and chairs that were perfect for pirate watching.

"What is it? What did you find?" I approached her with the plastic terrarium.

It all started with one of her first homework assignments to collect a couple of bugs in a homemade terrarium. We'd created the environment with soil and leaves, branches and rocks, and filled it with inhabitants. But when the assignment was done, she'd wanted to make another.

And another.

And another.

And here we were, in search of inhabitants for terrarium number four.

Lainey stuck her finger next to a mound of dirt, an earthworm wiggling through it.

"Oh, look. Mr. Worm." I smiled and knelt beside her.

"Do you think he'll like his new home?" She pulled her hand back quickly, regret scrunching her chubby cheeks.

I opened my mouth but didn't immediately respond when I saw the expression on her face for emotions she probably wasn't old enough to describe but was old enough to feel.

"I do," I said quietly. "We worked so hard to make it nice and comfortable. It will be a new adventure for him." With that assurance, I picked up the earthworm which immediately wiggled and curled between my fingers.

Lainey let out a squeal of delight, the sound making me chuckle.

"Go ahead. Touch him." I held the worm out.

Hesitantly, she pointed her tiny finger and touched the slimy crawler. This time her squeal turned into a high-pitched cackle which was only adorable because it came from such a tiny human. I laughed harder as she kept touching and then cackling as the worm moved.

There was nothing as freeing as the laugh of a small child. Like a cloud, it carried no weight and simply followed whatever breeze of happiness picked it up. And every time Lainey laughed, I hoped that breeze would make the loss she'd experienced just a little bit lighter.

I showed her how to pick up the slimy crawler and plop him in his new habitat. "What do you think?"

She peered through the plastic. "Does he have a mommy and daddy worm?"

A balloon inflated in my throat. *She'd never asked these kinds of questions before.*

We hadn't spoken about her parents or their death at all. It was obvious she missed them—obvious the way she hurt. I'd talked to Roman—*Mr. Knight*—about her visits with Dr. Shelly, and maybe this was a result of those, he'd said it would take time for her to open up. I understood. I'd learned a long time ago that just because something was broken didn't mean it was ready to be fixed.

"I'm sure he does."

"What if they're gone?" She drew circles with her finger in the dirt.

"That happens," I said because it was the truth. "But that doesn't mean Mr. Worm is all alone. We're going to find him some friends to make sure of it." I extended the terrarium to her and pointed to another worm crawling a few pavers away. "Like that one."

She looked uncertain for a moment.

"We can call him Mr. Slime," I added with a wink.

Just like that, the giggle was back and then she was off to add another friend to her collection. I straightened, about to follow her when another shiver trickled down my spine, stronger now. *Roman.*

No. Mr. Knight.

After that night in the rain, I forced the correction every time. I couldn't risk this job. And I definitely couldn't risk falling for my boss.

I looked over my shoulder, a strand of hair hooking between my lips as I inhaled, and saw my boss approaching. Lainey was in her own world, searching for more worms next to a tree and leaving me once more as the barricade between her and her uncle.

If there was one thing I wished I could ask, it was why she wouldn't talk to him. Yes, he was grouchy and imposing and gruff. *But not to her.* The way he looked at Lainey—and the agony he felt when she pulled away—melted my heart. The way he looked at me, on the other hand, melted things a little farther south.

"Is everything okay?" He asked firmly before he'd even reached me.

I nodded. "We're just collecting worms for her newest terrarium."

He adjusted his glasses, wearing them like the most advanced form of shield—made to make you believe you could see right through him when they might as well be made of bulletproof glass. *Transparent yet untouchable.* For all my heart ached for Lainey, it ached in equal measure for the man in front of me who was hurting too, but old enough to pretend like his pain didn't matter.

"About next Friday," I began hesitantly.

"What's next Friday?" He scowled and demanded before I could even finish.

"Halloween."

"Oh." He blinked twice.

"I don't know if you've thought about a costume for her, but there's a small parade at the school at one," I told him hesitantly; it was all Lainey wanted to talk about when I picked her up from school, though her teacher, Sister Mary, had mentioned it, too.

"Shit." He ran his hand along his jaw, dragging my attention to the shadow of stubble coating it. "I... forgot... about Halloween."

"It's okay. There's still time," I assured him.

"Yeah." He crossed his arms and stared at Lainey. She was carefully riffling through the dirt in search of an earthworm for her collection.

"She wants to be a pirate," I offered, adding, "She told me earlier on the way home."

"There's a costume store in Monterey, if you want me to—"

"Is it open now?"

"Now?" I heard the way surprise threaded my voice. "Probably..."

We were in the days leading up to Halloween, the store was probably open late for last-minute purchases.

"Lainey!" he called to his niece.

She jumped, eyes wide like she was in trouble, and then slowly trudged back over to us.

He crouched, his pants fitting tight to his muscular thighs, drawing my attention for much longer than was appropriate.

"I heard you want to be a pirate for Halloween, Bug," he murmured, the endearment holding even more weight now that Lainey was obsessed with making homes for her own bugs. "Should we go pick out your costume tonight?"

Her gaze slid to me and then back to her uncle.

"Stevie is going to come with us," he said without asking.

My mouth dried up. I hadn't meant that—hadn't meant to suggest that. I really needed to pick up more evening Uber trips until the end of the year, and every night this week had already been sponged up by dinner and puzzles with Lainey and Roman. *Mr. Knight.* And now costume hunting.

I opened my mouth to refuse, reminding myself that I had my own future to think about, one that existed outside of this haven, unfortunately. But then I felt it—tiny fingers as they curled into mine and tugged expectantly. The matching look in Lainey's eyes pierced my resolve, and it deflated like a broken balloon.

"Yeah," I agreed with a smile. "We'll get your costume for the parade."

It was my own fault. I didn't want to leave them. They were like two puzzle pieces who didn't know how to connect without me between them.

"What do you say, Bug?" Roman prompted.

Lainey stared at the three worms in her terrarium. The faintest hint of a smile tugged onto her cheeks and then her little chin bobbed in a nod.

THE PLASTIC CRACKLED as my fingers traced the individual packaging. *Vampires. Witches. Nurses.* There was every costume under the sun in this store, and I'd wandered away from Lainey and Mr. Knight when they'd found the kid's aisle, hoping to hide how enthralled I was, as well as give them a moment alone.

I'd never dressed up for Halloween. *One of the many rules of my childhood.* No costumes. No pets. No sleepovers. Dad had been particular about certain things that I'd never understood. Now, I didn't want to understand them. I was afraid to—afraid it might make me more like him. Because, for better or for worse, Lee Nelson Turner's blood ran in my veins; I just prayed that it wouldn't make me as broken as he was.

Superhero. Marilyn Monroe. Lancelot.

"Stevie?"

I jumped, lost in thought, and then realized my fingers had paused on a *Dexter* costume. I yanked my hand away quickly. *No.*

"Yeah?" I faced my too-handsome boss. "Is Lainey done?"

As if in answer to my question, the little girl came skipping up the aisle to me, her smile piercing her chubby cheeks. She held out the bag with her costume. *A girl pirate.*

I admired her choice. *Girls should take no prisoners.*

"That's perfect," I explained, examining her choice.

She took a glance at Roman and then shifted so that she could whisper in my ear. As soon as Lainey leaned in, my eyes connected with Roman, his expression hardening. The intensity of his stare was strong enough to make every breath a tug-of-war with the atmosphere.

This was the first time Lainey was speaking in his presence. The first time that she'd give more than a nod or a shake. Even if he couldn't hear the words, this was the closest he'd come to hearing her speak in over a month.

"I want you to be the fairy princess," Lainey whispered.

My eyes sprung wide, heat dumping into my cheeks.

"Lainey, I can't—"

"What is it?" Roman interrupted me.

"Nothing." As soon as the word was out, Lainey whimpered. *Crap.*

"Ms. Michaels." His low-tone warning made me shiver. "Tell me."

"She wants me to dress up, too. As a fairy princess." I made a point to look at Lainey when I continued, "But the parade isn't for me. It's only for you, Little Miss Pirate."

The way her face fell broke my heart.

"Go find her a princess costume," Roman told her before I could say anything else, sacrificing my refusal in order to see his niece's face light up. *And I couldn't blame him.*

Lainey scampered down to the Disney costumes at the end of the aisle, her big smile pinned back in place.

"You really don't have to do this." I straightened and folded my arms, feeling my nipples pebble when his eyes dropped to my chest.

"I do," he grunted, his tone making it clear that I did, too. And then, watching Lainey, his expression softened. "Val loved Halloween."

I heard his pain. I *knew* his pain. I felt it in my chest. A twin flame of loss that burned bright. Even though Mom was sick for a long time, there was no runway long enough to prepare you for the tailspin that grief sent you into.

"She had a party every year and made everyone dress up," he went on, living in the memory.

"Even you?" I couldn't stop the words before they were out.

He didn't reply for a few seconds, and I wasn't sure he was going to before he said, "I never came prepared, but Val always had something waiting for me." His gaze dropped to the ground. "Last year, she dressed Lainey up as baby Yoda and gave me a Mandalorian helmet."

I smiled, but before my imagination could run wild with the image of the man dressed as the Star Wars character whose stoic, grumbly, and businesslike personality so closely resembled his own, Roman held up his phone, showing me a photo of the two of them in costume. Both smiling.

If ovaries could in fact squeeze, that was what I felt low in my stomach at that moment. *And boy, were they flexing hard.*

"I don't know what happened." Pain streaked through his voice.

I tore my gaze up, struck by the tortured look ravaging his face. I was seeing behind the glasses—behind the shield. The man in front of me wasn't as bulletproof as he made himself seem.

"Loss," I answered. "Loss happened."

"She used to love me," he said it like he wanted to prove those times existed—like he needed to. To me and to himself.

I wanted to comfort him. I wanted it so bad I felt it like a bruise on my bones, the strength it took to hold myself back damaging me almost as much as giving in to the urge would have done.

"She still does," I murmured, giving him the only assurance I could.

He only saw all the ways she was holding back. I was the one who saw the way she watched him when he wasn't looking. I was the one she asked when I picked her up from school if Uncle Roman was home even though she knew he wasn't.

She loved him, but she was afraid to show it.

And it was entirely understandable, she'd just lost the two

people she loved most in the world.

Roman's rapid inhale cut through the moment and made me wince with its force. Once more, the man was gone and the shielded, stoic protector remained.

"And what about you? When was the last time you dressed up for Halloween?" His eyebrow arched.

My mouth opened, paused, and then shut. *Stay calm.* I brushed off the question with a smile and small laugh. "I've actually never dressed up for Halloween."

Too late, I realized I'd opened a door.

"Never?" His head cocked, curious, of course, because who had *never* dressed up for Halloween? "Not even when you were little?"

I shook my head, thinking carefully not only about what I was going to say, but to the questions it would lead to. "Dad didn't believe in certain… kinds of things. Halloween was one of them."

"No?"

Breathe, Stevie. He'll never know.

"Dad was a pastor and very involved in our church community and youth groups." I kept my voice steady, part of me wanting to give him enough rope to lead him to me, another part knowing too much rope was just enough to hang myself. "He didn't believe in Halloween. Too much devilry."

Roman—*Mr. Knight* hummed low, but before he could ask more, I redirected the conversation.

"We had our own tradition. We'd go to the movie theater that night, and not only did we get tickets for two movies, but I'd get to buy whatever candy I wanted."

"What did you pick?"

I smiled. "We both loved Swedish fish."

He made a horrified face and then we both laughed. "Sounds like a good tradition."

The happiness of the memory faded like the shine of a firework. "I guess."

"You were close with him," he asserted, his gaze narrowing on me like a fisherman reeling in a catch that has snagged on his line.

I was in too deep, and I hadn't realized until it was too late. The last person I wanted to talk about was Dad—the memories of who I thought he was or the harsh reality of who he'd been.

"I was," I admitted softly. "But he wasn't a good man."

"Is that why you and your mom moved to California?" Suddenly, those glasses of his weren't just bulletproof, they were a one-way mirror, and this conversation was on the verge of becoming an interrogation.

"We needed to be... safe."

His lips pulled into a firm, angry line.

I knew what I'd let him think. I'd led him right to the well of domestic abuse and let him drink, knowing it wasn't the truth. *But neither was it a lie.* We hadn't been safe. And according to Mom, no one was.

Thankfully, Lainey chose at that moment to return with a princess costume

I smiled and suppressed a groan.

I'd grown up with plenty of princess stories. They'd all gone down the tubes when I learned the truth about Dad—when I learned that the man Mom had fallen in love with and loved for fifteen years was not just a lie but a monster. There were a lot of things that could turn a person off to the idea of love, but what Dad did—*who Lee was*—it didn't flip a switch, it fried my whole fairy-tale circuit.

"Are you sure—"

"I think it's perfect," Roman jumped in and took the costume from Lainey. "Hopefully these wings will help prevent you from falling into the ocean again."

I glared at him. "I didn't fall into—" I broke off when his eyebrow started to rise. Stamping a tight smile on my face, I returned, "If I'm going to dress up, so should Uncle Roman."

He froze, and I realized what I'd done. I'd seen the photo—I saw what the two of them had—and I'd just inadvertently dangled it in front of him like a carrot on a stick held in front of a horse.

I had to fix this.

Panicked, I grabbed the first costume I could reach and pulled it from the hook, examining the man in the image wearing chain mail and a leatherlike draped belt. "How about... a knight?"

I winced. Well, if that wasn't appropriate.

The unwavering tilt of his mouth soured, began to dip when Lainey took the costume from me. We both held our breaths while she regarded it and then hooked it back on the shelf.

Roman rocked back on his heels, defeat nailing him like a blow to the chest, but before he could fully mask his emotions, Lainey grabbed a different costume and handed it to him. The massive bag much larger than the other one because of the feathered hat shoved inside it.

"Captain Hook?" Roman hid the break in his voice almost perfectly.

A small victory welled in my chest, watching her choose to include him for the first that I'd seen.

"Looks like Lainey needs a few more scallywags for her crew," I said with a teasing grin.

"As long as she doesn't make me walk the plank," he replied just as my phone began to vibrate in my pocket.

I missed whatever was said after that when my eyes zeroed in on the screen. *Reality was calling.*

"Ms. Michaels..."

I looked up. "I'm so sorry. I just need to take this," I apologized. "I'll meet you outside."

Spinning on my heel, I practically ran out of the costume store, answering the phone just in time.

"Hello?"

"Hello, Ms. Michaels? It's Linda Hale from the Monterey Community College."

I swallowed hard and looked down at my feet. "Yes, hi."

"I was just reaching out because we haven't received the rest of your payment for your spring semester classes, and I was wondering if I could get that squared away while we are on the phone?"

"Oh, yes. Of course. Actually, now's not a great time..."

"Ms. Michaels, if you wanted to apply for financial aid, that would take care of everything. I'd be happy to walk you through the process."

I bit my lip, locking my breath in my lungs until I could be sure that I could exhale without faltering.

"Promise me you'll be careful, baby."

Since the moment we moved to California, Mom went to extremes to keep our identities and our lives protected. Even though she'd changed our legal names, the records sealed for our protection, she never trusted any kind of massive system. Not public schools. Not even a hospital; It had taken me breaking down into sobs and losing my voice in our argument to finally convince her that she had to get treatment at the hospital—that we had to go back to the city so she could get the help she needed.

Community college would've been another one of those arguments, but there was no other way for me to follow my calling. Still, it was the reason I stuck to online classes… and refused to apply for financial aid.

I had no idea where that information went—what kinds of databases it ran through. I had no idea if I'd need to apply with my original or changed name. *I had no idea what kind of dangers it could unravel.*

"Thank you, but I'm not interested in aid. I can afford my education, I just have to move some things around." *Like people… in my car.*

"Okay, but the deadline is only a few weeks away, and if we don't receive payment before then, I'll have to remove you from the courses you've enrolled in, so that other students who are on waiting lists can join." Her tone sharpened, making me feel even worse about my situation.

But I didn't want pity almost as much as I didn't want help.

I could tell her the truth that I'd spent our savings on Mom's medical bills, so every dollar of the thousands that they wanted was a dollar I'd scrounged up on my own. But I didn't want pity *almost* as much as I didn't want help.

"I understand, and I will absolutely have the tuition payment to you in plenty of time—"

"Ms. Michaels?"

I whirled around, seeing Roman and Lainey exit the store, both his hands carrying massive bags; it looked like they'd picked out some accessories after I'd left the two of them alone.

I turned my head away and said quickly, "I'm sorry, Ms. Hale. My boss just came in, so I have to go. I will call back and get this sorted out right away. Thank you so much for calling, have a good night."

I hoped my cheerful voice made up for the less-than-courteous way I hung up on her.

"Coming—oomph!" I'd been so worried about having Roman hear me on the phone with the school that I didn't realize how close he'd come. At least, not until I ran straight into him. Again.

My palms connected with the muscled slabs of his chest. *Was it normal for muscles to be that hard? Or was he wearing chain mail underneath his shirt?*

I stared at the bronze triangle of chest that peeked out from the open *V* in his collar. Just like Lainey had been loosening in inches, so had the rigidity of his clothes. My tongue teased the barrier of my lips, wanting to taste him. Like the mix of salty and sweet, I had a feeling his impossibly strong yet achingly soft persona would be just as addictive.

Jeez, Stevie. Get it together.

"Sorry about that." I jerked my hands down to my sides and stepped back.

"Is everything okay?"

I shouldn't have looked at him. *The one-way mirror was back.*

"Yeah." I nodded and faked a smile.

"Are you sure?" He definitely didn't believe me. "You seem upset and your pulse is elevated."

My hand shot to my neck. There was something far too intimate about him watching my heartbeat. *Intimate and vulnerable.* Two things I refused to be around a man.

"It was just my school calling about my classes for next semester. Just confirming some things," I said breezily and then sidestepped his interrogation.

His scrutinizing stare suctioned to my back as I went to the Bronco.

Too bad, Mr. Former FBI, I might be your nanny, but I'm not your next case to be solved.

CHAPTER SEVEN

Roman

"Come in!" Dex called when I knocked on his door.

I pushed into the ops room at Covington Security, the state-of-the-art security building far surpassing my office back at the FBI.

The table in the center of the room was framed by a projector screen on the right wall, racks and shelves along the back with hard drives, servers, and the network hardware that ran the whole operation. Opposite the projector was a substantial desk that supported three computer screens on top of it and one quiet computer wizard behind it.

"Hey, Dex."

He slid to the side and peered out from behind his computer, his longer hair framing the hard angles of his face. The reflection of the screen glinted off his glasses, and his forehead creased immediately when he saw me.

"Ahoy?" he drawled slowly, arching an eyebrow.

Right.

"Lainey's got a Halloween parade at her school in forty minutes. This was her pick," I explained and motioned to the Captain Hook costume I had on.

Red jacket. Short black pants. Boots. Massive black hat with a feather. I even had a damn stuffed parrot that Lainey had picked out in the store, but I'd left that in my car.

"I won't have time to go all the way home to change."

"Anybody else see you like this?" He wondered.

"No."

"Probably for the best."

I let out a little laugh and nodded in agreement. All the guys —especially Dante and Reed—would have a field day with Captain Hook visiting Covington.

"What can I do for you?" Dex asked, returning his attention to his computer. "I've already uploaded your analysis of the arsonist that Hazard is dealing with; he confirmed they got it this morning and sent their thanks."

My chin dipped.

I came to Covington with a unique skill set, and a majority of the kinds of cases they handled here didn't require a psychological profile of the perp (because most criminals weren't complete psychopaths), so Ace had—after confirming with me— offered my expert knowledge consultatively to other well-regarded security firms in the country like Reynolds Protective Group in Wyoming and Armorous Tactical near San Francisco.

"I was wondering if you had access to the school's database over at Monterey Community College?" I asked with a low voice.

The fingers that were quietly tapping away in the background came to a marked stop.

"I don't." He paused. "But I could."

I read between the lines. Dex formerly worked for the CIA and had the skills to rival the best hackers in the country. If anyone could get access to any information anywhere, it was him.

"You need me to register you for Pirating 101?" he deadpanned.

"Ha." I grunted and swatted the damn feather that kept falling in front of my face. The truth was going to be the price I paid for the favor. "I was hoping you could look into Stevie's enrollment status for me."

There was a piece to her I was missing.

When we'd been about to leave the costume store the other day, Lainey's shoe had come untied, so we paused right by the front door for her to fix it. While she did that, I saw Stevie in the parking lot through the glass.

I saw the flush in her cheeks. The rigidity in her spine. The way she kept biting on her damn lower lip. She held herself together though it was clear the conversation made her want to fall apart.

I believed her that it had to do with school because I could tell when someone was lying—the blessing and curse of being a good profiler. But I also could see when someone was holding back, and Stevie's answer was only a piece of the whole picture.

Granted, I shouldn't care about her whole picture. Her school was her business. Her personal life was her business. But having her in my home, watching my niece, it blurred the lines of which parts of her were my business.

I was being honest, sometimes it was easier to figure out someone else's secret than it was to deal with your own.

And my secret was that I wanted all of her to be my business.

It was a few moments before I realized I'd received no response from Dex. I turned and found myself under his steady observation.

"I could."

I read the unspoken warning in his gaze. *But only if I was sure that I wanted to cross that professional line to know more about my nanny.*

My mouth firmed. "Please."

At that moment, the door swung open, Dante filling the frame, followed closely by Reed. They both gaped at me, looked at Dex, and then back at me.

"Did I miss the memo about Covington costume day?" Dante smirked.

I folded my arms. "I've got a Halloween parade at Lainey's school at one."

"You need backup? Dante's ready to morph into a Backstreet Boy at the drop of a hat," Reed joked and walked around the other man to fully enter the room.

It was no secret—not even to a newcomer like me—that Dante had a small obsession with the Backstreet Boys. In fact, his hallway karaoke was so prominent that I'd grown accustomed to it even when I'd been working virtually.

"Lucky for you, Reed, you're already in costume," Dante quipped, and when everyone gave him a confused look, he added, "As a proby."

Reed rolled his eyes and took a seat at the table, leaning back and crossing his ankles out in front of him. "Any chance you can make this Backstreet Bro walk the plank?"

"Backstreet Bro." Dante threw back his head and barked out a laugh. "Those are fighting—"

"How are Isla and Jackson doing?" I broke in before a scuffle broke out.

About a week ago, Jackson's pregnant girlfriend had been kidnapped in an attempt to get back at him. The former SEAL had stopped at nothing to rescue her, and even though she hadn't been harmed, she'd also gone into early labor and had their baby prematurely. And just like Ace had done for me, the owner of Covington Security told Jackson to take as much time as he needed at the hospital with his woman and their new baby girl who'd be living in the NICU for a few weeks.

"Good. Really good." Dante nodded. "I didn't know it was physically possible to wrap a Navy SEAL around your finger, but that little peanut managed it without even trying."

I smiled a little, remembering how Bill and Val had looked when Lainey was born. *Remembering the photo Val took of me when I'd held my niece for the first time.*

"And what about your sister and the baby?"

And if one baby for the team wasn't enough, Rocco's wife, Carina, had given birth to their baby last week, too. In the last two weeks, the baby-to-bodyguard ratio had rapidly increased at Covington Security, but that meant my work schedule was packed. Between profiles, finishing up jobs that Roc and Jackson were responsible for, and sorting through new cases, I hardly had any downtime.

A good thing.

No downtime meant no time for my thoughts to stray to my damned tempting nanny—*or the way I'd almost kissed her three weeks ago.*

"Perfect." Dante beamed. "Gets her good looks from her uncle. Obviously."

"Hopefully not her singing voice," Reed quipped.

A low rumble of laughter spread through the room.

"Is there a reason all of you are in my office?" Dex grumbled, wanting to get back to his peace and quiet.

I wanted him to get back to work, too; I wanted to know why the hell my nanny, who seemed to do nothing more than eat, sleep, nanny, and study, was worried about school.

"I should head out—"

The door opened again, Dex's low curse stifled when his older brother strode into the room.

Naturally, the bright-red jacket and red feather in my hat drew Ace's attention.

"Roman didn't get the memo that we only dress as Vikings here." Dante took the opportunity to crack another joke.

Reed snorted.

"Halloween parade," I muttered for the third time. A parade that I needed to leave in ten minutes for.

Ace's chin dipped. "Well, I'm glad I caught you before you left." He looked at his brother. "Detective Werner is emailing over details on a case now. When it comes through, can you pull it up?"

"Werner?" Reed sat forward, having worked closely with the detective when he'd been on the force.

I'd also worked with Werner briefly when the BAU had been brought in to consult on several murders that turned out to be mob related.

"They need our help on a case?" Dante probed.

Ace looked at me, an ominous preface to what he was about to say. "They have two bodies."

A hum started in my blood, electricity ready to be tapped. It was the same hum that came with every case folder placed on my desk at the BAU: the charge to stop a killer.

"They think it's serial?"

"He wants our help—your help." Ace's deep voice was pulled tight under the strain of bringing this to me.

"Of course, I'll take a look," I told him, but as soon as the words were out of my mouth, I knew there was more to this.

"I've got the email," Dex interjected, and a second later, the projector screen lit up, mirroring Dex's computer.

On the screen appeared basic information on the two victims.

"Estimated eighteen to twenty-one. Brown hair." I read through the listed physical attributes. "Victimology seems consistent." And I was sure the attached photographs would confirm my assessment.

"Jesus," Reed muttered. "Raped and strangled."

I knew what he was feeling. Sick. Disgusted. But years of dealing with the world's worst had numbed me to the nausea of these moments. I couldn't afford to be sick. I couldn't afford to be emotional. This was why I'd ruled out a family and children early on. Not because of the danger, but because of the kind of man I had to become to catch these kinds of twisted psychopaths.

Hollow.

"Neither identified?" My head cocked and I looked at Ace.

"Rorik is working on DNA, but the victims didn't have any identifying information on them and no one reported them missing locally, so Werner thinks they came from another city or out of state."

Rorik Nilsen was the chief medical examiner for the city. I'd met him a handful of times, not under the best of circumstances obviously, but I knew he was a longtime friend of Ace's. Between his work for the city and the way he moonlighted as part of the Covington team, it was no surprise that Rorik's personal life was nonexistent. For some, the dead were easier to deal with than the living; *understandable since the dead couldn't lie.*

"Runaways," Reed muttered. "The city is no stranger to vagrants and homelessness."

A chill ran through me.

There were estimated between 1.8 and 2.6 million runaway youths each year. If the victims were older than eighteen, it made it even less likely that someone reported them missing and more probable that they'd arrived in San Francisco and faded into the eight-thousand-plus homeless population.

"I would look at missing persons from neighboring states to start," I suggested and checked my watch. Twenty minutes until the parade. Ten until I had to leave. "Dex, can you forward me the file? I'll take a look over the weekend—"

"Roman." Ace's deep rumble halted me. He took a deep inhale before laying his next bomb on me. "Rorik found something on the bodies—something that Werner said won't be in the report."

Dread dragged its icy fingertips down my spine.

"All the victims had skin cut from their chest… in the shape of a cross."

Fuck. The world rocked under my feet. *Fucking fuck.*

"The Archangel."

There was a pause—the kind that comes between the pin pulled on a grenade and the explosion.

"Who?" Dante finally rasped.

"The Archangel," I repeated. "A serial killer that I've been tracking for almost a decade—that the BAU has been tracking for almost three."

"Three decades?" Reed gaped.

"The most prolific of our time… if I'm right." I swallowed hard. "If he's truly back."

"Back? Like he went on vacation?" Dante choked out.

"Something like that," I rumbled and then delved into the SparkNotes version of the sordid tale. "My predecessor at the BAU had been tracking a killer they'd called the Archangel for a decade. He targeted young women around his age who were known in their communities and involved in their church in some way. They were all assaulted, strangled, and left with crosses cut from their chest."

"Fuck."

"The BAU profiled him as a religious zealot who, after having sex with his victims, then believed they were immoral and needed to repent and then be sacrificed in order to be redeemed. They gave him the name Archangel."

"An angel sent by God to destroy sinners," Dante murmured. "Jesus… and I thought the Catholics were merciless."

"But he stopped?" Reed cocked his head.

I nodded again. "For fifteen years. And then, six years ago, I got a call—a voice mail at my desk, the line from a community center in Wyoming near Casper. The woman on the voice mail said she'd just found a box full of cross necklaces. Underneath the jewelry was a stack of playing card-sized, vacuum-sealed sheets containing preserved flesh. She said he was there—that she hoped I would get him."

Dante lifted his fist to his mouth. "Jewelry and skin? Fucking hell."

"She didn't leave a name? An address?" Reed asked.

My fist flexed against my side. "No," I said through tight teeth. "She was afraid." I could still remember the slight quiver in her voice. "She thought what she'd given me was enough."

"How'd you know what she gave you was legitimate?" Reed sat forward, resting his elbows on his thighs.

"For every victim, he took two tokens. Photos of the victims before they were killed confirmed he kept their jewelry for himself, and we only revealed to the media that he carved into the chest of his victims, but we never shared the shape." I notched my glasses higher on my nose. "I believe the caller saw the jewelry and the preserved flesh and knew exactly what it was even if she didn't say it."

"What happened?"

Failure.

"We landed in Wyoming that night. By the next morning, there was already one body, but it wasn't quite like before." I gritted my teeth together so hard I was surprised one of them didn't give way and snap. "That victim—that kill… it lacked his previous finesse. If the tokens weren't the same… if I hadn't gotten that call… I would've said the body looked like a first-time killer. But the details… the marks… they were all his."

"A copycat?" Dex probed.

I exhaled slowly. The thought had crossed my mind a million times, but I just couldn't get it to stick.

"If it is, it would have to be someone who knew the Archangel. The cross cut was his signature, and even after all those years, it was never made public." I paused, tasting the bile of defeat on my tongue. "That first kill was messy, and the age of the victim tracked with how old we estimated the Archangel to be. Early fifties." I shifted my weight. "It was sloppy and we were able to track him from Casper through Jackson and up to Wisdom…"

"And then he took Lydia," Ace prompted, familiar with this segment of the case.

I nodded. "He took Lydia Reynolds for his next victim—Archer's mom," I clarified when the guys all raised their eyebrows at the connection. "But we were too close on his trail, and he was too… out of practice, for lack of a better term. We found where he'd taken her and got there in time to save her… but not in time to catch him."

"Did she see him?" Reed asked, his fists knotted tight together.

"Not a good enough look. All she could give us was that he was a six foot white male with a beard."

"So, all of Wyoming," Dante said, running a hand along his jaw.

"But these…" Reed spun his chair back to look at the screen. "These are all younger females."

"I know." I swallowed. "So, it could be a copycat, but I believe that whatever happened to him—whatever made him disappear for over a decade—it altered something that when he went to give in to that urge to kill again, it wasn't the same; something was off. And after the mess of a job he did in Casper and his failure in Wisdom, I think he changed tactics—I think he switched his target victims."

"To young, high-risk females."

My head bobbed again. "Women who wouldn't be reported missing right away."

"Should we call the BAU—"

"No." I shook my head. This was still my case—*this would always be my case.* "I need to see the bodies for myself to confirm. I won't bring Koorie out here unless I'm sure it's him. She's tracked his trail of bodies to Arizona but weeks behind the kill. If this is him… these victims will be the ones found closest to their time of death."

"Roman—"

"I'll head up to the city tonight," I declared, interrupting my boss because my mind was set. "Once I check the bodies and confirm, I'll reach out to Koorie's team if necessary, but I need to see them first. I'm the only one who will know."

My eyes didn't waver when they met Ace's.

He'd never ask me to do this—not after everything that had happened. But it had been six weeks since Val died, and most days, it felt like I was no closer to helping Lainey than the moment I'd picked her up from the hospital.

"But who will—"

"I'll have Stevie stay the weekend," I answered before he could finish, feeling the weight of everyone's attention on me. *I was sure Lainey would prefer it anyway.* "I have to do this, Ace."

If I couldn't help my niece, I could at least rid the world of one more monster for her.

CHAPTER EIGHT

Stevie

"My favorite beach is right over there." I pointed past the playground fence to a secluded portion of the shore.

Lainey followed the line of my finger, distracted by the low roll of the waves before her head turned back to the parking lot, a worried expression dotting her forehead.

I'd arrived half an hour ago to help her change into her costume. Black leggings, a yellow sash around her waist, a red jacket that matched Roman's, and red bandanna. I'd corralled her wayward waves in two little braids, and held them down with the bandanna. There'd been an eye patch in the bag, but she didn't want to wear it.

"He'll be here," I promised, scanning the parking lot for Roman's Bronco and wondering why he was cutting it so close.

I wished he could see her like this—looking for him in her little pirate outfit, waiting for him to get here.

I turned and then apologized to the mom behind me when I tapped her with my fairy wings. A giant blue tulle skirt, sheer white wings, and a matching flower crown... *This costume was ridiculous.* But Lainey was happy, and that was what counted.

Sister Mary walked along the line one more time with a

serene smile, prompting Lainey to tug on my hand. The parade was about to start and Roman still wasn't—

Here.

My breath caught. A red coat and frilly white feather came into view, but it was his stride that was unmistakable. Determined. Uncompromising. It fit the man as well as the character. And the glasses... with the costume... not even J.M. Barrie could create such a hot, nerdy Hook. My lower parts tingled at the sight of the nerdy pirate.

Roman stalked across the parking lot, the wide brim of his hat not enough to mask the shadow that darkened his features.

Something was wrong.

But when his eyes connected with mine like lightning striking the sea, I quickly looked away.

"Uncle Roman is here," I nudged Lainey and then pointed in his direction.

There was a small bustle in the crowd that signaled his approach before the low tenor of his voice rappelled down my spine.

"Well, ahoy there, Captain Lainey."

He was close. I could smell his amber-and-citrus musk as it mingled with the sea air and burst into my lungs. And then he was in front of us, enacting a bow of deference to his niece and me. The white plume on his hat shimmied in the wind and then fell into line as he straightened to his full height, presenting himself with the full effect of his costume.

Lainey smiled, but I couldn't.

Costumes weren't made to fit people well. My own fairy dress case in point; the sleeves were too big for my shoulders, forcing my back ramrod straight so they wouldn't fall down my arms. On the flip side, the mock-corset torso was too small for my *conspicuous* chest, smashing my breasts up along the edge provocatively.

But I couldn't bear to let Lainey down, so I wore it anyway. *We were only trudging around a parking lot and playground after all...*

Roman's costume though... it was made for him. The short pants cut off right below the knee and molded to his strong thighs. The red jacket stretched along his broad shoulders and chest like he'd been sewn into the damn thing. Even the ridiculous white collar of the shirt that I could only describe as frilly, framed the strong cut of his jaw and softened the classically hard lines of his face.

"Mr. Knight," I murmured, feeling his stare rake over me and leave the familiar trace of icy-hot tingles on my skin, intensifying the ache between my thighs.

"It's First Mate," he returned. "First Mate Roman Knight to my captain, Lainey Nobeard, lady of the seven seas."

Lainey giggled, the small sound in his presence making him jolt and reach up to steady the fake parrot on his shoulder.

The black hat, fake sword, and stuffed parrot were unnecessary in my humble opinion; the man standing in front of me exuded the fierce lawlessness that no props could ever mimic though it was odd to think of a former FBI agent as lawless, but when it came to protecting his niece—his most valuable treasure—it was the only description; Roman would break any rule, battle any force, and utterly destroy anyone who tried to harm her.

"Princess Stevie."

My mouth went dry. He'd used my first name, and in an instant, it felt like I was no longer wearing a princess costume, but standing naked in front of him. All this time, I hadn't wanted the formality of "Ms. Michaels," but no one warned me of the coarse intimacy that came with the way he said *Stevie*. The lower rumble of his voice held something in those words that it hadn't before. Something decadent but also dangerous.

"Roman."

His eyes flared.

"Sorry I'm late," he apologized gruffly, turning his attention to Lainey.

"We didn't start, so you're not late," I assured him.

For weeks, I'd watched a six-year-old wade through the impossible depths of grief, tipping through distraction, ignorance, and inconsolable sadness with the force of a Tilt-A-Whirl. But the man in front of me remained as unmoving as a stone, as though he thought the slightest crack would send everything crumbling.

If we'd been at the house—in normal clothes and surrounded by our normal environment—I would've found a way to hold my tongue and stay silent. But out here… we weren't nanny and boss; we were pirate and princess. And there were no rules out on the open seas.

"Is everything okay?"

"Fine," he clipped and then nodded to Lainey who'd wandered a few steps to the side of us, toying with her fake sword. "How is she?"

"Excited…" I answered slowly, confused for a moment.

"She was up most of the night crying," he confessed quietly.

After everything he'd told me about how his sister loved holidays, I wasn't surprised that this was hard for Lainey. But she still wanted to come today and dress up as a pirate.

My throat constricted. "Well, she's here now. And happy," I told him with a brave smile. "And that should count for something, too."

He grunted.

"She was waiting for you."

Now, I had his attention.

He turned, our eyes connecting. "She was?"

I felt my mouth go dry as I nodded. "Watching the parking lot, waiting for you to get here."

The way he looked at me, it was like he knew she hadn't been the only one.

"She needs you, Roman. She just doesn't know how to say it," I promised softly, reaching for him and resting my hand on his forearm.

I hadn't just slipped out of the formality we'd maintained, I'd leaped from it.

Tension rippled through his muscles and his eyes snapped back to mine, twin pits more tumultuous than the stormy seas.

I realized just how much he'd needed to hear those words. He wanted to fix her pain, believing it would fix his, too. But there was a hurt inside him that had nothing to do with his niece —an uncertainty he didn't know how to face. And I wondered if the man who spent his life saving the world was afraid to let anyone save him.

"And what about you, Stevie?" he rasped, angling toward me. "Do you know how to tell someone when you need them?"

My lips parted. *What did he mean? What did he know?* Worry knotted like packed-up Christmas lights in my stomach.

For so long, I'd convinced myself I didn't need anyone to take care of me—*and I didn't.* But then I met him. I met him, and I saw the way he cared for this little girl and for the first time, I ached to know what it would feel like to have a man like him care for me.

"Stevie..." He breathed my name, our bodies swaying just a little closer.

Before he could say anything, the sound of plastic hitting plastic rang through the air and Roman's arm jostled forward; Lainey had knocked her sword against his and looked up at him with a lopsided grin.

She wanted to play.

Roman adeptly fell into character, pretending to spar with Lainey's sword and grunting in mock pain every time hers grazed him. For a moment, I let myself fade into the background, leaving the two of them in this world where they could grieve and grow together. And then that thought spread like daffodil seeds in the breeze to a place where this life we'd been living for the last four weeks didn't have professional boundaries or an expiration date.

"Princess Stevie." Roman brushed my arm with his fingertips, and my eyes sprung open. "Time to move."

The parade had started. The line of parents and children moved ahead of us, a small gap forming because I'd been stuck in a daze.

"Sorry." I gathered the froth of my skirt and quickly caught up.

Lainey took my hand and I smiled. We laughed and enjoyed the large loop around the parking lot, Roman on one side of her and me on the other. But the entire time, all I thought about was the hot stamp his fingers left on my bare skin, wondering how long I could make that heat last before solitude chilled it away.

I was hardly out of my car in their driveway before Lainey took my hand and pulled me in the direction of the wooden door tucked into the fence.

I looked for Roman so he would know where we were headed, but he'd answered a call on his cell and was talking in low tones in the garage. I thought I'd heard him say the name Dex, but the creak of the wooden gate that led into the garden drowned out anything else.

"Where are we going?" I asked with a laugh as she led me along the pavers through the garden.

She swished her fake sword in the air and then pointed it at the guesthouse. "The fairy princess castle."

My worn sneakers—*not standard fairy or princess attire*—crunched on the dirt before we reached the cement walkway.

We'd walked around the magical structure countless times, but Lainey never asked to go inside, so I never had reason to ask Roman for a key. Instead, while she scouted for pirates, I peered through the windows, noting how the house was already furnished though large sheets were draped over the furniture, shielding it from sight.

"See anything?" I crouched by Lainey, staring through the rungs of the railing at the ocean that frothed in front of us.

Her head shook.

"Do pirates have homes?"

I started, immediately wondering if that was why she'd chosen her Halloween costume—because she didn't feel like she had a home.

Sympathy clogged my throat, but I forced myself to speak through it.

"Of course they do," I assured her like I was a pirate expert. "A pirate's home is his or her ship." Two big brown eyes stared at me. "It might not look like everyone else's home, but that ship is where they live—where they come back after every adventure and where they feel safe during every storm."

"What about a bug's home?"

"Well, a bug's home is in the dirt. Or trees or bushes," I said. "They make their own special homes."

"What about your home?"

I sucked in a breath, unprepared for the unabashed curiosity of the six-year-old to turn to me.

"I..." I swallowed. "I'm still looking for mine."

Maybe I shouldn't have said anything—or should've made up something happy. But I believed kids deserved honesty. Not honesty as in I was about to confess that I hadn't had a home since my dad had broken ours. But measured honesty.

"You can have this one," she offered with her toothless smile.

"I can't have this one. This one's yours," I said simply because all the real reasons went beyond *measured* honesty.

She giggled. "No, silly. We can share it."

My stupid costume felt even tighter on my chest.

I wouldn't mind sharing this home with this little girl and her guardian. I wouldn't mind at all.

"We can just stay for a minute before we have to go inside and change," I said softly after a minute. We needed to get back to the routine of the night. "We have homework to get done before dinner."

Since Roman left work early for the parade, I was hoping I'd get my own early dismissal tonight; Halloween would be a night of high demand for Uber trips, and I needed them all. Especially because I wished I could just stay here, playing dress-up and pretend with my tiny charge in the company of a handsome pirate.

Lainey was having none of my structure though, still high on the excitement of the parade and her love for her costume, she released my hand, drew her fake sword, and charged down around the back deck of the guesthouse like it was the pointed prow of a ship.

"*Stevie.*"

In costume, we got rid of the facade we'd maintained before. It was just Stevie now. No Ms. Michaels. Not even Princess Stevie. Just me.

Roman came down the walk, each step rumbling the earth underneath us. Something was wrong. More wrong than earlier.

"Sorry, she wanted to play down here," I called out, shifting my weight.

He didn't respond. Instead, his expression crystallized into something inarguably infuriated the closer he got.

I gulped. Before I lost my nerve, I needed to ask to leave early tonight. I'd avoided the issue for as long as I could, but the call from the school last week reminded me that this wasn't my life. This was my job. A means to support my education—my dreams.

"Mr. Knight, I was wondering if I could leave early tonight?"

He stopped immediately.

"I have some school things—"

"No. I need you to stay here with Lainey for the weekend," he interrupted, his statement not even feigning choice in the matter.

My mouth fell open.

"I need to go to San Francisco for a case."

"Okay, but I—"

"It wasn't a question, Stevie."

Seriously? My spine straightened. As much as I wanted to help him—help them, I had to think about my future, and I would make way more money filling my weekend with trips than I would staying here.

"Well, maybe it should be," I replied firmly. "I have other things I need to do this weekend that I really can't—"

"What things?"

I bristled and folded my arms, a petulant fairy facing off against a persistent pirate. "Personal things I need for school," I caged my answer; I didn't need anyone's help, least of all his.

"I'll pay for the rest of your tuition for next semester."

Whatever I'd imagined or expected his response to be, it wasn't that. I stepped back, reeling with the force of his words.

"Wh-what?"

How did he know? How could he know?

"I'll pay for the rest of your tuition," he repeated. "One weekend for all of it."

Pay it. *Three thousand dollars.* He said it like it was the equivalent of the twenty-dollar Halloween costume he'd bought for me.

"I don't need you to pay for my school. I'm perfectly capable of paying—"

"I know you haven't paid the full tuition for your classes next semester," he interrupted my blatant lie.

Anger lashed through me like a whip. "How do you know about my tuition?" I demanded. "Are you... spying on me?"

He didn't even have the decency to appear remorseful. "After you looked upset the other day, I had someone check into it."

My hand shot out, spearing a finger directly into the bulk of his chest. "You had no right to do that," I seethed, tempted to add he had no legal ground to do it either.

Strong fingers manacled my wrist, shackling it in his hold as he lifted my hand to the side. He moved forward, not leaving even enough space for a sword to slice cleanly between us.

"I have every right to look into the person I'm paying to take care of my niece—every right to know if you're in trouble or need help," he declared, his voice shredding into a rough rasp. "I just want to help, Stevie."

I wanted to be angry—*was angry*—but I was also... *warmed*. It wasn't just Lainey he wanted to protect; *he wanted to protect me;* I heard it stacked into every syllable he spoke, like dynamite lit with the heated charge in his gaze.

The thought paralyzed me.

Yes, Mom wanted to protect me when she moved us out here. Yes, we went through crazy lengths to make sure our new lives stayed under the radar. But because of her illness, I'd been the one taking care of her in those last years, and once she was gone, I had no one left but myself to rely on.

Safer that way.

But boy, did he tempt me.

"I'm not in trouble, and I don't need your help," I replied firmly, yanking my arm out of his hold.

A small whimper cranked both of our heads to the side. *Lainey.* I wasn't sure how long she'd been there, but it was long enough to know we were arguing, and it brought giant tears to the corners of her eyes.

"Lainey—" Roman broke off and moved toward her, but as soon as he did, she bolted for the house. "Dammit."

"You shouldn't have spied on me," I said lowly.

He spun and then he was towering above me, his deep growl drenching me with all of his frustrations as they boiled over.

"I shouldn't have looked into it, but I did. I couldn't stop myself. I can't seem to stop myself when it comes to wanting to take care of you." He reached up and cupped his palm to the side of my face.

It was the first time he'd touched me that wasn't either saving me or warning me or accidentally. It was the first selfish touch. For both of us.

I shivered as his thumb stroked my skin, but his expression was what captivated me. Tension tempered with tenderness. Like a slingshot pulled taut and ready to release, he vibrated with the strength it took to hold it back and the fear of what would happen if he let loose.

His head drifted lower. Low enough that I felt the brush of the feather from his silly pirate hat. My lips peeled apart, easily convinced that kissing him—kissing my boss—was an acceptable resolution to this disagreement.

It certainly would be the resolution that would cost me the most.

Because who could kiss this sexy, brooding man and be content with only giving him a single kiss?

"Please," he pleaded hoarsely. A single heart-wrenching word that undid me.

I sucked in a breath. I was wholly unprepared for the real Roman that lived behind his myriad of walls. And seeing this man hurting—no matter how angry I was—would always be something I would need to try and fix.

"Okay." My wants made me a traitor to my reality. But I didn't care.

They say like is attracted to like. Well, in this case, maybe broken was attracted to broken, each of us hoping to make the other whole.

"Good girl," he uttered without reserve, catching himself and the wholly erotic yet inappropriate response and trying to erase it with a loud clearing of his throat as he tugged his hand away. "I'll pay your—"

"You can pay me double my hourly rate," I declared without

qualm, knowing the total would still be far less than him paying the rest of my tuition. "And I'll stay."

"Stevie…"

"Take it or leave it." I folded my arms.

His jaw clenched. "I'll pay double your hourly rate…" His eyes flicked behind me, too late did I realize what he was going to suggest. "And you'll move into the guesthouse, rent-free, while you work for me."

Jesus.

Protests clung like dew on my lips, but how stubborn was I really going to be for the sake of principle? The expense of my tuition loomed over my head like a dark cloud, and I'd refused his offer to clear it. Was I really going to turn down the opportunity for rent-free lodging for the next couple months, too? All to claim 'independence?'

No. I was only slightly irrationally stubborn, but I wasn't stupid.

"Okay." I'd worry about straddling the line between accepting his help and becoming dependent on him another day. "I'm going to check on Lainey."

I sidestepped around him and sped up the path, vacillating with each step whether I'd just made the smartest or most foolish decision of my entire life.

CHAPTER NINE

Stevie

"I'm back," I called quietly into the house.

Lainey had immediately stopped crying earlier as soon as Roman told her I'd be sleeping over for the whole weekend. He saw her exuberance. He missed the fear in her eyes when he mumbled something about packing his things and she realized my presence meant his absence.

Lainey and I had finished up her homework, and then once Roman started dinner I left to go back to my apartment and pack a bag to stay. And change out of my ridiculous costume.

It wasn't lost on me how little my apartment felt like home each time I returned to it. Whereas, when I was at Roman's house it felt like where I was meant to be. And now, it would be.

Guesthouse. Rent free.

If I hadn't been so angry at the way he'd gone about it, I would've cried. It was incredible how one thing could take so much weight off my shoulders.

I can't stop myself from wanting to take care of you.

That was the part I couldn't wrap my head around. *That and the "good girl."*

I set my bag on the dining table, straightening when I heard the approach of heavy footsteps.

"Stevie?" Roman appeared. "Are you okay?"

My brow furrowed. "Yes..."

"You took a while at your apartment and didn't make it back for dinner. I saved you a bowl." He tipped his head to the counter where a foil-wrapped bowl sat waiting for me.

My cheeks grew hot and my throat felt tight. He was impossibly thoughtful—sometimes infuriatingly thoughtful—and I wasn't prepared for it; no one had prepared me for a man like him.

"Thank you," I said. "I thought you might want to spend some time with just Lainey before you left."

His eyes narrowed accusingly on me. *"Boyfriend?"*

Oh. Right.

"No," I replied and began to shake my head when he took two steps to stand in front of me. "Roman, about—"

"He's not allowed here," he warned without warning, and I wasn't sure my eyes could get any wider—or that this situation could possibly get more misconstrued. "No one is allowed here over the weekend without my permission, and I'll tell you right now, your piece-of-shit boyfriend will never have my permission to be here. Not this weekend, and not when you move into the guesthouse."

I didn't know whether to be shocked or amused or pleased... though the warmth spreading through my lower parts definitely had its preference.

Roman's gaze raked over me. I'd changed into a pair of yoga pants and a tank top with a sweater to cover my shoulders. However, from his vantage point, I was pretty sure he could see right down my shirt.

And the thought was not upsetting. *Not at all.*

Roman inched closer. "If it were up to me, Stevie, he wouldn't have my permission to be around you at all."

My breath caught. I tried to tell myself that it was only Roman's standards for how he cared about the people in his life that made him say these things, but the hunger in his gaze called me a liar.

The warmth I'd felt ignited into an inferno, kindled by the rough possessiveness in his voice. I felt my nipples harden against my shirt. Painfully. Wantonly. But more importantly, it didn't feel wrong though I knew it should. Wanting my boss—wanting something I shouldn't have was the most unoriginal original sin.

"He's not my boyfriend," I murmured a little breathlessly. *But anyone would lose their breath realizing a predator has marked them as prey.*

"What?" He winced in surprise, his gaze sliding down my front, blazing when he saw the pebbled outline of my nipples through the fabric of my thin bra and shirt.

"Colin wasn't my boyfriend," I explained slowly, figuring out how to tread the line between truth and transparency.

I still needed the flexibility to drive for Uber, and if this afternoon was any indication, he'd probably use his connections to shut down the whole app if that was what it took for me to accept his help.

I'd already accepted his help. I wouldn't make myself completely dependent on him. *I couldn't.*

"I was just giving him a ride. He just had Lasik done and couldn't stay out in the rain." I inhaled and then repeated huskily, "He's not my boyfriend."

I didn't know what upset him more—thinking I had a boyfriend or knowing that I didn't. The lines on his face grew more prominent, the pulse of his jaw strengthened, and the curl of his lip tightened like it took his all not to let his mouth come for mine.

And then I realized. I hadn't just been his nanny. Or too young. I'd also had a boyfriend.

He wasn't prepared for that barrier to evaporate.

"Stevie…" he growled low, and his face drifted toward mine. Inch after inch after inch. Like an anchor finally finding a place to settle.

My eyelids grew heavy, about to shut when his head tore to the side so fast, it made me gasp.

Before I could say anything, he whipped around and stalked away from me. *What just happened?* It took a moment to collect myself before I could follow him, and when I did, the sight left me speechless.

Roman stood in front of Lainey's door, his hands gripping the doorframe with a force that carved out every muscle of his forearm and embossed every vein. His head hung between his shoulders as though his body was bankrupt of strength.

As I got closer, his tortured eyes lifted to mine, and that was when I finally heard it: the soft sobs coming from her room.

I knew she cried at night, but I didn't know it was like this.

"I'd do anything to make it better," he said, his low voice cracked raw. His gaze drifted back to the door as though he could will it and every other barrier between him and his niece away with the sheer force of his determination. "If I go in there, she'll pretend she's okay."

"Let me try," I offered, letting my bag slide down onto the floor at my feet.

He stepped to the side, but I moved so quickly that my shoulder brushed his arm in the transition and brought goose bumps to my skin. It was obnoxious how this attraction wouldn't leave me alone, especially now when I should be focused on Lainey.

Under his watch, I knocked softly, the rumble making her cries instantly cease like he said they would.

"Lainey?" I slowly opened her door and peeked my head inside. "It's Stevie. Can I come sit?" I asked the tiny form buried under the covers and facing away from me.

The covers moved in what I *thought* looked like a nod—at least, that was what I was going to take it as.

I looked at Roman once more, gratitude softening his pained expression.

"I'm going to shower," he murmured, heading for the bathroom as though just being outside her door would bring her more harm.

Slipping into the room, three steps brought me to the twin bed and I sat on the mattress, propping my back against the headboard.

A few seconds later, the covers began to shake again with her cries.

"It's okay to miss them," I murmured and placed my hand on her shoulder. "You don't have to hide that you're sad."

Lainey moved under my hand, and then I realized she was

turning over. Her small face appeared from the edge of the blankets, ruddy and red nosed.

"D-do you miss your mom and dad?"

My throat constricted. "Yes."

I missed Mom every day. And Dad… deep down, I missed Dad. I missed Dad just as surely as if he'd died when I realized who Lee truly was. In so many ways, "Dad" was one more of Lee's victims—the one I'd never forgive him for.

"Uncle Roman doesn't miss my mom and dad," she said thickly, wiping her nose on the blanket.

"Why do you think that?"

Her head ducked. "He's not sad. He never cries."

"Is that why you hide when you cry?"

She sniffled and nodded. "If he doesn't cry, neither should I."

Oh, my heart.

He thought she didn't love him when here she was, trying desperately not to disappoint him.

"I know your uncle misses your mom and dad," I assured her, reaching out and peeling a strand of hair from where it stuck to her damp cheek. "I think he's just afraid to be sad."

Lainey moved closer, curling her head onto my lap. "But Uncle Roman catches bad guys; he isn't afraid of anything."

I rested back on the headboard, letting my fingers begin to absentmindedly comb through her hair.

"Sometimes, we don't know our biggest fear until we have to face it." I paused for a second. Roman thought he was protecting her by only showing strength, instead he was turning her into a little island, cut off and surrounded by grief. "Maybe you could show him that it's not scary to be sad."

She was quiet for a few seconds, and I wondered if I'd put her to sleep, but then her tiny voice squeaked out, "Maybe."

Maybe was enough for tonight.

"Stevie, can you tell me the pirate story?" she then asked, her voice tipping from sad to sleepy.

"Sure." I smiled and then delved into the silly pirate tale I'd been spinning for weeks.

Five minutes later, Lainey breathed heavily on my lap. Careful not to wake her, I moved out from under her and slid her pillow underneath her head. Opening her door, I turned and backed out of the room, making sure she continued to sleep calmly until the door was shut.

Taking a deep breath, I straightened my spine. I had to tell Roman that he needed to stop being so stoic. Lainey didn't need someone who was strong, she needed someone who was sad just like she was—who missed her parents just like she did.

My exhale sped from my lips and I spun directly into something hard, hot, *and half-naked.*

"Stevie," Roman rasped, taking my arms in his hands and forcibly steadying me away from him.

I gulped, drinking in the sight of him.

The buttoned-up former FBI agent stood in front of me wearing nothing but a towel. And because he'd reached out to grab me, that towel hung precariously low on those notches below his hips.

"Roman..." I stammered, my eyes counting each muscle knot in his abdomen like I was marking their attendance in Perfect Core 101. *All eight present and accounted for.*

"Is she okay?"

I snapped my attention to his face, heat dumping into my cheeks like some kind of visual truth serum.

My head bobbed for a second before I found my voice. "She's sad," I began dumbly and then added, "She doesn't think you miss her mom and dad."

"What? How could she think that?" Roman reared back, and it took everything in me not to watch the way the movement rippled over his broad chest.

I gulped. "She doesn't think you miss them because you're never sad."

Instantly his face hardened. "Please tell me you told her that wasn't the truth," he rasped.

"I did." I bit my lip. "But I think it would be better... for both of you... if you shared your sadness."

At first he looked insulted. Then affronted. And finally, indignant. And when indignant took over, it carried him a single step forward to tower above me with a menacing glower.

"You don't know what you're talking about."

My chin notched up. I knew I was crossing lines, but I didn't care. If I needed to be the casualty that brought the two of them together, then so be it.

"I know that you're afraid to be sad—that you're afraid to show her anything that isn't strength, but all you're showing her is that it's weakness to miss her parents," I charged, my words landing with the precision of the tip of a knife. "That's why she cries alone."

Roman's eyes swirled like a whirlpool of anger and lust, frothing and foaming as the two emotions worked each other into a frenzy.

"To do what I do, Stevie, you have to not feel," he confessed, his body vibrating with tension. "You have to take emotions—all of them—and lock them up tight because if you start to feel, you realize you can't stomach reality. And if you can't stomach reality, then there's no one to rid it of its monsters."

He had to be talking about his job with the FBI. I didn't know what kind of criminals he'd dealt with, but his broken tone testified to the toll it had taken on him.

"But you're here now. You have a different life now," I said, drawing a shuddered breath. "And this life needs you to feel."

I'd seen it call to him for weeks now, but he refused to give in, preferring to stand on its sidelines as a protector rather than risk pain as a participant. My heart clenched. Lainey was right; on the surface, I'd never expect this man to be afraid of anything. But here he was, afraid to let anyone in—a gladiator unwilling to take off his impressive armor, afraid he might be hollow underneath.

"It's okay, Roman," I promised him in a husky whisper, and then, before I realized what I was doing, my hand flattened on his left pec, the velvet steel came to life under my touch.

"Stevie..." His gaze sparkled with warning.

I breathed deep, his amber-and-citrus musk permeating my nostrils with deceptive ease. My tongue slid over my own lips, and even though I continued our conversation, my thoughts drifted somewhere else—somewhere warm and forbidden—as I swayed toward him.

"What's the worst that could happen if you let yourself feel?"

I asked, my voice barely recognizable through the thick layer of husk coating it.

He jolted as though I'd struck him. *Or unlocked him.* Our eyes collided—two different galaxies crashing into one.

"*This*," he growled a second before his mouth claimed mine.

I gasped against the onslaught, instantly quaking apart under the storm of his kiss. Hard lips forced mine apart, baring what felt like the deepest parts of me for his scrutiny.

He cupped both sides of my face, stepping forward until my back hit the wall. Distantly, I knew this was wrong. Distantly, I knew this could jeopardize everything. But as I shuddered and melted into his heat, winding my arms around his neck, I wondered if wanting to do what was wrong was something I'd inherited from Dad.

If wanting what was wrong was built into my genes.

Perhaps it was in my blood to cross lines that should never be crossed. *And kissing Roman Knight was one boundary I never should've broken.*

I felt his low growl all the way in my bones, calling to something deep inside me that I'd never allowed out before.

He wasn't the only one afraid to feel.

The hot steel of his tongue plundered into the depths of my mouth, licking and stroking and searching for every hidden piece of desire it could find. I'd never been kissed like this. *Ever.* Frantic and fraught with hunger.

On the outside, he might be a protector, but when it came to giving in to his feelings, he was as ruthless as a pirate.

My back bowed, pressing my chest to his. I was drawn to his strength just as much as I wanted to see his weakness. His hands angled my head harder against the wall, kissing me until I swore his tongue carved his name into my soul. But it was the way his hips pinned mine that stoked a flame I'd never fueled.

Ache knotted in my core. I knew what my body wanted. Every so often, I'd touched myself to feed its cravings. But mostly, I did everything I could to ignore them because I was afraid to feel, too.

But now, I kissed him like the hypocrite I was—demanding

he make himself vulnerable though I was unwilling to do the same.

"The things you do to me, Stevie," he growled and snared my lower lip between his teeth, biting down until a shiver cascaded down my spine.

I felt the things I did to him, specifically the hard ridge of him that jutted through his towel like a weapon angled against my stomach.

"All I want is to take care of you. Your school. Your home. Your body," he went on, sounding mindless with desire. "The idea of taking care of you makes me lose my mind... and makes me so fucking hard."

"Roman," I whimpered loudly, rocking my hips into him, wanting every layer of fabric and fear to disappear until there was nothing left except me and him. *The nanny and the pirate.*

My underwear slid along my pussy with how wet I was, delicious friction eating away at my cells. I'd starved myself of intimacy for too long, one taste turning me into an innocent beggar.

"*Please.*" The plea ricocheted against his mouth, piercing holes in the bubble of vulnerability we'd locked ourselves in.

I felt the sharp intake of his breath like a knife dragged along my lips a second before they tore away and the word "Fuck" spilled out.

He stepped away from me until his back hit the other side of the hallway, both of us facing each other, gasping for some sanity.

"Shit, Stevie..." He trailed off, regret lacing every inch of his expression. He dragged the back of his hand over his mouth like he could wipe away the last several minutes of our make-out session.

I wished I could erase it that easily, but my mouth felt scorched—burned by a passion I'd never felt before. It was going to take more than a brush of my hand to forget the heat of his mouth or the promise of his kiss.

"I need to get going," he said, clearing his throat and completely bypassing the whole boss-just-kissed-the-nanny situation.

I nodded, muted momentarily by the lump in my throat.

"If you just want to give me the keys to the guesthouse, I can unlock it…" I trailed off, watching his expression morph into confusion.

"You're not staying in the guesthouse this weekend," he said matter-of-factly. "Lainey can't sleep alone in the house…"

Shoot. Duh, Stevie. One kiss and I'd lost all my marbles.

"Oh. Of course." I nodded furiously and spun toward the living room. "I'll just grab a blanket for the couch—"

"Jesus, Stevie." He grabbed my arm, stopping me on a dime, and then released me just as quickly. "You're not sleeping on the damn couch." He pointed over my shoulder; I knew what was there without looking. "I changed the sheets for you. You're staying in my room while I'm gone."

In his room.

In his bed.

The instruction passed unspoken between us, and my mouth went dry. I couldn't stay in his bed. Not tonight. *Not after…* His hold tightened like he heard my thoughts.

"Just give me a minute to change and grab my stuff, and then it's all yours," he declared and then disappeared into his room.

Two minutes later, he returned with his weekend bag, and I followed him mutely to the front of the house. He waited until he was halfway through the front door before he faced me to say goodbye.

"Stevie…" He trailed off, bringing his hand up to cup my chin, the pad of his thumb brushing over my lower lip, still tingly and swollen from when he'd bit it. "Have a good night."

It wasn't a pleasantry. It was another order. A deep, seductive order.

Before my jaw could hit the ground, he was gone.

I'd kissed my boss. I'm going to be sleeping in his bed. *And he wanted me to pleasure myself in it.*

Deep in my stomach, I knew that this was one more wrong thing by the way I wanted it so badly.

CHAPTER TEN

Roman

My hand flexed on the frame of the window, frustration rolling through me in waves as steady as the sea.

It was him. The thought haunted me every mile from the city back to Carmel.

The Archangel was in California. *An hour from here.* And he'd killed two women.

The weekend hadn't been a weekend. It had been work. *Part of the hunt.* And I drank in every moment of it, letting the adrenaline of the chase drug me to distraction.

"Roman."

I tensed. The sound of her voice did things to my body I couldn't justify. Turning, I faced the woman I couldn't stop thinking about.

When I was tense, I thought of Stevie. Angered, I thought of Stevie. Worried, Stevie. Lonely, *Stevie.* Her and the memory of that damn kiss hunted me like I was the psychopath. And maybe I was for lusting after my young, innocent nanny.

I turned. Stevie stood in the hallway wearing an oversized Monterey T-shirt and a pair of sleep boxers. *Fuck.* My dick that had been semihard from the moment I stepped through the door this morning, knowing she was asleep in my bed, now hardened into steel imagining her touching herself wearing that.

"Good morning." There was a roughness to my voice that the stress of the weekend and the strain of my dick made it impossible to erase.

"When did you get back?" she asked, her voice still adorably hoarse from sleep.

"Last night—early this morning, technically." I'd pulled in the garage around one thirty.

I'd finished up late with Werner, and when I got to the lobby of my hotel, I realized I didn't want to be there anymore, even if it was for only a couple of hours to sleep. I wanted to be back here—back home. So, I left.

Stevie said I had a new life here, and all it took was one weekend away to realize just how quickly I'd gotten used to that new life.

In the city... hunting the Archangel... that was the old Roman. And I thought I'd relish the chance to be him again, even just for a short while. Instead, I'd only thought about them—about her.

It was a damned nuisance that I couldn't get my nanny off my mind.

"Oh." She blushed, noticing the unfolded blanket on the couch.

I wished I could say I'd gotten some sleep, but I hadn't. All I'd done was lay and wonder what she slept in. If she'd slept well. If she'd done as I'd imagined and touched herself, thinking of me.

Fuck knew I'd fisted my dick far too many times in the last two days thinking about her.

Even with sleep eluding me, I was glad to be home. So, I'd made a cup of coffee, sat to watch the ocean, and let my mind ponder when it had become safer to focus on serial killers rather than sexy nannies.

"How was she?" I rasped, reminding us both why we were here.

"Okay." She padded into the living room, her bare feet hardly making any noise for how dangerous her presence was to me. "She missed you."

My stomach tightened. Words I wanted to hear.

Stevie's eyes slid over me for a brief second, and I bit my tongue hard to stop myself from asking if she did, too. I wanted to know if her nights had been as fitful as mine and if her days had been caught up in the memory of our kiss. I blinked and realized her gaze now lingered on my lips. *I had my answer.*

Lust pumped through my veins. I thought two days away would dull this, but it only seemed to make it stronger. We should talk about the kiss—I should tell her it was a mistake and apologize. But it wasn't a mistake, the apology would be a lie, and I wasn't a liar.

"Did everything go okay with your case?" she asked, quickly snapping her focus away from my mouth as though we both didn't know where it had been.

My gaze retreated back out the windows.

Lainey's silence. My damned unquenchable desire for Stevie. All things that felt destined to remain unresolved. But the Archangel case... that I had a chance to solve, a chance to finally catch this fucker. Out of everything, catching these kinds of monsters was what I did. Unless I'd become incapable of that, too.

I grunted, unsure how to answer her.

"I confirmed that the murders were related to a case I was working with the FBI. I don't know if that's good or bad." Just more pieces to fit into the puzzle—pieces I hoped would finally lead me to answers after all these years.

"Murders?" she choked out behind me.

I ducked my head, closing my eyes as I recalled my visit with Rorik. Seeing the bodies—the crosses cut from the chest—it was like a punch to the gut that no matter what I did, this case would continue to haunt me. *He* would continue to haunt me.

"Two of them. Young girls." My jaw tightened. "Numbers twenty-three and twenty-four."

"Numbers... you mean... that means..."

"A serial killer." I exhaled slowly, folded my arms, and spun toward her. In slow motion, I watched the color bleed from her face.

Shit. I'd said too much.

This was why I didn't get involved—didn't get close. Talking about my job wasn't the same as everyone else. My job was gruesome and deadly. My job was the kind of thing people loved to watch TV shows about—how mind hunters caught the world's worst—but when they faced it in real life, no one wanted to know the horrifying details.

No one wanted to be with a person who got into the mind of psychopaths.

"Sorry."

"No. I'm sorry." Her throat bobbed and she asked, "What did you do for the FBI?"

My head tipped. I thought she knew though I don't know why; I'd never talked about it.

"I led a team at the Behavioral Analysis Unit," I explained, taking a few steps into the living room. "We profiled and hunted serial killers across the US."

"Profiled... serial killers..." she said like she was in a daze.

I understood. It wasn't an easy thing to think about—to know that there were enough fucked-up people in this world to justify a whole department of the FBI to hunt them.

Again, why my life was meant to be lived alone.

"Yeah," I said and then walked into the kitchen to pour myself a second cup of coffee. "Anyway." I brought the mug to my lips and took a gulp.

My keys on the counter caught my eye, and I remembered the other part of our arrangement. Taking the ring, I pulled off the key for the guesthouse, warming it in my fingers for a moment, wondering if this was one more decision I would come to regret: having her so close all the time.

"Here's the key to the guesthouse." I turned and set the key on the island, sliding it across the granite. "If you need help with any of your stuff—" I broke off when I saw the ashen look on her face. *What the...*

"Stevie..." I growled low, a second later my feet carried me to her. *Christ, she looked like she was about to pass out.* "Are you alright? What's—"

Just as I reached for her, she shook her head and snapped herself out of it. "I'm fine." She jerked away from me, *clearly* not fine. "I should go—need to go." Her head bobbed like a metronome.

Shit.

I knew I'd fucked up with that kiss. Knew it. She was my nanny. And she was the only one who could get through to Lainey.

And I'd royally fucked it up.

"Look, about Friday—about that kiss," I began, and if anything, her expression only looked more horrified.

"It's fine," she assured me. "I just remembered something I have to do for school, and I—"

Before I could head off her excuse that was clearly a lie, Lainey's bedroom door opened and she came into the hall. Her hair was a disaster, her pj's mismatched, but she looked well rested. *Thank god.*

Lainey saw Stevie first, a small smile creeping to her cheeks until her eyes found me.

"Hey, Bug."

The start of her smile fell, and that familiar feeling of failure washed over me again. But then she took off. Her bare feet slapped on the floor until she reached me and flung her tiny arms around my legs like she used to do every time she would see me before... *before.*

I stood paralyzed with fear and hope, my arms slightly ajar from my sides, afraid to touch her and pull her close—afraid to breathe and shatter this fragile bridge.

My gaze was the first thing that wavered, sliding across the floor until it reached shapely, bare legs, up to boxers and a tee, and finally to Stevie's choked-up expression. There was color back in her cheeks now, but damn, did we need to discuss that kiss.

I swallowed hard, resting my hands so lightly on Lainey's back as though one more ounce of force would dissolve her into sand.

"I missed you, too, Bug," I said lowly, allowing my hand to move in slow circles on her small back. "I missed you, too."

Not just this weekend. These weeks. This entire time, I'd

missed my niece who was finally coming back to me in pieces. *Thanks to Stevie.*

She felt so tiny—tinier than I'd ever noticed before. Or maybe it was just the comparison I had now to the amount of pain and loss her little body had to bear. Like an ant carrying three times its weight, she shouldered it all with a fortitude that no six-year-old should have to have.

"Lainey, why don't you show Uncle Roman what you made for him?" Stevie suggested softly when Lainey started to release me.

A tiny smile dimpled her cheeks as she ran to the shelf on the side wall in the living room and picked up something from it. As she brought it over to me, I could see it was a picture frame.

I crouched down, taking it from her when she offered.

"It's us," I said dumbly, surprised to see a photo of Lainey and me dressed as pirates from the parade on Friday.

I knew Sister Mary had taken photos of all the kids with their parents at the end of the parade, but it looked like Stevie had managed to snap one, too.

"Do you want to tell him where it's for?" Stevie prompted.

Lainey took a step back and looked at her, still not ready to speak.

Stevie smiled and didn't make a big deal about it, instead adapting to my niece's needs. "We thought you might need some photos for your office, isn't that right?"

Lainey nodded and faced me again. She put her fingers on the edge of the frame and gave it a little push in my direction.

"It's a perfect first photo for my desk." And a perfect reminder of my new life—one that I needed to do better at.

"I'm just going to get my things and get going. I have class," Stevie murmured once more, taking the opportunity to disappear into my bedroom and gather her things.

She could run for now, but eventually we were going to talk about that kiss. I didn't care what it took—I'd pay for every semester of her schooling if it came to that—but I was going to convince Stevie I was sorry for kissing her. I had to, even though I'd never regret that single taste of heaven.

The thing was, Stevie was magic. She was what made this

new life here work. And short of castrating myself, I swore to keep my emotions in check in the future because I couldn't risk losing her.

Thirty minutes later, Lainey and I were on our way out the door and that was when I noticed the key to the guesthouse still sitting on the counter.

Dammit.

We'd had an agreement.

"I TAKE it that things didn't go as planned?"

I looked up at the door. My laptop was in front of me but I'd stopped scrolling through the autopsy reports on the screen a few minutes ago, resting my head on my linked hands and staring at the photo of Lainey and me instead.

Dex entered my office, watching me with eyes that somehow knew my mounting frustration had to do with more than this case.

He was running a bunch of system updates this morning, so with the ops room down for the next couple of hours, Ace said they'd come to my office.

My space at Covington was big compared to my office at the BAU. I could fit a whole four chairs in front of this wide mahogany desk compared to the two I'd squeezed in front of my old one.

"Do they ever?" I replied rhetorically.

"When it involves a woman, usually not," he ignored the cue and answered anyway.

I didn't flinch—didn't move. I was prepared to take my unacceptable attraction to my nanny with me to my grave, along with the rest of my damn emotions. But then I remembered Lainey's arms hugging around my legs. Her smile when she gave me the framed photograph. Even though she still hadn't said a word, this was the first time she'd reached for me since her parents died. And it was all because of Stevie.

"She makes everything better," I rasped low, locking my hands in front of me. "And I think I've made everything worse."

"Then make it unworse," he said flatly.

I gave him a blank stare. "Really?"

"I never claimed to be a relationship expert." He pulled out one of the chairs on the other side of my desk and sat down. "But if it's any consolation, you're well on your way to fitting in with the team."

I cocked my head, prompting him to explain.

"Well, Dante ended up with a client. Roc ended up with Dante's sister. I guess technically I ended up with a client, too. And Jackson wound up with the sister of a vigilante MC president. So, if you end up with the nanny, that's right on par with the rest of us."

"Except Ace. And Reed."

Dex tipped his head back. "Of course, Ace. But Reed… who the hell knows what kind of woman will bring him down, but I have a feeling he'll put us all to shame."

"Did I hear my name?" The door widened, allowing Ace's massive body to shoulder through.

"Just saying that you're the only one of us who found your woman in a quasi-decent way," Dex returned.

"You mean because I helped Addy fake her death, promised we'd never be more than friends, and then broke that promise?" Ace countered with an arched brow.

Dex sat back and folded his arms. "He tries to make it sound worse than it was to make the rest of us feel better."

One side of my mouth tipped in a smile. When the rest of the team was around, the Covington brothers assumed their individual roles—quiet genius and fearless leader. They left the bantering to Dante, Roc, and the rest of the guys. But every so often, when I caught the two of them alone, their normal, brotherly relationship showed through.

My chest tightened.

Val and I never bantered like that. She was always too busy trying to take care of me—trying to involve me in a life outside of my job. My eyes drifted to the framed photo sitting proud and solitary on my desk. I had a life outside my job now, but the cost was too high.

I bit my cheek until I tasted blood and the bitter thought that I miraculously managed to keep to myself: *it should've been me.*

I should've been the one in that car. I should've died. The only person to miss me would've been Val, and she would know how to grieve. She would know how to move on. And my niece would still have her parents.

"Before we switch gears," Dex started and held up his hand. "I wanted to let you know that you and Lainey..." He paused. "And Stevie"—Ace's eyebrows rose—"are welcome to join us for Thanksgiving at our place. It's going to be a full house, so no pressure, but if you think it would be easier..." He trailed off and cleared his throat. "We'd love to have you."

Thanksgiving.

The band around my throat notched tighter. It was November. We were on the precipice of holiday season, and like Halloween, Val overdid it for every holiday. How the hell was I going to give Lainey something to enjoy when the best part about the holidays was family and her family was gone?

Fuck.

"Thanks," I managed. "I'll let you know."

I'd have to ask Lainey. And Stevie. Assuming I fixed things with Stevie.

Ace stepped forward when the door opened and Dante joined us, sinking into the chair next to his younger brother, any levity he had leaving his features.

"Don't mind me," Dante murmured, snacking away on a bag of M&M's.

"So, you've confirmed it's him?" Ace continued.

I nodded. "The methodology. The trophies. It's all the same. It has to be him." I turned my screen to show them the autopsy photos that Rorik forwarded to me, not even thinking twice that the men in front of me—while they had seen a lot of horror in war—they hadn't really seen evil like this.

"Jesus," Dex muttered.

Ace maintained his composure.

"The cross from the chest is his signature." I pointed to the injuries on both the female victims. "According to Rorik's time of death, this first victim was killed about a month ago, and the second victim less than a week." I paused. "His time line was always about a month between victims, and that doesn't seem to have changed." I enlarged the face of the second victim. "Less than a week… that's the closest we've been to his trail in a long time."

"Did Werner call Koorie?"

"No. I told him I would call her as soon as Rorik got me these images."

"Have they been following this guy?" Dex asked.

I nodded. "The BAU has been tracking him all over the Midwest. Last I heard, they had a body in Arizona that might fit the signature. The problem is, we've always been so far behind him that with disruption and decomp of the bodies, trying to follow his trail was like trying to find footprints in sand left two months ago."

"Arizona. Now, California," Ace muttered.

I clenched my jaw and clicked on another window that opened up a map with all the Archangel's kills pinned to it. "Blue pins are his original murders." I gestured over the smattering of dots in the states between Illinois and Wyoming. "Those track along major interstate highways." I clicked a button that bolted the roads. "The red dots are the kills since his hiatus. Dark red is the oldest, light red is the most recent." My palm opened up because the red pins were widespread across the entire Midwest.

"So, his victimology isn't the only thing that changed."

I shook my head. "The kills now don't follow any kind of pattern—at least, not to anyone besides him. There's no single highway. No connecting bus routes. I've checked for businesses that have offices in all these states. Rental car companies. Traveling sales jobs…" I trailed off and pinched the bridge of my nose. "It's one of the main reasons he's eluded us all these years because for the life of me, I can't figure out where he's going next."

Ace hummed low and crossed his arms, thinking for a second. "Whatever happened in his period of dormancy is what caused him to change his choice of victims."

"Yeah."

"And is what connects all these seemingly unconnectable dots." Ace motioned to the random array of red pins.

I grunted in agreement.

"So, we need to figure out what caused him to go dormant." Ace rubbed his hand along the shaved side of his head.

That was almost as hopeless of a task as trying to figure out what connected the dots.

"Incarceration or death." The two usual suspects. "Obviously, death is off the table," I remarked. "As for incarceration, I've asked Lydia Reynolds to look through so many prison photos of inmates who fit the Archangel's stop-and-start-again time line, it's a wonder she can see straight." I exhaled deeply. "But nothing. Even though she didn't get a good look at him, no one jumps out. So, it's still a possibility, but..."

"But?"

"Prison doesn't usually make a serial killer change his victimology," I continued, flattening my palm on my desk. "And in this case, he's obsessed with morality. Even though it's twisted and causes him to enact these heinous kills in order to correct some kind of moral failing, ironically, I don't think the Archangel would be tempted to commit lesser crimes."

"So what else would put a man like him on pause?" Dex broke in, demanding we think outside the box. "What else could cause you to change your entire life?"

"Having to raise a kid," I muttered ruefully without thinking, shocking not only myself but the two of them with how viable a reason it actually was.

We all looked at each other, gazes ping-ponging from an off-the-cuff retort.

"Do serial killers even have kids?" Dex rumbled, bringing to life the suggestion that rippled silently through the room.

I balled one fist into my palm and cracked my knuckles.

"Not usually." For obvious reasons. Psychopaths didn't typically have the personalities that would attract someone into a relationship with them. *Typically.* "But he could be another Bundy. Charming enough to convince a woman of anything."

"He was dormant for fifteen years." Ace ran with the idea. "So, if he picked back up when the kid turned eighteen, maybe left for college or whatever, that would mean he took custody when the child was only three."

What were the chances that the man I was hunting also had his own twisted life turned upside down for a child?

Still, what Ace said gnawed at me.

"What if the kid wasn't eighteen?" I rasped, looking at the ashen faces and bruised necks in the images of the victims on my screen. "What if she ran away?" My stomach curdled. "Just like all the victims."

A shiver ran through me, chasing the thought into my bones like it was the seed that needed to be watered.

"You think the kid—the daughter—called and left that voice mail?" Ace sat forward. "Did it sound like a kid?"

I gritted my teeth. "The voice on the line was hardly more than a quivering whisper—like whoever she was expected the Archangel to be able to hear her fucking thoughts."

"I don't know if I like the kid for it. How would she even know about the kills that happened before she was alive?"

Using the back of my knuckle, I notched my glasses higher on my nose. "Podcasts. YouTube. There are dozens of crime bloggers that have covered the case over the years."

"Plus, Harry figured out that Dexter was a serial killer, so why couldn't this kid?" Dante interjected.

Dex rolled his eyes. "I don't think that a TV show is the best basis for a working profile."

"If it was the daughter, it would explain why his victims turned younger if she was the one who betrayed him," I went on, watering more life into this profile that made more sense than any other explanation we'd had before.

"So, he's killing girls that remind him of his daughter?"

"It's common for serial killers to choose their victims based on a similarity or similarities to someone who has wronged the killer—or who he perceives as someone who has wronged him," I explained low, my mind working two steps ahead of my mouth. "The daughter's betrayal must've trumped whatever caused him to kill initially and broke his dormancy."

"So, if we can find the daughter, she could lead us to him," Ace rumbled.

"Even now?" Dante asked. "It's been seven years. Assuming she hasn't had any contact with him."

"It's the best lead we've got right now," I replied and looked at Dex. "Cross-reference adoptions from twenty-two to twenty-five years ago along with missing person reports from seven years ago. See if there are any matches."

"In Wyoming?"

"What if he moved them to Wyoming after the kid came into his life?" *Like you moved across the country when you became Lainey's guardian,* went unspoken by Dante.

My fingers drummed on the desk, adrenaline thrumming through my blood.

"We'll cross that bridge if we come to it. Wyoming is where he picked back up, so start near Casper and work your way out." I exhaled a tense breath.

Ace clipped his chin down in a nod. "Alright. I'll give Detective Werner a call and let him know where we're at."

"I'll update Koorie and see if she has any other insight that might narrow our search." I reached for my cell, my thumb poised to dial Koorie as soon as everyone cleared out of my office.

As hopeful as I was, I was also realistic. Even if we were right about this, orphans... adoptions... runaways... that was a lot of data to sort through for just Wyoming.

"Can you also get me all the previous victims' information and photos for the last seven years?" Dex asked as he stood.

I looked up at him, a little surprised by the question. "Yeah, it's not much though and we haven't found any other correlation between them." And I was now even more convinced we wouldn't.

"I want to run them all through my system just in case," he said. "I like to unturn every stone."

I gave him a half smile and nodded. "Thanks."

Ace offered a low goodbye before disappearing into the hall, but Dex didn't leave right away. He waited until Ace was gone.

"Let me know about Thanksgiving," he added, returning to our earlier conversation. "And the reason I brought up this team's habit of finding hard love is because we're the kind of people who've been trained to recognize right from wrong—to feel right from wrong. No matter the scenario." He picked up his iPad and held it to his side. "We all recognize when something is right even when that something is hard… or impossible. Love included."

Love.

I sat back in my chair, kept a straight face, and murmured some kind of unintelligible thank you just to get him out of my office.

I never said anything about love. Lust? *Definitely.* Knowing I'd be sleeping in my bed tonight where Stevie had spent the weekend was going to drive my dick insane. But love…

Loving Lainey was one thing. Loving a woman… *loving Stevie…*

That wasn't in my cards, no matter what life I led. *And it was all the more reason to convince my too-damned-desirable nanny why that kiss should've never happened.*

CHAPTER ELEVEN

Stevie

"A-HA!" I CLICKED ANOTHER PUZZLE PIECE INTO PLACE, MORE OF the tail on the Little Mermaid puzzle Lainey and I were working on.

"This one," she whispered, looking over her shoulder toward the kitchen—and Roman—as she pushed another green piece my way.

"Thanks," I whispered back, fitting the edges into its spot.

The soft click flattened it into the picture, but instead of searching for another piece, I rubbed my finger over the small portion I'd put together, feeling for the seam.

Puzzle pieces.

That was what my life over the last five weeks had felt like—a puzzle piece snapped into a bigger picture that involved my endearing charge and her reserved guardian. Homework. Games. Bugs. Dinner. Days passed, more pieces fit together. And when he'd kissed me… and it hadn't felt out of place.

It was just one more piece… that fit perfectly.

But then Monday happened.

"*Stevie,*" Lainey whisper-hissed and pushed another piece under my fingers, reminding me that we had a task to complete.

Stevie. Stevie Michaels. *Not Stephanie Turner.*

I shuddered, fitting the piece in all the wrong spots because I couldn't focus on the puzzle any longer.

He doesn't know who you are. He doesn't know who your father is.

I repeated the mantras over and over again all week—morning, noon, and night—but it hadn't changed a thing.

He doesn't know that you're a product of the very brand of criminal he hunts.

Dad was my memory, but Lee was a mystery.

When we first moved, Mom absolutely forbade me from any attempt to reach out to him or anyone from our hometown or even look him up. Though I missed him and was desperate to know what he'd done to hurt Mom so badly, I obeyed because that was how I was raised: *to obey thy mother and father.* And when she finally told me the truth, it became a matter of self-preservation.

"You need to forget you ever heard the name Lee Turner, Stevie. Forget that he exists as though he died, too, because if there is ever a way to make you pay for my sins, he will find it."

Atonement and retribution had always been two very large staples of my father's personality. One time, I'd found a missing dog in the parking lot outside the grocery store. Mom had just run inside for some milk, and I was waiting in the car. The puppy had a tag on his collar, but he was so cute that I wanted to keep him. So, I hid him in my backpack in the back seat, turned the music up, and snuck him up to my room when we got home. Obviously, that plan didn't work out long term. That was one of the times I saw Dad really mad, though not violent. Ironically, never violent. However, he made me write a three-page apology letter describing in detail the sins of covetousness and theft; he had me rewrite it three times before it was acceptable and he walked me to the owner's house to return their dog.

That was only one instance of the kind of lengths we'd have to go to apologize for something. It just didn't seem crazy then, and neither did Dad disliking dogs.

So, for seven years I pretended like Dad was dead but his ghost could still find me. And after Roman kissed me, I did something I swore I was never going to do: I looked up Dad on the internet.

Typing the name "Lee Turner" into Google was the most painful thing I'd ever done; if I really wanted to be free from him—from his retribution—that meant I searched hoping that he was either dead or in jail. *My own father.*

Seven years of not wanting to know spared me from confronting what I'd hoped to find. My dad, dead, or a killer, arrested. Or a man still living his life under the radar, yet a threat to me.

Before I could decide which answer I was looking for, my search returned nothing. No mention of his arrest. No mention of his death. Nothing.

He was still out there. Maybe under a different name like I was. And that meant if given the chance, he'd find me and extract my apology and my penance; I refused to imagine what that would even be.

Lainey clapped her hands, finding another piece of the puzzle that fit, and the sound snapped me out of my past. I felt Roman's attention shift to us—*to me.*

He doesn't know who you are.

I hazarded a glance at the kitchen where Roman was making his famous BBQ pulled chicken mac and cheese. The aromas coming from the stove were enough to make my mouth water, but when they came up against the sight of the man cooking them—white tee, fitted jeans, and those glasses—they didn't stand a chance.

Four weeks ago, Roman wouldn't be caught wearing anything except dress pants and a button-down shirt, and I never would've been anything except "Ms. Michaels." Now, all those boundaries had disappeared.

I checked my phone; it was time to go. Roman's coworker, Dex, and his wife, Jo, were coming over for dinner, and I wanted to leave before they arrived.

For the whole week, I'd managed to make my exit from the house without further conversation with Roman about our kiss. I'd clung to our former routine like a lifeline while debating how to tell him I wouldn't be staying in the guesthouse.

Sure, the keys were burning a hole in my pocket, especially since I'd jumped the gun and made an online tuition payment first thing Saturday morning in the amount of my rent for this month… before I learned what Roman did. Now, I had four days to scrape together rent or I was going to be sleeping in my car in addition to working out of it.

Though the keys were very, very tempting, I couldn't take them. Not now. And it was better—easier if Roman thought my refusal was because of the kiss.

Just tell him the truth.

If I had a dollar for every time the thought crossed my mind, I wouldn't need Uber or Roman's help to pay for school.

But what truth would I tell him? That Lee Turner was… is… a serial killer?

How do you know? How can you prove it? Who did he kill? How did he kill them? Why?

"Because my mom told me" wasn't a good answer. And neither was "I don't know who he killed or how or why he killed them." Heck, I didn't know if Lee Turner was even his name anymore.

I hadn't seen the trophies, Mom did, and she wouldn't tell me what they were. *Always trying to spare me, even in the end.* All she said was that if I knew what they were, there wouldn't be a shadow of a doubt that Dad was responsible. I could provide no proof, and certainly nothing actionable after seven years.

The worst part about her confession was that Dad was a lie. The second-worst part was that no one could help us.

"Don't look for him, Stevie. Don't put your name out there. And whatever you do, don't go to the authorities."

It wasn't that she didn't trust the police; it was that she'd given them their very best chance at arresting her husband. She'd risked her life—our lives—to contact them and lead them to Dad, and they still hadn't caught him.

What could I possibly say now that would change that?

I was only fifteen when we left. A kid. And now, seven years have gone by. What I knew was enough to make me interesting—enough to make me a target—but not even close to enough to be useful.

Roman would want to help me, but he wouldn't be able to.

And he was already tortured enough, unable to change the past for one little woman in his life; I wouldn't add myself to that list.

Beep. Beep. Beep.

"Alright, Captain Lainey, it's time for me to go." I rose, rubbing my knees where they'd gone stiff from kneeling next to the coffee table.

She made a sad face and reached for my hand. Taking her palm between mine, I gave it a gentle squeeze.

At least one of us seemed to be doing better since Monday. She still wasn't speaking to Roman, but she was engaging with him more than before.

"I'll see you next week," I promised and kissed her small fingers.

"You should stay," came his voice before I'd even faced him.

Tucking my hair back behind my ears, I forced a smile.

"I have schoolwork to do. Finals are coming up." I grabbed my bag and notched it on my shoulder. "Plus, you're having guests—"

"Who thought you'd be here, too."

He wanted me to stay like I was a part of something that I could never be a part of.

"I appreciate the invitation, but it's not really my place." I inched closer toward the door with every word. "I'm just the nanny." *And it was better that everyone in the room remembered that.*

A spoon or something clattered loudly, capturing my attention before I had a chance to leash it.

My gaze connected with a tense Roman, anger thinly veiled behind his glasses.

I sucked in a breath and yanked the door open, determined to get out of there before he tried to correct me. As I bolted outside, I almost crashed into Roman's dinner guests, and I mumbled a quick "excuse me" heading to my car.

Dumping my bag in the trunk, I pulled out my cell, pausing by the driver's side door to open the rideshare app and start the scan for incoming requests. A ride request popped up from *Dean* who needed to be picked up at the Carmel Pub downtown.

"*Stevie!*"

I jumped, hitting the accept button on my screen in the process. *Ugh.*

Crap. If I'd just left a few minutes earlier... before there was anyone else in the house to keep an eye on Lainey...

Roman stormed toward me, a kitchen towel still slung over his broad shoulder and his jeans riding low on his waist.

"When do you want my help moving your things into the guesthouse?"

I gulped. So much for avoiding this conversation for a little longer.

"Roman, I appreciate the offer, but I don't think it's a good idea for me to stay here." I fished out the key ring and extended it to him.

He scowled at the keys like I'd just given him the middle finger.

"Which part of it isn't a good idea? The part where you save money for school or the part where you have a whole house to yourself that's about a thousand times nicer than the apartment you're currently renting?"

The part where I'm starting to feel things for you that I shouldn't—that I can't.

"Like I said, I'm grateful for your generosity, but I can't accept it," I insisted.

His shoulders dropped. "Stevie, look if it's because of the kiss, it was a mistake, and I promise it will never happen again," he swore so strongly I winced when it broke off a little piece of my heart.

"Are you sure?" I murmured, wondering how he could be so certain when we stood this close.

So close, it felt like our colliding breaths were strong enough to tip the world on its axis. So close, the magnetic pull between our bodies felt strong enough to shift the poles. So close, the tectonic plates of the planet would need to be sheared apart in order to keep his lips from mine.

"Yes."

I bit the inside of my cheek to stop any sound from escaping that would betray how I really felt about that kiss... about him. I'd only known Roman for a little over a month, but if there was anyone capable of tearing apart the fabric of the earth to hold himself to his duty and to a promise, it was him.

"I appreciate that," I choked out. "But I'd rather—"

"Dammit, Stevie, you don't need to be so independent all the time," he interrupted, frustration deepening his tenor. "I know you've only had yourself to rely on since your mom died, but you can't keep shutting yourself in this bubble where no one is allowed to help you."

I jerked back. "Are you… profiling me?" I wasn't sure what hurt more: his certainty that he'd never kiss me again or hearing him turn me into another work responsibility. "I'm not one of your suspects, Roman. I'm not one more problem you have to fix."

His breath released in a low hiss, realizing he'd crossed a line.

"We had an agreement," he muttered with regret but without apology.

My spine straightened. "The only agreement we had was an employment agreement."

"But you need—"

"What I need, Mr. Knight, is to work and focus on school. My financial arrangement with my school is not your concern. Again, I appreciate your offer, but I've changed my mind," I said firmly and reached for the door.

His palm slapped on the frame and held it shut.

"Then I'm paying you double for the hours you're here."

My mouth dropped open. "You can't—"

"It's my employment agreement. I can do whatever I want," he growled low, chasing a shiver up my spine.

I swallowed hard and kept my teeth locked tight. I could argue, but what was the point? I needed the money, and if he wanted to give me a raise for the job he'd hired me to do, then so be it.

"Fine," I said with a sigh, feeling the fight go out of me as my body preferred to fan a different kind of flame.

"What changed?"

Nothing.

I wanted to laugh. And cry. Nothing had changed; I'd only been playing the fool, pretending like it could.

"Why don't you want my help anymore?" he pressed, scrutinizing me like a cell under a microscope.

I shivered, not knowing what it was about Roman that made it feel like he could see past every defense I'd so carefully erected around my heart. *Maybe it was those damn glasses.*

"For the same reason you want to give it."

"What are you talking about?"

"You need to know that you can save the world. I need to know that I can save myself."

The more I depended on this man, the harder it would be to accept that he couldn't save me from my past any more than I could change half of my genes that belonged to Lee Turner.

"Stevie… it's okay to need help. You don't have to do everything alone." He read into my words just as surely as he read the minds of all the criminals he'd caught.

Not only had I been kissed by my boss, but now I was being profiled by him.

I notched my chin higher, pain angled like the tip of a knife under my jaw, and I blinked back tears.

"Says the man who planned on living his entire life emotionless and alone," I charged, the words thick like lava as I spewed them from my tongue. "We all have our reasons to do the things we do, but I'm your nanny, not one of your suspects; I'm not here to have my reasons figured out."

I forced the door open and he didn't fight it, allowing me to get in my car without argument, though he stood right beside the door the entire time, watching me like a menacing guardian angel on my shoulder.

God, that stare…

The intensity of it followed me as I backed up. It followed me down the drive. I swore it followed me through the trees that should've shielded my car from view.

It wasn't until I turned back onto the Coastal Highway that the heat thrumming through my blood began to die down.

Crap.

I fumbled to attach my phone to the holder on my dash, the map highlighting my route to the pub even though I didn't need the direction. Groaning inwardly, I wondered if I should just cancel the trip—*I wished that Dean would have.*

I was careful about the rides I chose, usually opting for female passengers when I could be picky, and definitely not picking up men from outside a bar on a Friday night. But it was one ride, and I didn't want my rating to suffer. Plus, it was still a little early.

I quickly tapped to see where Dean's drop-off was. The address showed a location on the other side of town in one of the big developments where the really rich people lived. It was deeper in that same development as the house Carina had stayed in when she first came to Carmel.

Not even two minutes later, and I was pulling up in front of the pub, scanning the few people outside for someone who looked like they were waiting for a ride.

There was a middle-aged man who looked to be waiting for someone and kept glancing at the sky; I hadn't checked the forecast, but a quick glance showed ominous dark skies and bloated gray clouds. *Maybe that was why Dean had called for a ride this early.*

I rolled down my window as I approached, about to call his name when his attention perked and he began to walk toward a red Honda.

Ugh. Not Dean, I guess.

Pulling up in front of the pub's green door, I went to reach for my phone so I could give Dean a call, but then thought the better of it; I could just go inside and check. It was probably so loud in there anyway that he wouldn't hear his phone or me.

I put my car in park and left my hazards on. A rumble of thunder boomed just as I darted across the small space between my car and the building.

It was packed inside the pub. *Good thing I didn't call.* There was a live band about to get started in the corner, the low lighting, tinted by the green lampshades, oozed over the crowd that buzzed like bees inside a hive.

I didn't go out. I didn't go to bars. So the sheer number of people and the energy of the room were enough to make me stop and catch my breath.

"You alright there, Miss…"

I turned, realizing it was the bartender who'd spoken to me. His familiar stare made me do a double take; I'd just seen that same stare arrive at Roman's house not even half an hour ago.

Bennett Covington.

The youngest of the Covington brothers owned the Carmel Pub with his wife, Cammie; I'd momentarily forgotten the connection; I'd only seen him maybe once or twice before.

"Stevie Michaels. Sorry, yes. I'm just looking for… Dean." I blanked for a second.

As soon as I said the name, a young guy to my right turned. *Of course.* Baseball cap turned backward, 49ers tee stretched over his growing gut, he looked like a frat guy. *A drunk frat guy.*

"You our ride?" He looked me up and down, a smile spreading up his face. "Won't complain about that." He laughed, and I didn't even have a chance to respond before he called over his shoulder, "Time to go, gents!"

The two guys he'd been talking to stood from their seats at the bar and joined him in an array of white pants and pastel polos. *Awesome. Three frat guys.*

My heart thudded wildly to cancel the trip, especially when it was obvious that these guys had been out golfing and drinking all day. *Don't be ridiculous, Stevie. It's going to be fine.*

"My car's outside," I said weakly, backing toward the door because I felt uncomfortable giving them my back until absolutely necessary.

The last thing I saw before I turned was the obvious displeasure and concern on Bennett Covington's face as I led my three passengers outside.

I beelined for my door, ignoring their low comments, laughs, and stumbles as they made their way to my car. I'd just reached for my seat belt when there was a knock on the passenger door. Dean was bent over, his face grinning in the window.

"Gonna need you to unlock, sweet Stevie."

Vomit.

Of course, they were too big to fit the three of them in the back seat.

Biting my tongue, I unlocked the passenger door, bracing myself as Dean sank into the seat.

Good god. The pub smelled... like a pub. And it adequately masked the way these three reeked of alcohol like they'd been bathing in it for a week.

I didn't bother to ask if everyone was settled. I put the car in drive and did my best to not look as eager as I felt to get them to their destination.

"So, you from around here?"

"Yeah." My foot pressed a little harder on the gas.

At that moment, a notification came up on my screen that Roman was calling. I let it ring through, but the sight sent a cold blast of determination through my blood. I'd been managing my life perfectly fine before him, and I would continue long after him.

After him. The phrase didn't register. Like an engine turning over, trying to start, it couldn't seem to make anything run on the thought of what my life would be without him and Lainey.

Oh god.

"What kind of name is Stevie?" Dean rested his arm on the center console and tipped his weight onto it, coming very close to invading my driver's seat bubble.

Stephanie was the girl with two loving parents and a normal life. Stevie was the woman who'd survived having a criminal father and a chronically ill mother.

"A short one." I shifted closer to the window.

"Everyone's been so nice around here to us visitors. We had a great day—great fucking day golfing." His fist-pumped the air and his friend hooted from the back seat. "Now we're just trying to have a good night, isn't that right, boys?"

They hollered again, and my teeth locked tighter.

We reached the development, but I didn't slow to the speed limit; I wanted them out of my car as quickly as possible. I pulled up to the curb in front of the address, ending the ride and remarking curtly, "Have a great night." *Now get out.*

"Oh, we will." Dean snickered, but they all opened the doors and got out without incident.

I didn't care if they tipped. I didn't care how they rated me.

The only thing I cared about right now was getting back to my crappy apartment. Obviously, my argument with Roman had completely thrown me off, and that was why I felt tied up in knots.

I shifted the car into drive when there was a loud thud and my car rocked along with the noise.

"Oh shit," I heard Dean exclaim from outside.

What the hell?

Had they just hit my car? Or drop something into it?

I cranked my head to try, but the back door was shut so all I could see was two of them steadying the third near the rear side panel before they pointed at the car.

No.

I let out a small whimper as I put the car back in park and threw off my seat belt.

"Hey, Stevie…" Dean trailed off as I rounded the trunk.

"What happened?" I stepped in front of them and scanned my car. The lighting wasn't that great but as far as I could tell, there wasn't any damage. *None that would make the car undrivable, that is.*

"Ben's a little fucked up." Dean appeared at my side and laughed like that made it okay.

I glared at him, watching in frustration as he crossed his arms and casually leaned against my car like it was his property.

"Whatever. My car's fine. Have a good night." I went to spin away when a punishing grip caught my arm.

"Well now, hold up a second."

Oh no. My heart beat wildly like an animal that knows it's in danger.

"Let go of me." I yanked my arm away, and I was surprised he released me.

I was less surprised when I turned again, only to crash into one of his friends who'd come up behind me in the meantime. Blood thudded loudly in my ears, pounding over and over again: *Danger. Danger. Danger.*

I shouldn't have gotten out of the car.

"Why don't you just stay and hang out with us for a little?"

Dean asked casually, like he was going to give me a choice. "It'll be fun, and I'll make sure to tip you good for your time."

My stomach rolled. If it was just him, I would've smacked him. But I was in danger, not stupid; I wasn't going to attack one guy who was three times my size when there were two more of them waiting in the wings.

"Thanks for the invite, but I'm leaving," I said firmly, daring any of them to stop me

Dean's head cocked, and the smile he gave me felt like an army of spiders crawling over my skin. Before I could even process what he was going to do, the drunk creep crouched in front of me and with one swift strike, punctured a hole in my back tire.

I let out a small cry and quickly covered my mouth. I hadn't even seen the pocketknife in his hand.

"No, you're not."

Cold, brutal panic set in, and only one thing came to my mind: I needed Roman. *I needed him to save me.*

CHAPTER TWELVE

Roman

"Looks like someone is still in the doghouse," Jo teased, returning to the kitchen after she'd said hello to Lainey and made her friendly offering of an additional piece to the puzzle.

They'd bumped into Stevie on their way out, and Dex gave me that all-knowing stare when I immediately brushed by them to follow her outside, but I wasn't surprised that Jo would be the one to say something. Her boldness was as bright as her smile.

"I don't know what you mean." I cleared my throat and began scooping my BBQ mac and cheese onto plates.

"With Stevie..." Jo drawled, sauntering up to the counter and lifting an eyebrow.

At least she hadn't called her my nanny.

"I offered to help her with school," I grumbled. "Not sure how that ends me up in the doghouse."

"Offered?" Her eyebrow arched. "Or you had Dex hack into the school and then demand to pay her tuition?"

My gaze narrowed on her innocent one before it shifted to Dex, leveling him with a flat, annoyed expression. *Dick.*

"Don't look at me." He shook his head from where he stood behind Jo and then rested his hands possessively on her shoulders. My fingers tightened for a second, having felt that same instinct to touch—*to possess*—countless times over the last few weeks. At the parade. At the costume store. *With Stevie.* "She's a journalist. I don't know how she finds this stuff out."

I rolled my eyes. "I was trying to do a good thing."

She huffed and wagged her finger. "Men."

"What? An offer of help is somehow offensive?"

"It wasn't an offer."

"It was still a nice gesture."

"Extreme independence is a trauma response," Jo said casually.

I notched my glasses higher on my nose.

"I interviewed a psychologist for a story a couple months ago," she explained with a shrug.

Trauma to losing both her parents and having no one else to rely on. At least Lainey had me; from what Stevie shared about her past, it was clear she had no one.

"Shit," Dex grumbled, releasing his hold on Jo as he pulled out his phone. "What the... Yeah, Benny?" he answered the call warily.

I normally wouldn't have thought anything of Dex's younger brother giving him a call, but the way his expression changed while they were on the phone... the way his eyes slid up from the counter to my face... it sent dread curling through my veins like a poisonous snake.

"Wait, you said her name was Stevie Michaels?" His eyes connected with mine. "You're sure?" *Fuck.* "I'll handle it. Thanks for the heads-up."

"What is it? What happened?" I didn't give him a chance to hang up before the questions flung from my lips like an arrow.

"Benny said a young girl stopped in and picked up three guys from the pub. He was concerned because they were pretty wasted—apparently they'd come in after they finished a full afternoon golfing on the Rock Beach course and had been drinking the entire time."

"What about Stevie?" I demanded, my breaths coming in hard spurts.

"Roman... Stevie was the one who picked them up."

I jerked back. "What? No. Three guys? Hell no." I reeled. He had to be wrong. My shy, kind, infuriatingly independent nanny wouldn't pick up three guys from a bar. "Did they force her to go with them? Can you pull up the video feed?"

Dex clenched his jaw. "He said she came in looking for them, gave him the one guy's name and the whole group got up from the bar and left with her, but Benny's worried because she didn't look comfortable and it's Stevie"—he lifted his hand, approximating her height—"alone with three drunk guys."

This made no fucking sense.

Was it about the money? Her tuition? Had she refused my help and decided to make up the difference by offering herself—*Crack.*

The wooden spoon I'd been using to serve the mac and cheese snapped in my hand. Every pair of eyes—including Lainey's—stared at me like I was about to turn massive and green and go full Hulk any moment.

"She was probably giving them a ride," Jo explained with certainty.

"What?" I asked through clenched teeth.

"A ride," she repeated. "You know, like an Uber."

An Uber?

"Why the hell would she do that?"

Jo folded her arms. "Because she is an Uber driver..." She stared at me like *how could I not know.*

Anger boiled in my veins, demanding the same thing. *How the fuck could I not know?*

"You didn't know?" Dex mumbled, grinding salt into the wound.

"It's not like it was on her résumé," I clapped back.

"That's how she met Carina," Jo explained. "It's how she was—is paying for school."

Did I know? Had I known? Had Carina said something about meeting Stevie when she'd given her a ride and in the chaos of my life I'd missed it?

Rationally, I knew I had no right to care what Stevie did in her time outside of my house. But the thought of her driving random people around—*random drunk guys*...

Snatching my phone from the counter, I tapped on Stevie's number. I needed to hear that she was okay. Every other conversation could wait. With each unanswered ring, my hand pressed harder onto the counter, and I prepared for a dent to appear any second.

"No answer," I said in a low, tight voice.

I'd been in countless high-stress situations before—situations where my team was down to the wire in hunting a killer before he claimed his next victim. But none of those situations made me feel like this; none of those victims were *my* victim.

"Can you hack the GPS on her car?" I rasped, burying the plea under a pile of roughness.

"What kind of car?"

I told him the make and model.

"Too old. It would take me too long," Dex replied. "But if you get me your computer, I can probably hack into the rideshare software and track the ride through there."

I bolted into the living room, grabbing my laptop from where I'd stashed it on one of the shelves. Handing it to Dex, I let him do his thing, pacing in the kitchen as he did. I counted the seconds, each one stacking like a brick on top of my chest that made it harder and harder to breathe.

"It's going to be okay, Roman," Jo assured me.

I wanted to believe her but I couldn't.

"Got her," Dex said four minutes and thirty-six seconds later. "Looks like the trip destination is on the other side of town, and she's arriving now."

Goddammit. "Send me the address. Can you keep an eye on Lainey? I need to make sure she's okay." And I wasn't going to wait and hope she'd call me back; I was going to see for myself.

"Of course," Jo said without hesitation.

"Thanks." I nodded and strode into the living room where Lainey retreated to after the spoon snapping incident.

"Hey Bug, I have to go out for a little bit to get Stevie, okay?" I asked even though I didn't expect an answer. "Uncle Dex and Aunt Jo are going to stay here with you and eat and puzzle until we get back, alright?" I brushed her hair back from her face.

God, if she lost someone else from her life…

Lainey looked up from her puzzle, her worried eyes mirrored those of her mother.

"Stevie?"

I sucked in a breath.

A word.

A whispered word. But a word nonetheless.

"Yeah." I nodded quickly. "I'm going to bring Stevie back."

And then I was going to handcuff her to this property, pay for her school, and endure whatever emotional repercussions she lashed at me because those were easier to manage than worrying if she was in danger.

I'M SENDING REED *for backup*.

I read Dex's message before it disappeared from my screen, grinding my teeth harder together. *Great.*

I dragged a hand through my hair. I was never like this. I assessed and analyzed. I was calculated and precise. I had to be because that was how my usual suspects were. They had no emotion and therefore, to catch them, I couldn't have any either.

But this, right here, was all emotion.

I had zero proof that Stevie was in danger. So, what if she gave people rides? Tons of people did that nowadays without any issue. I was probably a psycho for tracking her down right now, but God, if I didn't feel it in my gut that something was wrong.

I tried calling again. *No answer.* My foot revved the engine. Even if—even though she was angry with me, Stevie wasn't the kind of person who wouldn't answer. And the thought gnawed at me like cancer to my bones. I needed to know—needed to see with my own two eyes that she wasn't in danger.

Every mile that brought me closer lifted my heart higher in my throat until I tasted each beat of my pulse every time I tried to swallow. My tires screeched when I turned into the development; the Bronco wasn't exactly made for hugging corners.

My breath locked and loaded in my lungs as I made the final turn, and then fired round after round of unmeasured rage when

I saw Stevie's car—*and two big guys pinning her to it while the third had his hands on her chest.*

My vision went red. I sped up and slammed on the brakes right in front of them, getting out of my car before they'd even recovered from their drunken shock.

"FBI!" I roared, wielding a badge that no longer meant anything, but also a gun that sure as hell did.

Instantly, the two fuckers holding Stevie released her and stumbled away, cursing and looking at one another in pure panic like how the hell had the FBI found them?

"Roman…" Stevie's hoarse voice reached me, bringing every hair on my nape to attention and every cell in my body to full alert.

"Get in my car," I ordered without looking at her.

I knew if I looked, I'd need to touch—I'd need to assess and know that she was okay. I'd need to strip her like a savage and make sure every inch was unharmed.

"*Now.*" In my periphery, I saw her move, clumsily at first as she pushed herself away from her car, and then I waited for the sound of the car door to open and then shut.

"Dean…" one of them hissed to the guy who'd been *touching* Stevie. "What the fuck—"

"Look"—the fucker named Dean lifted his hands and had the audacity to smile at me—"I think there's been a misunderstanding—"

I fired one shot into the air, watching them all jump, and then aimed my weapon back in their direction.

"You." I focused on the one who looked like he was about to shit his pants. "Put this on your friend over there." I tossed him a zip tie, and he quickly fumbled to pick it up and then tie his friend's hands. "Sit on the curb," I ordered and then fished a second zip tie from my pocket. "Your turn." I waved my gun at the ringleader, instructing him to tie up his other friend.

"Yeah, no problem, man," Dean agreed easily, still looking at me like if he kept cooperating I was just going to give him a slap on the wrist and let him walk away.

As soon as Shitface Number Two was tied up, he went and

sat on the curb next to Stevie's car before I even had to ask. It was at that moment I realized that Stevie's back tire was flat.

My vision went red.

Behind me, I heard another car pull up slowly. *Reed.*

"Look, we were just having some fun," Dean tried to assure me as I advanced on him.

I left the other two for Reed to take care of. But the third—the one who touched her...

"Fun?" I let out a harsh laugh. "That what you call slashing her tire and holding her against her car?" I demanded, lowering my gun and holstering it in the back waist of my jeans.

He started to relax, as though me not having a gun was going to make this easier for him.

"Yeah, it was fine." He waved it off, mistakenly allowing me to get closer to him just because I wasn't holding a weapon. "She was going to have a good time, I—"

Crack.

My fist flew like the strike of a steel mallet against the side of his face. He whirled to the side, crying out in pain as he landed on his knees.

"What the—"

I grabbed the collar of his stupid fucking polo and flipped him over, placing one knee on his chest and wrapping my hand around his throat. His arms flailed for a second, but he was too wasted and in too poor of a position to strike me with any force.

"W-what are you d-doing?" he sputtered and gasped.

"Having a little fun," I rasped viciously right in front of his face, tightening my hold as I spoke.

"You're—you can't—" He broke off because oxygen was more important than words.

"I can do whatever the fuck I want to you, and no one would ever know."

His eyes went wider with each word.

"Knight!" Distantly, I heard Reed's shout but I ignored it.

"P-please—" Dean gasped and pleaded, but all I could think about was the way Stevie had done the same, and he'd ignored her.

Rage like I'd never felt before consumed me.

"I've killed murderers. Rapists. Monsters," I seethed low, the words leaching like acid off my tongue. "Do you know what it takes—what you have to be to kill monsters?"

His eyes stretched so wide I waited for his eyeballs to pop from their sockets as he struggled violently to breathe, but I wouldn't let him

"Roman!"

"*A bigger fucking monster,*" I spat and closed my grip, the tips of my fingers searching for one another through the meaty flesh of his throat.

His eyes bulged, his open mouth desperate for air, and it was just when his eyes started to roll back in his head when a strong grip curled into the back of my shirt and forcibly hauled me off of him and threw me back.

"Jesus, Roman," Reed swore under his breath, shoving me back and kneeling by the fucker. The younger man checked for a pulse, the slight dip in his shoulders indicating that he found one. And then he looked at me, disbelief mixed with just a hint of fear. "What the fuck were you thinking?"

"He touched her," I said low—a defense I would've staked my every subsequent action on even if that action had killed him.

We remained locked in a stare for another second before Reed snapped his chin down and shook his head.

"I'll handle this. Just take her home," he grumbled and exhaled deep. I waited another second before he snapped at me, "*Go.*"

When the red fog of rage cleared, I would owe my new teammate an apology and a thank-you. But for right now, that rage was too thick and crisp—a storm ready to destroy everything in sight.

If I hadn't worried about her… If I hadn't decided to check…

The what-ifs lashed against me like a whip to my back, making each step land quicker as I stalked back to the Bronco. Stevie's frightened face stared at me through the windshield.

I got back in the driver's seat and shut the door hard enough to make her jump. I wanted to apologize, but I couldn't. I was so fucking… afraid.

"Are you alright?" My eyes flicked between her and the road.

Her cheeks were still flushed except where I could see she'd been crying, tears leaving an ashen streak through the bright color. I followed the trail down her neck, my gut twisting when I noticed her shirt. It was ripped apart. *They'd held her while that fucker ripped her top open.* I tightened my grip on the steering wheel, wishing it was still locked around that motherfucker's neck.

She drew an unsteady breath, the movement making her tits tremble.

"Yes," she answered simply, her throat bobbing as she gulped.

I could see her bra. Black or navy, I couldn't tell, but it provided a hard contrast to the pale skin of her chest—a hard contrast to the full flesh that pressed against the rims. And then I saw it… the faint red marks of rough fingerprints on her right breast.

"*Fucker,*" I snarled.

My gaze snapped to the other side of the road, scanning for oncoming traffic. I was two seconds from shoving every emotion I had down deep in my gut, returning to that development, and committing murder. *But then there was Stevie…* strong and trembling beside me.

Realizing where I was looking, she reached up with one hand and cinched her tee closed with her fist. "Roman, I—"

"Don't," I clipped, my voice deep and strangled. "I'm taking you home."

She shuddered and settled deeper in the seat, sending a wave of self-loathing crashing over me. She'd just been assaulted—*I saw the fucking marks*—and I was treating her like an obstinate ass. But I couldn't think straight. My mind swerved side to side, veered over double yellow lines that marked boundaries that shouldn't be crossed; it sped past the limits of where rationality and restraint kept everything safe.

I couldn't think straight because my emotions had taken the wheel.

Wanting her. Wanting to protect her. Wanting to possess her.

It all collided and felt like it was turning me into one of the monsters I used to hunt—the ones that had no care or control except when it came to taking exactly what they wanted.

And what I wanted was her.

"Wait, where are we going?" she asked as my hand on her arm propelled her through the garden gate and down the path to the guesthouse.

"You're staying in the guesthouse," I ground out, though our destination was obvious.

"Okay, but—"

"No buts. You're staying here. End of fucking discussion," I declared, releasing her long enough to fit the key into the vintage rosette doorknob and unlock the front door, letting it swing wide. "Inside."

With her arms folded over her front, she walked into the undisturbed space. There was a stillness in the guesthouse that felt like we'd stepped into another realm. The seat of the cottage, perched at the edge of the cliff, was almost impossible to see from the main house, and the way the sea wrapped around almost every side… it was no wonder Stevie had made this the setting of a fairy castle.

I flipped on the lights, the warm haze sliding over the sheet-wrapped furniture.

Jackson said that his father had used this house for business associates when they'd come to meet with him in Carmel. When I'd bought the place, I'd had a cleaning service go through both buildings to get rid of all the dust, but aside from that, it had probably been a good decade since guests had stayed here.

She should walk farther into the room—farther away from me, I thought, feeling how every ounce of blood roared to touch her. *But she didn't.* She stayed only inches in front of me, within reach.

She dragged in a deep inhale, drawing my gaze to her rising chest, before she faced me.

"Thank y—"

"Where did he touch you?" I demanded, unable to erase the sight in the car from my mind.

"Roman—"

"Show me," I growled low.

Whether it was my tone or the unyielding look in my eyes, her arms lowered slowly, grabbing hold of the ends of her shirt and peeling them back.

Jesus.

Air hissed from my lips, the sound of my restraint slowly deflating as the fabric spread and revealed her stomach and chest. She was full of curves for being so small—*full of everything.* Beauty. Compassion. Strength. Heart.

So full... while I was so empty. It was no wonder my very cells ached to be around her.

Her eyes dropped and she pressed her fingers to the bruises that had started to lift to the surface. "I'm fi—"

I grabbed her wrist and held her hand away, breathing hard. Ever so gently I replaced her fingers with my own, tracing over the marks as though I were dragging the point of a pin along the skin of a balloon, determined not to puncture it. There was a line I wouldn't cross again—a barrier I refused to break. But damn if I wasn't going to toe that line with every inch of my sanity.

I touched along her collarbone, the skin raw from where the fucker had forcibly ripped her shirt, and then paused at the notch at the bottom of her throat.

"I'm okay," she murmured, and I felt her swallow against my fingertips, my dick hardened to granite. God, I wanted to feel that throat around me, trying to swallow around my length.

Don't feel, I warned myself, gritting my teeth harder as my hand moved lower, down her sternum, and then veered up the swell of her right breast.

Damn, she was so soft. Her skin, velvet smooth. Porcelain except for where blood vessels had been broken underneath the surface.

"Fucker," I rasped, laying my fingertips over the top of the spots where he'd grabbed her.

The worst part was, I wasn't talking about the shithead who I still wanted to murder—I was talking about myself. Because I shouldn't be doing this; I shouldn't be getting this close, but I couldn't stay away.

"I'm okay, Roman," she promised again, her voice hardly more than a breathless whisper.

My eyes lifted to hers—a mistake when I found them just as dark and tumultuous as the ache inside me felt. A perfect storm brewed between us, doing everything in its power to throw us together and drown us in desire.

I wanted to peel off the straps of her bra and fill my hands with her breasts. I wanted to know the color of her nipple before I stained it red with my lips. I wanted to be the only man to leave marks on my shy little nanny—to be the only man to make her scream.

I shuddered, my resolve bending against each fresh wave of lust.

"Roman," she inhaled my name, swaying forward just enough to press the full round of her breast into my grip. "Please."

Darkness ate away at the edges of my vision for an instant, lust driving my dick into the front of my pants. I wasn't even sure if she really said the last or if I imagined it in my lust-twisted mind, but god, I couldn't get her plea out of my head.

I ached to fuck her—to bury my dick deep inside her little cunt until all I could feel was her. And if I didn't get out of here soon, I was going to.

I yanked my hand away, caging it under my arm, and ordered gruffly, "You're staying here, and you're never driving for Uber again."

She rocked back, her lips—full and red from the way she'd been biting them the entire drive back—parted in shock.

"W-what?"

"It's not a discussion." I wished she'd step away—wished she'd walk somewhere else in the room where my fingers knew they couldn't reach her.

She crossed her arms but without her shirt over her chest, I was treated—*tormented*—by the way her tits shoved together, the crease between them deepening. I bit my tongue until it bled.

"What makes you think you get to decide that?" She countered. "You're not my guardian, Roman. I'm not yours."

I let out a bitter laugh that devolved into a groan—a deep, soul-sucking groan.

"Don't I know it, Stevie," I rasped. "Don't I fucking know it."

The tension layered thick like a heavy fog between us.

"And if I don't agree?"

"Then I'll find a way to lock you in here."

She started to laugh until she realized I wasn't joking. "So, you're threatening to keep me prisoner?" She gaped.

"No. I'm promising to keep you protected," I said. "You can trust me, Stevie."

Jo's words echoed in my head. Trauma turned into independence. Independence turned into instinct. But I would keep showing her she could rely on me—or forcing her to—until she reached for me when she was struggling instead of figuring out all the ways to handle the world alone.

She breathed deep, and then her shoulders slumped; the fight dissolved from her. For tonight, at least.

"Okay."

One word lifted a hundred pounds of weight from my chest. "Good—Thank you," I caught myself and mumbled. and then held up the key ring that had been permanently imprinted in my left fist. "These are the only set of keys. I'll leave them for you."

I went to set them on the small table by the entrance, but she approached and took them from my hand instead.

"Thank you," she said quietly, her gaze glassy as it found mine. "For saving me."

I ground my teeth. "Don't thank me." *Especially when she had no idea how close I was to ruining her.* "You should have everything you need in the house. Jo brought leftovers from dinner so you have something to eat tonight if you get hungry. The security system is hooked up to the main feed and there's a panic button in the bedroom downstairs. We can worry about the rest of your things tomorrow, and we'll file a police report on Monday."

Her chin dipped. "Okay."

I spun for the front door, taking the handle as some kind of support as I looked over my shoulder and said, "Lock the door behind me."

"So, I'm not being locked in then?" She teased gently as she approached.

"Not yet," I bit out, letting my eyes drown in hers once more until images of me fucking her all over this house poured into my mind. "Tonight, I'm the one who needs to be locked out."

I strode outside, telling myself it was only a gust of ocean air I heard, not the way her breath caught, hoping I'd break back in.

CHAPTER THIRTEEN

Stevie

I PULLED BACK THE SHEER CURTAIN FROM THE WINDOW, LETTING the fingers of the sunset stretch inside and stroke along my cheek.

Outside, I'd heard Lainey's squeal, and I couldn't resist the temptation to look.

Roman brought her down to the little seating outlook where he'd caught me that one day. He was telling her something about the terrarium in her hands. *No.* It was a Mason jar.

My head tipped, wondering what they were doing.

Roman stretched out his arms and then quickly cupped his hands around the air and brought it to the mouth of the jar. I hummed low. They were catching fireflies. Peering harder, I saw the faint flickers of light from the tiny bugs, blinking like little beacons in the sky.

I smiled, watching Lainey's happiness as she gave him the jar and mimicked his action and caught one in her hands, carefully dumping it into the jar. Drawing my lower lip into my mouth, my gaze stole back to Roman. The patience he had with her, the tenderness with which he helped her move the tiny bug into the jar... My heart squeezed until I thought it might burst. He'd do anything for her.

His head snapped up and our gazes connected, awakening

some kind of sixth sense in me. A sense that made me feel like he'd do anything for me, too.

I jerked my head away and covered the window back up.

Two days had passed since my assault—two days filled that had passed with endless hours. Yesterday, Roman had my car towed to a local shop to have the tire replaced; they said we'd be able to pick it up this coming week. Then, Jo returned to the house to pick me up and take me to my apartment to get my things. Thankfully, my minimal belongings were already packed up because of the whole "I spent my rent on tuition situation," so we'd loaded them in her SUV and brought them back here.

Home.

I gulped and looked around the guesthouse. It had come back to life as soon as the ghostlike sheets were removed. Warm, neutral furniture brightened the already well-lit room, similar to the bedroom decor that sat down a spiral set of stairs on the floor below. The bowed windows commanded an almost complete two-hundred-and-seventy-degree panoramic of the turbulent sea below.

Even though I was living on his property, Roman gave me my space to process and recover from Friday night. He and Lainey delivered containers of food and water to my door, one of them accompanied by Lainey's original artwork of me as the fairy princess in the castle. But aside from the text message asking if there was anything I needed, he respected my answer and my privacy when I told him no.

I drew down the edge of my tank top and assessed the purple bruises.

The assault felt like a lifetime ago rather than two days, but I guessed that was because I wanted to distance myself from what happened. Though the memory still made me shudder, I wasn't afraid. Maybe seeing my car—getting in it again—maybe that would send me cowering, but right now—*here*—I felt like I was wrapped in a shield of security that was unbreakable. *Because of him.*

The bruises were already starting to fade—Dean had only grabbed me hard for a second before the Bronco speeding toward us had spooked him. But Roman's touch... that still lingered on my skin like an invisible tattoo.

You're not mine... and don't I fucking know it.

I shivered, warmth cascading down my spine. That was what I was really afraid of—how I felt about my boss. The way I ached for his kiss. Craved his touch.

Sins of the flesh will be punished, Stephanie. The darkness they bring is from the devil himself.

Dad's warning when I became a teenager was on par with the pious path of my life. However, when Mom told me the truth, it turned everything my father had ever said or done into a lie... except those words. They still remained a warning, one that buried like the seed of an oak tree in my soul, its roots spreading and thickening with each passing day.

I wondered if giving in to his emotions was what turned Dad into a monster. *I worried that giving in to mine would make me one, too.*

What if darkness was hereditary? *What if the instinct to kill was hard-coded into my genes?*

The knock on the door made me jump.

I'd paced my way almost to the small kitchen without realizing it. Padding back over to the front door, I unlocked and opened it.

"Hi."

"Stevie." Roman's lip twitched, his eyes instantly dropping down to my bare neck to my shoulders and then to my chest.

Something bright flickered in his dark irises, cascading goose bumps over my skin and pebbling my nipples so tight they felt pinched as they poked against the fabric of my tank.

Crap.

I wasn't wearing a bra. I was hardly wearing a shirt. I was definitely *not* wearing the normal amounts of clothes I usually had on when I faced him, and my body now appreciated just how much those layers of fabric had been necessary armor.

"Sorry to bother you," Roman said gruffly, the noise dissolving against the crash of the waves. "She saw you at the window and wanted to show you her new bug family."

Pretending like my body hadn't just taken its first breath since the last time we'd stood in this doorway, I stamped a smile on my face and crouched in front of my little charge.

"What have you got there?" I asked and examined the jar, counting almost ten of the flickering flies inside it.

Lainey bent forward. "Fairy flies," she whispered in my ear.

"Fairy flies?" I arched an eyebrow, wondering where that name came from.

"Their butts light up!" She giggle-snorted, and I laughed.

I pointed to the one bug crawling on the inside of the glass. "Did you know they light up when they are looking for love?" I wasn't going to delve into the details of bioluminescence or bug booty calls with a six-year-old, but an elementary variation of the facts was something Lainey would enjoy. "The boy bugs flash and flicker to tell the girl bugs that they are in love."

Roman cleared his throat above me, but before I could look up, Lainey tipped forward again.

"Uncle Roman says fairy flies light up the night so the pirate can find the fairy princess."

A soft gasp siphoned from my lips, my tongue suddenly tied up. Of course, he'd heard bits and pieces of the tale I'd spun for his niece, and my stomach fluttered that he'd added his own magic to it.

"That too," I murmured, lifting my hand to the base of my throat, feeling it was impossible to swallow. *He couldn't be alluding to me.*

"We won't keep you..." The coarse vibration of his voice caught me off guard and captured my attention. But before I could look up, my line of sight snagged straight ahead at the level of his waist. There, the massive bulge of his erection was strapped to his thigh by his jeans and I couldn't look away.

Oh wow.

Heat pooled between my thighs, dripping from an ache that had been swelling for weeks. As if he felt my gaze, his body shifted, half turning away from the frame like he was looking to escape. Unfortunately—or fortunately—all that managed to do was give me a profile view of the thick rod I'd felt wedged against my stomach the other night.

My tongue traced along my lips. I'd tasted the heat of his

mouth, but I found myself wanting to taste this, too—wanting to taste the very moment this reserved man lost all his control. Granted, in addition to being a virgin, I'd never given a guy head before, but I'd seen and heard enough from the world around me to know how pleasurable it was for a man.

"Stevie..." Lainey whispered something else in my ear, and I tore my gaze to the ground, trying to focus on what she was saying. "I'm going to put this jar out tonight for the pirate."

"Good thinking," I choked out, but all I imagined was Roman showing up at my door in the middle of the night, my hands gripping his red coat, his feathered hat tumbling to the floor as he took and took and took.

"Let's go, Bug," the man from my imagination rumbled low and planted his hands on Lainey's shoulders, steering her away from my door. She snuck in a quick hug, causing the backs of his knuckles to brush against my shoulder for a second, before they both drew away.

"Have a good night," I said softly, watching them walk away and leave me to the quiet turmoil of the cottage. Maybe those fairy flies would at least bring a certain protective pirate to my dreams if not to my doorstep.

In my dreams, he wouldn't need to know the truth that I was fruit from a poisoned tree.

I JOLTED awake with a gasp as the vibration from the rough waves outside shook the house.

The clock on the small nightstand read that it was only a little before eleven, so I hadn't been asleep for long. I sighed and pressed my hand to my forehead, feeling how clammy my skin was.

My sleep had been fitful and fruitless, it was no wonder I'd woken so easily.

With another huff, I threw off the crisp white sheets and sat up, my gaze drawn out to the dark sea where it continued to thrash below. *Apparently, I wasn't the only one who was having a fitful night.*

My toes found the floor and I stood, welcoming the cool air over my flushed skin.

I needed a walk. I couldn't sleep like this.

I went upstairs, grabbed a water from the kitchen, and strode to the windows that paneled the back of the house with a view of nothing but ocean—or nothing but darkness at this time of night.

I wondered if Lainey had fallen asleep okay. I wondered how long Roman stood outside her door to make sure she wasn't crying... and to guard over her if she was. And then I wondered if he'd fallen asleep easily in his big bed—if he'd buried his desire as successfully as he buried every other emotion that threatened his unbreakable persona.

The full moon glittered off the midnight-moving water. It felt as though I were living on the very edge of the world with no other signs of light or life except the sea and its depths. Somehow, I felt lonelier than before—like I had something to lose whereas before I hadn't had anything at all.

I took another sip of water. *I should go back to bed.* Turning toward the staircase, a flicker of light from the front window caught my eye before it disappeared.

Next I knew, I stood by the front door, drawing back the curtain in search of the light.

Instead, I found him.

Standing once more at the spot where he'd caught me—*where he'd first held me*—Roman scowled out at the sea, a jar of fairy flies in his hold.

My pirate.

I should've stayed inside—behind the door he wanted locked to keep him out. But instead, I turned the knob and set myself free, letting my bare feet carry me over the threshold and along the rough path toward him.

He had on a gray T-shirt and dark sweatpants, the flutter of the fabric the only thing moving about him. His spine was ramrod straight and the line of his broad shoulders so stiff he looked as though he was nailed to an invisible wall. Not even his chest broke to breathe.

His dark hair, dark expression... everything about Roman dissolved him into the night except the fireflies and the glint of his glasses… and the anguish that rolled off him as violent as the waves that hurled themselves against the rocky coast.

This was a bad idea.

In my bones, I knew it would be safer to sacrifice myself to the rough sea than it was to throw myself into the attraction that sparked between us, hoping it would catch flame.

"Dammit, Val… dammit…" His low utterance gutted me, and I stopped several feet behind him, the overwhelming sound of the ocean spray masking my approach.

I drew a deep breath. "Roman."

He whipped around, surprise quickly igniting into anger in his gaze.

"Stevie." His voice crashed into my chest, and if it were possible for him to turn any stiffer, he did. His hands tightened on the jar as his eyes raked over me. I had on even less than before—the same tank but my sleep shorts rode high on my hips. "What are you doing out here?"

I gulped. "I came to ask you the same thing."

He looked away, shutting me out once more. "Go back inside."

I ignored him and instead walked closer.

"Stevie…" he warned this time.

"What are you doing out here, Roman?" I probed again.

He was silent for long seconds, looking toward the invisible horizon.

"She still cries at night," he confessed without turning around.

"She's grieving," I replied. "Like you should be."

His continued refusal to open up broke my heart just as surely as it caused Lainey to cry alone. Maybe it was wrong to tell someone how to grieve, but after knowing this man for the last six weeks, it was impossible not to see how he held back like a dam about to burst.

"You should go to bed," he said, trying to come off like he was talking to a child, but the thick husk of his voice betrayed him.

"What are you doing with the fireflies?" I asked instead, trying to calm my racing pulse.

His eyes dropped quickly like he'd forgotten he was even holding the jar. "Setting them free."

I felt a twinge in my chest. "But they're supposed to light the way so the pirate can find the princess."

"You know as well as I do that the pirate never gets the princess," he rasped low, covering the lid of the jar with his massive palm and beginning to twist it free.

"Roman—" I took several steps closer to him.

"Don't," he warned low, my body now inches from his.

Something broke inside me. Something that couldn't bear to see him suffer like this—couldn't bear to see him doing so much yet punishing himself for it not being enough.

"I want you to kiss me again," I declared.

My eyes locked on the jar of fireflies like he held a universe between his palms, and I wished on each and every flickering star in that glass-enclosed galaxy that he wouldn't pull away from me again.

A hoarse groan split from his chest as he quickly adjusted himself and crouched down. He spun the lid off the jar and let it clatter on the ground, freeing all my wishes and a sharp pain in my chest.

"No, you don't," he rasped, the fireflies creating a web of moving light around us

"But—"

"No buts," he snapped and stood so quickly, I took a half step back. "I don't think you understand. So let me explain it to you like I explained it to the fucker who touched you before I almost killed him." His eyes swung to mine, a riotous conflagration of self-loathing and lust, and he took a menacing step in my direction, burning up the remaining space between us. "To catch monsters, Stevie, I had to become one."

"Roman..." I let out a strangled cry.

"I made myself this way. I trained and sacrificed to become a man with purpose—a monster who could save the world. I'm not meant to have a life. I'm not meant to have children." His eyes darkened, and I shuddered in surprise when I felt the hot press of his knuckle underneath my chin, lifting it up so we were poised at the edge of a kiss. "And I'm not meant to crave my fucking nanny more than I crave breath. Not meant to kiss her or mark her or fuck her or claim her."

My hot whimper tangled with his rough breaths in the no-man's-land between our lips.

The fireflies, though they'd left the jar, continued to flutter around us, drawn to the invisible electricity sparking where we touched.

"I'm broken, princess."

Whatever reservations—whatever fears I had were washed away like sand underneath the powerful tide. Maybe this was what I'd been warned about when I was younger—this thing inside me that felt like a hungry beast that threatened to devour me from the inside out if I didn't find some way to reach this man and find the answer to my ache for him.

"You're not broken, Roman," I breathed out, daring as I did to reach up and slowly flatten my hand to his implacable chest. "You're unfolding."

Unfolding in this new role. Unfolding in the new life. Unfolding feelings that had been cocooned inside for so very long.

From fingertips to knuckles to palms, hot muscles rippled with tension underneath my touch. And before I could even register the sudden movement, he'd framed the sides of my face with both hands and pulled me flush to him.

All at once, I was trapped between cold cliffs at the edge of the world and the hard male at the edge of everything.

"Fuck, Stevie," he grated out. "*Fuck.*" And then he kissed me again.

ROMAN MIGHT CLAIM to be as impenetrable and unfeeling as stone, but his kiss turned his lips to liars.

His mouth ravaged mine with a ferocity that made my knees weak. Like the last time, this kiss was hard and bruising, demanding and desperate. It cemented him every inch the pirate as he plundered my mouth, fueled by pent-up desire.

My hands—both of them—filled with the fabric of his shirt,

pulling me tighter as his tongue seared my mouth with hard, sweeping strokes. I wanted more. I wanted closer. If he was broken, I wanted to be cut by his sharp edges, shaped to fit into this life he swore he wasn't made for.

Whimpering, I arched my hips, searching for his thick length. I didn't have to search far. The soft fabric of his sweatpants was no match for the weight of his erection. It dented into my quivering stomach and my inner muscles clenched, wishing it was denting me from the inside.

With a buried growl, his teeth snagged on my bottom lip and bit down hard, causing me to gasp in pain for an instant before he sucked on the injured flesh, soothing it with each hot pull.

"Please, Roman."

Insatiable want burned through me like wildfire. I wanted those lips on my neck. On my breasts. Around my nipples. I let out a small cry but it was swallowed once more by his consuming kiss.

For all my life, I'd been a good girl—first because I had to, then because I was afraid to be anything else. But this... this kiss was pure sin, and I craved more. No matter the consequences.

"Please, take care of me..." I pleaded breathlessly, rocking my hips against his, desperate to feed the wild need that tore through me.

"Shit—" he swore and pulled his lips to the side. "I shouldn't —we shouldn't—"

Once more, his lips tried to lie, but the rest of his body refused to move away, thrumming against mine for the relief we both craved.

My grip on his shirt tightened, holding on for dear life. I dragged in breaths like my head was held just above water and I was preparing to dive deep.

"It's okay," I promised him. Releasing one clenched fist, I fitted my fingers around his wrist and pulled his palm over my mouth. "It's okay," I said the words into his skin, punctuating them with a kiss.

His gaze sizzled with explosive lust, each touch burning his desire further down the fuse to a bomb that couldn't be contained.

I dragged his hand down along my neck, over my collarbone, and then finally pressed it over my breast, shivering under the wash of pleasure it sent through my body.

"Fuck, Stevie," he rasped, tortured, as his head drifted closer to mine, pulled by a gravity he couldn't resist.

"It's okay."

His hand tensed, and I thought he was going to pull away, but instead his big fingers began to squeeze—began to weigh and knead the weight of my breast in their hold, and I swore it wasn't my knees, but the whole earth underneath my feet that began to shake.

"No, it's not," he bit out, finding my nipple through my tank and plucking it between his fingers. "I don't know how to feel, Stevie. I don't know how to fucking feel."

But his protests didn't stop his touch.

Stars erupted in my vision, but even pleasure couldn't block out the pain from his voice. Gasping, I released his wrist and found his hard pec, desire weighing it down over the rocky planes of his abdomen that tightened under my touch until I reached the waist of his sweats.

Roman sucked in a sharp breath and held it like a knife pierced through his chest.

"Then let me show you," I begged and reached for the girth of his cock.

This time, I couldn't make out what choice swear words cemented the severing of his restraint before his hand raked around the back of my head and his mouth ravaged mine.

My tongue was caught in a tumble of waves, too pleasurable and too strong for me to catch my breath. The kiss carried me under, but it didn't matter. All I cared about was the throbbing part of him I stroked and the way it made him *feel*.

I wanted more. I ached for the heat of his bare skin—to feel how his body wanted me beyond all the ways he could deny. My fingers clawed at the edge of his pants, about to dive under the fabric when they were caught in his hold.

"Jesus, Stevie," he ground out. "How much more do you want from me?"

Everything, I wanted to say but somehow managed to hold back, replying instead with, "I want to taste you."

"Fuck," he groaned, and his big body swayed. It seemed incredible that my words—my touch—could shake such an unshakable man. "You don't want me to feel, you want me to fucking crumble."

I held my breath, wondering once more if I'd gone too far. But then his hold peeled away, finger by finger, and behind his glasses, his eyes drenched with lust.

"Please."

His other hand slid from the side of my face, his thumb finding the swell of my bottom lip and stroking over it like I was a child who had no idea what I was asking for.

"Have you ever sucked a man's cock before, Stevie?"

A shiver of warm heat zinged through my veins and sent a rush of wetness between my thighs.

"No." I gulped.

His jaw muscle flexed hard. "And you think you can take all of mine like a good little girl?"

I moaned and slid my tongue out to follow the trail of his thumb, but as soon as I did, that thumb snapped on top of it and pinned it against my lower teeth. I gasped, and he took advantage, sliding his finger deeper into my mouth toward the back of my throat.

"You have a tiny mouth, princess," he rasped. "Do you know what's going to happen if I fuck it?"

He had my tongue captive so all I could do was shake my head.

"I'm going to have to stretch those pretty lips wide just to get inside. Your tongue isn't going to know what to do because it won't be able to move—to swallow." To make his point, he pressed his thumb down on my tongue, forcing my jaw wider though I wanted everything he'd just said. "Then, I'm going to bottom out against the back of your throat, and you're going to choke on every plea you ever uttered for wanting to make me lose control."

His warning ended as he pulled his hands away, freeing my

mouth, and then he snarled, "So tell me again what you want, princess, because this is the last chance you'll have to walk away."

His eyes flickered even darker than the shadows as I sank to my knees. The gravel cut into my skin, but the small pain evaporated under the blazing desire in his stare. The moonlight glinted off his glasses, and for the first time they seemed to magnify his untethered emotions rather than shield them.

Once more, my tongue dragged over my lips, marking them for sacrifice. "I want to suck your cock." The sheer power of the words made us both shudder.

Roman's deep groan was as powerful as the dark waves that crashed against the rocks.

"Good girl." He hooked his thumbs under the waist of his sweats, pulling them out and over the heavy length of his cock.

My mouth went dry.

I didn't know if it was the midnight shadows or an illusion of the full moon, but what I saw seemed nothing like what I'd felt. What I'd felt against my stomach—against my palm—couldn't have been this big. *Could it?*

The root of his cock jutted out from a coarse net of dark hair, but instead of sticking up or even out, it hung low under its own weight. The thick trunk wrapped in pulsing veins. I traced them with my eyes all the way down the length and then choking on my own saliva when I saw how they swelled around a distinctly curved tip.

Could they... was that...

"I warned you I was a monster. You shouldn't have begged," he said as though answering my thoughts.

A monster. *Was that what they called a dick that curved at the end?*

"Open your mouth. Show me how good you are," he ordered, and my jaw immediately dropped wide.

My whole body felt jittery with his praise, like I was filled with lightning bugs that flickered and glowed with chemical want.

He fisted himself, his fingers just touching around the width, and guided the purpled head to my waiting mouth. He fed me the blunt tip, my lips wrapping around his thick flesh that felt softer than velvet.

I'd never felt anything like this, and my tongue instantly began to explore him, licking around the rim and flicking into the slit.

"Oh fuck, Stevie," he let out roughly.

I let out a small moan and felt how the sound made him swell and release a drop of moisture like a small burst of salt onto my tongue. Relaxing my jaw, I inched him in farther, wanting more of his groans of pleasure and words of praise.

Roman hissed, drawing my gaze briefly to his face which was tipped back, every inch of it strained with tension. His free hand cupped the side of my face and then tangled in my hair.

"You want me to lose my mind, then suck on me like a good girl. Suck like you want to swallow me whole."

For the life of me, I couldn't describe how turned on his dirty words made me feel. All I wanted was to obey and obey and obey and hope that he never stopped.

Unable to look away from his gaze, I tightened my lips down and followed his instruction, pulling him into my mouth as hard as I could.

"*Fuck.*" The word sent a thrill of power through me though I was the one on my knees. And the urge to do it again came instantaneously—like a reflex. So, I sucked again with instruction—even harder this time—and my reward was to be fed another thick inch of him.

"God, you're so good." He shuddered and fisted a handful of my hair. "So hot and incredible around me."

Need furled low in my stomach, and my core clenched to the point of pain. Again and again, I closed my lips as hard as I could and sucked on his cock, earning more of his length and more of his praise until his tip brushed the back of my throat.

The sensation surprised me and I tensed.

"This is what you wanted," he ground out, eyes wild with lust. "Your pretty mouth stuffed full of my cock." He pushed deeper, hitting that spot again; this time I tried to swallow, but couldn't. "Is it worth it to be choked in order to see me lose my fucking mind?"

I tried to nod and he felt it, pushing deeper against the back of my throat in response. The curve of his cock hit a spot that made me gag and jerk. *Oh god.* My eyes bugged wide, feeling my air supply suddenly cut off. An instant later, I could breathe again as his hips drew back slightly.

"God, you feel so good, drooling all over me," he groaned, his eyes glazed over with pleasure. "You have no idea what you do to me."

His thumb drew tender circles on my scalp for a moment before his feral need drove his hips forward once more. Knowing it was coming made no difference to my body's instinct to choke and then sputter with each thrust.

I had to look foolish—inexperienced in my eagerness to pleasure him. Maybe in the daylight, I'd be embarrassed by the scrapes on my knees and the splits in my lips. But right now, the wild expression on his face promised it wasn't what I knew or didn't know that drove him insane; it was just me.

"That's it, princess," he encouraged, cupping my head as he rocked deeper into my mouth. "Take my whole fucking cock."

Drool slid down my chin because it had nowhere else to go. I felt it leak onto the coarse hair covering his balls each time they brushed against me. He was too big—my mouth too full. Still, I tried to suck—tried to swallow each time he pushed deep because I wanted to consume him.

His thrusts grew wild, and I stopped caring about oxygen, living instead off of every hard pant from his lungs

"You're going to drink down my cum like a good little princess," he rasped hoarsely, driving against the back of my throat. I welcomed the burn—welcomed the bruise. *I welcomed every feeling that he tried to fight.* "That's it, Stevie. Fuck, that's it."

Between my lips, I felt him swell thicker. I felt the veins along his shaft distend and salty liquid leak from the tip.

Roman's wild eyes locked on me like he might not survive if he looked away. His fingers notched into my scalp, holding me in place.

He shunted his hips all the way forward until the angled end of his cock bottomed out in my throat, and he came violently.

His roar of release collided with the crash of the waves, breaking apart the man who was just as powerful and mysterious as the sea. Hot, thick spurts of cum jetted what felt like straight into my stomach as he held himself there for a few seconds before inching out enough to let me breathe.

"God, Stevie..." he groaned.

His eyes held mine, the touch of his hands relaxing while he continued to fill my mouth. "Good girl," he said over and over, swiping drool from my chin. I swallowed three times before his cock finally let up.

I never wanted this night to end.

Then, he carefully slid out of my mouth and tucked himself back into his sweats. Each of his movements slowed as regret stacked like weights onto his shoulders.

My chest squeezed. Like a rubber band, he'd stretched beyond his comfort zone, and now, here came the recoil.

"Stevie..."

"Don't," I warned him, rising and shaking my head in protest. "Don't you dare say this was a mistake and you're sorry."

His mouth narrowed into a thin line. The fact that he didn't say anything was even worse.

I turned away and wiped my mouth, feeling like the biggest fool.

"Listen to me—"

"Don't—" I broke off as he grabbed my shoulders and forced me to face him.

"Listen to me." He gripped my chin fast. "You're going to go back to the cottage, lock the damn door, and get back in bed, understood?"

His gaze roamed my face. From my eyes to my lips. It memorized every inch like I was a puzzle he'd have to put back together later from memory.

"Yeah," I murmured, suddenly overwhelmed with exhaustion and defeat.

I swayed, and he steadied me— always ready to protect me but never anything more. But then, instead of letting go, I watched his head drift down toward mine. For a second, I thought he was going to kiss me once more, and I tensed.

I could handle his rejection, but not when he made it seem like it was for my own good. But then he veered to the side, and I felt his mouth settle against the shell of my ear.

"Then you put your fingers between your thighs and touch yourself."

I gasped softly, forgetting in the midst of everything that my ache was still unsatisfied.

"You're going to rub and pluck and stroke your needy little clit as if it were me—as if it were my fingers making you wet and swollen and horny," he continued to rasp. "You're going to touch yourself until you come, and when you do, you're going to scream my name so fucking loud that I'll be able to hear you from my bed."

I whimpered. I could scream until my lungs gave out, but it would never be loud enough for him to hear me all the way in the guesthouse.

"Do you understand?"

No.

No, I didn't understand.

I didn't understand why it couldn't be him.

"Why can't it be you?" I asked breathlessly.

"Because I know if I touch you, I won't stop until I'm fucking you. Until I'm fucking those perfect tits... that sweet little ass... and finally your hungry little pussy. And then, I won't stop fucking you until you can't see straight. Until you can't fucking scream because your voice is gone. And until the only part of you that has strength to move is the part that's wringing every drop of cum from my cock."

My sore, swollen lips began to part in shock, but I forced them to work—to speak.

"I'm not that fragile, Roman," I insisted though the tremble in my voice diminished its strength. "I won't break."

He stood straight, his eyes smoldering with flickers of desire buried in ashes of pain. "You're not the one I'm worried about."

And then he turned and stalked toward the house, putting distance between us like his life depended on it.

I stayed rooted in place, watching him walk away several moments before I tested out my sea legs. I could feel my knees promising revolt, but my pace picked up as I got closer to the cottage.

Part of me wanted to go inside and go to sleep—to spite him

and deny myself the pleasure he wanted me to have. But I ached too badly to punish myself that way. My body needed release while I still tasted his on my tongue.

Retreating inside, I began to close the door behind me, not even realizing when I paused to take one last look at the main house until I saw a familiar shadow standing at its windows.

He was watching me.

In that moment, I knew Roman would be at that window until I finished myself off. Somehow, across the distance and over the sound of the waves, he'd be standing there until he knew I'd screamed his name.

I slammed the door shut.

Maybe he was right. *Maybe he was a monster.*

But even that didn't stop me from being his good girl and doing exactly what he wanted.

CHAPTER FOURTEEN

Roman

"Hey, Bug." I watched her eat her chocolate chip pancake. She didn't look up, but I knew she was listening. "Thanksgiving is coming soon, and we're going to spend it at Uncle Dex and Aunt Jo's house. You remember them from dinner the other night?"

She nodded slowly and started to play with her food rather than eat it.

God, why did the holidays have to come so fucking fast? Why couldn't we have had months before everything she lost was thrown in her face?

Maybe I should schedule some extra sessions with Dr. Shelly.

"I was thinking..." I cleared my throat and braced myself. "Maybe you could help me try and make your mom's famous cauliflower casserole?"

We always fought over Val's cauliflower casserole at Thanksgiving—Lainey and I having a contest to see who could eat the most of it.

I hadn't planned on mentioning it. Like everything else, I wanted to replace everything that might remind her—everything that might hurt her—with something new. And maybe I wanted that for me, too, because to try to live up to Val was impossible. So, if I just didn't do anything that she did, I couldn't be reminded of all the ways I was failing her and my niece.

But... *unfolding*.

Lainey's head snapped up, her little eyes wide. And then she floored me by smiling and nodding. My breath escaped in a rush, so afraid that she was just going to burst out into tears, I didn't realize I was holding it.

"Good," I rumbled low and then cleared my throat. "They also said we could invite Stevie. What do you think?"

I wasn't sure I'd ever seen her head move so fast, and my gut tightened, feeling the same way. When Stevie wasn't around, it felt like there was something missing.

"You could ask her this morning, if you want. She's going to come with us when I take you to school," I suggested, cementing myself as the biggest asshole on the planet.

Yeah, it was pretty damn obvious that Stevie was the only one who could make all of this easier for my niece—*for me*. But when I should be creating as many barriers between Stevie and me, instead, I was finding ways to justify taking them all down.

I was the asshole who wanted to fuck my nanny.

I was the asshole who took advantage—who couldn't control himself even though I'd spent my life condemning criminals for the very same crime. But there was no other word for it. When it came to Stevie—her tits in my hands, her lips suctioned around my cock... but especially that look in her eyes where it felt like she could see *life* in me when I swore I had none left—it tipped me over that edge.

As if cued by my thoughts, there was a soft knock at the back door. I looked up and caught Stevie's eyes, a wave of hot electricity ricocheting back so strongly, I was surprised it didn't shatter the glass. Her lips parted and my cock went hard instantly, remembering last night and those lips stretched around my dick.

"It's open," I called hoarsely.

"Good morning," Stevie greeted, and I had to be imagining the subtle husk to her voice.

This morning, she had on black leggings and a long sweater—an outfit that should hide everything tempting about her, except all it did was remind me just how much temptation there was to hide.

I wasn't used to seeing her this early. I was used to a full day of work and distractions to harden me before I had to face her soft compassion. But I needed to take her down to the station this morning so she could file a report with the police about what happened on Friday, and then I needed to take her for her car this afternoon. Between those two things, I'd planned on bringing her to Covington with me. An idiotic move in hindsight after last night.

After I'd fucked her mouth like it was my property.

I thought about changing the plans, but I refused to let anything change because of what happened. *Except the way the memory of her perfect mouth wrapped around my fat cock would haunt my nightmares for the rest of my life.*

Stevie's attention was wholly focused on Lainey who'd climbed down from her seat and bounded across the living room to hug her legs. I stared at the two of them. Stevie's flushed cheeks and warm smile, and the way her eyes closed for a second when she hugged Lainey back. The two of them loved each other. From day one, they'd been like two peas in a pod—a pod that I was slowly being let inside of.

Guilt sucker punched me in the gut. This was why nothing could change between us. My niece was and needed to be my first priority—my only priority.

"Good morning," she addressed me this time and the blush staining her cheeks deepened.

She'd done as I'd ordered—touched herself like I'd wanted to. God, I wondered if her cunt turned that same deep pink shade when she fingered herself. *Fuck.* I swallowed a groan as my heavy cock turned to stone.

"There're pancakes here for you if you want some," I said gruffly, turning away to hide the obvious stretch against the front of my dress pants. Her soft "thanks" was followed by two sets of footsteps in my direction. "We should leave in ten." I retreated to my room without a second glance in their direction.

I didn't have time to work one out—*again*—before we needed to leave, so I settled for splashing cold water on my face while I ran through the list of all the reasons I was fucked up. Broken.

Or unfolding.

I shuddered. The word haunted me—*tempted me to embrace it.* Maybe she was right. Maybe I was unfolding into this new life here, and maybe that was why it was so painful; because when it was all said and done, there would be no hiding from the fact that I was hollow inside.

I adjusted my damn dick once more and prepared for an erection that would be lasting more than four fucking hours if I was going to be around Stevie all day. Grabbing my laptop bag, I strode back to the kitchen.

"Are you guys ready?"

They were both hunched over the dining table, peering into the tower of terrariums that had become the centerpiece. I admired Stevie's perfect ass for a second. According to Stevie, all the bugs in each enclosure had names though she was pretty sure Lainey couldn't tell most of the inhabitants apart.

"Lainey asked me if I would spend Thanksgiving with you both," she said, facing me. After last night I didn't blame her for questioning the offer.

"Will you?"

I didn't want her to have a choice, and having Lainey ask her to come made it impossible for Stevie to say no—and made me a complete ass.

Her lips peeled open and then shut. "Okay." She gulped and then added, "I'd love to."

Lainey squealed and clapped—more sounds that I was now privy to—and all because of *her*.

"We should get going or you'll be late for school," I declared low, breezing by them and holding the front door ajar. I needed to keep this day moving; the longer I stopped in these moments, the stronger the temptation became to stay in them and the more precarious this situation became.

My innocent, irresistible nanny was like the very strongest of drugs—the kind that would steadily cure my niece while slowly killing me.

"THANK you for coming in with me," Stevie said softly once we were back in the car.

My palm stretched and then flexed around the shifter knob, the tension in my body making me want to rip it straight out of the transmission.

We'd dropped Lainey off at school and then went straight over to the Carmel Police Department. I'd already spoken to the chief on Saturday morning and given him a heads-up that we'd be in first thing Monday to report the assault.

My plan was to bring Stevie to the station, deliver her to the officers so she could file a report, and then wait for her to be done. I'd been enough of an overprotective brute in the last couple of days; for both our sakes, I needed to show her I wasn't going to cross any unprofessional lines again. But before I could walk away, she'd looked at me and asked if I'd stay with her.

Stay with her.

My independent fairy princess who fought tooth and nail against me helping her with school, against taking a bigger paycheck, against staying in my spare fucking house, asked me for help.

I wasn't the only one unfolding. And god, did my every protective instinct immediately shift into overdrive.

So, I went and sat quietly next to her, listening to every detail of what happened, and while I was prepared for a lot of things today, I wasn't prepared to be right back at the brink of murder by the time her story was done. I should be the one taking care of these fuckers. *For good.*

And when the detective said he'd follow up on the incident and get back to us, I didn't trust him. He hadn't sounded confident. He hadn't sounded like this was that important—*like Stevie was a priority.* And it enraged me.

I managed a low grunt in response to her and immediately dialed Dex. I needed to know what the fuck had changed between Saturday morning and now.

"Hello." His deep voice rumbled through the car as I pulled out of the station's lot. "You're on speaker, and Reed's in my office."

Great.

"I need you to find out everything you can on Dean Johnson and the two guys who were with him that night, Ben Lopez and Jared Greenfield." I ignored Stevie's stare as it widened from the passenger seat.

"What happened?" He asked, and I heard some commotion in the background.

I swallowed hard, wondering if I should've just waited until I got to the office to ask him. *Fuck.* I didn't want Stevie to worry about this any more than necessary, but it was too late now. Once more, I was acting emotionally rather than rationally.

Fucking unfolding.

"My gut says this isn't being handled properly," I clipped.

"Roman." Reed's voice came from the background, the former cop's tone edgy with caution. "Give them a couple days to figure it out."

"It shouldn't take a couple days to charge those fuckers with assault," I ground out as I gave the SUV some gas, translating some of my frustration into speed. "Something doesn't feel right."

I heard his loud sigh. "Let me call down there and talk to them. They seemed pretty on top of their shit when they hauled them all in the other night."

His words should comfort me but they didn't.

"Dean Johnson's mother is Congresswoman Johnson," Dex interrupted. "The other two are friends of his from law school."

My blood began a familiar boil.

I'd worked for the government long enough to come across my fair share of political oversteps—men, and sometimes women, who'd do anything to preserve their reputation and power. I'd worked cases—caught child pornographers who'd sold their... wares... to senators and congressmen who thought they'd covered their tracks.

"I need you to see if she made any contact with the police department or any kind of donation, above or below board, to the department or to any officer, detective, or the chief individually."

"Jesus, do you know what you're suggesting?" Reed gaped, bringing to life the wordless shock that radiated off of Stevie.

"I know exactly what the hell I'm suggesting, Proby," I said in warning. I might be the newest guy on this team, but I'd put away a helluva lot more bad guys than the golden boy detective. "And I'm making sure that someone wasn't paid to look the other way at the piece of shit who thought he could attack my—Stevie."

She was Lainey's nanny. She wasn't my anything.

"Look, Roman, you can't just go around investigating a whole damn department for being dirty just because you want to nanny the fuck out of her—"

"Jesus Christ," I snarled, and Stevie let out an audible gasp. "You're on fucking speakerphone, Reed."

Beside me, Stevie went completely still.

"Sorry about that," Reed muttered remorsefully and then cleared his throat. "Just meant that you're leaping—no, catapulting to a lot of conclusions."

He was lucky my fist wasn't catapulting down his throat. Not because he was wrong, but because he was right. There were a lot of things I wanted to do to Stevie, and *nanny the fuck out of her* seemed to crudely yet accurately describe them all.

"We'll be at the office in five, and if you have anything else you want to say to me, you can do it then." In private. To my face.

I ended the call and doused us in silence.

"I'm sorry, but I just want to make sure the police are doing their due diligence for the other night… for you," I explained, ignoring the elephant in the Bronco.

She sat quiet for a second. "And what about last night?"

"Last night…" I exhaled closely and forced my expression to remain unfazed. "Last night was a lesson. Today things go back to normal." I wouldn't say last night was a mistake or that it needed to be forgotten.

"I see," she murmured and swallowed. "What kind of lesson?"

Dammit. I ground my teeth together. I was trying my damnedest not to hurt her, but she just kept pushing for answers—for my emotions.

"One that I've learned from," I replied coldly. "You are... essential to Lainey. And I won't let anything jeopardize that."

Including how much I wanted to nanny the fuck out of her.

"You can kill him later," Dex said, joining Reed and me in the hallway outside of my office.

I forced myself to not give Stevie one more glance as I closed the door and gave her some privacy to work at my desk.

"No need," I grumbled, following them both down the hall to Dex's office.

In his defense, Reed immediately apologized to Stevie and then to me, but I still had the urge to give that pretty face of his a good knock.

In spite of his crass remark, Reed was a good guy. Honest, hardworking, loyal. Most days, I'd agree that his only fault was being too pretty for his own good. Even on Friday, Dex told me after the fact that Reed had walked out on his date without stopping to give the woman an explanation in order to help me find Stevie.

There weren't a lot of things that pushed his buttons or got him fired up, however after over a decade on the police force, hearing me accuse the cops of, at best, looking the other way and, worst, being dirty without giving them even an hour to follow protocol was the kind of thing that hit too close to home.

We reached the ops room and my brain turned on work mode. "What have you... fuck..." I trailed off, my gait slowing as I registered the image of the dead body up on the screen.

A new victim.

Then, I realized that in addition to Ace, who stood by his brother's desk, Rorik was in the room, too.

"Ace. Rorik." My chin dipped. "Long time no see." It was almost two weeks since I'd been up in the city, in his morgue, going over the details on the victims. I cleared my throat and looked back at the screen. "When?"

"Found this morning," Ace informed me.

"Once you confirmed we were looking for the Archangel, I put out a notice to the departments within our radius of San Francisco to be on the lookout for high-risk targets that fit the profile. We got a call from Monterey this morning. Local LEO just happened to find her body behind a dumpster near the beach."

"I can go up there with you—"

"I asked them to bring the body to Carmel's morgue," Rorik informed me.

"And they agreed?" I folded my arms. Jurisdiction was always a sticking point.

"They did when I told them she was a victim of an FBI case."

As if on cue, the door opened behind me and Dante ushered Agent Koorie in to join us.

"Knight." She greeted me with a tight smile and a tip of her head.

"Koorie." I exhaled and extended my hand in greeting.

Her black hair was pulled back into a tight ponytail, and she had on the same matte black suit she'd worn every day that I'd worked with her. I'd always admired her consistency and dedication, but now I looked at her and saw my former self—before Lainey. *Before Stevie.* I saw a woman completely enveloped by her job... and entirely unaware of it.

"Looks like the Archangel doesn't want to leave you." She took my hand and gave it a firm shake.

"Nightmares rarely do," I muttered and then looked to the guys. "Special Agent in Charge Sally Koorie, meet Reed Lockhard, Dex and Ace Covington, and it looks like you've already met Dante Lozano."

She nodded and briefly made her way around to shake everyone's hands, completely unintimidated to be the only woman in the room.

"Where's the team?"

"You're looking at it." She flashed a grin. "The rest of my team is on a case in Idaho." She sighed. "Not sure if we're short staffed or if world circumstances have bred more psychos, but that's where we are." She strode over to the table, planted her hands on the top and looked to Dex. "Alright, so what did I miss?"

I returned my attention back to the screen—and the newest victim I hadn't been able to save.

"Not much," I said, gritting my teeth.

Dex jumped in and ran through the list of victims, pulling up a digital map of the deaths and reviewing the time line, and adding the latest victim's death to the map.

"You know our working theory," I continued. "Hopefully, we'll get more answers with this victim."

"You really think a kid?" She rested her hands on her hips and shook her head. "The most prolific serial killer of our time took a break because *he had a kid.*"

I nodded, still struggling to wrap my head around it, too. Just like everything else, even serial killers had a stereotype. So, when there were ones that broke the mold—like Ted Bundy and the Archangel, whoever he was—it was hard to veer from our normal line of thinking.

"Okay, so what's our next step?" She deferred to me even though I was no longer FBI and this was definitely federal jurisdiction.

I looked to Rorik. "When will they have the body here?"

He glanced at his watch. "Within the next half hour."

"Okay. I'll go with you to the morgue to meet the body," I declared. I needed to be there to confirm this was another of his kills. A perverse kind of victim identification. I wasn't related to any of these women, but in my gut I felt responsible for them because I'd failed at catching the fucker who'd done this. "Ace, can you go with Koorie up to the site where the body was found?"

My boss nodded. "The police closed off the scene immediately once they realized what they were dealing with, and they're waiting for one of us," he said to Koorie.

"I'm going to see if I can get an ID on this victim," he said without breaking his gaze from his screen.

"Where do you want me?" Reed ran a hand over his buzzed blond hair.

"With me," I decided and opened the door to the hall.

All of us except Dex filed out of the room. Dante said to let him know if I needed anything, but he was running point on several other Covington cases and with Roc and Jackson home with their women for the next couple of weeks, I wasn't going to pull him off of the firm's work unless absolutely necessary.

We were halfway down the hallway when my phone buzzed. *The garage.*

"Shit," I muttered and looked over my shoulder. "Actually, Reed, I'm going to need you to do something else for me." I crooked my fingers, indicating for him to follow; Rorik came along, too.

I knocked lightly on my office door before opening it. Stevie's head popped up from where it was resting on her palm, and she swiped her cheek. *Shit.* Another burst of rage fired through my veins. She'd been crying.

"Your tire is fixed. I'm going to have Reed take you to the garage to pick up your car."

Her features went slack and paled in disappointment, and I winced.

She's not yours, I chided myself. If she were, I would be the one who had to take her. I would be the one who followed her and made sure she got home safely. I would be the one for everything because she would be mine.

But since she wasn't, I had to start treating her like any other woman I was helping; and that meant asking any one of my very capable teammates to help out because I was needed elsewhere.

"Her car is at Leed's Garage over on Fifth," I turned and said to Reed, adding with a lower tone. "Everything's all taken care of, just make sure she gets home okay."

I'd given the garage my credit card on Saturday when the tow truck delivered the car, instructing them to charge the full bill to it.

"Ready..." Stevie had packed up her things and now stood beside me, close enough for her scent to paralyze my brain. Warm sugar and peppermint. And it called to me like a damn siren.

"Stevie, this is Rorik Nilsen. San Francisco's medical examiner," Reed jumped in and made the introduction because my brain misfired over her seductive scent. "Rorik, this is Stevie Michaels, Roman's nanny."

I caught the subtle break in his voice on the word nanny, but I didn't think anyone else did.

"Nice to meet you," Stevie greeted him with a hesitant smile.

"You, too." Rorik's pale-blue eyes flicked between us.

"I might be home late tonight."

"Okay." Her throat bobbed and I felt the suction like a ghost grip around my cock.

Yeah. No idea how late I would be, but it was going to be late enough that I didn't risk more than five minutes in Stevie's company.

"Thanks, Reed," I clipped and strode away without another word, Rorik following behind me in unnerving silence.

"How's it going?" Rorik asked, his metallic gaze never leaving the road in front of us. "It's been what… two months since the accident?"

When I was up in the city, we hadn't really had a chance to talk in private. Rorik had been dealing with other cases in addition to the bodies I was there to see, and there was too much going on to really talk. Which, honestly, was fine with me. *Especially with Rorik.* The medical examiner didn't waste time— didn't try to small talk his way around the subject like most. *Maybe working with dead people all the time had dulled his people skills.*

"It's going," was all I could manage. *What else was there to say?* Time didn't stop for grief.

"Death is strange, isn't it?" he mused. "It's the only thing that changes everything yet changes nothing."

"Is that why you work with the dead? Avoiding change, Mr. Deadman?"

A ghost of a smile tipped his lips. "The dead are honest. That's more than I can say for the living." His lip twitched for a second, like the memory poked at something sleeping inside him, and then his cool facade returned. "So, you and the nanny?"

"Stevie," I clipped, further betraying my weakness. *Dammit.* "I take it you heard Reed's comment on the phone earlier."

I turned onto Main Street in Carmel, heading up the road toward the municipal complex that housed the morgue.

"I did," he confirmed. "However, I prefer to see things with my own eyes before making any assessment."

"Well, there was nothing to see."

"If you say so," he drawled low. "You're the behavioral specialist, Roman. You know better than I do."

Was he toying with me? I gritted my teeth. Rorik was so damn reserved, I couldn't fucking tell if he was serious or if there was a shadow of mockery in his reply—like I was blinded to my own reality.

"She's my nanny, and she's too damn young," I practically spat the truth that chastised each and every one of my cells. "It's fifty shades of wrong, so you can save your breath if you're going to try and give me relationship advice."

It was a little harsh, but I was annoyed. Annoyed about my feelings for Stevie and annoyed that everyone around me could see them.

"I'm not," he said flatly. "I know nothing about relationships and even less about good ones. There's only one thing I recognize."

I exhaled through tight teeth as I parked the car out front of the building. Turning, my gaze met Rorik's and immediately, I felt a cold burn. If fire could be freezing, that was what it felt like to share a stare with him.

Of all people, I was qualified to say that Rorik wasn't a psychopath, but damn there were times when his unemotional austerity and almost painful perceptiveness really made me question just what the hell had happened in his past. But I didn't.

Instead, I asked the question he wanted me to. "And what's that?"

His expression was changeless. "Inevitability."

Of course, death was inevitable.

His eyes glinted just before he exited the car though he said nothing more.

But apparently, so was Stevie.

CHAPTER FIFTEEN

Roman

Once I'd finished filling out the necessary chain-of-evidence paperwork, I joined Rorik in the morgue. Carmel's medical examiner had worked with Rorik and Covington before, so all my signatures were just formalities that the FBI and their associates were taking over the case.

I yanked open one of the large metal double doors and found Rorik already hunched over the sheet-clad body. He'd folded the fabric below the victim's neck and his gloved hands examined and confirmed what we both knew to be the truth.

She was the newest victim in our case.

My gut tightened as I approached. She was so young. We'd be so far behind the Archangel on his previous victims that decomposition of the bodies obscured the realness of their features. But not this one. Her death was recent and her features all too real.

Fuck, she couldn't be much older than Stevie.

I tried to shake off the thought, but it was pretty damn hard when the girl on the table even looked similar to Stevie with her dark hair.

"Strangulation." Rorik pointed to the marred flesh of her throat. "And a cross of skin cut from her chest."

"Yeah." *The Archangel had done this.*

Laying a towel over her chest, Rorik folded the sheet lower. He took a probe from the tray beside him, palpated her abdomen for a second, and then inserted it. It beeped a second later and he pulled it out.

His jaw flexed. "Body temp matches the ambient temp which is no surprise, but I always confirm every reading I can when possible," he said and straightened, wiping off the probe and replacing it on the tray.

Walking to the other end of the table, he lifted the sheet from her leg and tried to bend her knee but it didn't move. Then he returned to her head and tried to tip her chin; it moved a little.

"Rigor mortis has reached the larger muscles but has started to disappear from the smaller ones." He pointed to her leg and then her throat respectively. "So, if rigor mortis is fully set in within the first twelve hours and completely gone within thirty-six, my educated estimate is that she's been dead fifteen to twenty-four hours."

"Shit."

A day ago. The vise around my chest tightened. *I knew it.* I knew we were closing in on his trail. He'd been in Monterey a day ago. *He could still fucking be there.*

Locking my teeth, I stalked to the second table that had evidence bags stacked on top of it containing all of the victim's clothes and personal effects. It wasn't much. Her clothes and a messenger bag. The police hadn't gone through anything. As soon as they saw the cut on her chest, they'd called us. But I wasn't expecting to find much.

I peeled open the first bag and dumped the clothes onto the table, grateful that Rorik and I both preferred to work in silence. The ripped blouse had no signs of blood which I expected since the wound to the chest was always postmortem. Next came her jeans. According to the report, the victim had been found with her blouse split and her jeans around her ankles.

Bile rose in my throat.

Shoving everything back in the bag, I turned my attention to the second, larger evidence pouch.

My phone vibrated in my back pocket. Yanking off one glove, I reached for it and answered.

"Yeah, Dex. You're on speaker." I hit the speakerphone button and set my phone on the table.

"I've got an ID on our victim."

"What?" I gaped, gripping the edge of the autopsy table for support. We'd never gotten a match on the runaways so quickly before... *if we got a match on their identity at all.*

I wasn't complaining but *what the fuck?*

"Nancy Jones. Twenty-two years old. Current address listed as an apartment in Monterey."

I replaced my glove and dug through the messenger bag. Notebooks. Textbooks. A planner. *Fuck.* "She was in school," I rasped just as my fingers closed on the thin plastic of her school ID buried at the bottom.

Monterey Community College.

A student just like Stevie. The thought hit me like a sucker punch to the gut and I tipped forward, a low groan tearing through my lips before I managed to swallow it down. *Focus, Knight.* This wasn't about Stevie. This was about a serial killer and his victim, and I owed Nancy the respect of not being preoccupied with my damn nanny at a time like this.

"What the fuck?" I huffed aloud this time, cocking my head to the side. "He's changing his MO again," I rasped low; it wasn't a question to anyone except myself.

Why? Fucking why?

I yanked my glasses off and ran my fingers over my eyes. I was supposed to be the expert. I was supposed to be the one to figure this fucker out.

"I have her transcription for Monterey Community College right here. Sophomore majoring in nursing." There was a small break where I heard him typing and then he spoke again, "Both her parents are dead. No siblings. Got her California driver's license two years ago..." he trailed off suddenly.

My gaze snapped to my phone. "What is it?"

Another pause. "I'm not sure," he said. "I need to look into something. I'll get back to you."

The line went dead.

I looked at the ID again and then pounded my fist on the table. "Shit."

"What does it mean that he changed his MO?" Rorik asked without breaking from his task; he was measuring the size of the markings on her neck and chest.

"Usually it means the killer is devolving. It means his control over himself is diminishing, his methods more erratic, and his attacks more prone to error." I let out a harsh laugh. "It *usually* means I'm getting closer to catching him."

"But this case isn't usual."

"No," I said hoarsely. "No, it's not." I spread my hands over the contents of her school bag again. "The Archangel has too much control to be devolving. He disappeared for a fucking decade; no matter what the reason, no matter he's... changed... since he started killing again... this isn't him devolving."

I took several deep breaths, the face on the ID, the mutilated condition of her body, all of it blurred behind my eyelids.

"Every killer has a pattern that they follow to fulfill their needs," I began slowly. "Even now, he's been killing runaways for seven years—high-risk targets that are difficult for us to identify. But now, he switches to a student? She wasn't high risk and she had her fucking ID on her."

Rorik hummed low. I knew he said nothing because that was how he was. *Silent.* Allowing his subjects to speak to him. But I wasn't going to resent it. I needed a sounding board right now.

"He's working toward something—*searching* for something." I rocked back on my heels when the force of my next thought hit me. "Or someone." *The daughter.*

I hated to walk down a path made of assumptions, but if we were right about why he stopped killing and why he started again, then his victims weren't just young women who resembled the daughter who'd betrayed him. They weren't just young women who ignited his rage when they crossed his path—*they were his path.*

He was fucking searching for his daughter and killing women along the way.

"I need to call Koorie," I declared abruptly, my mind reeling with the possible breakthrough realization. I ripped my gloves off with a loud snap and tossed them in the trash. Grabbing my phone, I headed for the autopsy doors, so my conversation didn't disturb Rorik.

"It's going to take me several hours to document my findings and take photographs, if you need to go," he called after me.

I slowed, considering the offer before quashing it. "No, I'll work from here," I decided resolutely.

I had my iPad with me and there was a desk in the corner of the room that I could work from once I'd finished going through Nancy's belongings. There was nothing that I could or needed to do that couldn't be done from here.

I also didn't trust myself to leave.

When it came to Stevie, my restraint felt like a damn rubber band. Away from her, it was stretched taut—beyond its normal limits. And if given the chance, it would snap right back to its obsessive need to be around her again. So, my plan was to call Koorie and then spend the rest of the day locked up here with Mr. Deadman and the deceased.

THE DOOR SHUT with a soft click behind me, the faint light from the living room reaching its fingers over my shoulder like a warm grasp beckoning me to turn.

It was much later than I'd planned on coming home. Almost ten thirty.

I'd stayed at the morgue with Rorik until he finished late in the afternoon. From there, we returned to Covington headquarters and met back up with the team. Rorik provided Dex with all the findings from the autopsy. Koorie gave me a rundown of the dump site along with a list of businesses she'd requested camera footage from based on Rorik's estimated time of death.

There was a lot of data to go through—to piece together.

I would've stayed all night, but the other guys had their women to get home to. I, on the other hand, had a woman at home that I was trying to avoid.

Dex turned off his screens around six thirty. Ace took Rorik with him back to his place to "discuss business." Having been on the receiving end of Ace's "business discussing," I had a feeling he was trying to recruit the medical examiner to Covington, and I didn't blame him.

That left Koorie and me, and since it had been almost three months since I'd left DC and my protégé, I suggested grabbing a bite to eat at the pub, knowing we'd lose ourselves in a discussion about this case; I could always count on Sally to be a workaholic.

Sure enough. A couple of beers later and we were deep down the rabbit hole of the Archangel and his offspring.

There were a ton of flaws to the hypothesis. Would a teenage runaway have the resources to avoid a man who was a skilled hunter? Would she be able to live off the grid for seven years, so that he couldn't track her? Or, on the flip side, would she have the resources to change her name or minimally get a fake ID?

The theory fit, and then it didn't. It gave me hope and then deflated it. It was as fucking unsteady as my ability to keep myself away from Stevie.

Against my better judgment, I'd texted Reed when I'd left the morgue to make sure Stevie and her car had made it back safely to the house. In response, I'd received a photo of him, Stevie, and Lainey in the back garden; Stevie and Lainey looked like they were hunting for bugs.

Stevie must've picked up Lainey on her way back to the house, and Reed followed them both.

It didn't bother me that Reed was here with them while I wasn't. What bothered me was that it felt like he *should* be the one here with them—*with her.*

"Stevie?" I called softly into the house.

Lainey was asleep for sure by now, and I didn't want to wake her.

No response.

My heart began to pound as a too-familiar fear injected itself into my veins.

She was here.

She had to be here.

I set my keys on the counter and headed for the hall, stopping short when movement in the living room caught my eye. *Stevie.* She was asleep on the couch.

Shit. Instantly, I graduated from biggest asshole on the planet to biggest asshole in the universe.

Damn, she looked so much younger like this. Relaxed. Safe. *Mine.*

"No," I warned myself under my breath and stepped down into the room, prepared to wake her and let her know I was back when she shifted, sighed, and then snuggled deeper into… my pillow.

I groaned. After those couple of nights that she'd stayed in my bed, I hadn't washed that damn pillowcase for a week. Instead, I breathed her in every damn night as I jacked off like a fucking teenager to my fantasies of her.

Inhaling deep, I heard all the warnings go off like sirens blaring in my head… and then I ignored them. She looked so damn peaceful and *sound* asleep. She could say she was doing fine, but the bruised halos under her eyes told me she wasn't sleeping well. So, I couldn't wake her now, not if this was the first good rest she'd had in four days.

After everything she'd been through, I was going to take care of her in the little ways that I could. *Especially since I couldn't take care of her in the fucked-up ways I wanted.*

Walking to the couch, I crouched and peeled the blanket away from her.

Shit.

She only had on a tank top underneath, her damn incredible tits nearly spilling from the top.

Covering her back up with the blanket, I sat back for a second, staring at her face while I decided what I was going to do.

What I *should* do is take her back to the guesthouse. But that was far, at least when it came to not disturbing her sleep. And then to carry her down the stairwell to the bedroom—*no.* She had to stay here.

But I wasn't going to leave her on the couch.

Ah, fuck. I shook my head, swallowing a strained laugh at how much torture I was about to subject myself to—putting Stevie back in my bed and forcing myself to sleep out here knowing she was just down the hall.

Knowing she wanted all my damn broken pieces.

Knowing she wanted me to nanny the fuck out of her.

Gritting my teeth, I carefully wedged my arm underneath her knees and behind her back, sliding her gently off the couch and against my chest.

Thank god she was asleep because if she were awake, she'd hear just how damn hard my heart was beating right now.

When I stood, she let out a small mewl and snuggled closer to me. I waited until she took a deep inhale, thinking she'd settled, when instead she let out an audible soft moan.

"Roman."

How fucking hard was I going to be tempted? I tipped my head back and bit into my tongue until I tasted blood.

Just get her to the bedroom and get out.

I was pretty sure I held my fucking breath for the time it took me to carry her into my room. The bed was unmade, but I took her to the side I didn't sleep on since that part was basically untouched.

Tipping forward, I managed to shove the sheets out of the way and laid Stevie down at the same time, letting out my breath in a whoosh. *There we go.*

She was on her back and more importantly, no longer pressing her soft curves directly to my body. And I could breathe again.

Just a little more... I bit back a grunt as I removed my arm from under her legs, adjusted the blankets around them, and then pressed my palm to the mattress beside her. *Almost there.* Using my left hand as leverage, I started to slide my right arm from under her neck and pull myself away.

I only managed to free my elbow before she rolled toward me, this time, bringing her hand to my chest, tired fingers snagging on my shirt.

"*Roman,*" she murmured again and settled.

She wasn't awake—that was for fucking sure. But was she completely asleep? Did she know I'd carried her? Did she know she was in my bed?

Or was she dreaming of me?
"*Roman,*" she whimpered. "*Please…*"
Need tightened like a corkscrew in my gut.
"Please what, Stevie?" I rasped. *Please get her some water? Another blanket? A pillow? I'd do anything—*
"*Please touch me.*"
"Fuck," I hissed aloud and then whispered, hoping dream Roman conveyed the message, "I can't, Stevie."
"*Please,*" she begged again, a little drowsier this time. But whatever hope I held that she'd drift into a deeper sleep was demolished when her legs started to move—when she started to rub her thighs together.
Fucking fuck.
I thought there was nothing worse than having to walk away from her plea—nothing worse than my hard-on that, at this point, would only be cured by Stevie's cunt or complete castration. But as I knelt there, trapped to her side, I realized the situation *could* be worse if I was forced to watch her as she fucking orgasmed in her sleep. *Because of dream Roman.*
Fuck that.
Fuck him.
If Stevie was going to come in my house, in my bed, with my name on her damn lips, it was going to be because of my very fucking *real* fingers.
Somewhere along the way, I'd made myself responsible for her—all of her. Including every damn orgasm.
"Relax, Stevie," I bent forward and cooed next to her ear.
"Please, Roman, please."
"Shh," I soothed her. "It's okay, princess. I'll take care of you. I'm going to take care of you."
Even if it was at my own expense.
She inhaled unsteadily as I pushed back all the covers from her and let my hand rest first on the outside of her thigh before bringing it to her hip.
There was another small whimper of protest when I flattened that hip to the bed, but it died when my fingers skated back down her leg and wedged between her thighs, pulling higher until her legs were spread and my palm cupped over her pussy.

I groaned. The heat coming from her sex was insane. She must be fucking soaked. *For me.* My dick hardened to granite. Forget stretching my pants to the limit, the damn thing stretched my skin to the very brink of breaking and my mind to the edge of insanity.

"That's it, princess," I coaxed with a low rasp, applying pressure from the meat of my palm against her clit.

She exhaled with such relief, I swore it was like she'd never been taken care of before—sexually or otherwise.

"I'll take care of you, don't worry," I swore, the promise insinuating more than just a damn orgasm in the middle of the night.

Slowly, I began to rock the base of my hand against her, applying steady pressure against her swollen bundle of nerves. I needed to make her come, but I was going to do it without touching her—without breaking the barriers of her clothes.

It started with a small moan. A mewl of pure, innocent pleasure. But as I continued to give her pussy the pressure it craved, her hips began a fervent rock up to meet my palm, aching for more. And then it wasn't just heat against my palm but wet. Slick, warm want began to trickle through the fabric of her shorts and stain my skin.

"Good girl, Stevie," I praised, my mind so damn screwed up with pleasure.

I stared down at her, writhing in my damn sheets. Her hair was loose and strewn across the pillow. Her tank wrenched low on her tits, the shadow of her right nipple peeking above the edge. It would only take seconds to strip her. Seconds to get my mouth on that tit—teeth and lips marking her like a damned savage. My eyes traveled lower, over her stomach, down to my massive hand cupped between her thighs.

She was curvy but small, and her cunt would be small, too. But to see her like this—to see how huge my palm looked—all I could think of was how my fat cock would look clutched in her body. *Probably like I was about to split her in two.*

Air hissed from between my teeth and I clamped my eyes shut. I couldn't keep looking. Not when my dick throbbed like it did. Fuck, I'd never been so hard. Not in all my thirty-seven years of life had I *ever* been so fucking erect. It didn't seem possible, and definitely didn't feel safe. My cock didn't feel like steel in my pants, it felt like lead—heavy and lethal.

Her shorts began to slide with my palm along her cunt, adding another layer of friction to her clit. "God, you're drenched, Stevie. Soaking through your shorts and into my bed." A strangled groan tore from my chest.

"Roman..." She started to arch, and my eyes sprung open just in time to see her tits pushing toward my face.

"Is this what you did last night? Rubbed your pussy like I told you while you thought of me?" I pressed harder against her core and dragged my stare to the rumpled sheets on my side of the bed. "Because that's all I could think of when I climbed into bed last night. All I could think of when I jacked off right there—right fucking next to you."

She bucked against me. Meanwhile, my hips started to move in time with my wrist, pressing my dick against the side of the bed as my palm ground into her sex.

Christ, this was a dangerous game. My jaw muscles were locked so tight I started seeing double from the tension ravaging my body. I let out a low hum when her whole body started to tremble.

"Roman... please..." Her head thrashed side to side and she let out a small cry. "Please, Roman, please..."

"What? Please what?" I pressed harder—faster. Her body was flushed and trembling—it wanted this orgasm as much as I wanted to give it to her, but something was off. *"Tell me."*

Her hand shot up. From my chest to my neck, her nails dug into my skin and pulled me to her.

Fuck. Her eyes were open. *"Touch me."*

There were two things that hit me in equal measure. One, she was definitely awake and we both knew it. And two, I didn't give a single fuck. Her strangled plea killed me—ripped my restraint right from the center of my chivalrous chest.

I was a dead man. A devil for wanting her. *A pirate for taking her —for taking what shouldn't be mine.*

"Fuck, Stevie," I growled, lifting my hand away from her heat. "You want my fingers in your pussy? Is that it?"

Her head bobbed greedily.

"Say it."

"I want your fingers... on me," she panted. "Inside me. Please."

I groaned. I wasn't going to survive this.

Delving my fingers under the side of her shorts, I swore a part of my dick died when they slid into her soaking hot cunt.

"Fuck." It was the only word left in my vocabulary as my fingers delved through her folds. "Is this what you wanted, princess? My fingers on your needy clit? Buried in your little cunt?" I plucked and rolled the sensitive flesh, sending her hips bucking up against my hand. "You're so wet. So fucking wet for me."

Every word made her wetter—brought her higher. And I couldn't stop them. Like a cup tipped over inside my chest, the dirty praise spilled from my lips without restraint.

My fingers slid in and out. Somewhere, I knew I should test her—ease her. But she was too wet, and all I wanted was to keep feeding her more of my fingers and feel her come apart. A hungry growl snaked through my lips when her inner muscles clamped around me.

"Good girl," I coaxed roughly, loving the way her body tightened with each word of praise. "Squeeze my fingers," I ordered. "Make me wet. Make me crazy."

Her pussy tensed and gushed against my hand. My gaze locked on my wrist, watching the tendons flex and fire as I pushed two fingers deep inside her tight cunt.

Her throaty moans were my own brand of praise. Wordless and intoxicating. They drove me beyond my limits. Beyond my sanity. I was going to explode or die or both... but it would be worth it for this. When she'd taken all of my fingers, I ground my palm to her clit once more and savored her sharp gasp of pleasure just before I curled my fingers into her G-spot again, stroking hard until she bucked off the mattress.

"*Roman!*" Stevie gasped my name and a twisted smile of triumph spread over my face.

"You feel that?" I rasped, dragging my fingers over it again. "Answer me," I ordered.

She gasped loudly and garbled, "Y-yes."

"If my dick were buried in here, this is where it would hit." My voice was low—threadbare with lust. "Over and over again."

It would stretch and bend into her muscles, shaping her to only fit me—to only take care of me. And in turn, I would be the only one who could take care of her.

Grunting, I rubbed her G-spot with unrelenting strokes, my eyes screwing tight because I couldn't fucking process anything except how she felt around me.

"I want that. I want you," she begged with a small cry. "Roman, please."

Hearing her beg for me did things to my body that I'd never be able to describe.

"I'd fuck you until you couldn't think, princess. Until you couldn't see or breathe or speak. Until there was nothing left of you but your orgasm and nothing left to do but give it to me."

Her nails scored into the back of my neck, jostling my head in a way that dislodged my glasses. It didn't matter. I didn't need to see.

Her fractured cries grew louder, spiraling like she'd never climaxed before.

Fuck. She was going to scream. I felt it building with every squeeze of her tight cunt. She was going to fucking scream her perfect little head off when she came. And that scream was going to wake Lainey who would then bolt into this room to find me on the verge of fucking her nanny.

But I couldn't stop my fingers. I couldn't stop myself from giving her this. And I couldn't free my other arm from underneath her.

And that left only one other way to silence her.

"Roman... oh god..." She squirmed around my fingers, gasping and panting as her muscles wrenched tighter and tighter. "I need... I'm going to... I need..."

"*Me*," I growled and sealed my lips over hers, plunging my tongue into the very depths of her mouth as I drove my fingers hard into her G-spot.

Sure enough, she came like a fucking hurricane. A torrent of heat and tension along my fingers, waves of pleasure rocking her body, and a riotous cry buried into the depths of my lungs.

Her hips jerked against my hand, coming and coming until my whole palm was covered in her pleasure. White bursts erupted behind my eyelids, my own need threatening to consume me if I didn't do something to alleviate it. But I couldn't. All I could do was drive my cock against the side of the bed and hold on through the storm of her orgasm.

It took several minutes until she finally began to come down —until her breathing began to steady, until the muscles of her cunt fluttered instead of fisted, and until her hand uncurled from the back of my neck. I slowly released her mouth, our breaths colliding as I drew back. My eyes found hers, dark and foggy with exhaustion and release. *There was no pretending now.*

I slid my fingers from her tight clutch, righted her shorts, and buried her back under the covers like I could bury the erotic evidence of what I'd done, though my hands might as well have been stained red with her pleasure.

"Roman," she breathed out.

My throat burned as I swallowed. "Go to sleep," I ordered as though I were telling her to forget this ever happened.

Because that was exactly what I planned on doing.

It was childish and ridiculous, but I had no justification for what I'd done and no footing to stand on if I said it would never happen again.

What the hell was wrong with me? So much for last night being a fucking lesson. *I hadn't learned shit.*

I couldn't touch her. I couldn't take her. I couldn't have her. But none of that mattered now because apparently the only lesson I'd learned was that rules were meant to be broken.

CHAPTER SIXTEEN

Stevie

"She's beautiful," I murmured, staring unabashedly at the perfect round face and plump little cheeks of the baby in my arms.

"The word you are looking for is boisterous. Trust me," Carina joked, delving into the bowl of raspberries in her lap.

I felt a little guilty for it taking so long for me to get over to visit Carina, Rocco, and their newborn baby, Serena, but what could I do? My life was a little bit of a mess right now. Thankfully, Carina was one of the kindest and most understanding people on the planet.

"No," I feigned disbelief. "You're not loud at all—not even a little bit, right, Serena?"

"Just stick around for half an hour when she gets hungry," Carina grumbled. "All hell breaks loose when she wants the boob."

My friend and I both chuckled.

"She gets that from her father," a deep voice rumbled behind me just before Rocco walked into the room. Carina's husband was tall, dark, and bearded—and when it came to his wife, a hot-blooded Italian. His gaze first went to his child as he greeted me, "Hey, Stevie."

"Hey." I could've said anything really because as soon as his eyes hit his wife, it was as though the world fell away for a second and there was only her.

I'd only seen some of the Covington team with their significant others, but that unabashed possessiveness seemed to be a trait they all shared. And it was intense enough to make me catch my breath because it made me think of Roman.

There were times I swore my hot boss looked at me the same way—times like the other night when he held me with his hand buried between my legs. It was a stare that swore to raze the whole world if anything tried to keep him from me. But unlike Rocco, who greeted his wife with a hand cupped around the back of her neck and sealed her to him with a fierce kiss, Roman managed to kiss me… touch me… and then let me go.

There was no earth razing when he was standing in his own way.

"Well, you're right about that," Carina replied cheekily with a coy smile up to her husband.

"That set of lungs though…" Rocco trailed off and shook his head. "That she gets all from you."

"I don't think so. Have you met my sisters? My brother?" She scoffed. "I'm the quietest one."

Rocco's grin tipped deviously to one side. "Not when you scream, *ragazzina.*"

My cheeks flamed with heat. Carina's eyes bugged wide for a moment before she reached for a neighboring pillow and swatted her very large husband on the arm.

"*We. Have. Company,*" she hissed.

"No," he corrected smoothly. "We have Stevie. And if the rumors are true, that's not the most perverse thing she's heard this week."

My head tipped, and I looked at Carina sheepishly. I couldn't argue with that if he was talking about what I thought he was talking about.

"What? What does that mean?" Carina's head whipped in my direction. "What happened?"

I gulped. This wasn't the conversation I planned on having. I *planned* on spending some time with my friend and away from *all* thoughts of Roman. Of what he said. Of what he did. Of how he pretended like none of it happened the following morning… and every subsequent morning through today.

Though I was no better.

Part of me couldn't believe I wasn't dreaming when I woke up in his room, the hand between my thighs feeling all too real. I'd never felt the way he made me feel. It was more than the orgasm. More than the rush. It was the safety to feel. The safety to release. And… it frightened me. I hadn't been willingly vulnerable to someone else since… before I'd left Wyoming.

"Speaking of." Rocco folded his arms. "Did Roman give you the morning off?"

"The whole day," I replied, rubbing the pad of my thumb over Serena's tiny hand where it curled against her chest. "There are parent-teacher conferences at school, so he took Lainey and planned on spending the rest of the day with her."

I knew her silence still ate at him, but Roman had to see how things had improved since they'd first come to Carmel. She might not say words, but she spoke to him in gestures and smiles. Hugs and laughs.

"Ahh." Rocco nodded and then checked his watch. "Got big plans for your day off?"

"Just this. And then maybe the beach for a little."

I hadn't been in so long.

He looked at me strangely—assessing my answer before the professional-like expression disappeared and he said, "Well, I've got to make a diaper run." He bent and pressed another kiss to Carina's head. "When I get back, I'll watch Serena, so you can take a nap."

"Thank you." Carina's eyes practically smoldered, looking at her husband as though he'd just promised her a yacht and a château in the South of France.

"Good seeing you, Stevie. Enjoy the beach."

The alarm beeped when Rocco left the house a few minutes later.

"What happened?" Carina immediately probed.

"It's nothing."

"Don't make me swat you with a pillow, too," she warned

with a glare. When I pulled my lips tight, she added, "Stevie. Please. I've been elevated to the supremely revered position of glorified milking cow for my beautiful daughter whom I love more than anything in the world. However, please don't deny me the excitement of living a little vicariously since I was the one who set you up with Roman."

"What?" I gaped. "You didn't set me up—"

"I got you—"

"An interview. Not a date."

Carina shrugged like there wasn't much difference at this point.

My eyes locked with hers, and I held out for another second before my breath released in a long sigh.

"I was in the car with Roman on Monday. My tire was being fixed, so he took me to the police station to file a report and then on the way to Covington, he called Dex. The call was on speaker, Reed was in the room, and the conversation was a little bit of a blur until Reed accused Roman of wanting to 'nanny the fuck out of me.'" I used air quotes as I spoke.

Carina's jaw dropped. *"Does he?"*

I let the question linger in the air for a few moments, distracting myself with the sleeping baby in my arms.

"Does it matter?" I finally replied, lifting my head up. "He's my boss, Care. And now I'm living in his guesthouse. It's just… complicated."

She gave me a flat stare. "You do know I married my brother's best friend, right? The guy who was disavowed by the CIA and basically left for dead?"

"Yeah." I managed a half smile. But that wasn't the same as the man who hunted serial killers falling for the daughter of one —without even knowing it. "It's just too much. He needs to focus on Lainey… focus on himself right now. Not continue down a path with me."

"Do you believe that?"

My posture stiffened. I kept telling myself that, but it wasn't the same as believing it.

"Something's happened." She squinted, and I felt a blush come on.

"I don't know what you mean."

"I have mom eyes now, Stevie. That means I can tell when you've done something naughty."

I chuckled. "I don't think that's how it works."

"Then tell me I'm wrong." She waited, and I couldn't. "Or tell me what happened."

Sighing, I cupped my palm along Serena's head, covering her tiny ear with my fingers like she could actually understand what I was about to say. And then I delved into what happened at the end of last weekend. First, outside, and then in Roman's bed.

Carina practically squealed when I was done. "Ugh, I'm turning into my sister." She shivered at the horrifying thought and explained, "Juliana is a glutton for rebellious romances. Anyway, so what's happening now? Are you a secret thing?"

I choked. "If we're a thing, it's a secret from me, too."

"Ugh. Men." She shook her head. "They're so stubborn."

"No, it's better this way," I assured her.

She didn't look convinced. "Well, I don't believe you, which is why I'm going to give you some advice from my sister," she declared. "Sometimes, all men need to get their head on straight is a little competition. So, if you want to know whether or not you are *a thing*, it sounds like Reed wouldn't mind a little harmless flirting."

"I'm not interested in Reed." Though it would be a lot easier if I were.

"Roman doesn't need to know that," she murmured slyly and winked.

THE SAND WAS cold under my bare feet but it felt good. Refreshing.

I tugged my sweater tighter over my chest and meandered toward the water's edge. This stretch of beach was basically empty which made sense since it was the middle of a Friday afternoon in November.

The water stretched over my toes and then retreated. Ebb and flow. The way Roman wanted me was the same. Ebb and flow. And I was the cliff he beat against, trying to remain unchanged by the way he crashed into me—trying to pretend like it didn't erode my own barrier and reservations.

I checked my watch. It was almost four. Roman and Lainey would be back at the house soon, and since Roman had taken the day off for the parent-teacher conference, I wanted to be there to watch Lainey in case he had work he needed to do.

Retreating from the shore, I pulled my sweater tighter across my front and then watched my feet press into the sand and leave behind a mark that I'd been here.

Maybe that's what I'd been feeling ever since I got a glimpse behind Roman's armor—that his jagged edges had pressed into the deepest parts of me and left behind their own trail. One that had me returning to him.

Sand crusted my feet by the time I made it back to the parking lot. Sighing, I pulled my sweater sleeves over my hand and used it to brush off as much as possible so I wouldn't make my sneakers too sandy. Sliding on my shoes, I straightened and stopped short—a familiar face grinning at me from beside his motorcycle.

"Reed," I blurted out and walked quickly over to him. "Is everything okay with Roman?"

"Perfectly fine as far as I know." He paused and corrected himself. "Well, not perfectly… but I'm going to continue to keep my mouth shut about that before I talk myself into another hole."

I hummed. "Thinking before acting. A novelty," I teased gently. He'd already apologized around a thousand times since the speakerphone incident even though I told him it was fine.

"For me? Yeah." He chuckled.

"What are you doing here?" I probed and then had a thought that sank like a stone in my stomach. "Did he send you?"

If this was how Roman was going to continue avoiding me, we were going to have to talk.

"Roman? No. Rocco did," he revealed.

Carina.

"After what happened, everyone is a little worried about you." He sighed. "Roc said you were headed to the beach alone and asked if I could swing by and make sure you were okay."

I sighed, grateful for my friend's involvement in my life but fully aware that this move wasn't entirely altruistic.

"Well, here I am. Sandy but safe." I flapped my arms out and then let them fall to my sides.

"I have something for you," he revealed with that dimpled half smile that made him an internet sensation.

When Reed had taken me to pick up my car the other day, he'd gone on about his former life before moving to Carmel. He'd interpreted my silence as anger because of the comment he'd made, but that wasn't it at all. I was quiet because I was shocked at how Roman had passed me off with such casual ease. However, Reed's charming personality was an easy and vibrant distraction. And so was his story about how he became San Francisco's Hot Cop.

"For me?"

He nodded and then flipped open the seat of his bike and pulled out something wrapped in a black pouch.

"This way," he said and headed for my car.

"This isn't a drug deal, is it?" I asked from behind, partially joking though that was kind of what it felt like.

Reed tossed back his head and laughed. "No, but if you want some weed, I have some of that."

"I'm fine, thank you." Even though alcohol and marijuana were both legal in California, I had a lot of good reasons for why I avoided any kind of… altering… substances. How I'd been raised. The job I wanted to do. But the real reason was fear. Because at the end of the day, I wasn't part Mom and part Dad. I was part Mom and part serial killer.

I unlocked my car when Reed approached the passenger side and opened the door. Only then did he hold out his palm and pull back the covering.

"You're giving me a gun?" I balked, staring at the handgun underneath.

"Look, we all want you to feel safe."

"But I'm not Ubering anymore," I blurted out.

"Right, but you're going to school. At some point, you'll have your own place..." Whatever he said after that faded for a second.

My own place. Because my job with Roman would be over. Even if I finished my degree mostly online, then it would be time for me to get a *real* job. And Roman would let me. In fact, I had a feeling he'd somehow manage to get me my dream job—which was ironically teaching at a school like Lainey's—and he'd do it without a second thought.

"Just keep it in your glove box in case of an emergency." He reached inside and popped open the compartment. Then he pointed to the gun. "Safety and trigger. Hold the safety down to be able to fire."

I swallowed hard and stared. A week and a half ago, I never would've accepted a weapon. Weapons made me think of killing, and killing made me think of Lee—

"I don't have a license."

"You will," he replied. "I'm having Dex apply for one for you since you reported the assault to the police."

Apply. License. Goodness, were all of Roman's coworkers this protective?

I felt hot. Really hot. And not the good kind. Not the kind I felt when Roman was close—when he touched me. This was the panic kind of hot.

"But I don't want to hurt anyone," I protested weakly, feeling myself start to sway as my head began shaking, slow at first and then more wildly.

"Stevie." Reed set the gun on the seat and grabbed my shoulders, steadying me. "Having a gun doesn't mean you want to hurt someone. All of us carry weapons. The police carry weapons. Do you think all we want to do is hurt people?"

I hesitated. "No."

But none of you have sick genes.

"Look, you don't have to take it if you really don't want to, but I..." He exhaled loudly. "I know Roman would feel better about you having it."

His words gave me pause.

"You were in his car the other night by the time I got there, but when I pulled him off of the guy assaulting you—I didn't think I was going to be able to stop him the way he looked—" he broke off and dipped his chin for a second. "I'm not afraid of a lot of things, Stevie, but damn if that look didn't stop me cold." He gulped. "That look is... why I said what I said. Because I could see he would do *anything* to protect you."

Anything. *For me.*

"Okay." I heard myself say.

He sighed in relief and then reached for the gun again, about to place it in the compartment when I stopped him.

"But I don't want it in there like that..." *Exposed.* I glanced around for something to wrap it in.

"I can get you a holster for it—"

"Just use this." I took off my sweater, shook out the sand, and shoved it toward him.

"You sure?"

"It's dirty anyway." I shivered as he wrapped it and set it inside the otherwise empty glove box.

"Fine, but then you're borrowing this," he said and flapped open the long-sleeve T-shirt that he'd had the gun wrapped in.

"For what?" I stepped back.

"Because it's cold out here and you just used your sweater."

Except I was only getting in my car and driving back to the house, but at this point, I was sure Reed had a quick response for that, too. *These Covington men.*

With a sigh, I took the shirt and held it up in front of me. "Armorous?"

"Armorous Tactical," he explained as I put it on over my tank. "An elite tactical training facility in the San Francisco area. The owner, Hazard, is good friends with Ace, but they train a lot of police and private security."

I slid into the driver's seat and then rolled up the sleeves that were about half a mile too long.

"Thanks." I looked up at him.

"Oh, I'm following you back to Roman's," he said with a wink and then closed the door.

Of course he was.

The loud rip of his motorcycle trailed me all the way back to the house. I was hardly in the driveway before I saw the front door open and Roman stepped out onto the stoop, watching as I parked and Reed made a circle around my car.

Reed stopped next to me when I got out of the car. He flipped up his visor and looked at the darkening sky. Thunder rumbled in the distance.

"I was going to stay for a minute, but sounds like I've got to jet before the rain starts."

I didn't realize they were calling for storms tonight either.

"Thanks," I murmured.

"Don't take it too easy on him," he drawled and nodded to Roman whose gaze I felt grinding into my back. "Sometimes stupidity tries to disguise itself as stubbornness."

I chuckled and shook my head, and I swore I heard a growl make its way over to me.

"See you around, Stevie." The wide white flash of Reed's smile appeared effortlessly for a moment before he flipped the visor back down, revved his bike, and then shot off down the driveway.

He was a hot cop alright. It was an objective assessment. Like looking at a candle and claiming the flame was warm. *But as far as being attracted to him?* Well, that would be like only having that candle for warmth in the dead of winter. And Roman... he was the equivalent of a volcano. Silent and dormant for stretches of time. But when he did open up, the kind of heat that erupted from him was all-consuming.

I grabbed my bag and rounded my car.

"What were you doing with Reed?"

His harsh question slowed my pace. Roman stood barefoot on the stoop. He had on those gray sweatpants and a plain white tee that stretched across his shoulders, straining because he'd folded his arms.

I furrowed my brow. "I was at the beach, and he showed up," I explained, wondering why he was upset when he was the one who always wanted someone around me. *This couldn't be what Carina was hoping for, could it?* "How was the conference? How's Lainey?"

"Fine. Good," he clipped. "She's doing well in school, so I told her we could celebrate with a pizza and movie night."

"Oh, good." I smiled.

"How did Reed know you were at the beach?" He reached up and bumped his glasses higher on his nose. I'd come to realize it was his tic to keep himself under control.

I shrugged. "Does it matter?" And that was the point. "Do you want me to sit with Lainey for a little so you can work?"

"No—"

"Okay," I replied, cutting him off and heading for the garden gate. "Well, then I'm going to get a jump on some schoolwork. Let me know if you need—"

"How did he—" He stopped himself, his dark eyes narrowing on my chest—*on my shirt.* "Whose shirt is that?" The low rumble of his question was more menacing than the tumble of thunder that followed it.

A storm was brewing. Above us. *Between us.*

I gulped and then lifted my chin. "Reed's."

"Why the *hell* are you wearing Reed's shirt?" he practically snarled.

My lips popped open, about to just tell him the whole story, but then Reed's words came to my mind. *Sometimes stupidity tries to disguise itself as stubbornness.* I drew my lips back together, straightening my spine like it was coated in steel.

I was tired of the ebb and flow. I was tired of having to tie the hope I had to the weight in my chest and watch it sink. I shouldn't want this man—*shouldn't want my boss.* But I did. And if I couldn't have him, fine; it was probably for the best, and I would find a way to survive. And if I could have him, I'd find a way to survive that, too. But what I wouldn't survive was this slow and steady erosion.

"Stevie." He advanced a step, sending a wave of powerful heat through me. "What were the two of you doing at the beach?"

Roman looked like he was about to explode. He was breathing heavily—smoke practically fuming from his nostrils. His eyes were dark and electric—twin live wires just waiting to set something aflame.

And, god help me, I liked it. I liked when his emotions broke through his wall even when those emotions were anger and jealousy rolled into the perfect storm. I liked it because it fed the little balloon of hope in my chest.

"Why the *hell* is it any of your business?" I mimicked him, tasting the bitterness on my tongue that had been building. "I'm just your nanny, remember? You're the one who set the boundaries. You can't just choose to cross them whenever *you* want. They aren't a dotted yellow line that you can veer through but I can't."

"Dammit, Stevie—" He dragged his palm over his mouth like he was having to use his hands to hold back the things he really wanted to say.

Well, he could do that if he wanted, but I had no reservations.

"I'm either the nanny or I'm not. I'm either a lesson you've learned or a rule you're going to break," I declared firmly, eyeing the wooden door to the garden and my escape path. "And if I'm the nanny, then what I do—who I see—on my day off is none of your business, especially when it's a man you know, work with, and trust."

His lip curled at the last, unsure if he really trusted Reed anymore.

"*Everything* about you is my—" Roman started to roar before a high-pitched voice interrupted.

"Stevie!" Lainey exclaimed, startling us both as she barreled through the front door and straight into my legs.

Roman told me about how she said my name to him the night I'd been attacked. It was now the only word she'd say out loud in front of him, but it was a word, and it was more than before.

"Well, hello there." My heart squeezed as I bent to hug her. The sound of our rising voices must have topped the movie and brought her out here. "I heard you had a good day."

Her chin bobbed. A glance at Roman revealed his deep scowl, his fingers stretching because he wasn't done with our conversation, but I was.

Lainey motioned me lower so she could whisper in my ear. "Do you want to eat pizza and watch a movie with us?" She didn't whisper as quietly anymore, so I knew Roman heard what she said.

My stomach grumbled. *Crap.* "I'll take some pizza, but I can't stay for a movie tonight. I'm sorry," I apologized with a sad smile. "I have homework I have to do." *And a guardian to avoid.*

She pouted, but got over it a second later, taking my hand and dragging me into the house.

Roman fumed. His furious stare followed me like a thundercloud, booming when I couldn't see it and flashing when our eyes connected. Lainey made me a plate of no less than eight slices of pizza with a giant smile on her face.

"Stevie..."

I trembled hearing my name, the courage I'd had outside leaching from my skin like it was a sieve.

"Thanks, Lainey." I beamed and took her hand with my free one, my dinner plate in my other hand. "Can you open the back door for me?"

It was a cheap shot—making her my willing escort to the back door, so that Roman wouldn't press. But I panicked.

"I'll see you tomorrow," I told her even though tomorrow was Saturday. I still always saw her on the weekends, and I had zero complaints about it.

She wasn't just a job to me. And unfortunately, neither was her guardian.

She opened the door, and I slipped through it with a little wave goodbye and without looking at Roman again. When the latch clicked into place, I exhaled the breath held hostage in my lungs and power walked to the guesthouse.

He watched me the entire way, but I knew he wouldn't follow me. Not when he was spending the night watching movies with Lainey. His relationship with her was too precious and too fragile for him to risk any damage to it by coming after me to finish our argument.

Maybe some time and a few Disney princess movies would make him realize there was nothing to finish; it would give him time to remember that I was the nanny, and he was exactly right to stay within his own limits.

CHAPTER SEVENTEEN

Roman

Until tonight, I believed it was either genes or environment or a combination of both that created a psychopath. Now, I decisively added jealousy to that list.

Watching Stevie walk away from my house, knowing she'd spent the afternoon with Reed at the beach, and came home with his shirt—*Fuck.* There was only one goddamn reason a woman returned anywhere wearing a shirt of Reed's. And it made me lose my mind.

The line I'd been treading so closely, determined not to cross it, disappeared into my rearview in that moment. All the things obscuring my vision evaporated and left only her—like the sun from behind a lifetime of clouds.

Like sand in an hourglass, my sanity bled out second by second as I sat on the couch and watched every *Ice Age* movie known to man. *Since when were there so fucking many of them?* Part of me laughed with Lainey at Sid and Scratch and the whole damn gang. But the other, primal part of me counted down like a predator waiting for nightfall to go hunt my prey.

The bathroom door opened and Lainey appeared.

"Washed your hands?" I asked and she nodded. "Brushed your teeth?"

She bared them and nodded again.

"Alright then, to bed you go." I ushered Lainey from the bathroom to her bedroom and watched her climb into bed.

Thunder boomed outside, but she didn't even flinch. I had no idea how the hell Val managed to raise a kid that wasn't afraid of thunderstorms, but if anyone could do it, my sister could.

Crouching by her side, I pulled the blankets up to her chin and brushed her hair back from her face.

"I'm going to go check on Stevie in the fairy castle, alright?" I rasped.

I felt guilty leaving her even though I was just going next door and she was going to bed. In the weeks we'd been here, she'd never come out of her room overnight. Not once. Still, on the off chance that tonight was the night she did, I wanted her to know where I was. *Even if I had cameras on every inch of the property and house and would arm the security system as soon as I stepped outside.*

Her little head bobbed rapidly.

Of course, it was okay. My niece would do anything for her nanny. *And apparently so would I.*

"You okay?" I swallowed, feeling my throat tighten.

Lainey smiled small, but it was when she whispered "Yeah" that my throat opened up and air released in a whoosh.

I gritted my teeth before I broke down in tears from a single damn word, and bent forward and kissed her head. *Damn emotions.* But I couldn't reel them back in now even if I wanted to. And I didn't.

"Good night, Bug. I love you."

I shut her door with a soft click, and that was it. That was the end.

The end of the man I was. The end of the man I'd tried to be. The end of every version of me that thought I could keep myself from Stevie.

One minute, I was standing in front of Lainey's bedroom door and the next, I was at the front door of the guesthouse, my clothes drenched from the rain, and banging so hard the raindrops bounced off the panel like they were jumping ship.

"Oh my—Roman." Stevie whipped the door open in a tank and those little shorts I knew she slept in. She smacked her hand to her sternum, chest heaving, and looked at me with panic. "Is everything okay—"

"*No.*" Growling, I grasped her face in both my hands and cut her off with a hard kiss.

There was no more line. No more anything between us.

She gasped, and I took that, too, spearing my tongue deep into her warmth and lashing it against hers. The way I kissed her was punishment and possession. It was a week of frustration steeped in a lifetime of longing for the kinds of things only she'd made me feel.

For long minutes, I consumed her mouth while standing in the open doorway. The wind gusted cold rain against my back. Thunder shook the ground under my feet. But none of it undid me like the taste of her.

"What are you doing?" She panted when I finally dragged my mouth from hers.

I stroked my thumbs over the blushed swells of her cheeks, a haze of lust glazing her luminous eyes.

"Making it clear that there's no more fucking line," I rasped low, sliding one hand down to her throat. Her eyes widened when I applied pressure and tipped her head up. "I've learned my lesson, Stevie. I've learned I can't resist you, and I'm tired of trying."

"Roman…" She swayed into me.

A shudder racked my body as I took her lips again, kissing her deeply until I felt her hands curl into my wet shirt.

"Do you understand?" I demanded, biting on her lower lip and sucking on it until she gasped. "Do you understand there's no more line?"

"Yes." She angled for another kiss, but I held back.

"Good girl," I ground out and then backed her into the guesthouse, kicking the door shut behind me. "Now tell me what the fuck happened today with Reed."

Her eyes popped wide and she shook out of my hold. "Is that why you're here?" A wounded look came over her beautiful face. "Just so you can have answers?"

I chuckled low and advanced on her like a predator following its prey. *Or a pirate chasing down his princess.* She crossed her arms and backpedaled into the small living room where there was only one lamp turned on, a pile of empty Hershey's Kisses wrappers collected under the base. If I had to take an educated guess, she'd only turned the lamp on when I knocked; I had a feeling she'd been sitting in the dark, eating chocolate, and watching the storm strike out over the ocean.

"If I just wanted answers, princess, I would've demanded them from Reed," I said as I stopped and towered over her. "I'm here because I'm going to have you—because you're mine. But before I do, I need to know if I'm going to have to kill my coworker for touching you."

"No!" She gasped and whipped her head side to side. "He didn't—nothing happened."

I reached up and placed my palm over her heart, feeling it thud wildly into my hand. My jaw tensed and released as I stared down the valley of her tits before my gaze traveled to their hard peaks. She was ready for bed so she wasn't wearing a bra; her nipples pebbled into the fabric that was damp from where she'd brushed against me.

All I wanted was to drop my hand—to let my fingers catch on the edge of her tank, drag it down, and free her lush breasts. I swallowed a groan, my cock straining painfully to be set free. Sweats weren't meant to be rigid or confining, but when my dick was as hard as it was, everything except her sweet cunt was a cage.

Growling low, I slid my grip up to her throat again. It was a grip of dominance—of possession. And she didn't fight it. No protest. Not even a tremble of uncertainty. And that display of utter trust was the most erotic thing she'd ever done.

"Tell me, Stevie." I dipped my head back down and nuzzled my nose to hers. "Tell me, please."

The little noise she released made my dick throb with ache. "I went to the beach after visiting Carina, and she was worried I was going alone, so she asked Rocco to have Reed check on me."

"And the shirt?" I bit out through locked teeth, the caress of her pulse against my hand driving me wild.

"He gave me a gun to keep in my car," she murmured, every

unsteady breath dragging her tits to meet my chest. "I didn't want it... visible. So, I used my sweater to wrap it. Then he insisted I borrow his shirt because it was cold and told me he was going to follow me back here."

Fucker.

That wasn't why he'd given Stevie his shirt—*this was.* To fuck with me. But I'd deal with my meddling teammate later.

"Were you jealous?" she murmured huskily when I didn't say anything more.

But it wasn't a question. It was foreplay.

"No." I felt her quick intake of breath. "Jealous isn't a strong enough word for what I was."

"*Roman...*" She shivered as I dragged my teeth along her jawline, bringing my lips close to hers but without kissing her.

"Tell me what you want, princess." My mouth hovered over hers, our breaths sparring in the slim space. "Tell me."

Her tongue slid out, grazing my lower lip as it moved to wet hers. *Fuck.* My dick jolted painfully.

"You, Roman," she pleaded and planted her palms against my chest. "I want you to nanny the fuck out of me."

Jesus fucking Christ.

"God, yes." And then my mouth took hers in a rough kiss— one I had no intention of stopping this time.

Teeth and lips and tongue moved in a brutal symphony of want. Like a starving beast given its run of the most forbidden feast. She tasted like chocolate and a kind of sweetness that only comes from innocence, but even that couldn't change the demands of my kiss.

My tongue moved in powerful strokes through the honeyed depths of her mouth, reveling in the way she tried to keep up with its ravenous movement. She'd curled her hands into my shirt and flattened herself to me—needing more of the desire that was already drowning her.

My free hand that at some point cupped her waist, slid around to her ass, filling my palm with the soft flesh and dragging her hips hard against mine. And then I lifted her with just one arm. Her legs immediately locked around my waist, and her mouth opened with a gasp.

I buried my tongue deep as I carried her across the living room until her back was pinned to the glass.

"You've no idea how you torture me, Stevie." My voice was hoarse as I ducked my head and sank my teeth into her neck, growling low as my hips began to grind against hers. I couldn't stop them. Her mouth, her tits, her ass—she was so damn soft everywhere, but especially the part of her pinned against my cock.

I licked over the flutter of her pulse, and she let out a small mewl of pleasure. *Fuck.*

"So good. So responsive," I rasped and then sealed my lips back over the velvet skin of her neck and sucked.

She moaned, so I sucked harder. And back and forth we went until the hickey I gave her was sure to last for months.

She wriggled, and at first, I thought she was trying to get out of my hold, but then realized she only wanted my shirt off. Growling, I released her and yanked off my wet tee, tossing it to the floor.

My chest heaved from wanting her so fucking bad. I'd never wanted someone like this. More than food or oxygen or life itself. If I had... my life wouldn't have turned out—*I wouldn't have turned out the way I did.*

Stevie fingered the hem of her shirt, about to mimic my action, when my growl of warning came a second before I took her wrist with one hand and pinned it to the window, my other hand fisting into the fabric on her stomach. With one quick tug, I pulled her tank off with one hand.

My jaw latched tight as her tits popped free, their cherry peaks giving the same kind of warning as holly berries: *one taste would be my undoing.*

I cupped my hands over each weight. "Jesus, Stevie." I groaned.

Her breasts were so damn full for someone with her stature. They spilled from between my fingers, and made my palms work to knead all of them.

"Roman." She moaned loudly when I plucked at her cherry nipples.

"Fuck." I dropped to my knees in front of her and latched

my mouth over one peak, drawing the sensitive bud deep into my mouth.

I sucked on her like she was oxygen, and after weeks of holding my breath, I was finally taking her in. Her mewls of pleasure were exquisite—innocence made audible—and I couldn't go soft or slow. I devoured every inch of her tit with my mouth, my hand toying with the other, until she began to shake. I bit and sucked, flicked and laved like I'd never get enough.

"Please, Roman…" she begged.

Her fingers found their way to my head, clutching me like I was the life raft in the storm. I sensed the way she squeezed her thighs together, trying to ease their ache.

I let her nipple pop free, memorizing the sight of the wet, ruddy peak before I tilted my head up.

"Look at me, Stevie," I ordered.

With intoxicated-like movements, her gaze floated to mine.

I took my hand and wedged it between her thighs, dragging it up roughly to split them open. "I'm the only one who eases this ache. Do you understand?" I cupped her pussy.

Her lips peeled apart. "Yes."

"That's what it means to nanny the fuck out of you," I growled. "To fucking take care of your *every* need." I pressed the heel of my palm against her clit and she jerked against me, crying out with pleasure.

It was a mistake. I should've kept my hands on her tits—my attention on those perfect nipples that were begging for my mouth to abuse them. But I didn't, and now all I could feel was the heat of her cunt—the way she'd drenched through her sleep shorts from wanting me.

"Fuck. You're soaked, princess." I swallowed my groan, but it burned my throat like alcohol the whole way down.

Growling, I pressed my mouth to her other breast, taking her nipple between my teeth hard enough to force her to tip forward while I found the waist of her shorts and shoved them off her with violent eagerness; next time, I'd rip them. *As if she didn't already know I'd destroy anything that I didn't like touching her.*

Finding the back of her knee, I lifted one leg up onto my shoulder, resting it there as I allowed my mouth to drift lower.

First, over the curved flesh of her stomach, my tongue dipping into her navel.

She might be sixteen years my junior, but her curves were just as mature as her mind though other parts of her were as equally innocent.

Thank fuck I was already on my knees because my vision blurred as my mouth made a sloppy path toward her cunt, everything about her drugging me.

"Roman…" She trembled when my mouth was level with her pussy.

"You're perfect," I promised her, staring at her slick, pink folds and the swollen bud peeking through them. "So fucking perfect."

I inhaled deep, succumbing to her scent as I flattened my tongue against her slit, dragging it through her folds firmly until I reached her clit.

"Oh my god," she cried out and her other leg buckled.

"You taste so damn good." I quickly lifted that leg over my other shoulder and covered her with my mouth. I didn't need air—I didn't need anything except for more of her, so I took it. I ate hungrily at her cunt until I forgot about everything else except the sounds she made when I pleasured her; they were like sex to my ears.

Outside, the storm raged, thunder shaking everything around us, but I swore it was only Stevie that shook the foundation of the guesthouse. Her hips knocked against the window and then rocked toward my mouth. Her head rolled against the glass, the fingers of one hand digging into my scalp, the other palm flattened and smacking against the window.

"I can't—oh god," she panted, her thighs tightening around my neck. "Oh god, oh god…"

Her head thrashed back and forth against the window, hard enough to make me concerned she'd end up with a lump tomorrow. But I couldn't stop. I lapped along her cunt, drinking every ounce of desire I could find, and then set my tongue on her clit, screwing it into the sensitive bundle without remorse.

"You're going to come for my tongue like a good girl," I hum low, scoring her clit with my teeth. "Only good girls get my cock."

God, the way I spoke to her should make her angry—should make me sick, especially given our age difference. But it didn't. I was desperate to be trusted and she was desperate to be taken care of, and somehow, it made us perfect together.

It let us completely unfold.

"I'll be good—I'm good..." she trailed off with a cry that turned into a moan when I pushed two fingers inside her.

God, she was even tighter than before. Hotter. Sweeter.

My dick was on fire. The damn thing pumped like pure fucking magma flowed through my veins.

"Come for me, princess," I growled like it was an order she had no option but to obey.

And she did. *Exquisitely.*

I curled my fingers against her front wall, hitting her G-spot with deadly accuracy at the same time as I sucked on her clit. Truthfully, it was a cruel thing to do to a virgin. It didn't matter if she'd orgasmed or how she'd orgasmed before, to hit both spots at the same time to send her over the edge was like packing dynamite around a nuclear warhead: unnecessary and excessive.

But I wanted to break every inch of her. I wanted to watch her crumble for me—disintegrate from pleasure so that I wouldn't feel like such a broken bastard for taking her.

And she did. She broke so damn beautifully I could've cried.

Stevie screamed as her orgasm ripped through her, her hips jerking against my mouth as a rush of moisture coated my tongue.

"So fucking beautiful," I groaned, kissing just above her pussy and then higher on her stomach.

"I need you, Roman," she whispered, knowing just what to say to undo me—to remind me just how fucking badly I'm tethered to my need to consume her.

"Does your little cunt want my cock? After all that?" I growl, carefully sliding her one leg and then the other from off my shoulders.

Her head bobbed. "Yes."

I straightened in front of her and took a half step back. "Then take it out."

Her eyes snapped to mine—a split second of surprise before she scrambled for the waist of my pants, the material still damp from the rain. I couldn't stop my hands from reaching for her tits while she fumbled with my sweats for an instant before she worked the fabric over my massive length.

Here, it was different.

When we were outside, it was only the moon and the damn fireflies lighting us, but in here, even with only the single lamp on in the room, her arms dropped to her sides and her eyes grew round.

Maybe I was bigger tonight. Maybe all this wanting her grew like a cancer in my cock, engorging and distending it beyond what was normal. But there was no going back. Reaching down, I fisted the thick girth and dragged my hands all the way to the meaty red tip, pulling a drop of precum from the small slit.

Jesus.

My hands snapped out and caught her arms before she could drop to her knees.

"If you put your mouth on me, princess, I won't make it to your pretty pussy," I warned. "And fuck, do I need to make it there."

She was innocent but uninhibited, and it was the most intoxicating combination I'd ever experienced.

Her throat bobbed and then she nodded.

"Good girl," I rasped, inching her back against the windows, noticing for the first time how the rain splattered against the other side of the glass like even nature was locked in our tense turmoil.

Stabilizing her by the waist, I found her shadowed gaze.

"Are you a virgin?"

The red in her cheeks intensified—an answer if I ever saw one.

I took her throat in my grip once more, feeling her very life in my hands. Stevie tipped her head back ever so slightly, an erotic display of vulnerability, and then rolled her lower lip between her teeth. I wanted to tell her her virginity didn't make a difference now. I was too far gone—my dick too far gone for this night to end any other way except with me buried inside her. But I didn't because I wanted to hear her answer me.

"Yes," she replied throatily.

"Good girl." I kissed her again.

I didn't know how I would feel if she'd been with someone before. I wouldn't—couldn't hold it against her; she was an adult. But at the same time, neither could I imagine it. From the moment I met her, something in me had claimed her as mine, and that meant my cock being the only one inside her.

And that led me to my next confession.

"Stevie, do you trust me?" I asked with a low rasp and then gritted my teeth.

She swallowed and nodded. "Of course."

"I've never done this unprotected before, but I swear I'm clean." I paused, waiting until her eyes focused before I dropped the real bomb. "And I had a vasectomy six years ago."

Her hooded gaze widened. It was enough of a surprise to inject a dose of reality through the haze of desire. There were a million questions to be asked—to be answered. But not tonight. Not now.

Now, the only thing that mattered was her knowing I was going to come inside her but wouldn't get her pregnant.

I grabbed her chin between my thumb and forefinger.

"If I'm going to take your virginity, I'm going to do it bare," I rasped. "If I'm going to break you, I want your blood smeared all over my cock and your cunt filled with my cum."

"Oh, yes, Roman," she whimpered, her eyelids falling shut. "Please, yes."

A sense of pure power jolted my dick like lightning.

I jostled her chin. "Tell me you trust me."

Her eyes fluttered open. "I trust you," she swore with the sweetest innocence.

A mistake, maybe. Maybe in the morning. Maybe in the light. But tonight, the words brought me back to life. My head angled to the side, a ripple of tension running through me like she'd freed something that had been caged.

With one swift motion, I lifted her back up, this time

wrapping her legs around my waist so my cock notched at her entrance. Air hissed from between my lips as I rocked my hips, dragging my blunt tip along the seam of her folds until I was so fucking wet with her desire, even breathing could send me slipping inside.

"You're so wet for me, princess," I praised, pain and pleasure forming knots inside my body. "You came like such a good girl to make yourself so hot and slick for my cock."

"Yes," she purred, urging me on.

My hand cupped her jaw, forcing her eyes to mine. "I need to fuck you now," I rasped. I felt the air rush past her lips—felt time fucking stop for this. *For us.* "Hold on."

Her ankles locked around my back, her implicit trust baked into every movement.

"Good girl."

I shoved my hips forward, impaling myself into her soaked center with a roar of pleasure from my chest that shook the thunder into retreat. In the midst of it all, I heard Stevie's small cry of pain, but I couldn't stop until I sank completely into her tight heaven.

It was... obliterating. The spread and cinch of her uncharted muscles. The ripple of resistance before it was gone. The consuming heat locked inside her.

She felt like heaven on fire around my cock.

Dragging in choppy breaths, I searched for her eyes. I scoured her face—a sight I wanted burned into memories that even age couldn't erase. The flutter of her eyelids wide, the peeled part of her lips, the sensations of shock and pleasure and pain all muddled together when my fat cock invaded her body. But it was the way her irises darkened—clouded with a craving for more that unfolded me.

"I promise I'll make it better," I swore from between tight teeth.

Sliding my hips back, my gaze snapped to where we were joined. Her puffy pink folds were spread wide around me—split apart to fit my girth. And my cock, a fucking monster wrapped in angry pulsing veins, was streaked with red—marked with her blood.

Fuck. A groan split from deep in my chest.

It was the most possessively erotic thing I'd ever seen. Proof that my body had taken something that no one had before. *Proof that she'd given me something I didn't fucking deserve.*

I'd never been with a virgin before. Too complicated. Too many expectations I knew I couldn't meet. But Stevie... I wanted every hurdle. I wanted every hard thing that should keep me away from her because it made taking her all the more consuming.

"Breathe," I ordered, and she immediately complied. "Good girl." I rewarded her with a long, slow kiss, teasing the tension from her body.

I kept kissing her and began moving in steady strokes. There was no stopping; she felt too good.

"I can't stop fucking you, Stevie," I groaned, shunting my cock deep and feeling the pleasure of it rip the very blood from my veins. "You feel so fucking incredible."

Her small gasps turned into moans of pleasure, and it wasn't long before her nails dug into my back, clinging to me, pushing her hips to meet mine, as I slammed into her even harder.

"This what you wanted, princess?" I growled, my forehead dipping to hers as I thrust my cock all the way inside her until I felt her womb. Her muscles rippled and a tiny mewl escaped her mouth. "All the times you touched yourself... the time you begged me to touch you... this was what you were begging for."

"Roman..." she moaned, her head angling back into the window with nowhere to go. "I feel... I can't..."

I drove inside her again, the window rattling. I knew the glass was bulletproof, so it better be fuck proof, too, because I wasn't moving her. The way I wanted her was savage and uncontrollable—a goddamn force of nature. So the storm raging outside could watch us—could feel the crash of my hips into hers, could hear the rumbles of my need and see the way pleasure arced through her lighting up every cell.

My lip curled. "You feel me all the way inside you—feel that curve in my dick hitting your sweet spot?"

She whimpered, her hands on my shoulders digging her nails into my skin, a painful plea for more.

Screwing my eyes tight, I fucked her without control. Harder. Faster. Again. Again. Again.

Each time, my tip stroked over her G-spot demanding more pleasure from the tiny bundle of nerves.

"God, you feel so fucking good. Like heaven." I couldn't fucking breathe, she felt so damn tight around me. "I could live in your perfect cunt. Fuck you forever."

My hips smacked into hers, the sound echoing through the room. It was impossible to not move faster. She was so damn wet, every time I pulled out, her heat slid me back in deep.

Her head dropped to the side, whimpers and pleas escaping between gasping breaths, and it made me lose whatever was left of my mind.

"I need..." she let out a strangled moan. "I can't..."

"You can," I ground out. "I'm going to take care of you, Stevie, and you're going to come around me like a good girl. I promise."

I slammed my cock into her. The windows—the whole damn house felt like it was shaking around us, but I'd happily watch the whole thing crumble if it meant I got to feel her come.

I tested my grip on her throat, careful to tighten it only a little bit. Breath play wasn't my thing, but being in control was. Of her orgasm. Of her oxygen. I wanted to take care of it all—*I wanted to take care of her.*

My pace turned wild. Spearing my thick length through her tightening inner muscles over and over again, stroking her G-spot and bumping her clit each time I bottomed out. Her legs tightened around me and her nails dug deeper. Fucking her was like the perfect storm of pleasure, pain and possession.

"Please, Roman." She thrashed against me, so damn close to coming apart. Lightning ruptured across the sky, giving enough light to her face for me to see the tears of want that streaked it. "Oh god, please..."

My cock felt swollen to the point of rupture, and each thrust into her tight clutch had devolved into nothing short of pure torture.

"I've got you, princess," I rasped, my voice breaking at the end along with my thread of control over my own orgasm. "I'm here. I've got you." I gritted my teeth tight, feeling her cunt start to seize around me. "I told you I'd take care of you, so come for me."

Her eyes found mine, and her mouth fell open in the slow-motion surrender to pleasure. And then she seized with a violent scream as she came.

Light fractured across the night sky at the same exact moment, striking the earth with the same force as her orgasm struck her—*and me.*

A roar tore from my chest, unprepared for the way her cunt strangled my length. I was determined to ride through this—to watch her come before driving my own release home. But the tight grasp of her muscles, milking my heavy cock that was already beyond desperate to unload, it was too much.

I pinned the tip of my cock to her womb and let myself erupt. My roar rattled the room as my dick pumped jet after blank jet inside her, filling her up until I felt her desire and mine start to leak down my balls.

Neither of us spoke for several minutes. Instead, we traded emotions in a different currency. Soft kisses I placed to her neck. The gentle stroke of her fingers along my jawline. The warm exchange of air between our lips. The tender way she adjusted my glasses back to the bridge of my nose.

"Stevie," I finally rasped, pressing a kiss to her swollen lips.

"That was…"

"Insane."

Her breath hitched. "Magic."

Fuck.

"Hold on," I instructed and then carefully slid myself out of her. She started to try and lower her legs, so I gripped them harder. "No."

"But—"

"Just hold on," I repeated, sliding one arm around her back. She sighed and sagged against my chest. "Good girl." I kissed her forehead. "I'm not quite done nannying the fuck out of you."

Gritting my teeth, I carried her down the stairwell to the guest bedroom. I wanted nothing more than to spend the night —nothing more than to fuck her a half dozen more times before the sun came up. But I couldn't leave Lainey in the house by herself all night. So, I settled for bringing Stevie to bed and taking care of her sweet little pussy that my cock just destroyed.

I took my time wiping the blood and cum from her with a warm washcloth. Yeah, it was for the best that I had to go. If I stayed, I'd fuck her again, and I'd really be an asshole to fuck my little virgin nanny again so soon.

"Good girl," I purred when I was done and pressed my lips directly on her clit, smiling when I heard her loud gasp.

I bit down on my tongue to stop it from sliding out to taste her, drawing back and tugging the covers over her waist.

"I have to go." I found Stevie's eyes.

It was the only option right now. I couldn't stay the night, and I couldn't bring her back to the house. Not with Lainey there. Not yet.

She looked wounded for an instant before it was gone. "I know." She dragged the covers up to her chin, and then her natural compassion and the way she cared about my niece spilled out, trumping the aches of her own wants. "Is Lainey okay?"

I nodded and brushed a lock of hair back from her face. "She's not afraid of the storm."

There was a subtle pause, and then Stevie murmured, "Neither am I."

Everything stilled. She wasn't talking about the thunderstorm. She was talking about this—about us. And if it wasn't for my niece, I never would've walked out of that room. *Never would've had the strength to walk away from her.*

"Good night, Stevie."

"Good night."

I gathered my things and jogged back to the house, consoling myself with the reminder that Stevie was living on my property —that I would see her tomorrow. It was only a couple of hours until I'd be able to douse my ache to be around her.

Unfortunately, tomorrow was distant consolation for a man on fire.

CHAPTER EIGHTEEN

Stevie

I squeezed my thighs together and provoked the soreness between them. *It wasn't a dream.*

I never expected to see him after we argued. I'd figured he'd fume all night, avoid all weekend, and by Monday, we'd be back to normal—*trying to pretend the attraction between us didn't exist.*

But he'd come for me. *My pirate.* He'd made us *something.* And I'd eagerly lost my virginity to the consuming, magnetic power that was Roman Knight. No matter what consequences might be in store.

Until last night, I'd been a collection of unfortunate circumstances—of broken little pieces I kept trying to hold together like handfuls of sand. And then Roman appeared at my door, broke all the rules, and irrevocably changed me. He struck all my tiny kernels of sand like lightning, and created something I never could've imagined—something magical and exquisite and incredibly fragile.

I opened the cupboard to pull out the box of cereal I'd been eating all week when there was a knock on the front door. My brow scrunched. It was a little early for Lainey to be up and outside on a weekend, and if Roman needed me, he usually texted first. Or, at least, that was how things worked before last night. Before we'd slept together.

Before I slept with my boss.
With the kind of man who hunts the kind of men like my father.

My head was still shaking when I opened the door, startled to see *both* Roman and Lainey on the other side. Lainey was already in jeans and a sunshine T-shirt, her pigtails lopsided just like her smile. And Roman...

Our gazes locked and the memory of last night passed between us like an electric current through water, heat seeping down between my thighs and disintegrating whatever soreness remained.

God, he looked so good. So... relaxed.

The stubble on his jaw had darkened slightly in the last couple of hours, but it was his eyes... he wasn't trying to hide behind his glasses anymore. There was no mistaking the heat in his stare or the way it raked hungrily over me. I bit the inside of my cheek and wished I'd thought to put on something attractive this morning.

Unfortunately, my mind was still a little... well... *fucked...* from last night, so when I woke up without clothes, I grabbed the first thing I could find which was an old pair of sweats and a baggy tee.

"Hi." One syllable and my voice couldn't even keep it together for that, cracking on the end of the word.

Lainey immediately rushed my legs, and I grabbed hold of the doorframe to steady myself.

"Good morning," Roman greeted with a low rasp. "Hope we didn't wake you."

My breath caught. "No." I gulped. "You—I was already up."

To say he didn't wake me was a lie because the dream that woke me was a continuation of what happened last night.

Lainey tugged on my shirt, so I immediately crouched, grateful to give my attention to something other than the sudden ache gnawing low in my stomach.

"We're going to the beach," she whispered loudly. "Can you come?"

My mouth parted and I choked, hating myself for how my

brain immediately defiled her innocent words. Maybe I'd knocked it one too many times on the window last night because it felt like he'd been literally making my body come apart at the seams.

Roman cleared his throat, and I couldn't stop my eyes from straying to his groin. Even with his hands clasped in front of him, it was impossible to miss how his jeans stretched over his hard-on.

I gulped. *Wow, this was bad.*

"I received a note under my door this morning requesting to go to Stevie's beach," he explained and then looked at his niece. "Right, Bug? You heard Stevie went to the beach yesterday and now you want to go."

Her head bobbed eagerly.

"Oh," I replied, catching the tic in his jaw when my lips formed the sound. "Sure." I straightened and folded my arms, glancing over my shoulder for no reason other than if I kept looking into his eyes I felt like I might combust. "I just need a couple of minutes to change, and then I'll come up to the house?"

Lainey clapped and then grabbed Roman's hand, tugging him back up the path like the quicker they left, the faster I would be ready.

She wasn't wrong. When it came right down to it, there was nowhere else I'd rather be than with the two of them.

THE SHORELINE WAS CLEARER and calmer than yesterday. The clouds which ushered in the thunderstorm were gone, leaving the sun in their place. The water was still the rough equivalent of an ice bath in temperature, but kids never cared about those things. Lainey took her little shovel and plastic container to where the water ebbed, eagerly searching for snails and any other kind of creature to put in her tiny habitat.

"She likes making homes," I said, sliding my lower lip between my teeth.

Roman and I stood a few yards back from where she played,

both of our eyes locked on Lainey, though our minds were preoccupied with a much different topic.

"I never..." he cleared his throat. "Thought of it that way." The way he watched her shifted, like he was being forced to see her in a new light—one that didn't cast him in complete shadow. "Do you think it's a good thing?"

"Maybe it means she's making a home here, too."

We stood shoulder to shoulder in silence for a minute.

"Stevie..." His head half turned. "About last night."

My pulse picked up speed. I'd never had this conversation before—never had to have it. And certainly, never imagined having it with my boss.

"I should've been gentler."

"What?" I blurted out, clapping a hand immediately over my mouth. Heat blazed in my cheeks, but it didn't stop me from correcting him. "No. You were... perfect."

I swore I heard him growl.

"I thought..." I paused and rolled my lip between my teeth. "I thought you were going to tell me it wasn't going to happen again."

He laughed roughly and let his gaze drop pointedly to his waist. *He was still hard.*

"I don't think I would survive not fucking you again, Stevie," he said, his voice dropping at the end as the color of his eyes darkened. "I'm barely surviving keeping my hands off you for a few hours... in front of my six-year-old niece."

I shivered with pleasure, my whole body coming to life with his words.

"Can I ask you something?" The question kept bubbling its way to the top of my thoughts ever since he'd dropped the bomb last night. When his chin lowered, I continued quietly like Lainey would be able to hear my almost whisper from so far away, "Why did you have a vasectomy?"

His gaze drifted to the ground for a moment; he had to know this was coming.

I knew the procedure wasn't a *big* deal and that it could be reversed, but it wasn't like Roman didn't like kids—at least, the way he was with Lainey would never make me think he didn't want kids of his own.

"Six years ago, my predecessor stepped down as the special agent in charge of the BAU because the killer we were chasing threatened his family—kidnapped his son."

I sucked in a breath. "Oh no…"

"I'd seen plenty of horrible things on the job up to that point. I'd seen family and friends threatened—harmed before. We hunted psychopaths, some of them obsessed with the game—the chase. And sometimes, we became the pawns."

My stomach turned, but I didn't dare look at him. Instead, I kept my eyes trained on the water.

"Did he… did the boy…"

"We rescued him and caught the killer, but it destroyed Aarons—Agent Aarons; he blamed himself for what happened and resigned." Roman sighed, pain slashing over his features.

I understood more than most that just because you healed from a wound without major catastrophe didn't mean the scars didn't run deep.

"In the middle of it all, Val had Lainey," he went on. "And I'll never forget the moment I walked into her hospital room and she put Lainey in my arms for the first time. So small. So fragile."

Pigtails whipped in the wind as the subject of our conversation bent down and scooped up another tiny shovel of sand for her container.

"I'd do anything for her." *And he had.* "And all I could think was what I would do for my own kid… that I would put them before everything else, and that meant jeopardizing my ability to do my job well." He cleared his throat. *Twice.* But it didn't clear the emotion from his voice. "I wasn't in a serious relationship—hadn't been for a long time. I was a workaholic and loved what I did, so I made a choice. At the time, it was a no-brainer. Children had no place in my life, and I wouldn't put that responsibility on a woman if I accidentally got her pregnant, so I took away my ability to have them."

"And now?" It took a second to realize I'd asked those words.

"Now, I'm on a path I never could've seen coming…" he

trailed off and looked at me. "I never planned on any of this. Not Lainey. Not leaving." Our eyes connected. "Not you."

My breath caught, feeling the gentle touch of his fingers to mine. The way he was positioned, our hands were shielded from Lainey's view, so he could hold mine without her seeing. His long fingers threaded through mine, holding them like he never planned on letting go.

I'd never seen such emotion from him. Never seen a man so torn apart trying to do the right thing.

"Roman..."

His gaze glittered hungrily, and I swore I saw his head start to dip down for just a second before tiny footsteps smashed toward us.

"All done?" He released my hand and reached for her container to see what she'd gathered. "We have to stop at the store on the way home so I can get the stuff we need to make cauliflower casserole for Thanksgiving."

I made a low hum. That sounded delicious—the casserole and the idea of spending the holiday with the two of them. *Like a family.*

I shivered.

I'd lost my idea of family seven years ago and any hope of my own not long after. But here... now... I felt like I'd stumbled into one that I only could've dreamed about.

"Every holiday, Val would try to make... something... and invariably call me in tears, needing my help," he said as we gathered our things, letting out a soft laugh at the warm memory of his sister. "Isn't that right, Bug? Your mom struggled a little in the kitchen."

We almost missed it—how Lainey shook her head, but the sound of her tiny voice pierced the silence and captured our full attention.

"No."

Roman stopped in his tracks, looked at Lainey, and then to me to confirm that I'd heard her say the word, too.

"What do you mean, no?" I crouched in front of her and asked gently.

Lainey looked sheepishly up at Roman and then hung her head, sliding her foot along the sand.

Roman moved beside me, his big body coming down to our level. "It's okay, Bug," he said hoarsely, concern etched into his features. "You can tell me."

Her little lips pulled side to side and then she slowly lifted her gaze to her uncle. "Mommy pretended."

Deep lines pulled over his brow.

"What do you mean pretended?"

I bit my cheek and breathed so slowly, afraid to move, afraid that anything could break the fragile conversation between the two of them. Whatever Lainey was holding on to was important enough for her to breach her silence.

"Mommy pretended to mess up when she called you," she said, her voice so small that it was only Roman's broad back shielding us from the breeze that didn't blow the sound away.

"Why would she pretend?"

Lainey held the plastic terrarium tighter to her chest, rocking slightly side to side. Another several beats of silence passed and my legs started to burn from holding my position.

"Mommy said we had to pretend to need you otherwise you might not come." Her lower lip quivered.

Roman rocked back on his heels as though he'd been struck. "What?" he croaked. "Why?"

Oh god. My heart ached.

He was as unmoving as a statue, the only indication that her words affected him was the tic in his jaw and the turmoil in his eyes.

"She said you were so busy saving the world that sometimes you forgot to save yourself, so we had to help remind you."

I tasted blood from biting my cheek so hard. All the holidays he'd told me about... all the things his sister had gone over and above for... needed his help for... she'd done it to remind him he needed a life outside his job. She'd done it to keep his heart from hardening from all the terrors and tragedy he tried to prevent.

"To remind me..." Roman said with a voice made of grieved gravel. And then, right there on that beach, the world shifted on its axis and a single tear leaked down his cheek.

"I'm sorry I didn't save them," he rasped brokenly, another tear finding its way out. "I'm sorry I didn't save your mom and dad, Bug."

The pure pain distilled into his voice was the most heartbreaking thing of all. He didn't grieve because he held himself responsible. He grieved because he was supposed to be the one without a future and a family, not them. And he couldn't forgive himself for that.

Until now.

My eyes swung to Lainey as she shifted, extending one tiny hand and placing it on Roman's cheek, the tiniest fingers sent to soothe the biggest hurt.

"How could you have saved them, Uncle Roman?" She whispered.

How could he have saved them?

She was six. Not even close to an adult and even further from being philosophical. So, her question was purely from the perspective of a child who'd been in the car with her parents when the accident happened. Who knew it wasn't possible to stop any of it or save them. And who couldn't understand how the adult in front of her could ever think that he could.

Sometimes, the hardest thing in life was accepting that there was nothing you could've done to change the circumstances you were in. And until this moment, Roman couldn't accept it. The FBI agent who'd spent his career saving people, who'd given up —by drastic measures—his own ability to have a family in order to save people, couldn't accept that there was nothing he could've done to stop the accident or save his sister or her husband's life.

"I couldn't," the broken confession bled from his lips before his head hung and he sobbed.

There was nothing quite as strong as finally letting go of a weight you weren't meant to carry.

Roman pulled his glasses off his nose, the tears he'd bottled up for months since Val's death finally breaking free. And Lainey, after setting her terrarium down on the sand, wrapped her arms as best she could around his broad, shaking shoulders.

"I'm so sorry, Bug," he rasped, engulfing her in his embrace. "I'm so sorry…"

He wasn't sorry for being unable to save her parents; he was sorry for believing that being strong meant he had to be unbreakable.

For long minutes, they held each other and cried on the beach. Part of me felt like an impostor trapped in their very private moment, but another part of me felt like a guardian, protecting something that was precious—something that I'd become a part of long before last night.

"Let's go home," Roman finally said, stealing my attention to find his locked on me.

With one arm, he picked Lainey up as he rose. I gathered up her things she'd left in the sand and walked beside them to the car.

"How about I make my famous hamburger mac and cheese for dinner? It was your mom's favorite," he rasped when we got close to the car. "And I know for a fact, she didn't fake the fire alarm that went off the one time she tried to make it."

Lainey laughed into his shoulder, their shared grief easing them into a place that both hurt and healed.

While Roman shared the full story on the drive back, I stayed quiet in the passenger seat, my thoughts drifting to my own dilemma.

I didn't know what we were or what was going to happen, but if it continued down the path I hoped it would, I couldn't keep the truth from Roman. I was carrying my own burden, and though I had about as much control over who my father was as Roman had over the accident that killed his sister, it wasn't as easy for me to uproot the weed of fear in my chest that once he knew the truth, it would change things between us forever.

So maybe I would hold on to this dream filled with tiny captains, handsome pirates, magical fairy castles, and nights that could reshape the world for just a little while longer.

CHAPTER NINETEEN

Stevie

I STAYED FOR LONGER THAN I SHOULD HAVE.

After we got back from the beach, I wanted to slip back down to the guesthouse and let Roman and Lainey have some much-needed time alone together. Since I'd met him, Roman had shied away from talking about his sister or her husband in front of his niece except when they were at therapy. It was as though he'd believed, or maybe wished, that if he didn't speak about them, then it wouldn't hurt.

But he wouldn't let me go.

"Please, stay."

"It should be just the two of you," I'd insisted.

"It's never been just the two of us," he'd countered. *"Please."*

I couldn't say no to that.

So, I stayed while Roman cooked dinner. Bits of hamburger meat. Two different kinds of cheese. And then something mixed into the sauce that he demanded both of us leave the kitchen for.

While he cooked and then while we ate, he shared stories of Val—from when they were kids to when she'd had Lainey. I couldn't have said more than ten words while an entire life of a woman I'd never met unfolded in front of me. She became as three dimensional as the two people sitting in front of me who loved her more than anything.

"Your mom was the real pirate," he said, pointing his fork in Lainey's direction. "Hijacking me into all of her crazy schemes."

Lainey's toothy smile lit up her whole face. "So, I'm really part pirate?"

"Of course," he assured her without hesitation. "You can't escape genetics. Both your parents will always be a part of you."

My fork slipped from my fingers into my empty bowl, clattering and drawing their attention. I murmured an apology and quickly fished it up from the floor. *Nice, Stevie.*

"Let me take those," I offered quickly, grabbing the dirty dishes from the table and carting them to the sink.

My heart thudded so loudly, I worried they'd still be able to hear it even from a distance. It was ridiculous to be so affected by what he said; they were talking about pirates for Pete's sake. But his tone was so unshakable... *What if I couldn't escape my genetics?* What if there was something broken in me, too?

As I rinsed the bowls and tucked them into the dishwasher, I heard Lainey's small voice. "I miss Mommy and Daddy."

My breath caught.

"I miss them, too," Roman rasped.

I gently closed the dishwasher and looked back to the table. Lainey was folded into Roman's chest, her tiny shoulders shaking into his broad ones. His eyes met mine glistening for a second before he rose and carried her to the couch. There, he rocked her, comforting them both with whispered words I couldn't make out.

Locked in their own world, I was left alone with the doubt that gnawed a hole in mine.

It was a cheap trick—taking the long way to the guesthouse by going back out the front door and through the garden gate instead of using the sliding back door. But if I didn't, I risked Roman's gaze and another plea to stay, and what I needed was some time alone.

Last night changed everything—we'd took a major detour off the boss-nanny track and onto the sex express, and if spending the entire day with Roman had shown me anything, it was that I

BROKEN

couldn't think rationally in his presence. Around him I wanted to give and give and give… and then take and take and take… and pretend like the way all our broken pieces fit together was meant to be.

Settled into the turmoil of my thoughts, I showered, changed and then pulled out my laptop to review my notes for my Language and Literacy in Early Childhood course. It was the only one of my classes that finished before Thanksgiving, so I needed to prepare for my final on Wednesday morning; Roman had already—thoughtfully—told me he'd pick Lainey up from school on Tuesday, so that I could have the whole afternoon uninterrupted to study.

I wished there was a way to feel prepared for how it made me feel when he took care of me without question.

My color-coded outline blurred into a rainbow by the time there was a loud knock on the door. I looked up. I hadn't even noticed when it turned dark outside.

I slid my things off my lap and went to the door, already knowing what—*who* would be on the other side.

"You left." His rough accusation made my body heat almost as much as seeing him in those sweats again.

"I shouldn't have stayed. You and Lainey needed that time together." I held on to the door, feeling the army of goose bumps rise up against my skin.

He stepped closer, hardly leaving any space between us.

"You're the reason for that time together." He reached out and cupped my cheek, and my traitorous body turned into the warm spread of his palm.

"What time is it? Where's Lainey?"

Last night, everything happened so fast, I didn't have time to think; I only had time to feel. But right now, my nerves felt like a ball of Christmas lights that I was trying desperately to untangle.

"Showered and in bed sound asleep," he assured me and then added after a hard swallow. "She didn't cry alone this time."

I pulled my lower lip between my teeth, clamping down hard for a second. Still, it didn't prevent the small sound of relief from leaking through my lips.

"You're her hero, Roman," I murmured. "If you didn't show

her it was okay to be sad, she never would've believed it from anyone else."

His thumb stroked my cheek, and I saw the flick of his jaw muscle ripple the stubble of his beard.

"And what about you?" He rasped. "How do I become your hero, Stevie?"

My jaw dropped, feeling as though my heart slammed against the front of my rib cage in order to get closer to him.

"Y-you already saved me," I stammered. "Gave me a job when I had no references. A place to stay. An unreasonable nanny salary—"

His head dipped, his lips now gently brushing over mine. "I want to give you more."

More.

My chest felt tight with a balloon of hope stretching against the binds of worry.

"Roman—" I broke off, hearing the loud buzz of a cell phone an instant before Roman jerked back and dug in his pocket, worried it was an alert from Lainey at the house.

I could see exactly what he wanted to give me outlined in the shadows of his sweatpants. Long and thick, his erection stretched the soft fabric. My teeth sank into my lower lip as my core clenched painfully, aching for more of that.

"It's Dex..." he said with a slow drawl, staring at the screen. "Why the hell is he calling me on a Saturday?"

For something important went unspoken.

Frowning, he backpedaled and turned away to answer. Meanwhile, I replenished the oxygen in my lungs and scrambled to figure out how to tell him I wanted everything he could possibly have to give.

"*Are you fucking—*"

Roman's shout broke my train of thought, and I instantly stepped out of the doorframe toward him. He spun and took several large strides away from me, doing his best to not let me hear what he was saying even though his agitation was obvious.

He went quiet when Dex replied and then his chin dropped with a sharp nod a second before he ended the call.

"What is it? Is everything okay?" A ball formed in my throat. *Was it another dead body?* But I couldn't bring myself to ask that.

Roman yanked his glasses off his face and pinched the bridge of his nose, the flex of his muscles cracking through the tension.

"Dex found the money."

I jolted. "Money? What money?"

He slid his glasses back on and faced me, the darkness in his gaze harboring something deeply and violently possessive. "The money funneled from Dean Johnson's mom to the police to bury their investigation into your assault."

I let out a small cry and before I even realized I was swaying, Roman was there—catching me.

"I'm okay," I protested immediately even though I wasn't.

He was going to get away with assaulting me. *Just like that.* And what could I do? What did I do? Who could I turn to? I gasped for air between the thoughts that hit like straight punches to my stomach.

By now, I should be used to fate ripping out from underneath me all the things that most people had to protect them—a father, a mother, and now, the law.

"No, you're not," he growled and lifted me in his arms, kicking the door shut as he carried me through the guesthouse and down the small stairwell to the bedroom.

My thoughts spun out in a million directions, my head swaying side to side trying to follow them. But when my back touched the bed, I returned to reality and found myself curled and clutching Roman's chest in a way similar to how Lainey had earlier—like he was the only thing stable when the storms swept everything else away.

"I'm going to fix this." He laid me down and then climbed in next to me, half covering my body with his.

"How?" I asked even as my head shook in disbelief.

By now, I should know how dangerous it was to hold on to anything or anyone—even someone who was as strong and steadfast as Roman. But at every turn, he didn't promise to be different, he just was. He took care of me when he had no obligation to. He protected me when I wasn't his responsibility. And he wanted me... he wanted me against all odds.

"I'm going to call Zeke Williams tomorrow—Addy's twin brother. He's a lawyer, and we're going to press charges against all of them," he declared, his steely, unwavering tone belying the rage that boiled underneath the surface.

Tears welled in my eyes and my lips peeled apart, speechless. I didn't even know that Ace's wife had a brother, let alone a twin who was a lawyer, and I couldn't believe Roman already had a plan.

"Why?" The word was barely a sound as a tear streaked down my cheek. "Why are you doing this?"

He didn't need to do this—he didn't need to do any of this. He'd already rescued me that night; that was more than enough. I was an adult. I'd been responsible for myself—for myself and my mom—for long enough to age me out of innocence, to age me out of the belief that someone would always be there to take care of me.

"Jesus, Stevie." Roman exhaled loudly, claiming the droplet with the pad of his thumb, his gaze burrowing into mine. "How can you fucking ask that? Because you're not just my nanny, dammit. I care about you."

I shook my head, but before I could even open my mouth, he cut me off.

"And not because I fucked you," he warned low before I could even think it. "I cared about you long before last night."

Cared about me? I'd lost anyone who'd ever cared about me, and it would be foolish to think that Roman would be any different, especially given everything that should keep us apart.

How could he ever truly care for the daughter of a serial killer?

His warm breath caressed my skin right before he pressed his lips to my forehead, kissing along my brow, then the damp corner of my eye, and then down my cheek.

"That doesn't mean I can't take care of myself."

I sighed at the impossibly soft caress of his mouth over my skin, especially when his lips found the tender spot below my ear.

He drew back, placing his face directly above mine, desire practically dripping from his gaze.

"Is that what you really think I believe?" He rumbled low, daring me to claim he thought so little of me.

Knowing I would—could never.

"No," I whispered, feeling the hot shadow of his mouth approach mine.

I gasped when his grip closed on my chin, forcing it up so I looked straight at him.

"Good. Because I see you, Stevie. I see the way you're strong for yourself—the way you fight... the way you risk... to chase your dreams. I see the way you do it all while continuing to take care of those around you."

"Roman—"

"But part of taking care of yourself means knowing when to let someone else take care of you." He thumbed my lower lip. "When was the last time you let someone take care of you, princess?" He wondered and then added, "Before the morning at the police station."

That was my answer, and it died in my throat. I'd asked him to stay with me that day—to sit beside me as I told a bunch of strangers how I'd been attacked, and it was the first time I'd let myself need someone in a long time.

Of course, he'd taken care of me in countless other ways before and after that moment, but never because I'd asked him to.

"I don't... remember," I confessed. The answer existed in the time before Mom and I fled from Wyoming. Before the bubble had popped and I realized I wasn't being taken care of, I was being conditioned.

"Well, I want you to remember this. To remember me." His low voice skipped along my spine and made me squirm in the bed. "I want you to trust me to take care of you, Stevie."

I stilled.

Trusting Roman to take care of me was the most intimate thing I could ever agree to. More than sex. More than taking his body in mine or giving him my virginity. Trusting him to take care of me was the first step on the path to trusting him with all my truths—with all the things that had the power to break me.

He nipped his teeth along the edge of my lip, paining and then soothing the flesh with his tongue. That was Roman—pain and pleasure wrapped in one exquisite package.

"Trust me, princess," he murmured, kissing along my jaw and then back across my cheek until his lips hovered over mine.

I inched my lips higher, needing the kiss that hung between us. Desire steamrolled over everything else except the man in front of me. To just let go... to give in to that possessive gaze, those strong arms... to give in to his golden promises was so tempting... too tempting.

"Say that you trust me."

Emotion burned in the back of my throat. If I said it, it made my vulnerability real. But I wanted more than anything to be real with him.

His hand moved to my thigh, massaging there for a minute before sliding up to my hip and then to my waist, gripping me firmly.

"There hasn't been a moment of this day that a part of me hasn't ached for you," he growled. "Ached to touch you. To taste you. To bury my cock inside you so deep, I'll feel every vibration when I make you scream my name." His thumb dragged along the underside of my breast, tracing the curve as far as he could but not far enough to graze my nipple that furled painfully for his touch. "So tell me you trust me, Stevie, because god help me, the only thing I want is you."

It was too much. The way I wanted him was too much, and the way I trusted him was too strong to deny, no matter how much it was a risk to do so.

"I trust you," I blurted out breathlessly, overwhelmed by the twin aches in my chest and my core.

"Good girl," he ground out and then claimed my mouth in a searing kiss, taking my gasp along with it as his tongue dove deep, striking the farthest corners like it was a bolt of lightning and he was the storm itself.

"All I want is to take care of you, Stevie. All of you."

If fate thought to mock me with everything I'd never had but always wanted, she couldn't have done a more perfect job than with Roman. Giving him the name Knight was an unnecessarily sweet taunt on top of the torture.

I drew a trembling breath and exhaled, "Yes."

Groaning low, he kissed me again, this time with rich

tenderness. His lips played over mine with exquisite purpose and breathtaking restraint. I felt like one of the puzzles that Lainey and Roman and I worked on when we first opened the box, all my pieces severed and strewn apart, too overwhelmed to even tell which ones were upside down and which were right side up.

But Roman knew.

With each press of his lips, each soft swipe of his tongue, he coaxed my mouth apart and began to piece me back together. He gave me a safe way to break apart and the confidence that he'd put me back together again.

"Tell me what you want," he ordered firmly, dragging his mouth lower along my jawline and down onto my neck. "I want to hear you say it, Stevie."

I let out a small moan when his mouth latched on the side of my neck, sucking directly over my pulse like he knew all the beats were for him. His hands slid lower, teasing the rim of my shirt and making my stomach tighten, needing more.

It was dangerous. The level of intimacy I'd opened the door for was way more than just my body. If this was just about sex, he wouldn't have tried so hard to keep his distance. And he certainly wouldn't need to hear me say how I needed him.

"I want you to take care of me." The reckless words tumbled out, but I couldn't hang on to my own reservations any longer. Not when the flesh and blood man begging for them had proven at every turn that he would.

"Good girl," he rasped with a powerful shudder. With that praise, he began to methodically strip me of my clothes. My shirt tickled my stomach as he hauled it over my head and tossed it onto the floor, leaving my breasts bare for him. Without taking his eyes from mine, his hands moved lower, hooking into the waist of my underwear and peeling them from my hips.

"Such a good girl." He groaned once I was naked, his big palm moving from my side up to cup my breast.

Roman drew back and watched himself knead the weight… the way he stared at how my pale skin spilled out from between his strong fingers… it made me not want to breathe.

My eyelids fluttered shut when he plucked at my nipple, turning it red and firm like a berry waiting to be eaten.

"So fucking perfect."

I didn't know what was sweeter—the words or the hot, steady pull of his lips when they closed over my nipple. This was different than last night. Last night was rough and intense. Tonight, it was his tenderness that was the powerful wave sweeping me under.

Every touch. Every kiss. It felt like he was trying to heal me and please me at the same time. I wanted to tell him that I was okay—that I wasn't broken by this. But that wasn't the truth.

"Trust me," he cooed, bringing his mouth to my breast so his hand could move lower.

My head tipped back when his fingers dipped inside me, ripples of want heating my skin. My hips rocked toward him, searching for relief. My eyes drifted shut, and with each rush of pleasure dragging me deeper, I realized I did trust him to take care of me. I more than trusted him—I wanted him to take care of me.

"I do trust you," I murmured breathlessly, feeling his fingers curl right where I wanted them. "Ahh…" My legs clenched in pleasure, and Roman hummed low with satisfaction.

I had no idea what a G-spot was until Roman; I'd swear it never existed until he brought it to life.

His fingers stroked inside me, working me into a frenzy until everything felt like too much and not enough. Until it felt like up was down and down was up. Until it felt like I couldn't bear it anymore.

"I'm going to come," I panted, feeling his deep groan rumble against my chest as his fingers picked up speed and dragged me over the edge.

I cried out as my body disintegrated with pleasure, my back bowing off the bed from the force of my climax. The euphoric buzz in my body lingered for long minutes. Roman tenderly kissed my breasts and collarbone and neck until I started to come back down.

He made me want to be vulnerable—he made me feel safe to be vulnerable. And if that wasn't the direct shortcut to love, I didn't know what was.

Carefully, he drew back and rose next to the bed, removing

his own clothing in rough gestures. As soon as his swollen cock hung free, I turned on my side, my mouth parting hungrily to give him the same release.

"Not tonight," he said, tugging his cock up away from my mouth. "You see what you do to me?" He shuddered as his hand stroked hard up his length. "I'm so fucking on edge right now, I won't survive your tongue."

He placed one knee and then the other on the bed. My stomach quivered with each breath, my legs tipping open, a brazen invitation for him to settle between them.

"Fuck…" he ground out, his gaze locking on my pussy. "If you knew how beautiful you look right now. Those red tits. Your little pink slit all wet for me."

Without warning, he reached out and dragged one finger along my sex. My hips bucked when the touch grazed my swollen clit.

"Such a good girl." He brought the finger to his lips and sucked off my desire, stroking himself hard once more. This time, a bead of moisture pooled at the tip of his cock, milky white against the purpled rim, and every muscle of his torso flexed and released.

"Roman, please," I begged, my hand landing impatiently on my hip, about to touch myself if he wasn't going to.

His stare snapped to mine. "I promised you I was going to take care of you and your needy little cunt," he warned lowly. "Now spread her open for me."

If it was possible, my cheeks grew hotter with each inch of skin I touched until I reached between my thighs. I heard my sharp inhale when I reached my sex, my fold sliding through my fingers at first because I was so wet.

There was a part of Old Stevie who wondered if she should be embarrassed at her body's reaction to him—embarrassed by how badly I wanted every carnal pleasure locked into his stare.

"Perfect," he rasped with a strangled voice. Inching closer, he grabbed a pillow and motioned for me to lift my hips. "It'll be easier for you this way."

With my lower half tipped up, I was spread even more prone to his devouring gaze.

His free hand took my knee, steadying himself as his other hand positioned the head of his cock to my slit. A low hiss ripped through his lips as he dragged his tip through my folds.

My jaw dropped when the blunt flesh bumped over my clit, a firework of pleasure exploding low in my stomach.

"Ahh... that's it," he rumbled, his eyes locked between us. "Each orgasm gets you an inch, princess," he revealed. "So, if you want my cock, all you have to do is come."

He circled his tip over my clit again, and that first orgasm washed over me like warm summer rain, gently drenching all of my cells with the promise of life.

My moan hadn't even tapered off, my inner muscles still in the throes of contracting when I felt the fat head of his cock push inside me.

"Good girl," he praised with a strained voice.

I had no idea what to expect, and even if I did, he didn't give my mind long enough to clear to consider it before his fingers found my clit and began plumping the sensitive flesh. It was a different sensation than before—than when he'd rubbed over it—and suddenly I was being dragged back out to sea.

Back out to crest another wave.

My hands curled into the blankets, the ache threatening to tear me apart. Before I could even try to move my hips, Roman took his hand from my knee and placed it over my lower stomach, holding me in place so there was nothing that I could do except squeeze the tip of his cock and orgasm for more.

"Fuck," he bit out between locked teeth, his thumb searching for my clit and rubbing me with sure strokes, his touch leading me to another release.

"Oh god," I cried out, my body convulsing once more. *Harder this time.*

Roman's deep growl when I came around him was feral, and I felt him let my inner muscles pull him in deeper, gripping his thick length like it was the only support in the middle of the storm.

This time, I knew what was coming even though I wasn't prepared for it. I was still panting when he started to squeeze my clit. First soft, then hard, then harder. And each time, he held the bundle of nerves for longer, increasing the strength of sensation that rushed through me each time he released.

I didn't know orgasms could build. I didn't know orgasms could have differing degrees of devastation. Until now. Each time he pleasured me it felt like I made it to the summit of a mountain, only for him to send my cells climbing toward another higher peak.

But this was trust. This was vulnerability. This was giving more and more of yourself, sharing broken piece after broken piece, knowing the person I shared them with was putting them together.

My third orgasm, I screamed.

My fourth, I cried.

"That's it, Stevie. You feel so good, so tight." He groaned. "I never want to leave your cunt."

Each time, he inched deeper like he said he would. He spread my muscles that were sore—sliding farther into my pussy that both protested and then welcomed the invasion. And each time he gave me more. More praise. More promise. More cock. More pleasure. And it wasn't long before I wanted more of the pain.

I whimpered and clawed at the bed—at him—as he dragged me toward another climax.

I lost count of what number it was, and I couldn't give a name for the sounds that came out of my mouth when I found it. My body flew apart again and again, and each time, Roman coaxed me back together.

"Tell me you trust me." From somewhere close, I heard his rough whisper.

"I trust you." I moaned from the very base of my stomach when I felt him push deeper. I didn't know how there could be more left to him, but there was.

"Say it again."

I gasped for air, reaching for something—anything—to hold on to, and ended up clutching his forearm attached to the hand on my stomach. He must be able to feel himself underneath my skin, the way his size rearranged all my insides to make room for him.

"I trust you, Roman. I trust you," I cried out when his hips jerked forward and bumped into the spot inside my pussy that was like a detonator switch.

"God, yes," he growled savagely and then began to slam into me.

My jaw dropped and my back bowed. If I thought the trail of orgasms that brought me here was mind blowing, what happened now wrecked me.

His fingers took my clit once more, pinching the nerves until all its sensations felt clogged—bottlenecked—as his thick length took control. Driving his hips into mine, his curved cock pushing me higher. The sound of slapping skin drove me insane.

"Look at what you do to me, princess," he ordered and my eyes complied.

His muscles moved like a symphony of sinew, and his entire body glistened with the restraint it took to hold himself back while he made me come around him so many times.

"Roman," I begged for him—for everything he would give me. "Please..."

He slammed harder and harder into me, mercilessly grinding against my G-spot with each thrust.

"You're mine, Stevie," he groaned while driving into me. "And I'm never letting you go."

Those words were like the key to the very last recesses of my heart, and it felt like my whole body cried out to let him in. Every sensation he inflicted on my body magnified a hundredfold with those words.

"Oh god..." My eyelids fluttered. I was so close—*so close.*

"Break one more time for me like a good girl if you want my cum," he growled, and I felt myself start to fracture when his fingers released their hold on my clit, and that bottleneck of sensations assaulted me with blinding force.

I didn't simply break. My orgasm shattered me into a million tiny pieces. I screamed his name and came so hard, all my muscles seized. He thrust through the tightness in steady, powerful drives, and then his roar shook the whole room as he came, burying himself so deep inside me I swore I could taste his salty cum each time his cock pumped into me.

He moved slowly once the room stopped spinning, easing

himself out of me and performing the same ritual as the night before when he'd cleaned me. Sighing deeply, I watched him pull his clothes back on in a dreamlike state, every part of me from bones to brain reduced to a warm, glittery goo.

I didn't want him to leave.

The thought provoked the first real pain I'd felt since he'd knocked on my front door. But what choice did he have? Lainey couldn't be alone, and—

"Up you go."

I gasped as he hoisted me into his arms where I immediately curled to his chest like a moth to a flame.

"What are you doing?"

"What does it look like?" He asked, climbing the stairs *out* of my bedroom. "I'm taking you back to the house—to my bed."

"But—"

He stopped immediately, staring down at me with a resolved expression. "But what, Stevie?" He asked. "It wasn't my dick talking when I said you were mine."

"Oh." My throat tightened.

"I don't know about you, but my whole life has been spent around people whose lives have changed in an instant, right up until I became one of them," he rasped, tucking a strand of hair behind my ear. "In a moment, I lost a sister. Gained a kid. Lost a job." He sighed. "Moments are all we fucking have, Stevie, and I don't want to spend another one without you in it."

Oh my.

"What about Lainey?" I mumbled.

"Lainey will be so damn happy to have you in the house when she wakes up, she won't care about anything else, and you know that."

"Okay," I agreed, basking in the glow of his possessiveness as he carried me up to the main house and into his bedroom.

As I curled into his chest, I wondered if this meant I was no longer his nanny. I wondered if this meant we were in a relationship. But I didn't say anything, not because I was afraid to ask the question, but because I was afraid of the answer.

If he told me we weren't in a relationship, his truth would break my heart.

And if he told me we were in a relationship, my truth would break his.

So, I closed my eyes, listened to the steady thump of his heart, and drifted off to sleep, willing to linger in this wonderful limbo like a ship out to sea. Maybe one day, I'd figure out how to tell him I didn't need him to be my hero, I just needed him to be mine.

CHAPTER TWENTY

Roman

"Thank you for doing this," I murmured, thumbing through each paper in the file that Zeke put on my desk.

If there were an unsung hero in Carmel Cove, it was Zeke Williams. While Covington caught bad guys on a daily basis, and while Addy was superwoman in her own right as the blue-haired face of Blooms, the recovery house owned by her and her twin, Zeke worked silently in the background.

He not only coordinated everything for the recovery house on the managerial end as far as accepting applications, vetting and hiring staff, fundraising and procuring donations, but he also was the man in charge of the women in their charge. While Addy and the house managers might interact more with the Blooms women since many of them came from backgrounds of abuse, he was the one who laid out all the stepping-stones that would lead those women to their new lives. From therapy to job opportunities to classes ranging anywhere from cooking to self-defense, he made sure that each woman who walked through the doors of Blooms, stepped out with every tool in her arsenal to build a new life.

Sometimes those tools included restraining orders or divorces or custody agreements, and in those cases, Zeke put to use the law degree he'd earned just before he moved back to Carmel Cove to take care of Addy almost a decade ago.

"Of course," he replied with a nod, standing patient on the other side of my desk.

I'd invited him to take a seat, but he refused.

I couldn't help the way my brain was trained to interpret the refusal, wondering if Zeke Williams ever took a seat in his own life—ever stopped to do something for himself—rather than simply existing to stand up for others.

An admirable trait, without a doubt, but not sustainable.

"If it all looks good to you, I'll take this over to the prosecutor's office and hand them to her myself," he offered.

I'd told Stevie we weren't going to let the fuckers who assaulted her get away with it, and I wasn't lying. I contacted Zeke that very next morning; he was at the house that afternoon, listening to Stevie's statement, and then instructing us on what the next steps would be—basically gathering up all the evidence that the police had been paid off to ignore and then taking it directly to the prosecutor.

I had plans for the officers who'd accepted bribes from the congresswoman to leave her son alone and they involved a detailed exposé that I was going to enlist Jo's help to write and publish. However, I wanted the legal proceedings against Dean Johnson well under way first.

"You sure?" I glanced at him.

I flipped through Stevie's statement, the photos she'd documented of her injuries, the statements from Reed and me, user data and time stamps from the rideshare app, and finally screen captures from neighboring houses in that development that caught enough of the shadowed figure holding Stevie pinned to her car. We also had financials showing the money transferred from congresswoman's campaign fund in the days following the attack. Of course, Dex had traced the transfer to the accounts of the officers, however it wasn't done legally, so we'd left that part out for now.

I wasn't fluent in legalese, but that didn't stop me from scanning through each paper in the folder like I was. I was going to turn over every goddamn stone, even if it was a fucking boulder, to make sure Stevie got justice.

"I've worked with Delilah a couple of times. It's not a problem."

"Great." I sighed and closed the folder, sliding it back across my desk.

He picked it up. "I don't see how she wouldn't decide to prosecute this, but with the holiday on Thursday, I wouldn't expect any news from me until next Monday."

My head cocked. "Will I see you on Thursday at Dex's?"

Since Addy was Dex's sister-in-law and Zeke was her brother, I assumed he'd be at their house, too.

His expression didn't even falter. "I might stop by, but there's a Thanksgiving meal at the house, so I'll probably stick around there in case anyone needs anything."

I nodded and made a mental note to ask Addy if she'd checked in with her twin recently as he walked out of my office and shut the door behind him.

My gaze tipped to the photograph on my desk. My little pirate and my fairy princess. I never had photos on my desk before Stevie. And I never would've thought twice about the personal life of a friend—or lack thereof. But here I was… fucking unfolding.

I groaned and reached down to adjust my cock. Just the damn photograph made me hard knowing she was waiting for me back at the house—knowing she'd be in my bed tonight, taking my cock like a good girl.

I'd had a whole week of her. A whole week where I'd fucked her every chance I had. At night. In the morning. In the shower.

I couldn't get enough.

Sure, her soft curves and tight little cunt gave my body the stamina of a horny teenager, but it was more than that. I couldn't get enough of her smile that greeted me when I walked in the door. Enough of her laugh when we all dressed up as pirates, per Lainey's request, and puzzled together after dinner. I couldn't get enough of her profound comfort or soothing presence when Lainey and I talked about Val.

And I couldn't get enough of the way she continued to trust

me with piece after piece of her. Her sheltered childhood. The hurt she harbored when her dad was gone. The pain she felt watching and taking care of her mom as she deteriorated.

She was twenty-two. A college student. *A nanny.* But the way she pushed forward after every setback was nothing short of inspirational. Like a buoy stranded alone in the open ocean, she continued to rise back to the surface no matter the storms or the waves that tried to drag her under.

I might be Lainey's hero, but Stevie Michaels was mine.

The phone on my desk buzzed a second before Dex's voice came over the intercom.

"Can you come here?"

I didn't bother to reply since it was just as quick to walk down the hall and see what he needed.

"What's going on?" The door clicked shut behind me.

The projector flickered to life, tiled with images and information about each of the Archangel's victims, but they were so small in order to fit them all I couldn't read any of it.

"It took a little digging," Dex said and stood. "A lot of deep fucking digging," he corrected with a grunt. "But I think I found something."

He tapped on something in his left hand and the image on the projector shifted to the map we'd built before.

"A pattern for how he's moving?" I asked, staring at the dots that marked a trail all over the Midwest to the West Coast where his victims were found.

"No." He clicked the button again and at least a dozen of the markers turned red and moved to Wyoming. "Almost all of the victims except for the student, Nancy, were runaways. When I first looked through their files, it jumped out at me that a third of them had come from Wyoming."

The red dots pinned locations all over the state.

"It was where he started killing again. Where we almost caught him…" I trailed off. "It makes sense that some would be from that state."

"Not some," Dex corrected me. "All." The map shifted again. Another handful of markers changed color and slid to Wyoming. "I cross-referenced missing person reports, photographs, and any medical records that were available. And the more I did that"—another click turned more dots red—"the more I found that *all* the victims were runaways from Wyoming."

My eyes widened, staring at the map as it transformed from marking where the kills happened and bodies discovered to where the victims were originally from.

"Jesus…" I swore on a deep exhale.

"He's not just killing women who remind him of his runaway daughter, he's targeting only women from Wyoming."

My mind reeled. "How the fuck does he know this? How could he know these girls were from Wyoming when it took you this long to figure it out?"

It wasn't like there was a registered runaway database you could subscribe to, swiping right until you found a runaway from Wyoming.

"I'll pretend like that wasn't an insult because I know there is no one who would've figured this out any faster," he grumbled.

"You know what I mean." I sighed and shoved my glasses higher on my nose.

"I don't… have an answer to that yet," Dex replied, annoyed. "But at least we know how he's targeting them."

"Yeah." I glanced at the screen and then back to him. "And what about the missing person reports in the months surrounding Lydia Reynolds's attack, do any of them match the description of our victims?"

"Some," he said. "There's about a dozen that fit the current victimology, but it's taking time to go through them all—go through their lives to rule them out."

My head began a slow shake. "He's not just targeting runaways from Wyoming…" I drawled hollowly. "He's looking for her—he's hunting down his own daughter."

Dex's nostrils flared. "So we need to find the girl. That's how we'll find him."

I nodded. "And I doubt she's going to be any of those missing persons," I added. "Reporting her missing would only put obstacles in his way."

"Shit…"

I reached for my cell and realized I must've left it in my office. "I need to call Koorie and update her."

"What will he do?"

I turned. "He'll kill until he finds her."

There was no doubt in my mind of that. This was now his mission—his calling. Knowing his religious obsession, he was searching for his own lamb who'd strayed from his flock, and he'd stop at nothing to bring her home.

"I mean when he finds her?"

I coughed, feeling like my heart tripped in my chest.

The truth was that I didn't know what he'd do. If she'd betrayed him like I thought—she'd betrayed the commandment to obey thy father, and part of me believed he'd kill her for that. But another part of me was uncertain. The Archangel was an enigma—a killer with the self-control to quell his murderous drive for over a decade because of this child. It was completely possible that he'd be able to quell his need to punish her for the same reason.

"We're not going to let that happen," I declared. That was the only answer I wanted to focus on the only acceptable answer; we were going to find this fucker before he found her.

"This is everything we have for Stevie Michaels." The woman at the post office handed me a small carton of only three letters.

When I'd insisted that Stevie come live in the guesthouse, she'd put her mail on hold for pickup at the post office, unsure that she wanted it sent to my address because she wasn't sure how long she'd be there.

Over the last week, that had obviously changed.

Nothing was going to take her from me. *My good girl.*

So, with Stevie sitting on my lap, I'd watched as she completed the change of address form online, and then told her I'd swing by the post office to pick up any mail that was waiting on my way home.

I glanced down. Two of the letters were from the school's financial services office. *She wouldn't need to worry about that anymore.*

The third a promotional flyer from a church in Monterey. I almost threw them out then and there, but it was still her mail, so I decided to watch her do the honors.

"Thanks." I took everything and headed back to my car, checking my watch.

A few minutes later, I was back at the house, my blood thrumming when I walked in the door. I had a surprise that I'd been holding on to for weeks.

"Uncle Roman!" Lainey rushed over and hugged me.

The force of her hit me just as hard as the change that had occurred in her over the last two months. She talked. She hugged. She smiled. She laughed.

She would never be the same after losing both her parents—neither of us would. But just because things were different didn't mean there weren't new kinds of happiness to be found.

I picked her up and searched for Stevie who always lingered in the background, allowing me and my niece to have a moment before she stepped into it. She stood from the couch and smiled. One day, she'd understand she didn't need to wait. One day, she'd understand that she was a part of this moment because she was a part of us.

Setting Stevie's mail on the counter, I kept my palm over it so she couldn't be distracted by the school stuff as I declared, "I have a surprise for you."

"A surprise?" Lainey clapped. "Is it stick bugs?"

This kid and her bugs.

"Not stick bugs," I admitted gently. Though I was sure they would be involved in her Christmas present. Smiling, my gaze met Stevie's. "We're going to get a Christmas tree today."

Lainey's eyes turned as wide as some of her little bugs.

"We are?" She gasped.

"Yeah, so go get your coat and shoes on." I set her down and waited until she ran from the kitchen before I spoke again. "Val would kill me if I didn't get a real tree."

Stevie's full lips lifted easily in the corners. "Your sister was a smart woman."

Thinking of everything Val would do—and all the ways she'd do it better than I would—was still uncomfortable. But it was like the stretch of a tight muscle; it hurt and made me wonder if I was really capable of this since it felt like I was getting nowhere, but each time it happened, I realized I was further than before; the stretch still hurt, but I was growing into it.

"You should put on sneakers," I said, realizing she was wearing sandals. "And something warmer."

Her eyes flashed, years of instinctive independence making her want to fire back, but then it dimmed to a warm glow when I didn't back down—when she remembered my promise to take care of her.

Nodding, Stevie went back into my room. *Our room.* And when she returned, she had on sneakers, a light jacket, and wool hat, and all I wanted was to get her out of all the layers I'd demanded she put on.

I held open the door, unable to take my eyes from her as Lainey led the way to the car. When Stevie walked by me, her sweet scent made me inhale greedily.

"Good girl," I murmured and tapped her ass.

Her breath caught and pink stole over her cheeks before she jogged to catch up to Lainey. As she helped my niece into the Bronco, I quickly adjusted myself in my jeans.

The damn Christmas tree wouldn't be the only thing standing tall at the tree farm.

LESS THAN AN HOUR LATER, we were outside of Carmel at one of the few local Christmas tree farms in the area. Most of them didn't open until after Thanksgiving, but I wanted to go sooner. So, it didn't take more than a few minutes of online searching to track down the owner of the tree farm and pay him a few hundred bucks to open up the place just for us.

Just for her.

Anything for her.

"Alright, captain, it's up to you to find the best one," I told Lainey and then set her free down the long row of evergreens.

"Are we the only ones here?" Stevie asked when Lainey was out of earshot.

I grinned. "Val always had a real tree, and she always had it up before Thanksgiving so it was ready to decorate the day after," I told her. "None of the farms were open yet, so I got in touch with the owner and asked nicely."

"Asked?"

"Paid." The farm was a decent size, and since we were the first customers of the season, we had the pick of their full inventory. "Val would always get a tree for me, too. Not that I put it up in my apartment," I confessed. "She'd put it up in their study which was across the hall from the living room. It was Uncle Roman's tree, and Lainey picked every decoration for it."

She laughed softly. "So, you've never cut down a tree?"

I shook my head, my gaze drifting to her. "Another first for me." *Just like everything she made me feel.*

Stevie's lips parted and she tipped her head up, her cheeks delectably flushed.

I wanted to kiss her. Ached, really. And I was about to when the plod of small footsteps broke the moment and made both of us look forward. Lainey darted across the path, but didn't bother with us; she was still on the hunt.

"We always had a real tree, too, but my dad would take us out the day after Thanksgiving to get it," Stevie shared.

"One of the busiest days."

"He was very particular about everything… but he always let me pick out the tree," she offered. "Christmas and Easter. Those were the only two holidays we celebrated, but boy, did we celebrate. Especially Christmas."

"Oh yeah?"

She smiled. From what I gathered, her childhood hadn't always been the easiest, growing up with extremely religious parents. But then there were things like this that brought back fond memories.

"I'd always pick out the biggest one I could find, and he…" she trailed off for a second before finishing. "He would cut it down like magic."

"Not every day you get to chop down a tree," I murmured, anticipating the very task that was ahead of me.

The fondness that warmed Stevie's expression flickered and

then disappeared. We walked in silence for a few steps, watching Lainey scrutinize each option.

"What would you ask for for Christmas when you were a kid?" I wondered.

"The beach." She smiled. "Every year, I asked to go to the beach for summer vacation, but we never did."

My eyebrows rose. That seemed like a pretty easy gift to give, even if it was just once.

"Why not?"

"I don't know," she stammered, color rising in her face. "Too expensive? Or maybe my dad just had something against the beach..." She shook off that thought. "I eventually made it."

I made a mental note to take her to the beach on Christmas morning, but before I could say anything else, Lainey made another pass across the walkway and we both laughed.

"What would you have done if they didn't agree to open this place for us?"

"Broken in?" I teased and when Stevie gasped, I admitted, "I found a company last month that ships real Christmas trees all over the country, so I was originally going to do that."

"Oh?"

"I wanted a real one, but I was afraid that I was going to get it..." My throat bobbed painfully.

"Would make her sad," she finished.

I realized I didn't reply when she placed her hand on my arm. "I'd do anything to spare her sadness, but sometimes it feels like to do that, I'd have to spare her happiness, too."

She nodded slowly, searching for the words to respond. "When my mom knew... her time was short... she told me the truth about my dad. Before then, she never encouraged me to hate him, but when I asked, she would only tell me he was a bad man."

I stayed completely silent, knowing that talking about her father was one of the hardest and most vulnerable things for her.

"When she shared the truth, I was... horrified."

My jaw tightened. I couldn't imagine what it was like to hear how her father abused her mother, but the lingering look of pain on her face even now, years later, was a pretty good indication of how hard it was.

"I started to spiral because my whole childhood…" Her head ducked. I reached for her hand, linking her small fingers in mine. "But then she told me something that I've never forgotten; she told me I could hate the man, but I didn't have to hate my memories."

"She sounds like a smart woman," I rasped, echoing her assessment of Val from earlier.

"She was." Stevie looked at me with watery eyes and smiled. "But maybe for you and Lainey, the loss might always hurt, but the memories don't have to make you sad."

Before I could say anything else, a voice pierced our conversation.

"I found it!"

Both our heads turned in the direction of Lainey's voice.

"Uncle Roman! I found our tree."

I followed Stevie through the man-made forest until we reached my niece who was circling around her chosen Christmas tree like a vulture.

Really? I did a double take at her choice. To be honest, it was a little weak as far as Christmas trees went. It wasn't very full and sort of drooped at the top, and the one side had a pretty obvious dead spot where a neighboring tree had grown too close.

"You sure, Bug?" I kept my expression blank when I asked, not wanting to give away that it wasn't the greatest-looking tree on the farm. But when she had the pick of literally every possible tree for the holiday season, I wanted to be sure that this was really the one she wanted.

Her head bobbed.

"If you're sure, I'm sure," I declared and slid the saw from my shoulder.

"What made you pick this one?" Stevie asked as I approached and lowered myself to the ground.

Moving some of the drooping branches out of the way, I slid under them and positioned my saw against the bark but froze when I heard Lainey's proud answer.

"It looked sad."

"You wanted a sad one?"

I could only assume my niece nodded in reply because Stevie then asked, "Why did you want a sad one?"

The cold grip of fear closed around my chest, tightening with each thought that this was a mistake—that I shouldn't have brought her here for a tree. It was too soon. The loss too raw.

"Because everyone else will take the happy ones," Lainey answered quietly. "And then it will be alone."

Jesus. I gritted my teeth, fear releasing its hold only to allow a swell of emotion to crash over me. In the face of the greatest loss a kid could endure, this girl oozed so much empathy it seemed impossible for her tiny body to be able to hold it all.

"That was very thoughtful of you," Stevie replied after a second, her voice clogged, too.

"Yeah," Lainey agreed with childlike pride, and then tacked on, "It also had the most bugs."

A laugh burst free, breaking the tension in my chest, and I began to cut down our sad Christmas tree.

We'd stretched a little further today, and it hurt a little less. Val would be so proud of Lainey, and after all the times my sister told me I deserved more in my life than my work, I hoped she'd be a little proud of me, too; I hadn't been a complete idiot when it came to Stevie. Or maybe I had, but in a good way.

Wherever Val was watching us from, there was one thing I knew for certain: my sister was getting a good kick out of how far and how fast I'd fallen for my nanny.

Just because you set rules, Roman, doesn't mean life will abide by them, she'd warned.

Rules are made to be followed, I'd returned.

She'd smiled at that—a knowing, plotting smile that had, for the length of our childhood, always resulted in her outsmarting me one way or another.

And now, when I looked over the console at Stevie, I could practically hear my sister teasing me, *Rules are made to be broken.*

CHAPTER TWENTY-ONE

Stevie

"Don't forget to write your thankful notes and leave them in this basket." Jo lifted a small wicker bowl above her head and shook it, bouncing the few folded pieces of paper inside.

The very first thing we were told after Jo greeted us at the door to her and Dex's house was that everyone needed to write down something they were thankful for on a small strip of paper, fold it, and place it in the basket—but without our name. She said she'd explain the rest of the activity after dinner.

Well, it was after dinner. The twenty-two-pound turkey had been devoured; Dante had done the honors of cutting it to the tune of "All About that Baste." And there was not a single person in the room who hadn't begged, pleaded, bribed, and even threatened Roman to share his cauliflower casserole recipe; he and Lainey had made a double batch, but that didn't matter. It was the first thing that was gone.

Now, mostly everyone settled into the warm haze of the turkey and stuffing coma, except for Ace and Dex who were on cleanup duty. Dante and Reed argued at the kitchen island over who got to eat the last crescent roll though it looked like they'd decided to arm wrestle for the privilege. The rest of us lounged in the living room to the gentle amusement of *Planes, Trains, and*

Automobiles playing in the background because Dante insisted it was a Thanksgiving classic.

"Shoot, I didn't write mine yet," Carina said beside me. Her and Rocco arrived a little late because they hadn't wanted to wake the baby from her nap.

"I can hold her," I offered, happy to snuggle with the tiny bundle of baby who was sleeping again now that she'd just been fed.

I took the newborn when she rose, and Lainey immediately appeared by my side to peer at the baby.

"You like babies, don't you?" Rocco chuckled when she wedged herself onto the couch in Carina's former seat.

That was an understatement. Babies and bugs.

Lainey nodded. "She's so cute."

"Stevie does look pretty good holding a baby, don't you think, Roman?" Roc called.

I gasped, my gaze snapping to Roman and finding I already had his attention long before Rocco tried to tease him.

Roman watched me with fire in his eyes, and butterflies fluttered low in my stomach.

A baby. His baby.

Those kinds of dreams had been so far off in my life, I wasn't prepared to think about them. I loved kids—it was why I wanted to become a teacher and work with them, but I never thought I'd get to the point where I could trust someone else to love them let alone have a baby with them.

I'd been like a ship out to sea that never planned on finding the safety of shore. For years, all I'd done was prepare to ride the turbulent waves and steel myself for solitude. But then I met Roman, and the shore came so fast, I crashed into it. *Into him.*

"Yeah, she does." He shocked me even more with the deep drawl of his agreement, approaching the couch with a slow gait until he came and stood behind me, his hands resting possessively on my shoulders.

Heat flushed over every inch of my skin, and I knew I shouldn't have had that last Turkeytini.

His thumbs gently brushed along my shoulder, and each stroke felt more intimate than the last. All this talk of babies...

and the baby in my arms... I bit my lip to stop myself from moaning because all I wanted was to be back home and back in Roman's bed.

"So, what's on your list for Santa, Lainey?" Rocco asked, his eyes still teasing Roman even as he changed topics.

She blurted out with a wide smile. "Bugs. And a pirate ship."

Rocco's eyebrows rose. "How... varied."

"You'll get to enjoy these requests soon enough," Roman muttered to him, coming over to stand behind me.

Lainey wrinkled her nose. "I need more bugs for my collection."

"And the pirate ship?"

"For my crew," she replied like it was obvious.

Rocco nodded. "Seems legit."

"Alright, everyone!" Jo strode into the room, the obvious MC for this holiday get-together. "I have everyone's thankful cards, so if you want another slice of dessert, now's the time to grab it because we're going to get started."

The rest of the group gathered in the room, and when Carina returned, I offered her Serena's and my seat, but she refused, happily smiling and talking with Lenni.

"Okay, so what I'm going to do is read our thankful notes, one by one, and we have to guess which one belongs to whom. Okay, first up." Jo waved the paper like a tiny white flag before peeling it open and reading, "I'm thankful for..." She paused. "Drumroll, please."

I laughed when the room instantly came to life, all the guys tapping and drumming on whatever surface they could find.

"Bugs," Jo finished. "I'm thankful for bugs."

The group of us all looked at Lainey who couldn't keep a straight face to save her life, bursting out with a riotous laugh.

"I guess we all know who that one belongs to." She smiled and pulled out the next paper. "I'm thankful for... my wife's..." She trailed off, her eyes widening. Then she walked over to Lenni and handed her the slip. "I think everyone would be thankful if I didn't read that one out loud."

Lenni scanned the paper and then gasped, striding over to a chuckling Dante and swatting his arm. Everyone chuckled, watching the two of them argue until Dante put an end to it by kissing her.

"Looks like I need to emphasize a PG rating on the instructions next year," she mumbled, digging in the basket for the next paper. "Alright, who's going to be next…"

My heart began to thud louder—so loud that I passed a sleeping Serena over to Rocco because I was afraid the noise would wake her. Mumbling an excuse about the bathroom, I rose from the couch, feeling Roman's eyes on me the whole time.

I'd filled one out—the single word coming instantly to my mind as soon as the pen hit the paper, but now, the more I thought about it and the implication… I wondered if it was too much.

I made it to the edge of the room before my name rang out.

"Stevie."

I turned, but it took me a second to realize it wasn't Roman who called my name. Or Rocco or Carina.

It was Jo.

And she hadn't called it—she'd read it on the paper.

And now everyone was looking at me.

My cheeks burned, and thinking quickly, I smiled and met Lainey's gaze over the edge of the couch. "You were only supposed to write one, silly."

Her head swung wildly. "I only wrote bugs!"

If she didn't write it…

My heart tripped and stumbled, arriving slower to the truth than everyone else. *Roman had.*

Before I could even think about all the people around us, he was in front of me, blocking everything else from my view except him.

"I'm thankful for you, Stevie Michaels," he murmured, caressing my cheek with the backs of his knuckles.

In some ways, the declaration was more poignant—more potent—than one of love because it came from a man who never wanted anything for himself. And when you want nothing—when you actively try to ensure you have nothing to lose—to admit gratitude for something or someone was the height of vulnerability.

He'd confessed his vulnerability to me.

My mouth parted, but I couldn't think of a response.

No. That wasn't true.

I could think of a response but only one: *I love you.*

His eyes roamed my face and read my emotions—all of them, I was sure.

"Let's go home," he rasped.

As soon as I nodded, he took my hand and told the group we were going to head out.

If there were a time to give Roman crap for bolting a little early or beg for us to stay until the end of the game, this would've been it. But every person in the room seemed to sense that something had shifted for us, and though they'd been given a glimpse of it, they all knew—many of them firsthand—that it was an intimacy that deserved privacy.

So, the game paused so we could make our goodbyes. Fifteen minutes later, we left with enough food for a month, and Lainey garnered a promise from Rocco and Reed for a pirate ship for Christmas.

For all her energy at Dex and Jo's, Lainey was fast asleep by the time we pulled into the garage.

While I unloaded the two bags full of leftovers into the fridge, Roman put her to bed, and when we met in the kitchen, we were back in that moment at Dex's house, and I was on the verge of telling him I loved him.

"Stevie," he rasped and came to stand in front of me.

His hands cupped my face and then his lips were on mine.

We kissed like two people who'd been holding on for this moment for years rather than hours. It wasn't just pent-up desire that spilled between our lips, it was love. I felt it with every fiber of my being as his lips claimed mine with merciless demand, devouring my mouth to within an inch of still allowing me to breathe.

I felt the edge of the island hit my back a second before my feet left the ground. Roman lifted me onto the counter, never breaking our kiss as he wedged his hips between my legs. I let out a breathy moan when he started to grind against me, the ache inside intensifying into shots of arousal injected directly into my blood.

"I'm thankful for you, Stevie," he muttered against my mouth. "For your smile. For your compassion." He rocked forward, his length grinding harder into my sex, eliciting a moan. "For your strength and your drive." My legs locked around his waist. "For you. For all of you."

My head tipped back, and I felt his fingers grab the edge of my blouse, tugging it up and over my head. The thought that was distant in my mind—that Lainey could walk out of her bedroom any second and see us—worked its way toward the front.

"Tell me how much you want me."

I tensed and whimpered, realizing I couldn't do it.

I couldn't tell him I wanted him because it wasn't enough—it wasn't enough of the truth.

I did want him. I wanted his sweet kisses and dirty words. I wanted his protective nature and possessive desire. I wanted him to take control of all the things I fought so hard to do by myself because that was all I thought I'd ever have. I wanted him beyond all my doubts, but most of all, I wanted him to know how much I loved him.

"Tell me," he ordered, rougher this time, and even through his jeans, I could feel how impossibly hard he was.

"Roman, I need... we should..." I stammered, trying desperately to tell him we needed to move this into the bedroom, but I couldn't get that far, not when I felt the pressure of my bra release and the cool air rush over my breasts.

"Fucking tell me, Stevie," he demanded, dropping his mouth to my breast and locking his teeth on my nipple. I squirmed as my head tipped back with a loud gasp, desire tangling into a million knots between my legs. "Tell me because I... because all I need is you."

His lips pulled my breast into his mouth and sucked hard at the same time as he ground his cock against me again. Pleasure knifed through me, and the confession I'd tried to hold back bled free.

"I love you," I blurted out with a breathless moan, and everything stopped.

I felt his lips slide off my skin and watched his torso straighten with painful slowness in front of me. But when he looked at me, I realized I recognized his expression. It was the same one he'd had at Dex's house. It was the same one he wore every morning when we woke up. The same one I saw the night he'd carried me back to this house—back to his bed, and promised to never let me go.

He'd loved me all that time.

"Say it again," he begged, cupping the side of my face.

I licked my lips. "I don't just want you, Roman. I love you."

His big body shuddered. "I love you, too, Stevie. From the moment I met you, I knew you'd be my undoing," he rasped with emotion. "My unfolding."

I wanted to cry. Tears invaded my eyes, but then he kissed me so hard, so deeply, the riot of feelings in my body instead gave everything to that kiss.

I locked my legs around him, needing him inside me more than oxygen. I loved him. Desperately. Consumingly. *Vulnerably.*

I felt my butt peel off the counter, and I hung on tightly as he carried me into the bedroom, leaving a trail of clothing behind to be cleaned up later.

As soon as the door shut and the lock clicked, gone was the tenderness, in its place, pure possession.

He loved me. He wanted me. *My pirate.*

My back hit the bed, and then his mouth was everywhere. On my neck. On my collarbone. On my breasts.

"Please, Roman," I begged.

He growled and latched on to my right nipple. Filling his hand with my other breast, he expertly caressed me until my head thrashed from side to side. Everything was sensitive, as though opening my heart unlocked a level of pleasure I wasn't allowed to feel before. His mouth and fingers worked in perfect symphony until my whole body started to sing.

I arched toward him, unable to get enough of what he was doing. When he finally pulled himself up, everything swam in my vision but him. The man I loved. Reaching over his head, he pulled his shirt off with one swipe, keeping his eyes locked on me with wild hunger.

"I need to be inside you, princess," he said and untangled my legs from his waist.

I was halfway through a moan of agreement when he flipped me over and yanked me to the edge of the bed, my feet dropping to the floor. Next, my leggings and underwear came down in one swift motion to bare my ass. I shivered, the cool air its own caress against my slick sex.

I heard his growl a second before his fingers touched between my legs. I let out a strangled whimper. Hearing him tell me he loved me opened something inside me that made me impossibly turned on. He moved to peel my clothing from my ankles, but before he was done, he flattened his tongue to my pussy and dragged the velvet muscle through my seam, letting out a guttural moan in the process.

I cried out, jerking my hips back, on the verge of exploding.

"Always so fucking wet for my cock. Like you were made for me," he rumbled low, rising behind me.

I squirmed, hearing the sound of his zipper and anticipating what came next. A second later, I felt him line the head of his cock up with my soaking entrance.

"I love you, Stevie," he rasped once more. His hands locked on my upturned hips, holding me steady, and then he slammed in deep, the tip of him knocking against my womb as his balls rubbed on my clit.

He didn't pause, thrusting hard until my entire body shook with the force. "I love you so fucking much, you have no idea what you do to me."

I cried out, dying with pleasure as he pounded harder and faster into me, his body and his words breaking me entirely apart.

"Say it," he commanded.

My mouth opened, but only long, desperate moans escaped into the bed as the thickness of him fit into me with euphoric fullness. I arched back into him, needing more. Needing everything.

"Say it again," he groaned while fucking me, his hips

pistoning deep. Each drive rubbed his balls against my clit while his cock rocked into my G-spot. "Tell me you love me, and I'll let you come."

I wanted his control—all of it. And I wanted to lose all of mine. I'd been adrift, alone, for so long.

"I love you," I panted into the bedding, relinquishing my body... my heart... my vulnerability... all to him.

"Good girl," he groaned. "Forever my good girl."

Angling his hips, he drove even deeper into my body and sent me spiraling into ecstasy. I buried my face into the blanket, biting down on my lower lip and holding my scream inside my mouth like a ship in a bottle as my orgasm crashed through me in violent waves. His rough grunts coincided with each slow, hard thrust that buried him all the way to the hilt until he came inside me.

Sliding out of me one moment, I'm gathered into his arms in the next and laid properly on the bed. Minutes later, I was tucked into his chest, still trying to calm the rapid beats of my own heart.

"What did you write? On your thankful note," he rumbled as we drifted toward sleep. "What are you thankful for?"

"Pirates," I teased groggily.

His chest vibrated. "Seriously. What did you write?"

I let out a deep, satisfied breath, trying to recall another moment in my life when I'd been this happy.

"Family," I whispered, trembling with emotion.

I felt his breath catch. For some, being grateful for family was an easy gratitude to have on Thanksgiving, but not for me. My whole idea of family had been twisted—uprooted like a thorny weed. What I thought family was had been a lie; what I hoped family could be had been put out of my reach.

And then I came here.

And met them.

And without even realizing it—without even asking—they'd given me all the things I knew family to be. Honesty. Loyalty. Vulnerability. Safety.

Love.

Roman slid his fingers along the side of my face until they notched under my chin, pulling my lips up to his.

"You're what made us a family," he said, kissing me softly. "You, my love."

Happy tears leaked down my cheeks as he held me tight to him.

"I love you," he rasped like he wanted it to be the last thing I heard before I fell asleep.

The furthest corners of my hesitant heart heard him and hoped love would be enough when he learned the truth about my broken past because I couldn't imagine a future without him.

CHAPTER TWENTY-TWO

Roman

I ONLY WENT TO PUT MY TOOTHBRUSH BACK ON THE CHARGER, but I couldn't stop myself from settling my hands on Stevie's waist where she stood in front of the sink in the master bathroom. She had on one of my new Covington T-shirts and was putting up her hair, but her raised arms lifted the shirt enough to tease me with the globes of her ass.

"I love you," I rasped, dragging her back to my front and setting my lips on her neck. I inhaled the sweet lemon scent of the lotion she used and my cock thickened and pressed into the seam of her ass.

I hadn't fucked her there yet, but I would. Eventually. When my caveman needed to pump her pussy full of my cum subsided. Sometimes, I wondered if I was just desperate for my fucking vasectomy to fail—like if I came hard enough inside her, I could still get her pregnant.

"That's not the kind of wood we're looking for this morning," she murmured even as she tipped back into me.

"Are you sure?" I rubbed my cock against her and let my hand slide to the soft curve of her stomach.

I was going to reverse my vasectomy. That decision came like the flip of a switch the second I saw her holding Rocco's baby. I wanted that to be our baby in her arms. *My baby.* Of course, there'd be a conversation for when she was ready for that, but I was the kind of man who, once I knew what I wanted, I would pursue it to the nth degree.

And I wanted Stevie. In my life. In my bed. Wearing my last name. Pregnant with my kid.

"I can be quick," I teased, kissing her neck and reveling in the way she sighed. *Sometimes, speed was a virtue.*

She hummed, and my dick pulsed. Her moans were engineered to a frequency that drove a man insane. Like a damn dog whistle, one of those moans had my cock searching her out and panting for her.

My fingers angled for the waist of her underwear and her stomach quivered under my touch for a second before she practically leaped out of my hold, finishing her hair and shooting me a coy smile.

"We promised Lainey we'd finish decorating the tree before her school Christmas party," she chided, pointing a finger at me.

Grunting, I made a show of adjusting my erection as I approached her, palming it so the length jutted out against my sweats. I took her finger and pulled her hand to my face, pressing a kiss to her open palm.

"Then I want a promise that you're going to decorate my wood later," I rasped and flicked my tongue out against her skin. "I want it strung up and tinseled with your cum."

"Roman…"

"Promise me." I ordered and bit into the pad of flesh at the base of her thumb.

"I promise," she replied huskily.

"Good girl." It was only added torture to claim her lips in a hard kiss, but I couldn't help myself. "Now, put that ass away before I have to take an ice bath to look appropriate."

She chuckled, and I smacked her perfect ass when she turned and went back into the bedroom to get dressed.

It still took me a little longer to leave the bedroom, but by the time I did, Stevie already had a Pentatonix holiday playlist streaming through the TV and she and Lainey were sorting through the bags of decorations we'd bought for the house.

"Mommy loved blue and silver," Lainey declared, holding up a string of blue tinsel that was half unraveled and half tangled around her.

"She did." I nodded and walked to the kitchen, stopping short at the cup of coffee waiting for me on the counter.

It was the little things that continued to catch me off guard and remind me just how perfectly Stevie had fit into our lives —*into my life*.

"I think your mom and dad are going to love your tree." I heard Stevie say as she arranged the tinsel on the tree.

Lainey's shoulders slumped. "How will they see it?"

Stevie tugged out a string of Christmas lights. "Fairy lights," she said. "They work just like fairy flies… lighting the way for the people we love to find us."

Lainey's smile made my chest tighten, but it was nothing compared to the look Stevie and I shared when she went back to decorating.

"I will always find you," I murmured low as I joined her in the living room.

I went to claim a kiss from her inviting lips when my phone rang obnoxiously on the kitchen island. Frowning, I strode over and checked the screen. *Dex.* I ended the call and set my cell back down. I would be at the office in less than an hour, whatever it was could wait until then.

I was two steps away from the island when it buzzed again; this time, a rush of cold rippled through my veins.

Dex again. My eyes flicked up and caught Stevie's; she nodded that I should answer right before she reached for Lainey and distracted her with the boxes of Disney ornaments.

"Hello?"

"You have to get in here," Dex answered gravely. "There's been a murder in Carmel."

My lower back slammed into the edge of the counter when I swayed.

"What?" I hissed. "Where in Carmel? Who was the victim?" Immediately, I looked for Lainey and Stevie, like I needed them in my sights to know they were okay. "Was it him? Was it the Archangel?"

Stevie sensed something was wrong. She handed Lainey ornaments to hang on the tree, but she was only focused on me.

Shit.

I didn't want to worry her, so I gave them my back.

"I think so, but they're not telling us much—"

"What? Why the hell—why not?" I flattened my free hand on the counter, digging my grip into the granite like I could drive my frustration into it.

"I don't know. There was a body and the coroner called us—asked for Koorie."

"It has to be the Archangel." *Here. In Carmel.* "But why the fuck didn't the police call us? They know they're supposed to alert us with any victims who fit the profile." I drove my hand through my hair.

"My guess? We're not their favorite people right now."

I ground my teeth together. If the lawsuit we were bringing against those officers affected how the department handled the presence of a serial killer in town, there was going to be hell to pay.

"They wouldn't give her any more information over the phone, so I don't know if they know who the victim is or if they're not saying. She probably tried to call you, but just fucking get over here, Roman."

"Right. Yeah. I'll be right there."

I ended the call, my phone slamming on the counter with more force than intended. My body hummed with a mix of things I wasn't sure I'd felt before, but the biggest of them was fear.

The man I'd been hunting for as long as I could remember was here. In the town where I was living. Killing.

For the first time, my instinct wasn't to hunt; it was to protect.

When I worked for the FBI, I'd only had myself to worry about, which meant all caution would be chucked to the wind in order to catch this fucker. But now, I had Lainey. And a life. And

Stevie. And love. And goddamn if they weren't the only important things to me, and all I could think about was how to make them safe.

I spun and jolted when I realized Stevie was standing right behind me.

"What happened?" She was the picture of concern with her furrowed brow and folded arms.

Safe.

"We need to go." I stepped around her and walked into the living room, addressing my niece, "Hey Lainey, how would you like to go visit baby Serena today?"

She scrutinized me like only a six-year-old could. "Instead of my school party?"

My mouth drew tight and I nodded, silently praying that it wouldn't upset her. "Stevie can go with you, too."

That got her to smile. "Okay."

"Great." I'd never felt such relief. At Rocco's they'd both be safe, together and protected with him there while I got to the bottom of what the fuck was going on. "Alright, well why don't you get your stuff together, so Stevie can get going?"

Her curl-topped head bobbed on top of her tiny neck like a bobblehead doll, and then she scampered off to her room, completely oblivious to the emotional panic that was driving me.

Stevie, on the other hand, wasn't.

"What's going on, Roman?" she demanded again.

"You're going to take Lainey and drive over to Carina's house and stay there for a couple of hours, okay?" I clipped, determined to ignore her.

"Not until you tell me what's going on." She put her foot down. "I'm not a child, Roman. Protecting me doesn't mean you have to keep me in the dark."

I ground my teeth tight.

"There's been another murder, hasn't there?" she pressed.

"In Carmel," I rasped.

"Is it… the same person from before?"

I hadn't talked to her about the case since that morning when the discussion made her visibly ill, and it was why I was hesitant now. Except he was here. In Carmel. And I wouldn't let ignorance be the reason she could end up in danger.

"The Archangel." I shoved my phone into my pocket and let out a bitter laugh. "It's like he's following me. Haunting me."

"Why?"

"I don't know," I rasped. "Maybe because I almost caught him. Seven years ago, he came out of retirement."

Stevie flinched, but before I could regret answering her, she asked, "Retirement? Do killers… retire?"

"Sometimes. Usually when they get locked up or too old or sick," I said tightly. "But the Archangel was different. A religious zealot who… assaulted and killed women and then carved crosses from their chest." Her shocked gasp made me rein myself in. I cleared my throat and returned to the less-gruesome facts of the case. "He just… took a break. He killed for almost a decade without being caught—long before I joined the Bureau—and then disappeared."

She sank onto the couch, and I didn't blame her. To hear about so many deaths at the hand of one man made even my stomach turn.

"For how long?" Her voice sounded hollow.

"Fifteen years," I replied and then lost myself in the CliffsNotes of the case. "And then six years ago, I got an anonymous call that this killer was living in Wyoming, but the caller never told me his name. So, my team went, but by the time we got there, he'd killed one woman and had taken another—my friend's mom."

"Oh my god…" She covered her mouth with her hand. "Oh my god…"

I immediately reached for her shoulder and assured her, "We got there in time to save her, but we weren't able to catch him. Since then, he's been killing young women—runaways—all over the Midwest and western states."

"Runaways…" Her voice was thready.

"All from Wyoming," I revealed with a heavy sigh, her eyes locking on to me with the precision of a sniper, hanging on to my every word like her next target. "He's killing runaways, and I think it's because he's looking for his missing daughter."

"Missing... daughter..."

I wasn't sure when it happened, but looking at Stevie now, I realized her face had lost almost all its color, and I felt like an idiot.

"Shit, Stevie. I'm sorry," I rasped and pulled her up and into my arms, holding her tight. "I said too much. I don't want to keep you in the dark, but I also don't want you to worry—you have nothing to worry about. You know I'll do anything to protect the two of you, and sending you to Rocco's place is just a precaution. More for my peace of mind than anything else, okay?"

"This can't be happening," she murmured, stunned.

I wished I could go back three minutes in time and caution my former self from saying too much. But now, my whole life was the two of them, and though I wanted to share everything with her, I should've been more sensitive.

"It's going to be okay," I murmured, pressing my lips to hers.

"No, Roman." She pushed against my chest, and I drew back. Her eyes glistened and two tears coursed down her cheeks.

"Hey, hey... what's this?" I cupped her face and swiped away the drops of moisture. "Don't cry. It's going to be okay."

"No, it's not." She dragged in one pained breath after another—breaths driven by fear.

"Stevie, you're safe. You know I'd never let anything happen to you or Lainey. You know you're safe with me," I told her, shocked by her response. Even after her attack, I hadn't seen her this distraught. "What's wrong? What are you afraid of?"

She inhaled sharply and then, meeting my gaze, confessed in the smallest voice possible, "I'm afraid of losing you."

Jesus.

Suddenly, I understood. Everyone she'd trusted to take care of her... everyone she'd loved... she'd ultimately lost. And now, I'd just told her that the man I was hunting wasn't just a killer, but a good one. One who seemed to be toying with me by how close he was hunting to where I lived.

"You're not going to lose me," I declared fiercely, and then kissed her. I tasted her protest on her tongue and kissed her like I had the power to dissolve it.

"I am," she whimpered and shook her head. "I am because—"

"I love you, Stevie. You're *not* going to lose me," I promised against her lips.

"Ready!" Lainey declared, her backpack bouncing against her jacket as she ran over to us.

I pulled back, reluctant to take my attention from Stevie, but she turned away to wipe her cheeks on the backs of her hands so Lainey wouldn't see that she'd been crying.

"Ready?" Stevie replied, covering up all traces of her concern in front of my niece. "We're going to have to put your hair up when we get there." She threaded her fingers through Lainey's hair just like Val used to do. "You know baby Serena likes to pull."

"Oh yeah." Lainey's head bobbed.

"Alright, let's go," I said hoarsely, reaching for Stevie's hand and tugging her to my side. "Trust me," I murmured and pressed a kiss to the side of her head before I shuttled them both to the front door.

There were a million things that didn't sit right with me when I pulled out of the driveway. Why there was another kill here... in Carmel, of all the places. Why no one was telling us anything about the victim. But nothing so much as the look on Stevie's face when I told her about the monster we were hunting.

I'd seen her afraid before, but not like that—not the kind of fear that comes when you're faced with losing everything.

I swallowed hard, checking my rearview until Stevie made the turn off the Coastal Highway that would take her to Rocco and Carina's place.

She would realize... tonight... tomorrow... a week from now... a year from now... she'd realize there was nothing that could take me from her.

CHAPTER TWENTY-THREE

Stevie

I'D GONE FROM THE HIGHEST OF HIGHS TO THE LOWEST OF LOWS so quickly, I wasn't sure I'd ever get my stomach to drop down from where it seemed lodged in my throat.

"Hey, guys," Carina opened the door and greeted us. About half a second passed before she realized that there was something seriously wrong and quickly added, "Lainey, Uncle Rocco has Serena in the living room right back there"—she pointed down the hall—"why don't you go check on them?"

Lainey dumped her bag and shoes in the foyer and ran for the room at the back of the house.

"What's wrong, Stevie? You look like you've seen a ghost." Carina put her hand on my arm.

Worse.

"I can't stay," I told her, every breath growing more stunted.

I hadn't been able to find the words back at the house. How could I when it felt like I'd been swallowed up by something worse than a nightmare?

Roman wasn't hunting another killer—he was hunting my father.

I knew the day was coming when I would have to tell Roman the truth about my past—about my father. That he was a serial killer. But to hear Roman was hunting him. To hear that Lee had been killing this whole time... and all because of me... all because he was trying to find me.

"Oh my god, Stevie." Carina grabbed my shoulders and steadied me as I tipped forward, nausea crashing through me. "Just come sit down for a minute—"

"I can't." I pulled away. "I have to tell Roman the truth."

"Rocco said Roman is on a big case. Just come inside. Whatever you have to tell him can wait until tonight."

"No." I shook my head. "It can't wait. I have to tell him. Or Dex. Or... someone."

Someone who could do something because this was about more than just my past, more than just about my family now. It wasn't just a truth that needed to be shared, it was a problem that needed to be fixed—*that only I could fix.*

"Are you in danger?"

"Just please, watch Lainey. Please." Tears barreled down my cheeks. "I have to go to Covington."

Her mouth opened and shut, but ultimately, she knew she couldn't stop me. She recognized the urgency that vibrated from my very being.

"Then I'm coming with you," she declared.

"No, you—" I tried, but she was already gone, striding toward the living room with the commanding presence of a queen even though she had on sweatpants, a T-shirt, and a nursing bra.

It couldn't have been thirty seconds before she returned.

"Really, Care, you don't have to. You shouldn't leave—"

"Shouldn't leave Rocco alone with our baby and Roman's niece?" She chuckled. "He's survived family gatherings with my five sisters and Dante. He's prepared for anything."

I could only swallow and lead the way to my car.

"What's going on, Stevie?" she asked as soon as we turned out of the driveway.

Bitterness and regret and fear sat in my mouth like a melting ice cube, not only burning my tongue but carried into the rest of my body with each swallow.

"I didn't..." I trailed off and started over. "I kept from

Roman who my father was, and now it's going to break everything."

"Did you keep it from him to hurt him?"

"No." I shuddered at the thought. "Never."

"Did you know that I kept from Rocco that I was spying on him for the people trying to arrest him for a crime he didn't commit?" she revealed. "Sometimes, we start out on a path that we think it's best to follow, and when we realize it's not the right decision, we fix it. You're going to him to trust him with the truth and to fix it. He'll understand."

My chest burned, wanting to disagree. As a spy for the CIA, Rocco knew that lies could be essential for survival. In comparison, Roman's life was defined by the truth. By always doing the right thing. The man had surgically prevented himself from having children because he thought it was the right thing to do; that wasn't the kind of man who would *understand* why I didn't tell him I knew my father was a serial killer.

"I'm not sure this truth is something he'll be able to accept… or forgive." *How could he love someone who had the same eyes as the man he hunted? Who had the same blood as the man who'd killed dozens and dozens of women?*

"You know what, Stevie? Love is a truth, too. So, if the truth about your dad is more powerful than the truth about your love for him, then Roman doesn't deserve you."

My friend laid down the law from the seat next to me, and though I appreciated what she was trying to do, the idea of deserving better wouldn't spare the pain of a completely broken heart.

ONCE AGAIN, I found myself inching up the drive to the Covington Security headquarters, this time with my own answers to a deadly investigation. Carina remained quiet then beside me, and I was glad she'd insisted on coming because her words kept me calm.

Love was a truth.

We were buzzed through the entrance gate almost as soon as

I'd pulled up to it without having to stop at the intercom. The heavy tumble of my pulse tripped when I didn't see Roman's car in the parking lot. *He'd already left.*

Gripping the wheel tighter, I parked in a spot.

It didn't matter. I had to tell someone about Lee. They had to stop him. And then... then I'd handle the windfall that would come when Roman learned the truth.

"Stevie?" Reed was standing in the doorway by the time I was out of the car, concern scratching his handsome features. "Carina?" His blue eyes grew even rounder.

"I have to talk to Dex right now."

"Yeah, of course." He didn't argue with the two women charging at him, instead led us inside and through the hallways to Dex's office.

"Dex—"

"I need to talk to you about the case," I blurted out, barging right past Reed. My chest heaved. Maybe it was better that Roman wasn't here. If he was, I didn't know if I'd be able to speak the facts without drowning in emotion.

"The case?" Dex stood and scowled when Carina appeared behind me. "What's going on? Are you both alright?"

"No. Yes, but no." I gulped in air like it was my last breath before I dove into the deep, unsure if I'd make it back to the surface. "I know who you're looking for."

"What?" Dex rocked back. "You mean the Archangel? Did you see something—see him?" His eyes snapped to my friend. "Where's Rocco? Did he—"

"No." I flung my head side to side, strands of hair spilling free from the loose hold of my hair tie. "I mean, I know who he is."

The two of them stared at me like I'd just grown another head right in front of them.

"The Archangel?" Dex clarified, disbelief coating his tone. "The serial killer?"

My chin bobbed like a leaf on rolling waves, waiting for the one that would sink me.

"His name is Lee Nelson Turner." The truth was a knife to

my stomach, and I shoved it to the very hilt. "And I'm the daughter he's looking for."

To their credit, both Dex and Reed remained impossibly calm while the bombshell I'd just dropped on them continued to detonate. Carina also hung back in silence, but after our conversation in the car, I knew she had an inkling that there was some kind of tie between my father and this case.

"Jesus, Stevie." Dex's expression turned grim, but his next words surprised me. "I'm sorry."

Sorry? My mouth fell open a little. I was the one who should be sorry. I was the one who should've said something sooner—told someone sooner. Maybe then none of this would've happened.

Yet, he was the one apologizing to me.

I thought I could hold it together, but I couldn't. The warm rush of hope thawed some of the frozen fear in my chest and my shoulders began to shake as some of the weight I'd carried for so long slipped free.

I'd told someone who my father was, and he hadn't criticized me or held me accountable. He hadn't berated me or looked at me like I was guilty by association. *He'd apologized.*

Carina's arm slid around my shoulders, gently squeezing. "It's okay, Stevie. We're all here for you."

I bit into my cheek as more silent tears leaked free.

"I have to call him," Dex rasped. "He shouldn't hear this from anyone but you."

He was right. I nodded slowly, letting a single tear leak down my cheek.

"It'll be okay," Reed said beside me, offering a kind smile.

I watched Dex put his cell to his ear, and it must've rang only once before Roman answered.

"Turn around. You have to come back to the office," Dex told him, his eyes never leaving me. I figured Roman tried to argue with him because Dex's jaw tightened and he pulled off his glasses before ordering, "It's about the case, and if you don't come back here now, you're fired."

I choked on the ultimatum and watched Dex hang up.

"Well, that was a swift kick in the ass," Reed remarked, moving to the center of the room and propping his hip on the table.

"He's too damn stubborn for his own good," Dex grumbled as his excuse.

I smiled a little because he wasn't wrong. Roman was as stubborn as they came when it came to following his gut and doing what was right.

"I just need to know three things, Stevie." Dex met my eyes. "Do you know where Turner is?"

I appreciated that he didn't call him my father.

"No."

"Does he know where you are?"

"No." I shook my head wildly. "I mean, not that I know of."

How he would've found me, I had no idea. But I couldn't ignore that he'd made it to Carmel Cove out of all the places in the world, and the coincidence sent a chill through my bones.

Dex nodded and then posed his last question. "Why now?"

"I didn't know he was still... out there, and I had no idea he was who you were looking for." I exhaled slowly, trying to steady my pulse. "Roman didn't tell me anything about the case until today."

"Of course not," Dex grunted and then returned to his computer.

"Why don't you sit," Carina suggested, leading me over to one of the chairs pulled up to the table.

The next couple of minutes put my world on pause. The only indication that time passed was the soft clicks of Dex's keyboard as he went to work, presumably looking up everything about my father that would help them locate him.

After minutes that felt like hours, the door swung open so hard it bounced back against the wall. The anger on Roman's face evaporated as soon as he saw me, replaced with utter confusion.

"Stevie? Carina?" Even though Dex had called him to come

back, his questions were only for me. "What's going on? *Where's Lainey?*"

"She's at Carina's house with Rocco." I rose. I should've probably stayed seated because my legs were so wobbly, but I couldn't. I had to face him and the truth. "I need to talk to you."

The air went out of him in a whoosh. "Jesus, Stevie. Can't it wait? I don't want to be insensitive, but there's a killer in Carmel—"

"I know—" My heart pounded. I rested my fingertips on the table to steady myself.

"And I really need to get to Koorie—"

"Roman—" The rest of the room fell away.

"This isn't just any killer—hell, any serial killer." He drove his hand through his hair. He was so locked on his focus, like a top spinning on a single point—the only way to break him from it was to topple him altogether. "This monster—"

"Is my father!" I exclaimed, cupping my hand over my mouth as a small cry followed it. "That's what I came to tell you—what I had to tell you." I gulped in air though none of it seemed to reach my starving lungs. "I was born Stephanie Turner, and the monster you're looking for is Lee Turner. My father."

And that was how my happily ever after was broken.

CHAPTER TWENTY-FOUR

Roman

The monster you're looking for is my father.

I'd seen and heard a lot of fucked-up things in my lifetime—things that made me wonder what the hell could possibly fuck up a person or a situation to this point... things that I thought shocked me to my very core.

But none of those things had made me feel like this.

Even losing Val—the pain, the grief, it was mind numbing, but it wasn't *this*. This was consuming. Not like a wave or a storm. It was consuming like a bomb; it engulfed everything and left only ashes.

"Your father... you told me he abused your mother," I rasped low, betrayal morphing into anger.

"No, I said she left him when she realized he was a very bad man," she corrected, and the way those words split hairs fractured the hold I had over my control. "And he was," she insisted, drawing a trembling breath.

"You lied."

"Roman..." Dex's low warning to my side filtered into my reality.

I ignored him. She'd lied to me. I was a fucking profiler, and I hadn't realized she'd been lying to me this whole time.

"I didn't lie," she protested, voice growing thick with pain. "I just never told you about that part of him because it had nothing to do with me—because he has nothing to do with me. Not anymore."

"It has everything to do with you. You're his daughter, and he's a fucking serial killer!"

She flinched as though I'd slapped her, and truthfully, a physical slap would've been less abusive than the words that flung carelessly from my mouth. But I couldn't stop them.

"I'm not responsible for what my father did," she choked out, the tension in the room reaching volatile heights.

"And what about what he's doing now?" I charged. "What about what he's been doing for seven goddamn years, all because of you—all because you didn't say anything."

I could tell she wanted to cry by the way her chest spasmed, desperate to break apart.

"I didn't know, Roman," she confessed brokenly. "I didn't know what was happening. How could I? How could I know he was still hurting people when we left everything behind... including our freedom to start over."

"I want the truth," I ground out, my fist clenching and releasing at my side. "All of it. From the beginning."

Her lower lip quivered, the same movement I saw the night she was attacked and broke down. Like then, I wanted to go to her—to hold her—except now, I didn't feel like I knew who I was holding... or why.

She nodded and tangled her hands nervously in front of her, and I felt like with each passing second, I was watching her reel herself back in from where I'd promised her she could always reach for me.

"When I was fifteen, my mom came into my room, threw my things into a suitcase and told me we were leaving. She didn't tell me why or where we were going. We just left... while my dad was at church teaching a confirmation class."

Of fucking course, that sadistic motherfucker.

"When we made it to California, we went to... some place... and my mom changed our names." A tear bubbled down her cheek. "She told me my dad wasn't a good man, and that was why we had to leave." Another tear. "I thought maybe... he hit her or something. He was always... strict though I'd never seen him violent."

Everything she'd ever told me about her father made sense. Like blocks building on one another to construct the truth. Why they never had pets. Why he didn't want her dressing up for Halloween or watching certain movies.

It all fit with the profile of the killer that I'd hunted for the better part of a decade, and it was right under my nose this entire time. I felt myself starting to fume—from the heat in my blood to the burn in my cells.

This was what emotions brought—blindness. *Foolishness.*

"We lived in Monterey for a year or so before she got too sick and we had to move back to San Francisco," she said, crying as she spoke.

The primal part of me roared inside to go to her—to protect her, soothe her—but my anger beat it back down... beat it back into the damn box I'd locked all this shit in before.

"Right before she died, she told me the truth," she said, her voice becoming threadbare. "She told me she'd been listening to these true crime podcasts while she did housework. She told my dad it was Bible sermons." She clutched her arms over her. "She'd listened to one about a killer who was never caught and who cut crosses into his victims and took their cross necklaces as souvenirs. She said the image always stuck with her, and she was never sure why until she went to clean out the garage that day."

"She found his trophies?"

Stevie's chin quivered and then dropped. "She wasn't supposed to clean that area of my dad's stuff, but it had been there for fifteen years, and she said she just... ended up over there. Like something drew her to find it."

"And she called me." I knew this part of the story.

Again, she confirmed with a dip of her head. "She called, but knew we couldn't stick around. She was afraid the call wouldn't be enough. Not with how smart the podcast had made him to be. She was afraid he'd manage to evade you and what he'd do to her—*us* when he realized what she'd done."

"Well, if she would've given me his name, we might've had a better shot," I clipped.

"I'm sorry—"

"And you never had contact with him? Never tried to contact him?" I cut her off, knowing somewhere deep inside that she wasn't the one who needed to be sorry right now.

But I was the one with almost thirty fucking deaths on my hands because I'd been unable to catch him—four of those during the time when I'd been too preoccupied with fucking her —or wanting to fuck her—that I hadn't realized how all the pieces of her past fit the missing holes of my unsolved case.

"Why would I want anything to do with a man who's done the things he has?" Her voice broke. "It was bad enough when I believed for four years that he'd abused my mom, but when she told me the truth…" Her brow furrowed and for the first time, her gaze left mine and fell to the floor. "If she hadn't been dying, she would've never told me." She swiped more tears away. "She would've continued to protect me."

"So, you had no idea he was killing again?" I demanded.

Her cheeks turned beet red. "Do you think I would've kept quiet if I did?"

My teeth gritted. I wanted to respond, but I forced myself not to—forced myself to hold my gut reaction back because I didn't fucking trust the damn thing. I didn't trust anything, least of all the way I loved her.

"You kept quiet about all the women he killed before. Why should now be any different?" The words lashed from my mouth like a whip. But even if I wanted to, I couldn't take them back.

"I kept quiet before because I had no more information," she cried out with pure agony. "I didn't know Mom never gave you his name. And even if she'd confessed that to me, too, it would've been four years too late. You know him—that part of him— better than I do; you know he would've changed his name and appearance to keep you from finding him just like we did to keep him from finding us."

I dragged a hand through my hair with a snarl, too many fucking emotions pulling me in every goddamn direction, it felt like I was being torn limb from limb.

"I don't have evidence, Roman, only a young girl's memories." Her voice cracked, a small sob slipping through. "I never thought—"

"That he'd look for you? That he'd continue to kill? That you'd be able to put an end to this?" I snarled and advanced on her, losing all rein over the emotions I'd never let out before. "Is that what I'm supposed to tell the families of the victims? That you were too busy moving on with your life to save their daughters—"

"Roman," Dex boomed from his seat though he was no longer sitting. "Enough."

"No, it's not enough," I snapped back. "But it will be when I finally catch this fucker. Your father." I pointed my finger at Stevie like I was accusing her genetics. I spun to face Dex. "He's here. In my town. Find him, and call me when you do."

"Roman—"

"As for you"—I rounded on the woman I loved... the daughter of the serial killer I was hunting.

"Please," she said ever so softly. "You know I—"

"What I know is that I don't know you, and this is not over," I declared hoarsely, though my tone implied that we were. *Fuck.*

She blanched like I'd struck her.

"Of course," she murmured.

Stevie kept her head high as she walked out of the room because that was who she was—the one who kept standing tall no matter what wave crashed over her, even when that wave was me. My head turned, my eyes locking on her retreating form as it left a trail of all the ways I'd failed her in my wake.

Once more, this woman had lost someone who'd promised to stand by her and protect her. An hour ago, I would've killed the person who thought they could do that to her, and now that person was me. I was the one who'd cut off my love to spite my heart.

My view of her was broken by the small, dark-haired Italian demanding my attention.

"I guess you got lucky, Roman. Having to learn about all these monsters, and here, it only takes a mirror for you to profile an asshole," Carina charged with false sweetness and jogged after Stevie.

I turned to find both Dex and Reed staring at me, neither looking pleased.

"Don't," I warned them. "Reed, you're coming with me. I'll meet you in the car," I declared, wanting to focus on the case—on something—anything—about this fucking situation that was within my control.

The younger man held his ground for a moment before obeying and leaving Dex and me alone.

"You made a mistake," he said flatly.

"Me?" I growled. "She's the one who knew her dad was a fucking killer and didn't do anything about it."

Dex yanked his glasses off his nose and tossed them onto his desk.

"And what the hell was she supposed to do, Roman? Go to the cops with information they already had? Information on a man who hadn't killed in her lifetime? Information that was half a decade old? You're the one who said even the FBI wasn't sure that it was the same guy killing again, so what would they do? Look into it? And in the meantime, possibly put her at risk? Who would've protected her?"

"It doesn't matter! She knew her father was a killer, she should've said something—"

"She fucking said something now! Christ, do I have to do your damn job for you and profile the girl? The people meant to protect her, failed her. The people she should be able to trust, turned out to be some of the worst of humanity. Her mother *tried* to turn in her father, and he still wasn't caught. Why the fuck would she think that this time—*another seven years later*—would be any different? All this time, she's been shown she has no one to rely on except herself." He was practically shouting now. I'd never seen him shout before. "And you just proved her right."

Fucking fuck.

The more he said, the more I wanted to beat the shit out of myself. I was just so... shocked. And hurt and angry. And all I could see were all the things I'd missed about her childhood stories because I was too busy seeing her.

But that was the whole fucking point of love. To be seen by the person we loved, and to be safe.

And instead, I'd turned on her.

"She should've told me," I said between gritted teeth.

He let out a sad laugh. "When? Before you showed her that you were worthy of her trust? Before you loved her? Before she knew what you did or who you were looking for? Why would she tell you then?"

"I don't... fuck." I spun and slammed my fist into the door, feeling it rattle.

"After everything she's been through, you made her believe she could trust you, and you told her, in front of all of us, that you don't fucking know her. Jesus—" He turned away, shaking his head. "You should go. You have a monster to catch."

And it was pretty clear the monster he was talking about was me.

I let myself out without responding because there was no response. Or excuse.

She'd come to me with the truth, and I treated her like my feelings for her betrayed me; the reality was that without them, I wouldn't have the answers I'd searched for for so long.

Every step echoed *"fuck you"* like a ghost of guilt was stalking me.

I wanted to say fuck it to everything and head straight for Stevie, and I would've if there wasn't a serial killer on the loose. If it was anything less than life and death, I would've dropped it to fix this. But I couldn't, and she knew that. That was the worst part of all... she wouldn't want me to find her and fix this if it meant putting another innocent person at risk.

Her father might be a killer, but I'd never met a person more self-sacrificing and deserving of sainthood than Stevie.

I drowned in my emotions all the way out to the car. Regret. Self-loathing. Fear. And it wasn't until we were a minute or two away from the morgue when I realized Reed hadn't said a single word.

"I know I made a mistake," I offered gruffly, wanting to say something but not get into a conversation about it.

"My dad was a cop," he chose to reply, eyes trained out the window.

"I didn't know that." Granted, I'd only worked with Reed less than a handful of times when he was on the force.

"Because he was a dirty cop," he said, surprising me with a story that seemed wholly unrelated. "He was a dirty cop who'd smuggle drugs in my teddy bear when he'd take my brother and me to the park and then sell them."

"What the fuck." I swung my car into the parking lot at the morgue, reeling from the confession.

Now, it made sense why he'd be so irritated when I'd accused the Carmel cops of taking bribes.

"When my mom realized, she reported him. He never had a history of violence or abuse, but when he found out she'd turned him in…" Reed wiped a hand over his mouth. "He was a cop, so of course, they didn't arrest him right away. But that one night was all he needed. One night to come home, rip the rolling pin right from her hands, and start to beat her with it."

I was speechless as I put the car in park.

"If it hadn't been for my older brother, he would've killed her." He paused and cleared his throat.

"What happened to him?" I rasped.

"He overdosed later that night to avoid prosecution," he answered and finally looked at me. "How do you think the guys in the academy… at the precinct… would've looked at me if they knew my father was a dirty cop and drug dealer?"

I opened my mouth to reply and then shut it just as quick. I knew how I was looked at when I told people I hunted serial killers; I'd adapted how I described myself over the years as simply a behavioral specialist for the FBI.

People shouldn't judge you, but they did. They judged me. They would've judged Reed. And they sure as fuck would've judged Stevie.

But judged wouldn't have been the worst of it.

I'd seen what had become of parents and significant others of famous serial killers—the survivors. They spent their lives telling and retelling their story and traumas like they somehow had to make up for those crimes.

The point of his story hit me.

Even if turning in her father resulted in his capture, she

never would've been free of him. Especially as a child of a serial killer. She would've been questioned and studied. Poked and prodded. Her whole life under a microscope and then defined by who he'd been and what he'd done.

"Maybe she should've turned him in. Maybe she should've known he was still a threat." Reed shook his head and opened the door. "But if she was made to believe her mom gave you everything, what more could she have done except put herself at risk?"

I FOLLOWED Reed into the municipal building, but as soon as we turned down the hall toward the coroner's wing, he slowed, and I walked ahead of him.

Something was off.

There were too many people here—too many people in suits around a middle-aged woman in a red skirt and jacket who was simultaneously crying and giving orders to those around her. I couldn't hear what she was saying, and I was about to try and read her lips when my former agent stepped into my path.

"Come with me," Koorie demanded and practically dragged me through the double doors into the morgue with Reed close behind us.

"Koorie, what the hell—"

"You need to see this," she interrupted and pointed to the table—and corpse—in front of Rorik.

The medical examiner glanced up, steel-gray eyes piercing mine before returning to his subject.

"You got here fast," I remarked, striding closer.

"I never left," he replied monotonously.

I got the feeling that there was something in the works between him and Ace, but it wasn't my business, nor the time to ask about it.

"What the fuck—" I turned and coughed into my elbow; the brutalized body on the table took me by surprise.

It was almost impossible to judge any features of the victim, the way his face had been mutilated.

His.
His face.
The Archangel's victims were always women. Always.
"What's going on?" I demanded. "This can't be Turner's work."
"Turner?" Koorie's eyes bulged.
Right.
"We have an ID on the Archangel. Lee Nelson Turner. Dex is looking into him now."
"How did you—"
"I'll explain later," I interrupted and pointed at the dead guy, forcing myself to look at his head because there was something familiar there. "What are we doing here? This isn't one of our victims. He's a male, and judging by the crowd outside, not a run—" I broke off when Rorik flipped the body over and revealed a massive cross carved into the victim's back.
"Premortem."
My brows screwed together. This made no sense. If this was one of Turner's kills, it was a blatant violation of his victimology.
"Do we know who—"
Koorie slapped a folder to my chest, and I flipped it open.
Fuck. My stomach turned to lead. The victim's fingerprints had been matched to ones in the system. I looked at Koorie and then back at the paper.
I'd been grateful for death plenty during my career. I would prefer justice every time for a serial killer or rapist or pedophile, but death wasn't a bad second choice—knowing for certain the world was rid of them. But this was the first time I was grateful for the death of a victim. Then again, he'd been an abuser well before he'd ended up dead.
"Dean Johnson." I rasped and turned to Reed, handing him the folder with the fingerprint and DNA match.
"Yeah."
"Turner killed the man who assaulted his daughter."
Koorie's eyes bulged. "Wait, *daughter*—"
"He's looking for her," I murmured and walked away from them, distantly hearing Reed give Koorie the SparkNotes on Stevie and her relation to our killer and our victim.

No wonder they'd kept this under wraps. He was the son of a congresswoman—a high-profile target who'd paid off the police to *lose* Stevie's report.

And it was all because of her.

The Wyoming connection... the search for a runaway... everything fell like dominos into place. Except where we were wrong was that it wasn't Stevie who'd betrayed Turner, but her mother. And if Turner wasn't looking for revenge, then he just... wanted Stevie.

"If Turner killed Johnson, that means he found out about the lawsuit," Reed remarked, his voice breaking through my thoughts.

I spoke my thoughts as they came to me. "If he found out about that, he'd most likely be able to gain access to the address of her old apartment."

"Where is she now?"

"Safe," I replied with a strained voice as the image of her broken face flashed in my mind before she'd left with Carina.

Fuck, I had so much groveling to do.

"She's at Rocco's," I added.

And Turner wouldn't know she was there.

"You know what this kill is," Koorie said, meeting my eyes.

"Redemption."

Turner wanted his daughter back, and if Stevie knew he was a killer, then he was going to go with a gesture he believed above reproach—a kill she couldn't fault him for, *the death of the man who tried to rape her.*

"We need to get to that apartment," I said.

"Text me the address. I'll meet you there."

CHAPTER TWENTY-FIVE

Stevie

I HELD IT TOGETHER BECAUSE I HAD TO—BECAUSE THERE WAS A little girl depending on me to take care of her, not the other way around. But what it felt like on the inside was like I was in the middle of a boxing match, being hit over and over and over again, but every time I went down, I got back up. Not because I had any strength left, but because without the adrenaline, I wasn't sure I was going to survive.

"Stevie?"

I peeled my head up from my palms and looked at Lainey as she wandered up the path.

I faked a smile—the one I'd worn the entire drive home after picking her up from Carina's. Even though my friend wanted me to stay, I couldn't. I felt utterly broken, and the only place I wanted to be was here—the place that felt like home. *The place that wouldn't be home for much longer,* judging by Roman's reaction.

"Time for dinner," I told her, feeling the timer on my phone go off for the frozen pizza I'd put in the oven.

Her head tipped. "You look sad," she declared, not as easily distracted as I'd hoped.

"Nothing that some puzzling and pizza won't fix," I suggested and ushered her inside.

While the pizza cooled, we took our usual seats on the floor, and I lost myself for a couple of minutes in the simple task of matching pieces to their spots wishing life could be that easy.

"*I don't know you at all.*"

His accusation gutted me, and a fresh batch of tears tested the corners of my eyes when a steady knock on the door claimed my attention.

Who was here?

My first thought was Roman which made no sense because he wouldn't knock to get into his own house even if he had come with the miraculous intent to apologize. No. I shook my head and straightened. It was more likely Reed or Jo or whoever he could find to relieve me of my duties that was standing on the other side of the entry.

You're telling me that this whole fucking time, I've had the daughter of a serial killer watching my niece?

Whatever I'd been to him before was replaced by the stain and stigma of the label; I wasn't to be trusted, let alone loved.

"I'll get it," Lainey exclaimed when I didn't move from the floor right away, charging to the door with me only a second behind her.

"Lainey, wait—" I broke off with a stumble when Lainey pulled open the door and revealed my only nightmare on the other side. "*Dad.*"

DAD.

Lee.

I blinked in slow motion, unable to believe what I was seeing.

Older, but with eyes just as cold and decisive as I remembered, my father stood on the stoop of Roman's house, dressed in khakis, a blue polo, and a charming smile that had fooled me, my mother, and all the women he'd murdered.

"Stephanie." The voice of my father caused the room to tilt and spin. He was here. *He'd found me.*

"Who's Stephanie? Who are you?" Lainey's tiny voice broke my trance.

I bolted for the door, slamming it closed and locking the dead bolt. My heart pounded as I spun and braced my back to the wood like that was enough to keep him away.

It wasn't.

There was nothing in this house and no one who would get here in time to stop him from getting what he wanted—*me*. And we both knew it.

There was another light rap on the door, and I heard his low chuckle seep in from the other side.

"You know I don't like games, Stephanie," he called.

"Who's Stephanie?" Lainey asked, her tiny brow furrowed.

"Me—my real name," I panted, taking her arm and pulling her right in front of me. "We're going to play a pirate game, okay?"

"Why?" She frowned.

I flinched when my father knocked again. "Because that man out there is another pirate," I scrambled for a story. "He's a bad pirate, so you have to escape to the fairy castle, okay?"

She nodded slowly, sensing there was something wrong even though she couldn't comprehend it.

Lee banged on the door now. "Do not try me, Stephanie. There's nowhere for you to run."

Fear pierced my chest because I knew it was the truth.

I pulled Lainey to me, hugging her impossibly tight as I whispered, "Go to the fairy castle and press the magic button for Uncle Roman, okay? I have to go with the pirate and distract him, but if you press that button, Uncle Roman will come save me."

Her chin dug into my shoulder when she nodded again.

"I love you, Lainey."

"I love you, too, Stevie."

I released her. "Go!" I hissed, standing and holding my breath until she was out the back door and down the path far enough to where I couldn't see her.

I waited another moment before I spun, praying over and over again that she made it to the guesthouse and hit the panic button.

My fingers shook as they reached for the dead bolt, sliding

slightly on the metal. I inhaled deep and rolled my shoulders back. I wouldn't be afraid. Flicking the lock, I swung the door open.

He still stood there casually, his hands clasped behind his back like there was nothing to be afraid of.

"There's my little girl," he drawled slowly, and it made me want to vomit.

I ached for a world where I could be happy that my father had come for me—had found me and wanted to reconnect. But to know who he was... what he'd done... *what he'd done to find me...* it made that world an impossibility.

"I want you to leave. Now," I declared, hoping the tremor in my voice was so rapid it was impossible to detect. "And I don't want to ever see you again."

His jaw twitched. It was the same twitch I remembered from my childhood anytime I asked for things he viciously objected to. Like pets. And holidays. And vacations.

"Is that how you're going to speak to your father after seven years?" His tone sharpened.

"That is how I'm going to speak to a murderer that I have *no* ties to," I bit out.

His lip curled for an instant before he regained control with a quick chuckle. "You always liked to try my patience, Stephanie." He tsked like I was still a child. "Where's your little friend?"

I notched my chin up. "Safe."

"From me?" He balked and then laughed. "She's Agent Knight's niece. She will never be safe from me, not after what he did to you."

"What? What are you talking about?" I blurted out, realizing my mistake too late.

"He turned you into a whore, Stephanie. Spreading your legs for a place to stay," he snarled, the monster finally revealing itself after all this time. Shaking his head, he added with pained softness, "I should've been watching over you. If I had, this never would've happened."

The Archangel. For an instant, I saw my dad. After seven years with only memories, I saw the man who showed me how to ride a bike and kept me from falling. I saw the man who

BROKEN

taught me how to hunt and blessed our food before every meal. I saw the man who'd cut down whatever Christmas tree I picked with a smile on his face. I saw all the parts of him that genetics or past trauma or the devil himself had turned violent and remorseless.

"I'm just his nanny." If my heart was broken, the least I could do was use the sharp, jagged edges to defend myself.

"You're no better than the rest of them, falling into the trap of sin and losing everything because of it," he declared.

My broken heart stung from the acid in his words. I wasn't a whore, but I had fallen into a trap—a trap believing that love conquered all. A trap believing that I'd one day be able to be free from the man in front of me. And it cost me everything.

A tear leaked down my cheek, and I forced myself not to wipe it away. Lee already saw it, so wiping it away would only add to my vulnerability.

"Don't worry, Stephanie. I will cleanse you. I will help you atone for your sins, now that we're together again."

He'd kill me. *Just like the rest of them.* It didn't matter that I was his daughter.

He stepped closer, his arm shooting out and slamming his palm into the door before I could shut it. "Now get in the car." He angled so I could see the silver sedan still running in the driveway. "Or I will make you."

A glint of light caught on something by his waist. *A knife.* A nasty-looking knife.

The large leather handle tapered ornately into a curved blade that looked too artful to be dangerous. I thought of all the women he'd carved it into, and I lurched forward with the urge to vomit.

"Now, Stephanie."

I stepped out of the house, closing the door behind me like it could prevent him from going back.

Outside, the sky crawled with gray clouds that stained the sky ominously darker than it actually was. Maybe I was the gray cloud here, looming over this family with my dangerous past.

I should've told Roman from the start. I shouldn't have tried to hide my broken past, thinking I could build a solid future on top of it. All of those deaths were on my shoulders, and now Lainey, too, was in danger.

I had to think. I had to buy them time. My heart pounded so loudly it felt like footsteps in my head.

In spite of every loss I'd experienced in my life—every moment where someone or something I could count on disappeared out from under me—in this unbelievable moment, I believed in Roman.

I believed that even if he couldn't love me, he would still come for me. Because that was what he did—*who he was*. A hero. He would come find me in order to get to my father—in order to finally catch him and make him pay for his crimes.

At least if I could give him that, I could walk away from him and Lainey and the life I had here without feeling like I'd completely ruined everything.

"Wait," I pleaded, tugging on my arm and feeling the knife bite into my skin. I hissed in pain.

"No more waiting, Stephanie. It's time to go home."

My gaze went to my car. Blue and beaten up. *And armed.*

"I just want to grab a sweater," I stammered, driving down the ball in my throat. "I don't want to be out in this. It shows too much."

I held my breath, and though it took a moment, Lee's steps slowed. His black eyes ran over me with lingering disgust. It didn't change what he thought of me, I knew it wouldn't. Knowing how Dad was… knowing what Roman told me about the Archangel… I was the only one who knew every side of this man, and each and every one of them now only saw me as a sinner.

"I have an extra sweater in the glove compartment of my car." I gulped. "So that I can stay covered."

His strict religious views would also be his downfall. He wouldn't ignore shame. He wouldn't ignore repentance.

"Fine," he agreed and then warned, "But just remember, try anything funny, and I will go after that little girl who I'll let hide from me for now."

For now.

My gasp was muffled as he yanked me in the direction of my

car, his pointed blade digging into my back as we approached. When we were a few feet away, he shoved me forward. "Get it. We need to go."

My pulse fired off in my chest like an engine trying to turn over. If he caught me, that would be the end of it. I was no longer his daughter; I was a sinner. His flesh and blood was a sinner like all those other girls he raped and murdered. I tasted blood where I bit into my cheek as I whipped open the door, opened the glove box, and pulled out the dirty sweater I'd bundled around the weapon. My weapon.

Clasping it to my chest, I hung my head meekly—like I used to after Dad would rail at me for wanting to go to the movies with my church friends or, heaven forbid, asking to sleep over at one of their houses—and walked quickly to the passenger door of his car.

Ironically, I wanted to get out of there. I wanted him to take me far away from the house because then Lainey wouldn't be at risk.

The door was unlocked, so I opened it and slunk into the seat, locking my gaze with Lee's. Praying he couldn't see much below the dash, I dumped the gun into my hands and shoved it into the side of my boot; it dug into my ankle bone, but that was the only place to hide it. I dragged the hem of my jeans over it and then made a show of shaking out my sweater before sliding my arms into it.

The whole time, neither Lee nor I broke the stare as he strolled casually back to the car as though we were about to go to church.

This was why he was never caught. He was too methodical—the perfect mix of reserved yet confident. There was no emotion to him, like a tree without roots. He succumbed to his impulses but he never let them gain the upper hand.

He slid into the driver's seat and rested his knife on his left leg before looking at me with a sad, placid smile.

"I've missed you, Stephanie. After all this time, I've finally found you."

The switch of personalities gave me whiplash. It felt like I was interacting with someone with dementia—one moment, he knew he was my father and some part of that personality cared for me, and the next, he was emotionless—a human with a soul of stone.

My head turned, following Roman's house from the window and then the side-view mirror for as long as I could. *Home.*

Leaving this time was worse than Wyoming. Even as a teenager, I couldn't comprehend all of what I was leaving behind. But now, I felt every loss—loss of safety, loss of happiness, of family, of desire, of hope, of love—as though they were limbs from my body; and whenever we got where we were going, there would be nothing left of me. But it was the only thing I could do to keep Lainey safe.

I, on the other hand, was never meant to escape the monster next to me.

CHAPTER TWENTY-SIX

Roman

"What did you find?" I answered Dex's call through the car.

"Turner was a traveling minister. Best I can gather, he followed truck routes that his father used to drive."

"Was his father religious?" I interrupted.

"Yes and no. Looks like Turner's dad, Charles, went to church every Sunday, taught Lee's Sunday school and all that when they were home, but when he was out driving… Far from it. Reports of abuse and drugs and solicitation of prostitutes as well as assaults on minors." He paused. "There were some reports that mentioned he had a child with him, a few concerns about child abuse, but I'm guessing anyone who looked into it got as far as the leader of Sunday school and turned right back around."

My grip tightened on the steering wheel. It was all making sense. "Jekyll and Hyde. And Turner saw both sides to his father."

"Looks like it."

Maybe there were psychological, genetic factors to serial killers—something that predisposed them to need to kill more than the dozens of other abused and mistreated children in this country. But a traumatic childhood had played a role in almost every case I'd ever worked.

And if being schooled in religious doctrine by your father only to turn around and watch him commit sin after sin wasn't traumatic, I didn't know what was.

"Daddy Turner died on the road. He OD'd in a truck stop bathroom and wasn't found for three days. Meanwhile, Turner was locked in his truck with no food or water."

"Jesus."

"Apparently, there was a prostitute who went in with him, realized when he died, but didn't tell anyone about it or the fact that Turner was still in the truck because she didn't want to get in trouble."

My exhale racked my entire frame.

It was fucked up. The childhood was always fucked up by the monsters I chased. I wished I could say that Lee Turner's childhood was the worst of what I'd witnessed but it wasn't. And after living with Lainey these last months... seeing how resilient a kid can be to unimaginable trauma... I knew what happened to these kids to shape them into serial killers was beyond what could be described in a police report or psychiatric evaluation.

It was enough to tempt a person to wonder if anyone could come out of that pressure cooker of trauma and *not* become a psychopath.

But there were. There were kids who survived. Thrived.

Killing was a choice, and it was one that Turner had stopped himself from making for fifteen years once his daughter was born. And that told me it was a choice he could've stopped himself from making from the start.

"So, Turner went back along those roads as a traveling minister, probably approached his victims with some degree of charm. They felt safe because he presented himself as a man of God, and then he raped and killed them."

"Why?" Reed rasped next to me, shaking his head and rolling his shoulders against the seat.

"He probably viewed them as the reason his father fell from grace—viewed them as the temptation that caused his father to stray." I clenched my jaw. "They were probably some temptation to him, too, so he wanted to kill them before they turned him into his father."

Everyone was silent for a second before Dex continued, "I'm still waiting to hear back, but with Turner's photo, I reached out to some of the churches in the smaller towns where he found his most recent victims. I only have a response back from one though I'm assuming the rest I'll get will be similar. The Presbyterian church outside of Phoenix recognized Turner's photo but said he had a different name. Apparently, he came to the church and wanted to volunteer his time, specifically with their monthly community dinner that they offer to the…"

"Vagrants," I filled in. "A free meal for the homeless which could include runaways."

"I also went back to all the towns where the victims were from and realized that they were all stops on bus routes that left from the bus station in Wyoming."

"So he assumed Stevie's mom got them bus tickets and got out of town, figured that with no money and no job, they would've relied on a church community at their destination to help them get on their feet, and then would give back to that church with their time and volunteering." I sped through the facts as I spun the wheel with my palm and turned the car into the small lot at the run-down apartment complex that was outside of Carmel. "And while he looked for them there, he picked his next target."

"I still haven't figured out how he got onto Stevie's actual trail, but I'm working on it."

"Just got here. Talk soon." I hung up and instructed Reed. "Do a perimeter sweep. I need to call Rocco."

With a quick nod, Reed got out of the car and began to take a casual stroll down the sidewalk that went around the building so he wouldn't draw any suspicion.

I tapped on Rocco's name, the line ringing three times before he picked up.

"You know I'm risking my life to answer your call right now," he grumbled. "Carina would have my head—"

"I know. I won't keep you in danger. Just tell me how Stevie's doing."

Silence.

"Roc?"

"Roman, Stevie's not here. She picked up Lainey and left to go to your place as soon as she got back from the office... almost two hours ago."

"*Fuck!*" I slammed my hand against the wheel. "I have to go." I hung up.

This whole time, I thought she was safe at Rocco's—safe with Rocco, the man who was an expert at hiding from people who were trying to find him.

My fingers had never moved so sloppily as I pulled up the security cameras at the house. When I saw her car in the drive, I exhaled. When I tapped on the rear cameras and saw her and Lainey heading inside, I breathed in again.

She was safe, but I didn't want them alone. Not now. Not with Johnson dead. Not with her—Turner so close.

"Reed!" I bellowed just as Koorie pulled into the spot next to me. The younger man appeared a few seconds later, jogging over just as Koorie approached. "I need you to take my car and go to my house," I told him.

Someone needed to be with her. Someone who could protect her. Right now, I wasn't sure I deserved that honor. Not after the things I'd said.

"What's going on?" Koorie asked

I scored my fingers down my scalp. "I thought Stevie was with Carina and Rocco. She's not. She left and went back to the house with Lainey. They're fine," I assured them both. "I can see them on the security cameras outside, but I don't want them there alone. Not when I know this fucker is looking for her."

I held my keys out.

"On it." He took the key chain and added, "Perimeter was clear. I didn't see any sign of Turner."

As soon as I heard the Bronco start, I faced Koorie. "Turner's smart. He'd probably scope the place for a couple of days waiting for her, so let's split up and see who's home and if they've seen anyone who looks like Turner roaming around."

"I'll take the top floor," she declared and then beelined for the staircase.

It was a smaller apartment building with only two floors and five units per floor. Thankfully, it was after five, so there was a good chance that most of the residents would be home from work.

"Fuck," I muttered not even ten minutes later when the last door on the first level closed in front of me.

Only four of the five residents were home and zero of those four recognized Turner or remembered anyone religious or suspicious lurking around. I stalked back to the side of the building where the stairs to the second level were, praying that Koorie had more luck.

I kept my hand in my pocket—on my phone because Reed should be calling any minute now; the house was only about fifteen minutes away from the apartment building, depending on traffic and the time of day.

Koorie's footsteps on the stairs caught my attention. "Anything?" I demanded before she reached the bottom rung.

"All five were home, but no one recognized him," she answered and kept her cool when I turned my head down and muttered several obscenities. "It's getting dark, Roman, and I'm not sure how much more we're going to get tonight. There's a chance he might not know about this address. Learning about the lawsuit is one thing, but having access to the documents to find the plaintiff's address…"

"Right, but he was in San Francisco, then Monterey, and now Carmel. He's followed the places that she's lived, and none of that information would be in the police paperwork. He's tracking her somehow, and until I know how, I'm unwilling to put any information beyond his reach."

"Okay, well then we'll regroup tomorrow and set up surveillance on the apartment building and start searching in town. At the churches. The community groups. He might be following her, but we also know how he operates and we know he's sticking around because of Stevie." She put her hand on my arm. "We're not going to lose him this time."

A growl grated from my chest. "I want to stick around for a little longer, just in case he shows up."

"He's not here, Roman." Koorie folded her arms and tossed her long brown hair to the side. "And if you think that's what's eating you, you're in for a very long, very fruitless evening stakeout."

My gaze slashed to hers, but we'd worked together too long for her to even flinch at the daggers in my stare. "Don't profile me."

"Can't help it." She shrugged. "You taught me to profile everyone."

Dammit.

Before I could amend my former principles, my phone vibrated against my fingers.

Reed.

My finger swiped across the screen, prepared to answer the call, only to realize that it wasn't a call; *it was an alarm.*

"What the fuck?"

My fingers flew over the screen, bringing up the exterior cameras on the house and seeing Stevie's car in the drive.

"What's wrong?" Koorie asked.

"Someone triggered the silent alarm at my house," I told her and tapped on Stevie's number. I hung up on the fourth ring; she never let it go to the fourth ring. "It was at the guesthouse, so Lainey could've just been playing…"

Where the fuck was Reed?

I tapped to call him, my heart hammering even harder than when I'd thought Turner might actually be waiting around this apartment building.

"Someone or something just triggered the silent alarm from the guesthouse, and I don't see Stevie or Lainey anywhere. Where the fuck are you?"

"Just pulling down the drive. They were clearing an accident on Coastal, so I got held up," he said and then added, "Stevie's car is still here."

"I'm on my way," I told him and extended my hand to

Koorie for her keys. We were in her Nissan rental car a minute later, tires squealing as I peeled out of the parking lot. "What's going on, Reed?"

"No sign of anyone else. No sign of forced entry. One sec." There was a pause. "Front door was unlocked."

Wrong.

"Can't go in with my phone, Roman. I'll call you back."

He hung up and those next three minutes of tense silence were the worst of my life. My heart threatened to explode, waiting for the phone to ring again. Meanwhile, Koorie knew the only thing she could do for me right now was sit quietly and pray we didn't fly past a cop on the way to the house.

My breath whooshed out when my phone rang again.

"Did you find them?" I demanded when he called back.

"The main house was empty," he replied. "Stevie's phone was in the living room next to the table with the puzzle, but no sign of them."

I floored it through a stop sign, ignoring the blaze of horns that disappeared quickly in my rearview.

"I'm outside now, on the path to the guesthouse, but I don't hear or see anything."

Nothing.

Nothing paralyzed me.

It shouldn't be nothing.

It should be Lainey playing. It should be Stevie cursing me out for being a fucking asshole. *But it shouldn't be nothing.*

"At the guesthouse," he reported in a tight whisper. "Call you back in a minute."

As soon as the call ended for a second time, my screen lit up.

"I just got the alarm," I answered Dex without preamble, knowing all our systems routed through Covington first. "Reed's there, and I'm on my way. I don't see anything on the cameras and Stevie's car is still in the driveway, but Reed hasn't found either of them."

"It was the guesthouse bedroom alarm," he confirmed.

The one by the nightstand. It was close enough to be reached from the bed. Maybe they were playing hide-and-seek. Maybe Lainey bumped it…

"Reed was about to clear the guesthouse when you called," I said with a strangled voice.

"Is there any way Turner knows Stevie is living with you?"

My mind spun out for a second, flying fast and far like the hook of a fishing line being cast. And when I finally reeled it back in, the fear attached to the hook was something I wished I could throw back.

"How would he?" I croaked. "I only just changed her address from the apartment to the house last week…"

"But if he sent something to her apartment before that…"

He would've been notified of her new address.

"Pull up the security footage for the last half hour. Call you when I get there," I said with a strangled voice and hung up.

If Turner knew Stevie was there—*and Lainey was with her. Oh god.* My heart slammed against my chest like a weapon fired from the inside out.

It had never taken me so short or so long to get back to the house. I couldn't even remember putting the car in park before I was through the gate and heading for the guesthouse, oblivious to whether Reed was calling me back or not. I was here to see for myself.

"*Lainey! Stevie!*" I bellowed, head whipping side to side.

"I'll double-check the house!" Koorie called from somewhere behind me.

I drew my weapon and sprinted through the back door.

"*Lainey!*" I called again over the heavy pounding of my footsteps and the tumultuous crash of waves.

It was getting dark and hard to see, but if she was out here, she would've answered. *Fuck.* If anything happened to Lainey… *god.* I wouldn't know what to do. I'd sworn to do my best for her. Promised Val. Promised everything.

The fireflies were out in full force. Scattered twinkling lights like the brightness of a fairy tale broken into a thousand little pieces—remnants of the forever I could've had if I hadn't been a fucking idiot.

My eyes stung, but not from the brine-laden breeze whipping against my face. *If anything happened to Stevie…*

I reached the guesthouse and forced that thought away before it crippled me.

I opened the door without caution though there was no doubt in my mind something was wrong—that something bad had happened.

"Reed?" I called, scanning the room over the barrel of my gun.

He didn't answer. *Why wasn't he answering?* I cleared the living space and kitchen and then immediately went for the staircase. My heart didn't feel like it was pumping, it felt like it was bleeding out, and every second I couldn't find them was one second closer to the end of my life.

When I made it to the bedroom, I saw why.

"Uncle Roman!"

As soon as I heard her voice, my weapon fell to my side. Lainey sprung from Reed's hold, her face streaked with tears and barreled toward me.

I clutched her to me like she was the only air my lungs needed to survive. "I'm here. I've got you." My eyes squeezed shut, willing myself not to break under the relief I felt holding her in my arms.

"She was hiding on the bottom shelf," Reed rasped, drawing my attention as he nodded to the closed wardrobe in the far corner of the room. "If she hadn't come out when she heard my voice, I wouldn't have found her."

Locking my teeth together, I nodded and stood, picking Lainey up with me.

"You're safe," I rumbled, rubbing small circles on her back to try and calm her. The unimaginable relief of holding her tiny frame was mirrored by the indescribable pain I felt because Stevie wasn't here.

Reed didn't say anything else, but his stare mirrored the only question left.

Where was Stevie?

Her car was here. Lainey was here. But Stevie wasn't.

"I'm here. It's okay," I promised, drawing back so I could brush away the hair matted to her face. "Lainey, where's Stevie? Why were you hiding?" I asked as calmly as I fucking could even though fear and anger and self-loathing whipped through my chest like a tornado.

"Uncle Roman... Stevie... hide... gone." Her words were an unintelligible jumble as she started to cry harder again.

"Lainey... shhh... just breathe." I swiped the tears from her face. "You're okay now. Me and Uncle Reed are here." I tried to swallow but couldn't. "Just slow down and tell me, did you push the button?"

I had to start small. As much as it killed me, she was too upset to ask first about Stevie.

Her chin bobbed. "Stevie said to press the magic button to call you and then hide until you came."

My chest was on fire.

"Why did she tell you to do that?"

Her lip quivered. "I opened the door for the bad pirate." Big fat tears dripped onto my hands, burning the truth like acid onto my skin. *The bad pirate.* There was only one man that Stevie would describe like that.

Turner had come here. *He'd found her.*

"Then Stevie told me it was time to press the magic button and hide until you came."

Whatever was left of my heart shattered into a million pieces.

I told her to trust me and then betrayed that trust. I told her I would protect her, and I'd left her alone.

"It's my fault. I opened the door." She sobbed again.

"No, no, no. It's not your fault," I choked out. "Not your fault." I kissed her forehead.

"She told me she had to go with him," Lainey cried harder, snot running down her face that I used the edge of my sleeve to wipe away. "It's my fault she had to go."

No. It was mine.

Stevie was protecting Lainey from Turner, and she would've done anything to keep him away from her. *Anything.* And knowing her, knowing the woman I loved—*because I did fucking know her and her goodness and her strength and her bravery*—she did what she had to in order to get Turner off this property: she'd sacrificed herself.

"It's not your fault, Lainey. It's mine. But it's going to be okay." I forced myself through her wall of sadness.

"You have to save her, Uncle Roman," she begged, her little voice so thick and heavy. "You have to."

No promises. In my line of work, the only thing more dangerous than a serial killer was promising the victims' families that I would save their loved ones in time or that I would catch the perp if I didn't.

But this wasn't the case anymore.

This was my life. My future. *My love.*

"I promise I'll bring her back," I rasped deeply. It wasn't just a promise. It was a necessity. I clutched her to my chest for a long moment before I told her, "But you're going to have to stay with Uncle Reed while I do, okay?"

Her little chin dipped, and I handed her off to my teammate with immeasurable and wordless thanks, and then took the stairs two at a time as I reached for my phone. There was a missed call from Dex.

"Roman, you have to talk to—" Koorie didn't even finish her sentence before I picked up Dex's second call.

"He has her." I tried to keep calm, but I was fucking losing it. "Dex, he has Stevie."

I went outside and headed back up the path toward my car.

"I know. I have the security footage of the house. He's driving a dark sedan. I'm running the plates now and scanning traffic cams in both directions out from your place," Dex told me.

"What happened?"

"They spoke at the door for a few minutes before Stevie left the house with him. Turner had a knife, but it looked like Stevie went willingly," Dex told me. "The only thing was, he let her go to her car for something. It looked like maybe a jacket or a sweater or something that she got out."

I shook my head. That didn't make sense. *Why would she need a sweater? And why would he let her go get it?*

"I'm getting in my car. You have two minutes before I reach Coastal to tell me which direction I'm heading," I warned him, revving the car to life and speeding out of the drive.

"No pressure," he grunted. "Looks like the plates are registered to Our Lady of Mount Carmel." That made sense; the local Catholic Church. "There's no report that it was stolen, but the car would have to be missing for twenty-four hours before the police would file one."

"Thirty seconds."

The sound of him working was a variation on the ticking timer of a bomb, and my heavy breaths an indication that something was about to blow.

"I'm not getting anything on the cameras from the first intersections they'd reach in either direction."

No. "They had to fucking go somewhere," I ground out. "They didn't just vanish out of the driveway of my house. They didn't just fucking drive right into the sea—"

"What is it?"

"There's a beach on the way into town. Stevie's favorite." I wasn't sure if I had any real reason to believe that's where they were going, but there was no other option.

"And he'd take her there?"

A pit formed in my gut. "He killed a congresswoman's son for assaulting her," I said hollowly, pushing my foot to the floor. "Taking her to her favorite place is a small gesture in comparison if he's trying to redeem himself."

Dex grunted. "He can't really think she's going to forgive him."

The pit in my gut leached with icy dread. "He doesn't," I rasped. "And when that part of him overtakes the part that wants her to, he'll have no choice but to kill her."

Everything I'd learned about psychopaths and about the Archangel brought me to this moment and gave me the tools to find the woman I loved. *And the somber threat of what would happen if I didn't get to her in time.*

CHAPTER TWENTY-SEVEN

Stevie

"Where are we going?" I said, my voice cracking. Tears leaked down my cheek, but I didn't care if Dad saw them. It would be his mistake to underestimate me just because I cried.

His head tipped and then he smiled again. "To the one place I promised to take you."

I pushed back in the seat, surprised by his answer.

"The beach?" It was the beginning of December and dark out. The beaches wouldn't be crowded, but if even a single person were there…

He smiled and my stomach dropped. "Blessed is she who has believed that the Lord would fulfill his promises to her," he replied, adding. "Luke chapter one verse forty-five."

The fact that he quoted verses like he was the Lord—like he spoke for God would've been sickening if it wasn't completely overshadowed by the fact that his idea of the Lord's work was raping and murdering innocent women.

Maybe it was my fault that he'd made it this far—that he'd killed so many women. My fault for thinking that he'd just disappear into another life like we had. My fault for not asking better questions of Mom's confession, for being blindsided by the bombshell truth. But I wasn't blinded any longer.

"Up here is my favorite one." I pointed off to the left. At least there was a better chance of that beach being empty—a better chance for escape without putting anyone else at risk.

"Lead the way," he said with the same voice he'd told me to go pick our Christmas tree. *"Lead the way, Stephanie. It's your choice."*

I shuddered. How a person could have such two different parts to his personality was impossible to comprehend. He was my own version of Jekyll and Hyde. Lee and Archangel. Dad and serial killer.

I watched his thumb play over the blade of his knife in his lap, wondering if he was actually going to take me to the beach.

Part of me hoped he wasn't because I knew what it would mean if he did; it would mean we weren't running. It would mean he wasn't trying to kidnap me and take me with him. It would mean he wasn't trying to escape from anyone anymore and there wasn't a plan after this.

Not even a minute later, he followed my direction and pulled off down the drive to the secluded lot.

I swallowed over the lump in my throat.

He'd finally brought me to the beach like I'd always wanted, and it meant that this was the end.

"I'VE MISSED YOU."

I stopped short at the edge of the wooden stairs that led onto the beach. In the distance, the waves spurned the shore, trying to escape from him, too.

Turning, I met eyes that mirrored the color of mine but none of the character. I cared, whereas he was a cold-blooded killer. I cared too much—at my own expense—like it could atone for the crimes he'd committed.

"How did you find me?"

His head cocked, a serene all-knowing smile placating his features; I'd seen that smile a thousand times in my lifetime. A thousand times when he'd just been Dad. That was the hardest part about all of this. So much of what he did reminded me of who I thought he was and not the killer he'd always been—not the killer I'd never known.

"I never stopped looking for you, Stephanie," he drawled low, coming to stand beside me. "Never."

Fear and emotion tangled into a ball in my throat. "How?" I croaked.

"Methodically. But in the end, it was your mother who wanted to repent for her sins—for betraying me. Maybe she thought I'd never get the letter she sent to our home. Maybe she thought she'd disguised it enough that I wouldn't find her—who she'd become. But in the end, she'd died begging for my forgiveness."

Oh, Mom. A sob bubbled up. She'd written to him from the hospital. She's saved me from him only to lead him to me.

I'd always known she'd still loved him—that she'd saved us, but it hadn't saved her from loving a killer like she hoped it would. It was why she hadn't given Roman his name. It was why she cried every night and still had their wedding photo tucked into her nightstand drawer. And it was why, in her dying moments, she'd given in to weakness.

"It took time to follow the letter's trail, but I found her. I found Mary Michaels, and then I found you." He reached up and cupped my cheek once more with a tenderness it was hard to fathom a killer to possess.

I blinked rapidly, trying not to cry.

It was no wonder Mom's truth and warning had been so harsh that day. Guilt drove her to demand I protect myself at all costs… because she'd failed to do so.

"I have something for you," he said, dropping his hand.

Frowning, I looked at him warily as he reached in his pocket, his hand returning with a gold chain dangling from his fingers.

"I see that you don't have the one I gave you at your confirmation, so I brought you a new one."

A cross necklace. *Just like all the others.*

"Put it on," he ordered when I made no move to take it.

My throat tightened, making it impossible to swallow as I took the fragile chain. His annoyance grew when I fumbled for a few moments to undo the clasp and work it around my neck, but

I would take every extra moment I could, and he couldn't do it for me any faster without lowering his knife.

No matter how many moments there were that reminded me of my dad—reminded me of a man who managed to *feel* for fifteen years—there was no concealing a killer.

I hooked the chain and folded my arms across my front, masking the arctic chill that ran down my spine. Putting on the necklace was the equivalent of digging my own grave.

He extended his free hand, indicating for me to lead the way onto the beach. It left his gun exposed in his waistband. Right there. Right in front of me, taunting me to disobey him.

"Did you miss me?" he asked when my shoes hit the sand.

My heart constricted, the answer to his question painfully conflicted and complicated; I missed my dad, but I didn't miss him.

"How could I? I don't even know you," I said, repeating the words that had pierced my heart only hours earlier.

I didn't know him, just like he didn't know me. He wasn't the man I thought he was, just like I wasn't the same meek fifteen-year-old girl who'd learned to never to go against what her father said, who obeyed him as diligently as the Bible instructed.

He was a murderer, and I was a woman with her own weapon tucked to her leg, prepared to do whatever it took to stop him.

"I'm your father, Stephanie. Of course, you know me." His low chuckle clawed along my spine, and I inched my arms tighter over my front. "Stop," he ordered and my feet complied.

My breaths came in sharp bursts. Could he kill me? *His own daughter?*

"Turn around."

Slowly, I faced him, my mind moving wildly between the past and the present. Parallels from when I'd been in trouble when I was younger to being in danger now.

"Why are you doing this?" I asked, allowing the tremble of my voice to pass.

"Doing this?" Offense hardened his tone. "I'm your father. You belong with me."

I flexed my ankle, reassuring myself that the gun was still there.

"No, you're a killer," I countered, willing myself not to tremble when his lip curled.

This wasn't just an angry or violent man in front of me. He wasn't just some guy with a weapon. He was a serial killer. A *seasoned* killer. And he'd taken the lives of more people than years I'd been on this earth.

I wasn't going to make it out of this by being faster or stronger or better with any kind of weapon than him. I was only going to make it off this beach alive by being smarter.

"Our Lord knows that many devils and false prophets will be sacrificed on the path to righteousness." He stepped closer. "He even took your mother for what she'd done; God punished her for her betrayal. Her sickness was her penance."

I wanted to vomit. I wanted to tell him that her illness took her because he refused to get her real help all those years. I wanted to scream that her death was on his hands, but it wouldn't matter.

With all the other deaths those hands were responsible for, I doubted he'd feel an ounce of added weight.

"Oh, Stephanie." He sighed and shook his head, once again thumbing the edge of his blade until it drew blood from his own thumb but the wound didn't faze him. With a sad smile, he told me, "If she hadn't taken you, none of this would've happened."

"No?" I choked out. "You wouldn't have killed anyone else?" *Liar.*

"I didn't kill for fifteen years for you," he snarled, his composure fracturing to reveal the war between the man and the monster. "Fifteen years, and she took you because of a damned box of trinkets. Without so much as a *word.*"

Because she knew who you were. I held the words back.

"Fifteen years, I abstained for you," he said as though he'd given up murder for Lent. "I came to save you." He reached for my cheek again, this time leaving a trail of blood over my skin like he was marking me for sacrifice. "I even killed for you."

My eyes flung wide.

"W-what?" I stammered and turned my head away. "What are you talking about?"

Killed who? All those runaways?

"I killed him, Stephanie. I killed the man who assaulted you."

Oh god.

Dean Johnson.

I recoiled, hating the instant surge of guilt I felt for the death of the man who'd tried to rape me.

Dad—*Lee* sighed and then lost his hold on tenderness. His fingers reached out and grabbed my chin so hard I winced with the pain as he yanked my face back to his.

"I killed him only to find out you've been sinning—whoring yourself to the man trying to stop the Lord's work," he accused in a short burst of rage, pinching his lips tight and leveling me with a cold, intense stare. "Who tries to stop the Lord's work, Stephanie?"

When I didn't answer immediately, he brought the tip of his knife to my neck.

"Who?" His fingers bruised my skin.

"The devil," I choked out, gasping when he released me.

"On your knees," he commanded. "We all repent from our knees."

The sand dipped as I kneeled, but as I carefully sat back, I realized my gun was now within reach.

"I'm not a sinner, Dad," I said softly. "I love him."

He recoiled and stared at me with disgust and rage.

"No," he shouted, pulling his gun from his waist. "No, you lusted after him and fell from grace because I wasn't there to guide you."

I started to shake my head, but he went on with wild fervor, something inside him continuing to snap apart.

"But I'm here now, and I will fix this." Gone was any trace of the man I knew from his eyes, their depths filled with pure insanity even as they glistened, almost like they were filling with tears. "Therefore, having these promises, Stephanie, let us cleanse ourselves from all defilement of flesh and spirit, perfecting holiness in the fear of God."

He smiled serenely, his twisted adaptation of the scripture

soothing him. My father—at peace knowing he was going to murder me.

I felt the cool bite of the knife against my neck as I swallowed. He wasn't going to strangle me, I realized. He didn't trust himself.

"You're going to kill me," I murmured. "Your own daughter."

I grasped for straws while my fingers slowly inched down the side of my thigh toward the gun in my boot.

"The Lord our God knows that the greatest sacrifice we can give is the life of our child. For he gave his only begotten son…" The rest of the verse seemed lost to him or maybe lost to me, blood pounding so loudly in my ears that I struggled to hear anything except my hand peeling up my pant leg, searching for the cold metal underneath. "For the wages of sin is death, but the gift of God is eternal life."

Romans.

Tears pricked in my eyes. He quoted Romans to me. And then the tip of his knife dug into the side of my neck.

"Stevie!"

I was imagining it. I had to be. My brain was hallucinating in those few moments before death—those moments when they say your whole life flashes in front of you. And when I heard Roman's voice, I knew they were right. He was my whole life. My whole heart.

But it wasn't a delusion.

"Let her go, Turner!"

The voice caused Lee's grip to falter and lucidity to burst into my brain like a jolt of electricity. The knife disappeared from my throat as Lee stepped back, his chest heaving with the strength he'd had to find to kill his own daughter.

"Don't come any closer," Lee warned, whipping his gun up to the entrance to the beach.

I looked up, following his aim to where Roman approached. Hope burst into my chest. Roman was here. *He'd come for me.* I wanted to smile and sob in equal measure.

I took another look and realized that Lee only had his knife pointed at me... and that knife was now an escapable distance away.

As if hearing my thoughts, Lee snarled low so that only I could hear him, "Make one move to stand, and I'll shoot him."

The threat sucked all the air from my lungs. I'd risk myself, but I wouldn't risk Roman. I wouldn't risk Lainey losing one more person from her life.

"Put the weapons down, Turner," Roman seethed, keeping his gun locked on my father. "You have nowhere to run. The police will be here any minute."

Slowly, I pulled my pant leg up and found the grip of the handgun. If Lee looked at me again, he'd see what I was doing—what I had, so I prayed that Roman's presence was distracting enough to keep him from noticing.

"You cannot save her, Agent Knight," he replied calmly. "The Lord has chosen me to cleanse this earth of sinners and whores. In fact, it's because you've ruined her that only the Lord can save her now."

This was the man I didn't know. The killer. The monster provoked by my mother disobeying and abandoning him, taking me with her. The zealot who believed he was divinely justified for his sins.

"You're wrong." Roman punctuated his statement with a step closer. "If we confess our sins, He is faithful and just to forgive us our sins and to cleanse us from all unrighteousness," Roman replied. "So, let me confess."

I gasped, shocked to hear him quote the Bible. But then, this was Roman—this was what he did. He got inside the minds of psychopaths like my father. He inserted himself like a key into their locked-up insanity and broke in.

"No," Lee barked out.

"Let me confess my sins to you," Roman declared, except when he said "you," he didn't look at Lee—his eyes strayed to me.

His confession was for me.

"No, stop." Lee trembled with rage.

Roman didn't stop.

"I confess to sloth—to being so preoccupied with my work

and the world that I let the important things like feeling wither away," he rasped low, and I brought my hand to my mouth, stifling any sound caused from my heart bursting. "I confess to wrath—to being so angry with myself for my failures that I was blinded to what I knew to be true. I confess to gluttony—to devouring every emotion so there was none left for me to feel."

"Silence!" Lee roared, his eyes bulging with rage.

"I confess to envy—to wanting to be as kind and caring and trusting as you," he went on, making no move to hide that all his apologies were to me. "I confess to lust—to wanting you beyond all reason, beyond all measure. To wanting to be with you above any and everything else."

All I wanted was to go to him—to confess the same and tell him I forgave him and loved him, and to beg him to stop putting himself at risk for me.

"I confess to greed, Stevie. I confess to wanting all your laughs, all your smiles, all your happiness, as well as all your tears and frustrations and sadness. I want every moment of the rest of your life to be mine, but most of all, I confess to wanting all of your love for myself."

Tears streamed down my cheeks. It seemed like an impossible moment to feel the amount of love that I did. But I felt it. In spite of everything—the fear, the danger—for a split second, all I felt was love and the way it unfolded and enveloped me.

"Stop it! You defile her with your words and you will pay. You both will pay the price. I'm here to take retribution for your sins," Lee spouted off accusations with deranged fervor, sounding less and less like my father, and more and more like a man with a very sick mind.

He twitched and snarled where he stood. Gone was the composed killer who'd avoided capture for decades, who hunted with precision and without remorse. He'd stopped killing to be a father, and now that he'd killed again, his mind couldn't reconcile the two halves; he couldn't reconcile himself, and it felt like I was watching him split in two right in front of me; muscles tearing from bones, nerves ripping in half.

"And I confess to pride," Roman rasped, finally reaching the last sin. His eyes glistened underneath his glasses. "I confess to being too proud to admit I never doubted you when it came at my own expense. Too proud to admit I trusted you when you risked everything to trust me. Too proud to admit that it was pride that caused me to fail and not the way I love you."

"I will end you—"

"Maybe you will," Roman shouted at my father. "But these three things will last forever, Stevie—faith that I will always come for you, hope that you can forgive me, and love. All my love is yours. Forever."

"You're the devil—" Lee charged wildly.

"You're the one who has stolen Stevie from those who love her, the one who intends on killing her and destroying her life and mine." Roman walked closer—putting himself only a few feet from the psychopath aiming a gun at his chest. "And unless I'm mistaken, only the devil comes to do those things," he replied, the deadly low tone even stilling the waves into silence.

No. I started to shake my head. I saw what Roman was doing—trying to straighten my father's twisted perception of himself, trying to draw all of his focused rage inward where his mind was already breaking in the hopes that it was just enough for Roman to disarm him.

But Roman didn't know my father. He didn't know that Lee hunted every weekend in Wyoming. He didn't know that Lee was as skilled with a firearm as he was with his knife and hands. And he didn't know that my father would rather die believing himself a martyr than live having to admit he was a murderer.

Lee let out the twisted snarl of an animal going in for the kill, and time rippled in its progression. Fast, then slow. First, picking up as Lee cocked his gun. Faster when I screamed Roman's name in sheer panic.

And then slow as Lee's finger tightened on the trigger.

Slow as the boom of a gunshot echoed down the beach.

Slow when Lee turned and looked at me, his placid rage morphing into shock.

And then time stopped when I realized the shot fired was my own.

A dark stain bloomed in the center of his chest where I'd hit him. Lee Turner. *My father.*

A cry exploded from my lips just as loud as the gunshot. The weapon fell from my shaking hand into the sand, and then Roman was in front of me before I could see Lee's body crumble to the ground.

"Fuck, Stevie," he growled low, clutching my body to his. "I'm sorry, baby. I'm so sorry."

And then I sobbed, hard and violent, each cry like an elbow to my chest.

I killed him.

"I've got you," he promised. "I swear, I've got you."

I couldn't think—couldn't even be sure I was breathing. My body racked with furious sorrow for what I'd done.

I'd killed my father.

It was right, but it was wrong. Good, but bad. It was a pit of gray that seemed to open up in an instant and swallow me whole.

The beach disappeared from under me, and all I knew was the solid ground of Roman's chest. Vaguely, I heard sirens. Vaguely, I heard Roman muttering to people around us. Maybe Agent Koorie or maybe some of the Covington team; I didn't look.

Soon, all I heard was the heavy beat of my own heart.

I'd killed my father. Shot him to save the man I loved.

Yes, Lee was a serial killer. Yes, he was a monster. Yes, he was going to kill Roman and me.

But I wasn't him; I wasn't unaffected by taking another life, no matter how justified it was—no matter how right it was.

The world might only know him as the Archangel, but I knew better. I couldn't be unaffected by taking the life of the man who had been a father to me for fifteen years. Who'd loved and cared for me in the ways he was capable of. Who'd taught me how to ride a bike and instructed my Sunday school class. And who had… quelled… his sick desire or instinct or predisposition to murder people for fifteen years… for me. Who'd searched for me. Who'd killed the man who assaulted me.

Tears soaked into Roman's shirt, and I didn't know whose car we got in, but all I knew was that Roman wasn't driving. He held me in his lap in the back seat as the driver brought us back to the house.

I wasn't my father. I didn't believe there was only right and wrong. If there was one thing knowing Lee Turner had taught me, it was that even the worst people were not made of complete darkness. There were tiny tendrils of light that flickered for fifteen years, and those parts were the parts I grieved for having killed.

Those were the parts I grieved for because I'd make the same choice—fire the same bullet—every single time.

We don't get to choose the darkness that lives in all of us, but we do get to choose to focus on the light.

"I'm so sorry," he repeated over and over as he carried me into the bedroom. "I'm so sorry, princess."

The bed dipped as Roman laid us in it, but he didn't leave me. I felt in the way he held me that he would never leave me again. And for the first time in seven years, it felt safe to be sad. It felt safe to mourn who my father was. And it felt safe to accept that part of me would always love the father he chose to be separate from the monster he'd become.

"I love you, and I'm sorry." Roman soaked my skin with his words as he brushed my hair back and kissed my forehead. My brow. The top of my head. I felt the warm wetness of his tears coat his lips when they pressed to my skin.

The sincerity of his empathy overwhelmed me to my core. He cried for me and what had happened—what I'd done—when he had every right to feel satisfaction on the death of the Archangel, the man who'd murdered countless innocent people, almost including the two of us.

But he didn't.

Tonight, he mourned the loss of my father with me.

He held me and cried with me because we were all broken.

All of us.

And tomorrow, we'd accept the relief that Lee Turner would never harm anyone ever again.

CHAPTER TWENTY-EIGHT

Stevie

"THIS ONE, TOO!"

It was just over two weeks until Christmas and the holiday spirit felt as fake as the garland that Lainey was currently directing Roman to drape around every door and window frame. What happened four days ago hung like thick smog in the air, dulling every outlet of joy. Of course, it was Christmas, and above everything else, I wanted Lainey to have good memories of her first Christmas without her parents. So, even though Roman offered to tell her gently that we should wait to decorate, I wouldn't let him.

I wanted her happiness just as surely as I wanted my own. Like she knew just how to make me smile, Lainey rushed over and draped a strand of holly around my shoulders, clapping with glee.

I laughed and pretended like I was going to come after her before I returned to the pile of ornaments that I'd been tasked to attach the little wire hooks so they could be hung.

It felt wrong to celebrate a holiday when the three of us had lost so much. Roman, a sister. Lainey, her parents. Me, my father by my own hands.

After what happened, Roman requested the rest of the month off to just... be here. With us. And Ace had insisted he take it. The whole team, in fact, had rallied behind us with support in one way or another. Bringing food. Providing company. Distracting Lainey and letting her regale them with a million stories about the pirates she was waiting for, especially while Roman and I gave statements to Agent Koorie, the police, and finally met with Zeke to decide how we were going to handle the rest of the lawsuit. Through it all, Roman was by my side, his hands locked over mine.

It was startling just how... efficiently... death brought an end to so many things that had consumed our lives for months. It brought an end to the joint investigation with the FBI, and Agent Koorie had flown back east yesterday after officially closing the case. It brought an end to the charges against Dean Johnson though Zeke was still going to go after the cops who'd been bribed. And it brought closure to all the families of my father's victims, though ironically, it didn't feel like it brought closure to his own.

To me.

Instead, it felt like his death opened up a can of worms.

The saying goes that sometimes good people do bad things. Though less common, the reverse was also true: sometimes, bad people do good things. And Lee Turner had been a bad man who'd had moments where he was a good father.

"Tell me," Roman rasped, sinking down onto the floor behind me and sitting so that I was squarely between his legs. He tucked a strand of hair behind my ear. "Tell me what you're thinking, princess."

"Is it wrong to mourn him?" I looked at him and asked, having thought the question a million times over the last four days.

The media had gone wild with the news about the final capture and death of the infamous Archangel. It felt like the whole world celebrated his demise, and I was the only one left to be sad for him.

"You know it's not," he murmured. "Who he was to the world was not who he was to you."

I pulled my lips between my teeth and nodded. For so long, I fed my hatred for Lee because hating him for the truth was easier than admitting I was angry at myself. It was easier than trying to understand how I could care about someone who'd hurt so many people so horrifically.

"But that doesn't change what he did," I said low. "How can I be sad for a killer? What kind of person does that make me?"

"A good one. An empathetic one." He always had the answer to soothe me as I learned to navigate the loss of someone I loved and the relief that he couldn't hurt anyone anymore.

Thankfully, Roman and Agent Koorie had managed to keep my name out of the story. The fact that the Archangel was survived by a daughter wasn't something anyone but us needed to know.

He pressed a kiss to my forehead.

"Where do we go from here?" I murmured, staring so long at the twinkling tree lights that they started to bubble and blur. "It feels like we've all... lost so much."

"Not everything," he reminded me, turning me in his arms. "And we don't go anywhere from here." He tipped my chin up. "We stay right here, Stevie, and build a life full of happy days until the hard ones seem small."

I smiled though my eyes instantly watered. That seemed to be the norm lately—happiness and sadness existing in the same space. No, that was life. Life was happiness and sadness existing in the same space.

"I'm sorry," I said thickly. "I feel like a broken record."

"Not broken," he corrected, swiping a thumb over my bottom lip. "Just unfolding."

My breath hitched, my eyes connecting to his with a bolt of heat and the even stronger sear of love. And then he kissed me deeply, proving without a doubt that there was nothing I could say or do that would make him stop loving me.

Two weeks later...

. . .

"Merry Christmas, princess," Roman rasped in my ear a second before he slid into me from behind.

My gasp melted into a moan as his hand continued to casually pluck and toy with my nipple like he hadn't just ignited a painfully strong ache in my core.

The sorrow had eased drastically since the days following that night on the beach. It was hard for it to stay strong when every day it was diluted with love and happiness, friends and my newly formed family. And the moments where it did start to creep in, Roman was there. Always there.

"Roman..." I moaned. "What do you want for Christmas?"

I felt guilty that I had nothing, but time passed in a blur until I realized I didn't have a present for him.

"You mean more than your sweet little cunt wrapped around me like a good girl?" he ground out, pulling back and then thrusting deep in one swift, delicious movement.

"Yes," I said breathlessly, already teetering on orgasm territory.

He hummed low, his lips and teeth finding the skin on the side of my neck. "I don't know if you're ready to give me more than that..." he drawled low, working his fingers down between my thighs to roll over my clit.

"I am," I pleaded, white stars of pleasure flickering in my vision. "I promise I am."

He groaned low and began to move, sliding out and then burying himself deep. My cry of pleasure turned into a garble when he pulled around and in a swift symphony of movements, turned onto his back and hoisted me on top of him so I was sitting on his groin, his slick cock pressed under me.

"Ride me."

He didn't need to tell me twice. Lifting my hips, I notched the tip of him at my entrance and sank down, the curve of him angling impossibly deep.

"Good girl," he cooed with such pleasure I felt how my body squeezed and leaked onto him. "You're so good to my cock."

I flattened my hand on his chest. "This is more?" I panted, knowing it couldn't be. We'd fucked in this position before.

His jaw tightened once. Twice. And then the strong heat of his palm slid from my hip to my stomach.

"I want to have a baby with you."

My jaw dropped, and it took a good second before I was sure I'd heard him right.

"But you... you can't—"

"I can have it reversed," he rasped as his hips started to rock, needing something he couldn't keep at bay. "I want to have it reversed. When you're ready." He sucked in a breath, feeling how my body tightened around him. "I don't just want more with you, Stevie. I want everything."

Happy tears rolled down my cheek, and my head was nodding long before any words came out. And almost instantly, the nod translated into the rapid rise and fall of my hips as though I fucked my answer into him.

Our hips came together with frantic fervor. Lainey was always up early, and especially on Christmas morning, we wouldn't have a lot of time.

"Tell me," he grunted, holding my hips and pistoning his cock inside me.

"I want to have your baby," I whimpered and then gasped loudly when my orgasm took me by surprise.

Roman's hand clamped over my mouth, covering my cry of release as my body clenched around his. Pleasure reached up with strong fingers and strangled the air from my throat as my body started to convulse around his.

"Oh, fuck, Stevie." He drove deep once more, notching all the way against my womb, and then succumbed to his release, his cock pulsing heat deep inside my pussy.

A heady moan spilled from my lips as the last waves of pleasure coated my body in goose bumps. As soon as I shivered, Roman carefully guided me down to his chest, my long breaths matching up with his as his heart beat against my cheek.

My eyes had just drifted shut when a loud banging sent them flying open.

"Uncle Roman! Stevie! The pirates are here!"

Roman and I looked at each other. *"Pirates?"* we said in unison.

It was Christmas. Santa came on Christmas, not pirates. *What was she talking about?*

Aftercare and clothing had never happened so fast.

Roman was out of the bedroom first, but only because he didn't need a shirt. I was behind him by a couple of seconds. They both stood at the back door, a cold breeze blowing through it because they had it open. I wrapped my arms across my front and went to them. *My family.*

Roman's eyes met mine over his shoulder and he smiled.

"Look, Stevie!" Lainey pointed with glee as I rushed to join them. "It's my pirate ship!"

And it was a pirate ship.

Not a real one. But a *very* nice, *very* large jungle gym was built in the backyard by some very large men that previously looked more like Vikings than pirates.

"We'll be finished in a few minutes, Captain Lainey," Reed called, offering a tipped grin as he hoisted the black Jolly Roger flag from the single mast.

Ace and Dex were working on the small roof covering on top of the ship where a green slide descended down the far side. Dante secured the ladder entrance to the main deck, and even Rorik was there, attaching the multicolored grips for the small rock-climbing wall that led up to a different part of the deck. And they were all dressed as pirates.

"What is this?" I murmured to Roman, sliding my gaze to him.

"I'm guessing her Christmas present from the team."

Lainey was already outside, still in her pajamas, roaming around the ship with the widest eyes and biggest smile.

"You didn't know?"

"Reed said everyone wanted to get her a jungle gym if I was okay with it," he grunted. "He didn't exactly mention this."

I grinned.

"Alright, captain," Ace said. "I think your ship is ready to board."

Lainey squealed, taking a second to decide which method of entry she wanted to take before settling for the ladder and scurrying up to the deck. After a couple of minutes of watching her gleefully explore every nook and cranny, Reed engaged her in a fake sword fight.

"Come on, scallywags," Dante called out to us with a smirk. "Get up here."

"What happened to your shirt, Roman? Santa only bring you half a set," Reed joked.

"No, he just gave my shirt to you because he's tired of seeing videos of you without your clothes on," Roman quipped right back.

Reed clutched his chest, pretending to be wounded for a second before he threw his head back and laughed.

"What's a scallywag?" Lainey redirected the conversation as Roman and I climbed the ladder one at a time, joining Ace, Dex, Reed, and Dante on the deck; Rorik was perched on the climbing wall, gazing out to the horizon, half in our world and half not.

"Your pirate crew, captain." Dante laughed, holding his arms wide to mean all of us.

"No, not crew." Her little head swung in quick arcs from side to side. "I don't have a crew, right, Stevie?"

I balked, unsure of what she was getting at. She came over to me, so I crouched and said, "This is your ship…"

She gave a little nod. "But you said the ship is home."

"It is…" I swallowed hard.

"So not crew." Her small hand grabbed mine. "Family."

Everyone who heard her felt the ripple of emotion just as surely as if the jungle gym had been a real ship cresting over a wave.

"Family," I agreed, my eyes watering as I nodded.

She turned and went to Roman who immediately scooped her up in his arms.

"Love you, Bug."

Her small arms draped over his broad shoulders. "Love you, too."

"The women are getting Christmas brunch ready, whenever you guys want to come over," Dex said to me as the rest of the guys made their way off the ship.

"Thank you." I smiled.

I'd heard and experienced enough to know that Dex had been the most reclusive of the whole team before he met Jo... and now, he was the one hosting every holiday for everyone and their families.

As I looked around, I realized everyone here had thought life had broken them in one way or another. But life doesn't break you. It makes you crumble and retreat, afraid to trust and grow and feel until someone comes along, unafraid to grab hold of your pointy corners and sharp edges, unafraid to soothe you until you stretch, and love you until you unfold.

None of us were broken. We were all unfolding.

After a few minutes, it was just the three of us in our pajamas on top of the pirate ship.

"What are you going to name her?" Roman asked as we stood at the prow, the placement of the jungle gym making it easy to ignore the house on the left and feel like we were floating on the high seas.

Lainey looked at me, and I encouraged her, "Every pirate ship has a name. Like the Flying Dragon or the Black Pearl." One day, she'd learn about Captain Jack Sparrow, the most important fictional pirate to ever live.

Her nose scrunched, and she scanned over the yard to the horizon and then looked back at us. "I'll name her the Firefly," she declared with a toothy grin.

My gaze swung to Roman's as my heart squeezed.

"I think that's a perfect name," I murmured, feeling Roman's fingers slide gently into mine.

"Do you think Mommy and Daddy will see her then?" she asked more quietly. "Or does it need more lights?"

Roman tensed beside me, and I blinked rapidly so I wouldn't cry. "I think you are the brightest light there is, so they'll always be able to see you."

Lainey nodded, never losing her smile, and then, satisfied with that answer and eager to play on her new toy, she rushed to try out the slide and left Roman and me alone on top.

"I love you, princess." His head dipped close, heat blanketing my mouth a second before his kiss consumed me.

I smiled against his lips and murmured back, "I love you, too, pirate."

EPILOGUE

Roman

SEVEN MONTHS LATER...

"Are you sure?" I choked out the words, staring at Dr. Gibson like I hadn't heard her right.

Beside me, Stevie chuckled on the bed. "Ten tests and now, you won't even believe the doctor?"

"I'm positive," Dr. Gibson assured me with a small serene smile, clearly used to expectant fathers being in a state of shock.

"But how... is that possible?" We wanted more kids. We wanted to grow our little family. And I was going to be a damned gentleman about it. I was going to marry her. Wait until she was finished with school. And *then* reverse my vasectomy.

And in the meantime, I'd been perfectly content with fucking my woman like my life depended on it.

"Well, the odds are very slim, right around one percent, but it's still possible to create a pregnancy after a vasectomy."

My throat bobbed, and I remained silent for a second before I clipped to the doctor, "Can you give us a couple of minutes?"

Stevie's eyes widened, and I knew my tone worried her. *Good.* I wanted it to worry the doctor, too.

"Of course," Dr. Gibson murmured and backed out of the room.

BROKEN

As soon as the door closed, I grabbed the chair from the side of the room and wedged the top underneath the doorknob so no one could enter.

"What—" The word wasn't even out before I stood in front of Stevie, framed her face with my hands, and took her mouth in a rough kiss.

Her lips parted instantly, the silk of her tongue pliant as mine claimed every inch of her sweet mouth. Her hands found my waist, and her legs drifted apart as I stepped between them.

"Roman…" she panted. "Wait, Roman…" she moaned when my hand cupped her breast. "Wait, wait…" Her mouth tore from mine. "What's going on?"

"You're pregnant," I growled low, grinding myself between her thighs.

"And you're upset."

I took her wrist and dragged her hand to my crotch, letting her feel just how fucking hard I was. "Does this feel like I'm upset?"

Her eyes bulged. "But you…"

"Made it seem like we needed to be left alone?" I rasped, my lips tipping into a crooked grin. "Yes, I did."

Heat flooded her cheeks when she realized what I was about. "*Here?*"

"You're fucking pregnant, princess. With my baby," I groaned, my dick straining against my pants. "And you're wearing nothing underneath that gown." I reached for the edge of the fabric and pushed it up, baring her pretty pussy. With one hand, I undid my fly and then yanked her to the edge of the table. "So yeah, I do need to fuck you right here, right now."

A second later, I was inside her, thrusting hard and fast into her slick heat.

"Fucking pregnant," I growled low, feeling my balls tighten. "So perfect and pregnant." I splayed one hand over her stomach, feeling it move and shift each time my cock pushed deep.

"And yours," she added breathlessly, her cunt starting to squeeze me with more force.

No wonder she'd been orgasming so easily lately. Yesterday,

she'd come just from me sucking on her tits and it had been marvelous.

"All mine," I confirmed, driving into her hard. One brush of my thumb over her clit was all it took to send her bucking into her release, her cunt knotting around me in waves.

I kissed her, swallowing her cry as she came and let myself follow her over the edge.

"I love you," I rasped a few moments later, cupping her face and stroking her cheek with my thumb.

"I love you, too," she repeated with a wide smile.

The moment lasted about another second before Stevie remembered that we were in the emergency department of the hospital and then scrambled to make herself look like nothing had happened.

When we were both dressed, I freed the door, thanked Dr. Gibson for her time, and then snaked my arm around Stevie's waist as she buried her face into my chest.

"They know."

"They're doctors. They can't say anything," I told her with a grin and laughed when she buried her face deeper into me.

We reached the waiting room when I saw our friend, Gwen. She was an ER nurse, her husband a former DA, but it was who she was helping that made me slow my steps.

"Is that Reed?"

Stevie looked and confirmed, "He doesn't look good…"

Gwen was taking Reed's temperature with a touchless thermometer, but he looked like he had a hangover from hell. Face drawn, eyes bloodshot. I was about to head over to talk to him when I realized he wasn't alone; there was an unfamiliar redhead beside him.

And Gwen proceeded to take her temperature, too.

It wasn't a stretch to assume Reed and the redhead had spent the night together, but man, did they look worse for the wear.

"Maybe they have food poisoning," Stevie offered.

I grumbled and tipped my head, the suggestion fitting the scene well. "That would do it." But something gnawed at me that it wasn't what happened.

My plan to go talk to him was already crumbling, but when Gwen took them both through the double doors to the other hallway of patient rooms, I decided to wait and hear the whole story on Monday.

"Let's go home."

"She told me she's going to make a list of baby names." Stevie walked into the kitchen and said.

I was cleaning up from dinner while she put Lainey to bed.

We'd decided on the drive back from the hospital to tell Lainey right away because we were all on this ship together. One crew. One family. Of course, as our fearless captain, Lainey decided that she would be the one who gets to name the baby which left Stevie and me nervously smiling at each other.

"So, we're going to end up with baby Blackbeard?"

"Probably." She half laughed, half groaned. "I told her we would all vote on the names."

"Or we can take turns."

"What do you mean?"

"Like she can pick the name for this one. I'll pick the name for the next. I was thinking either Jack or Sparrow." I winked at her over my shoulder, drying my hands as I shut the dishwasher with my foot.

"The next?" She gaped. "There's not even this one yet."

"Right, but there's going to be plenty," I told her, rounding the counter and hugging her to me. "We have to create the whole crew for our ship."

"Oh yeah? And how many pirates does a ship need?" Her head tipped up, eyes sparkling.

"Five. Six. Maybe more if we get a bigger ship." I grinned and declared, "Come with me."

Taking her hand, I led her out the back door to the pirate ship in the yard.

The Firefly did indeed get more lights added—twinkle lights wound around the mast and flagpole and draped over the sides.

So even though there was still some light left in the sky, the structure glowed with warmth.

"What are we doing?" Stevie asked when I ushered her up the ladder.

Some nights, we'd make coffee and just sit on the prow of the jungle gym and talk about the future. Dream and plan for the family we were building.

Life had... and was still... unfolding unexpectedly. Beautifully.

"Well, with more crew, we're going to need to reorganize the ranks..." I drawled slowly, watching her walk to the edge of the deck and stare at the sunset.

Slowly, I reached into my pocket, finding the small box I'd hidden in my bag for two weeks now. I was going to wait until her birthday at the end of the month, but after this morning, I couldn't wait another second.

Stevie hummed and faced me slowly. My gut tightened, wondering how it was possible for her to be more beautiful each time I looked at her.

"So, with Lainey as captain and you as quartermaster, are you saying that I'm finally going to be promoted to first mate?" Her eyebrow arched teasingly.

I chuckled low, taking a step toward her and slowly drawing the ring box from my jeans.

"I was actually thinking... hoping"—I lowered onto one knee, watching her gaze widen—"to promote you to wife."

Her hands cupped over her mouth as I opened the lid and revealed the oval diamond ring.

"You're already my everything, Stevie," I rasped and tears sped down her cheeks. "Will you be my pirate wife?"

She was already nodding before I finished, smiling and crying and shaking as I slid the ring onto her finger and drew her into my arms.

"Say it," I begged with a chuckle, brushing her hair from her face.

"Yes," she exclaimed with a laugh and then added, "Wait, I mean, aye."

And that was how the pirate claimed his princess, on the prow of their home, with forever on the horizon.

The End.

I hope you enjoyed Roman and Stevie's story. Reed and Callie are up next in the Covington Security series. Get your copy of **BELIEVED** here.

OTHER WORKS BY DR. REBECCA SHARP

Covington Security

Betrayed

Bribed

Beguiled

Burned

Branded

Broken

Believed

Bargained

Braved

The Vigilantes

The Vendetta

The Verdict

The Villain

The Vigilant

The Vow

Reynolds Protective

Archer

Hunter

Gunner

Ranger

Carmel Cove

Beholden

Bespoken

Besotted

Befallen

Beloved

Betrothed

The Kinkades

The Woodsman

The Lightkeeper

The Candlemaker

The Innkeeper

The Odyssey Duet

The Fall of Troy

The Judgment of Paris

The Sacred Duet

The Gargoyle and the Gypsy

The Heartbreak of Notre Dame (TBA)

Country Love Collection

Tequila

Ready to Run

Fastest Girl in Town

Last Name

I'll Be Your Santa Tonight
Michigan for the Winter
Remember Arizona
Ex To See
A Cowboy for Christmas
Meant to Be
Accidentally on Purpose

The Winter Games

Up in the Air
On the Edge
Enjoy the Ride
In Too Deep
Over the Top

The Gentlemen's Guild

The Artist's Touch
The Sculptor's Seduction
The Painter's Passion

Passion & Perseverance Trilogy

(A Pride and Prejudice Retelling)

First Impressions
Second Chances
Third Time is the Charm

Standalones

Reputation

Redemption

Revolution: A Driven World Novel

Hypothetically

Want to #staysharp with everything that's coming?

Join my newsletter!

ABOUT THE AUTHOR

Rebecca Sharp is a contemporary romance author of over thirty published novels and dentist living in PA with her amazing husband, affectionately referred to as Mr. GQ.

She writes a wide variety of contemporary romance. From new adult to extreme sports romance, forbidden romance to romantic comedies, her books will always give you strong heroines, hot alphas, unique love stories, and always a happily ever after. When she's not writing or seeing patients, she loves to travel with her husband, snowboard, and cook.

She loves to hear from readers. You can find her on Facebook, Instagram, and Goodreads. And, of course, you can email her directly at author@drrebeccasharp.com.

If you want to be emailed with exclusive cover reveals, upcoming book news, etc. you can sign up for her mailing list on her website: www.drrebeccasharp.com

Happy reading!
xx
Rebecca

Made in the USA
Middletown, DE
18 February 2025